P9-CQQ-525

6599 A.D. The war between the Earth Federation and the Herculean Empire had been over for more than three centuries. The planet in the Hercules Globular Cluster was a cinder; the few descendants of the surviving Herculeans lived on Myraa's World, half a galaxy away, in what seemed to be a religious commune. But on an unnamed planet, deep within the Hercules Cluster, two survivors, father and son, gather their resources and plan a reign of terror against Federation worlds.

But the woman Myraa has a different vision—one which excludes empires and warring armies. Subtly, she strives to shape events toward a different end.

Rising to one of the most unusual climaxes in recent fantastic literature, this novel of chase and vengeance depicts a colorful, poetic future which is struggling to overcome its past. Filled with striking twists and vivid ideas, this is space opera at its most modern.

The Omega Point has appeared in Britain, Germany, Holland, Portugal, France, and Japan. This new one-volume edition, completely revised by the author, contains the never before published conclusion, *Mirror of Minds,* and a special afterword by the author.

Books by George Zebrowski

MACROLIFE

THE MONADIC UNIVERSE

SUNSPACER

THE OMEGA POINT TRILOGY

TOMORROW TODAY (editor)

HUMAN MACHINES (editor with Thomas N. Scortia)

FASTER THAN LIFE (editor with Jack Dann)

BEST OF THOMAS N. SCORTIA (editor)

CREATIONS (editor with Isaac Asimov and Martin H. Greenberg)

GEORGE ZEBROWSKI: *Perfecting Visions*, edited by Jeffrey M. Elliot

---

"The Omega Point Trilogy is an impressive achievement. It starts out as an exciting story, which also shows that man's future control of the environment, even of his own body and mind, will scarcely bring control of himself. From there it goes on to a cosmic vision of a scope rarely seen since Olaf Stapledon. Much recommended for readers who like thoughtfulness as well as sheer entertainment."

—Poul Anderson

THE OMEGA POINT TRILOGY

George Zebrowski

ACE SCIENCE FICTION BOOKS
NEW YORK

THE OMEGA POINT TRILOGY

An Ace Science Fiction Book/published by arrangement with
the author and his agent,
Joseph Elder Agency, 150 West 87 Street,
New York, N.Y. 10024

PRINTING HISTORY
Ace Original/November 1983

All rights reserved.
Copyright © 1983 by George Zebrowski.
Cover art by Attila Hejja
This book may not be reproduced in whole
or in part, by mimeograph or any other means,
without permission. For information address: The Berkley Publishing Group,
200 Madison Avenue, New York, N.Y. 10016

This first complete edition is based on material copyrighted © 1972,
1977 by George Zebrowski. Book One, *Ashes and Stars*, has been
revised; Book Two, *The Omega Point*, has been completely revised;
Book Three, *Mirror of Minds*, appears here for the first time.

ISBN: 0-441-62381-6

Ace Science Fiction Books are published by The Berkley Publishing Group,
200 Madison Avenue, New York, New York 10016.
PRINTED IN THE UNITED STATES OF AMERICA

To the first Clarion Workshop, 1968.

To my mother, who helped me attend.

To Don Wollheim, guardian of beginnings.

*Pat LoBrutto, defender of the faith
between author and editor, Susan
Allison, Patient Muse, and the
RPE Corps.*

CONTENTS

BOOK THREE: **MIRROR OF MINDS**

BOOK ONE

ASHES AND STARS

I. War Stars

"But what are kings when regiment is gone,
 But perfect shadows in a sunshine day?"

—Marlowe, *Edward the Second*

"The imagination enlarges little objects so as to fill
 our souls with a fantastic estimate..."

—Pascal, *Pensées*

THE WAR STARS burned brightly in his memory, each sun
a pulsing furnace of hate transforming plasma energies into the
frozen grimace of armor, creating the base for war's iron game—
machines, weapons, Whisper Ship hulls—power packaged and
stored until the moment of kinetic deployment. There was enough
energy here in the Hercules Globular Cluster for a million years
of conflict. Some had even dreamed of gathering a hundred
stars into a single unit and moving it through space as if it
were a ship. No enemy system could have survived a collision
with such a configuration.

As he walked down the stony corridor toward the war room
located in the center of the underground base, Gorgias almost
smiled at the absurdity of the scheme; but the bitterness set
into the muscles of his face resisted even a faint smile. Any
culture capable of calling up such a titanic force would have

had no need of warfare to gain its ends. Those who had dreamed such dreams had been mad. He imagined the red thread of insanity as a *thing*, a subtle, spidery network of impulses reaching upward out of some infinitesimal corners of space-time to lace the tender systems of biological structure. Where was the force-center of this willful bestiality, this evil within intelligent beings, so often wished away by well-wishers? The radiant energy of the Cluster had poured out with the martial will of its civilization; the suns of home had nurtured an armory of hate so powerful and tenacious that only the complete destruction of the home worlds had been enough to bring stillness.

Stillness, he thought, but not peace—there was no one to make peace with; New Anatolia and the twenty original worlds of the Empire would be lifeless for tens of thousands of Earth years. He felt the flow of hatred in himself, detachment followed by rationality, the silent shock of recognizing one's own workings. He remembered the sense of power that accompanied a noble ancestry, the prideful stance against death; a love of this power struggled to well up inside him and coil around his flesh. But at the same time he felt this strength passing from him, and he was not certain that he would miss it.

Once it might have won against the tall shadows from Earth, the pale Earthfolk from whose stock the Herculeans had sprung millennia ago, like sparks struck to light new stars. Earthfolk burned more slowly then Herculeans, reasoning, calculating, clinging to their leisure planet in fear of death. Or was this too an illusion?

He thought of his son. What was left for his namesake now? Should he encourage him to settle among the last Herculeans on Myraa's World? Should they continue to go out on nuisance raids against the Earth Federation? Or should they go back into stasis and pass into another time? As if from behind a mask he peered at possibilities beyond the dances of power which had consumed the life of his kind. Together with his son he still lived in the prison of their will; the will which had thrown a net across the stars, pulled together an empire, was ripped open now, lying on cold stones at the bottom of a dark sea.

The lights in the corridor flickered. A returning surge of hatred gripped him as he came to the door of the war room. He stopped and thought of the Whisper Ship lying in its berth in the bowels of the base; he knew what the ship could do, and it was only a matter of time before his son learned also.

The base was still an efficient military teaching environment, designed to bring one or a thousand students into full possession of its powers; it was the only school his son had known.

The door opened. Gorgias stepped inside, knowing that he would not try to stop his son; the pressure of the past was too great to permit alternatives, at least any that his son might accept.

In the darkened war room, a haze of projected light stood in a column on the polished surface of the meeting table, casting a three-dimensional starmap into the space of the large gallery overhead. A long-dead, encyclopedic voice was speaking. His son sat on the other side of the large table, a motionless figure staring up at the stars.

Quietly, Gorgias sat down and listened with him.

"Visualize an imaginary translucent tubeway through normal space," the voice was saying, "one end attached to Earth's solar system, the other to the Great Globular Cluster in the constellation of Hercules. . . ."

Overhead, the image showed the galaxy on edge. A glowing red snake grew out of the solar system, crossing the disk toward the center in short spirals and arcs until it buried its head in the cluster circling the galactic hub, 34,000 light-years from Sol.

"The fastest ships take five Earth months to pass through this winding volume of Federation Space, which varies from five to twenty light-years in diameter. A hundred thousand worlds circle their suns here, many of them earthlike; others are too young for intelligent life to have developed; some cradle prespace humanoid cultures; still others have in-system space travel; many are dead worlds. A continuous stream of human life colonizes these worlds, coming out from Earth as well as from other colonial planets. Rejecting engineered environments, this river of life hungers after natural worlds born of suns. . . ."

Now it seemed that he was rushing toward the Hercules Cluster at a fantastic speed. The image grew until it took up the whole view, dominating the skymap like a galaxy.

"The greatest object of colonization was the Cluster in Hercules. Its settlement led to a cultural and biological branching of humankind. The biological divergence was accomplished through genetic engineering, specifically through the mixing of human DNA with that of the cluster's original humanoids, whose civilizations contributed much to the style of the emerging Herculean Empire. This hybridization of humankind from Sol led to the greatest recorded conflict in history...."

He looked at the darkened figure of his son. Brought up in an atmosphere of disintegrating mobilization, pushed along by the pressure of a past he could never rejoin, the young man of two hundred and twenty Earth years had grown toward a breaking point; he had to recreate the past or die. Inside, his son was a fortress.

Suddenly the lights came on in the gallery, banishing the starmaps. The surface of the table below became a lake of light. His son glared at him from the far shore.

"I want to hear only one thing from you," he said, "that you will remove Oriona from Myraa's clutches."

"We can't; you know that your mother won't have anything to do with us...."

"We will bring her here and she will help us with our plans."

"Our plans mean nothing to her. How many times do I have to tell you?" Our plans, he thought, wondering at how the words now startled him. When had he changed, when had he started thinking differently?

"She'll think differently when she leaves Myraa's influence. Then she'll believe and live as we do...."

Once, long ago, Oriona had been his other half in everything. Yes, living on Myraa's World had changed her, probably for the better; she no longer hated the old enemies, she was indifferent to them. He looked at his son across the bright table. What could he say to him that would turn back his natural energy? The black uniform with its orange star of the Empire fit him well. There were enough uniforms in the base to clothe a planet.

Characteristically, after a few moments of silence, his son changed the manner of his attack. "You see, we have to be willing to hurt them badly, with small things perhaps, but small things of great cruelty, acts which can never be forgotten, wounds which can never heal. We must hurt them as they hurt us. We can do this."

"No action we can take against Earth can be decisive, ever."

"Unless we raise troops and strategic weapons. Meanwhile small sorties will hurt them and preserve our will for a better day."

"What weapons, what troops? Are you still dreaming of the troop cylinder?"

"There was such a thing toward the end of the war. One day I'll find it."

"Even a hundred would do no good—at best they stored ten thousand, one division of hastily trained personnel. Even if you found the cylinder, there is no assurance that you could revive those soldiers stored in that way. Actually, I never saw any evidence for the cylinders."

"But we have the tripod that fits a cylinder here!"

"So maybe there was one—only one."

"Under good leadership we can grow—the lives in the cylinder are not just for combat."

"You're talking of committing unborn generations to vengeance. It's over, let it die." Oriona, you are right, he thought, we must come to the end of our wars; if we do not, we will not see what lies beyond. What do you see, my love, what is there for you on that green world?

". . . In your weakness," his son was saying, "you fail to see that if we're terrible enough, often enough, we can blackmail a universe."

Perhaps he was right; what else was there beyond the old war? Inwardly he looked back into the past and saw a black pit.

"Only if we remain at large," he said to his son, "only if they don't catch us." The black pit was drawing him down; or was it rushing up to meet him?

"To remain at large is a matter of skill in avoiding a real test of strength," his son answered. "But consider—if we could destroy large populated centers, how long could they deny our demands?"

"You have demands? What could we ask for that they might not take back when we were made harmless?"

"The first demand is recognition of the need to rebuild our home world. . . ."

"Sometimes I think you're a complete idiot—what can their promises mean after the toll you plan to inflict? Don't you see—any guarantee would be observed by them at *their* pleasure, not ours." He looked at his son carefully. Was this the descendant of Gorgias the First, Uniter of Worlds, creator of the Herculean Empire? Perhaps there was more to his plan, some shrewdness he had missed.

"We would keep a hidden strike force. At the first violation we make them pay! If we can remain at large, you and I, then so could such a force."

Gorgias felt his head shake in denial, as if it had become independent of his body; his right hand trembled and for a moment he was unable to speak. His son's will had entered him and taken possession, half-convincing him, reminding him of his own earlier self, with its resolve and hatred. All that would be required to make his son's terrible vision work was an iron terror, a will that would be ready to do anything against the enemy, a resolve that would not crumble when confronted by pity. This would be the game Oriona feared, the iron game that would set father and son in the service of an old hatred, turning them into devices to serve the dead. Father and son had skirted the edge of this game; now, finally, they would be drawn into its merciless logic and cruel satisfactions. . . .

"One day," his son continued, "our worlds will be repopulated, our power rebuilt. We will have little need of threats then. But until then, you and I must be guardians of that future. Have you forgotten? Have you become a coward? Won't you even try—or will you abandon me as you abandoned Oriona?"

Gorgias looked into his son's eyes. *I won't need you,* they seemed to say, *I'll become my own father, I'll deny you if you refuse me and you'll be left alone. Without Oriona and me you are nothing.* A shuddering fear, like breaking metal, passed through him. He tasted its cold in his mouth. His stomach knotted in rage, and he knew for the first time that he would be able to kill his own son—if for no other reason than to abolish this monstrous resurgence of his own youth, this fortress self which had come out of him, out of the past, to stand alone in this way.

Oriona's eyes looked at him from beneath black eyebrows and black hair. "Well?" his son asked. "Will you plan with me?" The questions were now shouts, strong and insistent and convinced, assuming agreement. For a moment his son's shouting shape became a torso rising from the frozen lake of the polished table, an awesome creature imprisoned here by the sheer weight of its own hatred. His son was a creature of loveless power, making him doubt again, forcing him to feel once more the uncoiling insanity of the failed past.

"All right," Gorgias said softly, "but first—"

"Good!"

THE OMEGA POINT TRILOGY 9

"—but first we'll visit Oriona." Perhaps she may be able to quiet her son, he thought, even though the life she lives is a delusion.

"We'll take her away," his son said.

"Let's see how she feels." A lie might save his son's life. Any delay might change the future; once his son started on this new course, there would be no turning back; his life would become a hunted thing, and one day he would die. Any delay might save him. There were worlds aplenty outside the Federation, where a life might be started anew; a small community . . . simply existing . . . perhaps Oriona was living that life right now.

"I'll prepare the ship," his son said.

Gorgias nodded and tried to quiet himself.

II. Jumpspace

"It is natural for the mind to believe, and for the will to love; so that, for want of true objects, they must attach themselves to false."

—Pascal, *Pensées*

"A man knew himself as the product of this world. He sought to become its consciousness: a way of dreaming that would embody its salvation."

—Bousquet

A SHADOWED FACE floated in the stone ceiling, and faded; in another moment it would have spoken to him.

Cave eyes stared at a barrier of ice in a timeless place.

Outside the black walls, floor and ceiling of the doorless room, lay an infinite solidity; the cell was the only open space, cut miraculously out of a universe of rigid substance. The lonely lamp in the corner would go out if he looked away; the darkness would flow in around him and solidify, freezing his movement until his flesh also turned stony. . . .

The home world lay before him. He had never seen it after the holocaust, yet suddenly he was there. The land was an endless plain of ashes, the remains of cities and towns, the very mountains. The planet was a heated dust bowl, wind-whipped and sterile. Grief held back all his tender reactions, all regret and tears. He felt the hell wind on his face, tasted the baked ash in his mouth as the gray sea drifted around his feet.

He walked forward across the meadow of ashes. The horizon was a wavy line of heat distortions. He came abruptly to a large circular pit in the waste; stars burned below the world, glowing gravel floating in a subterranean universe. . . .

The dream was always the same.

A titanic fist pounded on the wall behind his bed, making the stone echo like metal; the black surfaces of the room became glassy and shattered, flowing away like water. . . .

He sat up suddenly and saw his father standing in the open doorway.

"Are you awake?"

"I'm ready," he said, feeling distrustful of the silhouette. His father's dark shape turned and went out into the corridor.

He looked at the dark lamp in the corner, remembering that in the dream he had believed that his life was somehow dependent on its continued shining; a curious absurdity.

He got up and prepared to follow his father to the ship.

The ramp tunnel exit loomed ahead suddenly and the Whisper Ship shot out over the barren surface of the planet. A glowing cloud of interstellar gas blazed from horizon to horizon as the vessel raced over jagged mountains, stone-filled valleys and dusty plains; airless, beaten by solar wind and heat, the lifeless world orbited faithfully, forever dead in the angry glare of its small, white-hot primary. Located near the center of the cluster, the entire system was wrapped in a cloud of gas and dust half a light-year across.

The ship lifted into the shining sky. Variations in cloud density let in the light of cluster stars, the glow fading as the ship shifted position.

With his father now asleep in the aft quarters, the younger Gorgias began his first watch. Without warning the ship slipped into otherspace, revealing the stars of the cluster as perfectly round black coals set at an indefinite distance. For the next one hundred and fifty hours the ship would push through this ashen sea, fifty thousand light-years across the top of the galaxy, halfway across the spiral, past where Earth swam deep in the spiral disk's outer arms, upward to the sparsely starred region where Myraa's World looked out on the dark between the galaxies.

* * *

All through his first watch, the younger Gorgias was irritated by the shroud of hyperspace covering the known universe, hiding the diamond-hard stars, abolishing the black void's comfort, leaving only the ash-white continuum dotted with the obsidian analogs of objects in normal space-time. The bones of reality, he thought, dry and lifeless; passing through this region was always a slow dying.

Did he really care about the Herculean dead? He searched himself, trying to feel the death of millions. The killing of ten would have been intolerable. Each of those hundreds of millions would have lived a thousand Earth years or more, each life an entire world of experience, now cut off. To remember their passing was to deny oneself all normal day-to-day living, all simplicity, all love; to remember their passing was to act in ways that would change him irrevocably, making him an instrument, a sacrifice to the fires of outrage. He did not, and never would, belong to himself, or to anyone else.

If he could hurt even ten Earthborn, the news would humiliate millions; the dead deserved that much. Each blow, however small, would be a reminder that the Federation's victory had not been complete. The dead were alive within him, sparks ready to flare up into an inner fire; his strength was the needed fuel; his strength was their will preparing to live again. Rest would come for him only when all the hatred he bore was spent.

The thought of his father's growing weakness made him angry again. He felt it as a coldness camped at his center, a promise of failure. He would have left the older man in stasis at their last waking and gone out by himself, but the ship was still tuned to the other's personality and would obey no one else. The ship could only be his by deliberate transfer of command; his father's death would not give him the ship. He needed his father's good will.

If only a second Whisper Ship could be found. Perhaps there was one somewhere on Myraa's World. He had always suspected that Myraa knew more than she was willing to tell. Maybe he could learn something from Oriona. Myraa or one of the other survivors might have revealed something to her, a piece of information that would not appear to be useful, but which might be crucial to one who could fit it into a large context. The visit might turn out to be useful after all.

He found himself thinking about Myraa—her nakedness, her long hair, her smile, the freshness of her skin. Thoughts of her always brought out his weakest feelings. The universe of time and space had cheated him (what was this effort of time passing?) of the simplest pleasures enjoyed by the humblest creatures on a million worlds. He was a thinking, self-conscious object living in a plenum where distance lay between objects that were made up of infinitesimally spaced small objects lying below gross perception. What was justice, or vengeance, in such a universe? Why did he crave closeness with Myraa, and why was he compelled to believe that distance from her way of life was necessary for him? In his way he loved her, but he would not give himself up to her; the cry of the past was stronger than her love; for him to ignore the past would be to die.

He would have to recreate the history from which he sprang; it would have to be a certain kind of living object, a network of conscious beings again holding the Hercules Cluster together. To this community he would give himself; there love might not be a fault; there he would shine as he had been meant to shine, a king from a line of kings; there he would know the past and future as they should be, unshattered and filled with the meaning of time; there the past would be pride, the future a distant glowing goal that would consume all things in its crucible of satisfaction and joy.

On the screen, the desolation of otherspace promised nothing as the ship rushed through its oblivion.

When his father came in to stand his first watch period, Gorgias rose and let the older man take the station chair.

"I've found a likely target for us," Gorgias said.

His father swung the seat around and glared at him. The face was pale, the blue eyes sunken from worry and doubt; the hands sought each other from fear, then pushed apart to hide the fact. "What are you talking about? We were not to plan anything until after the visit."

"Thirty light-years south of Myraa there is a frontier world, mostly small towns, not more than half a million people, an easy target."

His father gripped the armrests. "Later, we don't have time to discuss it now, get some rest."

"You said you would fight—"

"A world that size is unimportant, settled by rejects. Federation won't be impressed."

"We could destroy a town in a single run."

"They'd look for us on Myraa's World immediately, hold Oriona and others hostage..."

"We could do it after we take Oriona with us. Besides, what makes you so sure they are capable of holding hostages?"

His father was shaking his head. "There's too little thought and preparation. Don't be so impatient. Do you think that Federation military operatives are stupid? They'll pick up on every mistake. They won the war that way."

"But they never came up against a Whisper Ship."

"True, the ship is unassailable, but you might imprison yourself forever inside. Even the life-support systems require mass to synthesize food...."

"I could recycle indefinitely."

"But you would starve if something went wrong. Son, there are ways to trap or disrupt the ship. In time it would be possible to bring enough power to bear on it to tear it open."

"Things would never get that far," Gorgias said. He turned and started aft.

"Rest well," his father called after him just as the bulkhead door slid shut. There was no point in angering the old man now. Later, he thought, when the ship is mine, I can do as I wish, but I need him now to control the ship's programs. Suddenly, he feared that his father would never relinquish control of the ship.

At the end of the short corridor, another door slid open to let him into the aft quarters, containing a large bunk with gravity controls, bath cubicle and a small kitchen dispenser.

Gorgias lay down and tried to sleep, struggling to reach a deep calm, but rest charged a toll of memory before releasing him into its quietest realm. He was on Myraa's World for the first time. "Is this home?" he asked his father. No, it was another place, far from their enemies. Here the surviving Herculeans might live in peace. A green field showed a pit, a wound cut in the grass. Bodies lay in the pit, the corpses of Herculean animals, those that had been unable to adjust to the new planet. Later, fleeing warships had arrived, burning the grass into desert with their makeshift jets; only the crudest planetfall was left to them after their strained gravitics had failed.

Spring light was streaming through Myraa's window. Beams walked ghostly on the floor. Whole ships had been gutted to build the house on the hill. Sickness, suicide and lack of provisions had decimated the survivors, soldier and specialist alike; no hand or brain remained now that could repair, operate, or even understand the dead fleet. Only the Whisper Ship ran itself, demanding little direct understanding of its systems for effective operation.

Beams of steel passed through his body, pinning him in a place beyond sleep. There was no pain and no possibility of movement; in a few moments there would be . . . nothing.

He awoke and listened to the perfect silence of the cabin, imagining that the wintriness of hyperspace was increasing, pressing in on the ship, and would soon freeze it into immobility within the gray continuum. The cabin smelled of cold metal. He closed his eyes again and thought of entering stasis for . . . a thousand . . . two thousand years. Would the Federation still exist after ten thousand years? Would the machines maintain the stasis field for that long? What kind of universe would he find after a million years? No revenge would be possible for him in that universe. To step into it would require no more than a subjective moment of sleep, and all his purpose would be left behind. The idea filled him with a sense of loss. He saw himself going alone across time, the past a black pit behind him, drawing him backward, pulling him closer each time he fell asleep; one day he would not wake in time to save himself.

Then all thoughts and dreams left him, as he knew they would, as they always had; but again he wondered if he had won, or if a tide had simply gone out.

During his second watch he saw the ship's ghost on the screen, running ahead at a fixed distance. He wondered if an insubstantial copy of himself was sitting before the screen in that phantom vessel, watching a still more distant illusion, and if his father was resting in the aft quarters there also.

When he slept after his watch, the ship turned to glass, letting in the ghastly gray-white light from beyond, the glow of an overcast creation or the underside of a universe forever turned away from the living.

Opening his eyes, he longed for starlight, for sight of worlds, for living things. He looked at his hands. His skin was growing pale here, as if the few days had really been years. What was time in jumpspace? Perhaps time was lost in transit, then regained at the moment of exit, leaving in the traveler only the memory of long imprisonment.

He closed his eyes again. Memory was bare and clean, as stony as the halls and chambers of the base. He felt pity for himself, for his father, for Oriona imprisoned on Myraa's World, for his brother who had died there. Only revenge was left; nothing else would fill him up completely and quiet his hunger; nothing else would lead to renewal for his people. The only way to redeem the past was to bring it into the present and use it to control the future; he had to make memory a material thing, a force that would lash out at the Earthborn, making it impossible for them to ignore his demands. Revenge was the only way to kindle recognition in those who had taken everything from him, leaving this gray present, an old man and a black future.

If I do not reach out to hurt, he thought, I will not want to live.

A shadowed face looked down at him, and he knew that he would cease to be if it turned its gaze away. Again the pit of things past pulled him in, closer this time; he reached for a handhold to keep himself from falling in, but he woke up before he could grasp it.

III. Exiles

"The liberty of the individual is no gift of civilization."

—Freud

"There is nothing worse for mortal men than wandering."

—Homer, *The Odyssey*

THE ASHES of jumpspace faded; the black coals caught fire and became bright stars again. Nearby, the sun of Myraa's World burned with a yellow-orange life, its shouting light filling the screen, humbling the observer who had just emerged from limbo.

I have reached the complexity of hating myself, the older Gorgias thought. My son will begin to hate me and I will not want to live. I am not sure that his plans will be ineffective, I have simply lost...my taste for war. Reproaches rose in his brain, the dark shapes of Herculean soldiers going into battle, each one crying out for him to remember his training, his loyalty, the meaning of cowardice and treason. *I am not guilty*, he said to the shapes. Too much had changed.

Myraa's World grew large on the screen until it took up the whole view. The ship cut into the atmosphere and circled halfway around the planet before dropping to a few kilometers above the ocean.

17

His son came in and stood behind him as the screen showed the land ahead. The water grew shallow, revealing sunlit bottom. In a few moments the ship was past the rocky beach and rushing low over the land.

Oriona. He wondered how she would greet him this time. How would she greet her son? Would she continue to judge in her silent way? If she spoke to him, what would he say to her, what could he say to her after thirty years? She had lived those years while he had stolen them—stolen them from her and from himself. He would not see those years in her face; few Herculeans below the age of five hundred showed signs of age.

The ship turned north, running over worn mountains and grassy valleys. The yellow afternoon sunlight stained the greenery, making it look blue in patches.

"We're almost there," his son said quietly, almost as if he were afraid.

We're almost home, Gorgias thought. It always surprised him to think of Myraa's World as home; in a way it was home, the gathering place of almost all remaining Herculeans; it was home because Oriona was here, and because he was here with his son, however brief the visit; it was home because his son had once asked him if it was home, and he had lied.

The hill and house came into view. A circular design of panoramic windows drank in the western sunlight, though some shade was provided by six elegant trees standing in a carpet of tall grass. He saw that the trees were taller, their trunks larger. The branches were thicker with curving needles, and the red cones were as bright as the gem sands of New Anatolia's beaches.

The ship circled once and landed in a hover at the bottom of the hill in back of the house, where the evening shadow would cloak it.

He turned and looked at his son, but there was no sign of shared feelings in the younger man's face. For a moment Gorgias was afraid that his son would guess his state of mind and see it as yet another sign of weakness, but the other was already turning away to leave the ship.

He got up and followed his son out of the control room to the side lock. The mechanism had already cycled and they stepped out into a warm south wind which greeted them with the scent of living things. The effect was almost a shock after the sterility of the base and jumpspace.

The hill was a thirty-degree climb on a dirt footpath. His

son reached the door first and waited. They stood together for a minute until the door opened. Inside, they walked to the front room through a narrow corridor.

"There's no one here," his son said as they passed by the open bedroom door.

The black floor was dustless, as if someone had just cleaned it. The chairs sat alone, facing the massive bowed windows, waiting for visitors who would come out of time to seat themselves; the silence seemed eternal.

"Welcome."

They both turned and saw Myraa standing in front of the entrance to the corridor. She wore a simple blue robe which matched her eyes. A hood hid her long brown hair.

"Welcome," she repeated, "I knew you were coming."

She could not have known, he thought, but it gives her a sense of power to say so.

"Where's Oriona?" his son asked.

Myraa took a few steps into the room and said, "Oriona is no longer living—"

The sentence stopped for an eternity, preventing him from hearing the rest.

"—as you know it. It was her wish."

His son went up to her. "Wish? What are you talking about? How did it happen—an accident? Was she murdered?"

"It was her wish," Myraa said. "She left nothing for you, and she does not want to speak with you now."

"What are you saying?" his son asked. "Tell me where she is—is she dead or not?"

"She exists elsewhere, whether you accept it or not. I am telling you this so that you will calm yourself."

His son turned to him. "What is she saying?"

"Their belief is that, well—people are absorbed into others, like herself, becoming multiple personalities. I've never paid the idea much attention. Oriona is dead—Myraa is trying to . . . excuse me." He closed his eyes and felt a warmth spread through his body. He felt his head bow and a freezing weakness entered his muscles. He recovered and opened his eyes. Turning, he sat down in the nearest chair and looked out the window.

Behind him, he heard his son strike Myraa across the face. "Liar! What has happened?"

"I've told you," Myraa said, and there was no anger in her voice.

"Suicide?"

"No, but it was her wish."

"Do you hear yourself—which was it?"

"You've heard the truth."

"Explain it to me."

"She who was your mother lives . . . in a different way."

Oriona, Gorgias said to himself as he looked out the curving window, *now only your name is left to me.* A gust of wind shook the tree near the house, hurling a few red cones against the window in front of him.

"You'll tell me," his son was saying, "you'll tell me what you mean."

Stillness returned to the room, as if time had run backward to the moment when they had come in.

Then he heard a rush of air and a thud. He turned and saw that his son had kicked Myraa in the stomach. She lay on the floor, clutching her belly without a sound. He gave her a disgusted nudge with his boot, turned and sat down in the other chair facing the window.

"Oriona's death has affected her. Did you think before you hit her?"

"You didn't try to stop me."

He closed his eyes and turned his head away to keep his son from seeing the tears threatening to well out of his eyes. *Oriona,* he said to himself, almost singing the name. *So few, so few Herculeans left.*

"What is it?" his son asked.

Oriona, Oriona, I'll never see you again. All that might have changed between us is now impossible. How could that have been taken from us?

He opened his eyes and turned to his son. "Go pick her up."

The younger man laughed, and a look of contempt came into his eyes. "You've lost your mind. She lives here and does nothing but invent lies! We have only her word that Oriona is dead."

Alive—maybe she was somewhere outside walking, nothing more. In a moment he would get up and go find her. Then he realized how long it would be before he accepted her death; the slightest hope was a shock, pushing him into wish fulfillment.

"I pity you both," Myraa said from the floor. She sounded like Oriona.

"Dear father, we should be preparing for war!"

"At least her lies keep alive the few of us who are left."

"You and I live without her."

"She keeps the Federation from killing those who stay with her."

"How—by being meek and cowardly? They could all be killed in a few minutes."

"Then why haven't they done it?"

"The Earthborn are fools," his son said, "nothing more."

"Then being humble is a way to survive."

Myraa got up and came to stand between them. "Look," she said as she gazed out the window.

Wearily, the older man got up and stepped to the window; his son joined him.

At the bottom of the hill, a procession was starting to make its way up to the house, thirty people marching single file with hands linked. Each wore the black body garment of the Herculean military, but with no insignia. A body without a head, the older Gorgias thought, but they live while their leaders rot.

"What are they doing?" his son asked.

"They are your brothers and sisters," Myraa said. "All that your mother was is mirrored within them. She is more alive than ever."

"Idiotic nonsense," his son said.

Escape, the old Herculean thought. To leave all known worlds behind, to go outside the narrow Snake of worlds strung between Earth and the Cluster . . .

"It's true," Myraa said.

He thought of the worlds nearest Earth, where power for work was plentiful, where the only problem of life was what to do with one's time. There the problems of longevity were directing a different form of natural selection, one in which only the most ingenious and creative individuals would survive into advanced ages, beyond the one-thousand-year mark, while the rest died of accident and ennui. He remembered his raids against a number of those worlds just after the war's end, when his infant son and Oriona were hiding on the planet which later came to be called Myraa's World. He remembered the contempt he had felt for the long-lived, useless Earthpeople he had seen. He had disliked killing these temporal drifters. A pair of eyes, a face, an expression of vacant worry—images of various individuals still lived inside him. Too many had seemed content to die. He wondered if long life gave powerful individuals a proprietary view of reality.

Vaguely he noticed that his son was about to strike Myraa again. She retreated from him and his son followed until they were behind him. He heard the blow, followed by two dull sounds. Myraa and his son were struggling on the floor. Children playing, he thought.

He thought of worlds farther out in the Federation corridor, worlds teeming with colonists who had burned and reseeded whole planets. There life was more dangerous, yet death was not as feared as among the long-lived; but still the ties with the interior worlds were strong, since so many skills and services emanated from Earth. . . .

Behind him Gorgias and Myraa were quiet at last, but he did not turn his chair to look at them.

He thought of the fringe worlds of the Snake, scarcity-ridden places where Earth was almost unknown. Into this far end had come the ships of the Cluster, building, consolidating, gathering loyalty at the most distant nerve ends of Earth's influence; for in fact it was from these most distant worlds that his people were descended, having grown powerful within the rich environment of closely spaced suns inside Hercules.

Later had come the ambition of pushing through to Earth itself, of taking the entire Snake, fifty thousand light-years of space and worlds, for the Cluster. The introversion of Earth's stratified, immortalist society was supposed to have guaranteed victory. Herculean immortals had needed something grand to do with their existence, he thought.

But Earth had come to care. The takeover of the outer worlds had taken too long; one by one the outer worlds began to fight back furiously, and this led to the waking of the Earthgiant. His response brought back all that was strong and alert and clever in his nature, the same qualities that had built the largest human civilization in history, including Hercules. He had come breathing fire against Cluster worlds, until New Anatolia was burned into a cinder and all hope of winning against him became a sad joke.

Slowly he turned and saw that Myraa and his son were no longer in the room with him. Later, he knew, his son's rage would return, regardless of Myraa's efforts to quiet him.

He got up and wandered the large room, thinking about the possibility of life beyond the Earth-Hercules corridor; the Snake was only a thin thread of intelligence lacing the galaxy. Maybe there were other cultures in the central regions of the disk. Was there enough in the idea to interest his son? There had to be a way to change his plans, even if it was with the false hope of making his son think those same plans possible.

"How nice, Father," he imagined his son saying, "—you want me to become an explorer. For whom shall we explore, to what end shall we contact other civilizations? Behind me stands the ghost of a dead civilization. Shall we do it for them?"

Then, after a long silence, his son would continue, half-believing. "Will they give us the power to revive our civilization, Father?"

"Perhaps," he would answer.

"Why should they, whoever they are? And did you consider that we may be alone, that there are no greater civilizations in the galaxy? Even if they exist, they might not wish to be found. . . ."

Outside, the procession had reached the house and was now standing in front of the windows, peaceful faces looking in. He did not know any of them, and they gave no sign of knowing him.

There was dirt on their hands. He wondered if they had come from burying Oriona somewhere out there in the tall grass of the hilly countryside. They were too polite to come into the house, knowing that he was here with his son. He thought of them living in their monastic cells inside the hill beneath the house; there each occupant turned away from the universe of light and color and substance, in the name of seeing past life and death to some fabulous yonder. They might just as easily see through their cell walls, he thought bitterly. Reality lay not in their self-generated ecstasies, but in the cold ground of worms and decomposition outside their cells; in the life-giving ruin of nature which never gave the same thing twice, settling instead for a repetition of types and approximations, none exactly like the other; in the endless processes of star formation and universe construction, not in the wishes of creatures caught between the infinitesimally small and the infinitely large. . . .

Oriona. The thought of her pulsed inside him like a beating heart. His returning grief threatened to swell up inside him and tear his body apart. Ignoring the faces outside, he leaned forward in the chair and put his face in his hands, rubbing his eyes until they exploded into a storm of colors. At any moment he would fall back into the past; his eyes would fail to open when he took his hands away and he would be a stranger to his body while his mind drifted amongst the bloody images of war, in a limbo of sharp pains and shabby sights. . . .

Suddenly Oriona stood in his blind sight, as if thrown up to him by a merciful field of creation. Naked and beautiful, she stood with her legs together, hands folded across her breasts, eyes looking directly at him, long black hair flowing in a mysterious wind. . . .

He cried out and opened his eyes; the afterimage faded on the window before him and he was looking again at the mourners outside.

Oriona, he said to her memory, *your son will go out to kill now, and I am powerless to stop him; he is as I was.* Then a distant thought whispered itself to him: *If you died he would change.* And an even closer whisper hissed inside him: *You could kill him.*

As if something had spoken to them, the mourners outside turned and made their way down the hill.

IV. Sortie

"The passion for destruction is also a creative passion."

—Bakunin

"Life is impoverished, it loses in interest, when the highest stake in the game of living, life itself, may not be risked . . . [in war] Death will no longer be denied; we are forced to believe in it. People really die; and no longer one by one . . . thousands in a single day. Life . . . has recovered its full content."

—Freud

AFTER THEIR BODIES were quiet, Gorgias opened his eyes and watched Myraa as she slept next to him. There was no other woman for him among the survivors; she would know him as the son of leaders, to whom the future belonged even if that future were lost.

For a moment he considered what it would be like to come and live here with Myraa, but the thought shamed him; he felt weak before it. He must never forget that something greater had been taken from him.

Myraa opened her eyes and he smiled at her.

"Do you understand now," she started to ask, "that your mother—"

He turned away from her. "Stop telling me crazy stories—

they may help you but they do not calm me. Why don't you just tell me what happened?"

"When she was ready for passage, she did it herself."

"What?" He turned to face her, angry again. He had been getting ready to apologize for striking her. "What did it take to convince a mature woman to take her own life?"

"But she's not dead—"

"Then where is she?"

"Right here—looking at you through my eyes. One day, when you come to understand, she will speak. The passage she has taken—"

He hit her across the face with the back of his hand. She rolled away from him and lay on her back, saying nothing. He got up, put on his black uniform and boots, and went out into the main room where his father still sat looking out the windows. Gorgias went to the window and looked out into the start of twilight. He saw the group waiting at the bottom of the hill.

"What do the fools want?"

"They've come from burying Oriona."

"Where?"

"Somewhere out there in the tall grass."

"Then she is dead, no matter what Myraa says."

His father looked up at him suddenly. "What did she tell you?"

"That Oriona is alive inside her and will speak to us one day."

A look of naive hope entered his father's pale face.

"Don't be stupid," Gorgias said, "you're a fool if you believe any of it. They're mad here, comforting themselves with lies and stories—anything to forget."

"I don't take it seriously."

"They talked Oriona into believing it. She killed herself!" The older Herculean stood up. "Myraa said this?"

"Just a few minutes ago she tried to talk me into their madness. We've got to go. My way is the only way."

His father was silent.

Gorgias looked outside and saw that the mourners had disappeared. He turned again to his father and said, "Myraa and all the others are this way because of the war. Oriona's death is the fault of the Earthborn. We must strike back, we must make them feel our punishment in any way open to us. When will you share the ship with me?"

His father looked directly at him. The knitted brows seemed to be crushing the blue eyes peering out of the haggard face; his arms were pressed against the stocky body, hands closed into fists.

When his son came out from Myraa's sleeping room, a wave of pity and fear passed through the older Herculean. He watched his son go to the window and look down at the burial party still gathered at the bottom of the hill.

"What do the fools want?"

"They've come from burying Oriona."

"Where?" his son asked.

"Somewhere out there in the grass."

"Then she is dead, no matter what Myraa says."

He looked up at his son and asked, "What did she tell you?"

"That Oriona is inside her and will speak to us one day."

Could it be true, he wondered, was such a gathering of life after this life possible? If so, then immortality was a foolish thing. He thought of his vision of Oriona. Was she trying to reach him? Herculean women had been known for psionic abilities. Fool, he told himself suddenly, there is no evidence for anything like this; the universe had always been unfair and uncaring of wishes. Hope could not create life, or extend it into the void...

"Don't be stupid," his son said, "you're a fool if you believe any of it. They're mad ... comforting themselves with lies and stories..."

"I don't take it seriously." *And what lies do you live by, my son,* he said to himself, knowing that they were the ones he had once believed himself.

"They talked Oriona into believing it. She killed herself!"

He stood up. "Myraa said this?"

"...Oriona's death is the fault of the Earthborn," his son was saying... "when will you share the ship with me?"

He felt a sudden anger in himself, triggered by his son's demand for the ship; anger at Myraa and Oriona; anger at himself for not being able to regain his old strength; anger at the pitiless tide that washed from past to future and had left him here on this despairing shore.

His son turned and left the room. The back door opened and closed with a terrible finality; he would surrender to his son's will.

Surrender? They would lash out together, bringing a piece of the cruel past into the life of the Federation. There would be a public recognition of the past, however small; there was satisfaction in the thought, and he realized that this was how his son felt all the time. He would transfer control of the ship to him as soon as possible.

He started across the room toward the hall leading to the back exit, but stopped when something reached into him, filling him with sudden doubt and panic. *Oriona, forgive me,* he thought, *but there is nothing left for me. I cannot live without my son's approval. I have no one else now.*

He went through the hall. Myraa's naked shape lay on the bed, her body a deep blue from the twilight streaming in the east window. She sat up and looked at him as he hurried to the back door.

It opened and he stepped outside and went down the hill to where the Whisper Ship waited in a warm evening.

His father stood by his side, his face a mask as they watched gray jumpspace swallow Myraa's World. A reflection of them appeared on the screen for a moment, the ghostly images of two mournful men standing in an infinite sepulcher, faces in shadow. Then the black ghosts that marked star positions appeared, and Gorgias felt again as if he were returning to a vast universe of the dead lying beneath or alongside a continuum of color and life. Here death might dance with his will, fear make love to his courage and dream assassins slaughter his capacity for hope, if he stayed too long. . . .

"I'll match the ship to you," his father said.

The older Herculean had come to his senses at last, Gorgias thought as he sat down at the command station.

His father reached past him and touched the pressure panel. A sequence of numbers appeared on the screen, overlaying a view of subspace.

"The ship will know you by this number. If you ever have to assign the ship to another, you must cancel this number and invent a new one, as I have just done. The ship's internal fields will adjust to your body and brain-wave signatures within a day. If these are absent from the ship's interior for any great length of time, and you have left no instructions, the ship will destruct. Remember this."

"I will, Father, I will. . . ."

The board went dark and the numbers faded from the screen as the older man withdrew his hand.

It's mine, Gorgias thought.

"When we come out of hyperspace, you will be in command."

"Thank you, sir."

The older man turned and went aft, leaving him alone.

The oldest Herculean dreamed the past. It drew him into itself, to feel and live again. He was running down a long corridor with Oriona. The passage was filled with water to their ankles; the damp smell of sewage almost made them gag. The air was growing hotter as the city above them went through the stages of disintegration.

High above the planet, mobile fortresses the size of planetoids lanced energy into New Anatolia, incinerating whole cities, precipitating whirlwinds and earthquakes; floodwaters were crossing continents as the polar caps melted.

"Just ahead," he said, pushing his wife ahead. "There, it's there—where the General said he'd left it."

They came to the hidden Whisper Ship, the last possibility of retreat for a group of officers now dead, a gift of mercy for himself and Oriona.

"Our child will live," Oriona shouted as they scrambled into the side lock. It cycled behind them as they went forward into the control area.

"It's preset for its base," he said as he took the station chair.

"Is that safe?" she asked.

"It'll switch to jumpspace in the atmosphere, and it's faster than Federation craft." He touched the plate and fed in the numbers given to him by the General. Images of the streets above them persisted in his mind—metal flowing down from melting upper levels; people dying from sudden heat, exploding as steam formed from the water of their bodies; level after level collapsing as crowds fled downward. In less than a day the heat would sink the city, and dozens of others, into the planet.

The Earthgiant had come well prepared, with a large fleet escorting hundreds of brute-power units. The approach of this armada had drawn all Herculean forces back to defend the Cluster. It was clear now that those forces would not be enough to save New Anatolia or any of the Cluster worlds.

The Whisper Ship rushed out of the drain tunnel—into a

sky of red dust. Columns of energy pushed down from the sky, one for each city and town of the hemisphere. The atmosphere was blue around the frozen bolts as they pumped power into the screaming planet. . . .

"Stop it!"

A hand struck him across the face. He opened his eyes to see his ten-year-old son bending over him.

"Stop it!"

"The dream?"

"It hurts—it's so terrible."

His son was receiving his nightmares. The effect was not as violent as it was for Oriona, but it was bad enough.

"I'll wake up and it will be better," he said, "we'll take a walk down the hill . . ."

Then he opened his eyes again and found himself floating in the aft quarters of the ship. Time had rushed by; the boy of ten was a man; Oriona was dead; and when the ship came out of jumpspace, his son would be in command.

Thirty light-years south of Myraa's World, the Whisper Ship stabbed into the atmosphere of Precept, a frontier world near the end of the Federation's other corridor, a volume of space that was slowly being settled in the direction of the galactic rim.

The younger Gorgias knew that the thickening atmosphere outside the hull was beginning to howl from the vessel's intrusion, and there would be thunderclaps and vortices when the ship leveled off near the surface.

The screen showed swirling clouds and fleeting glimpses of brown and green surface. His father came into the cabin and stood silently behind him. Abruptly the clouds cleared and the ship was running level with the country below.

"How is it going?" his father asked.

"Very well—the ship pretty much guesses what I want it to do. The program plate is enough."

"You can override it with your voice, or add instructions."

"I'm well aware of that."

The first settlement became visible far ahead, a scattering of domes and primitive wooden dwellings on an open plain. There were few signs of vegetation inside the town. As the ship approached, groups of people looked up, toy figures on a dirt tabletop. A few were waving.

Automatically, the forward beam cannon lashed out with its tongue, flitting from one structure to the next; one by one, buildings began to blaze. In a few moments the ship was circling for a repeat run.

The cannon widened its beam and caught all remaining structures. The tabletop town was slowly being cloaked in black smoke. The ship shot past and circled again.

"What do you think?" Gorgias asked without turning around.

His father did not reply.

"You think this is too easy, and you're right. But the object is to hurt them, give them something to talk about, not fight a textbook battle."

As the ship continued to circle, Gorgias turned around in his station and glared at his father. "How many dead do you think?"

"This is not warfare."

"You wouldn't have said that once. Why do you care so much about being fair now?"

"But you can't win unless you can escalate terrorism into conventional conflict—destruction of Federation industry, and then invasion. You can't win..."

"I'm not planning to win. How many times do I have to say it? I want to hurt them, make them know that we live and remember."

"And you want to continue with that indefinitely?"

"Who's to say that we won't find wider support later," Gorgias said.

"I don't want to argue—I'm here, that should be enough for you."

The older man turned and left the cabin.

Gorgias shrugged and turned back to the screen. On the plain below, the smoke was a billowing, churning darkness pushing up toward the sky. Suddenly he wanted to hear the screaming rush of the ship through atmosphere, feel the kick of its shock wave pass over the dead town. He was just beginning on the road that would lead to the return of the Herculean Empire. He felt the will of his people surge through him as the ship shot through the curtain of smoke and out into a deep blue sky, which grew purple as he climbed, blackening into a void of bright stars. The nearby sun pulsed with anger, but could do nothing against him.

Gorgias touched the controls and the ship began to run at

the sun, accelerating to a few percent of light speed. Slowly the star grew in size, seething with the same energy he felt within himself; the star was his enemy, a watchdog that had failed to protect its planet.

When he had absorbed his fill of the star's intensity, he turned it off by switching the ship into jumpspace, abandoning again the universe of violent colors for the dead space of black suns.

For a long time he sat before the screen, thinking about his father's ambivalence. The gray-white jumpspace seemed a bit different this time, suggesting strong light trying to break in from a space beyond; maybe somewhere a waterfall of light marked the frontier between the two kinds of space. He imagined the light of a universe spilling over into an abyss, a cosmos dying in one place and being born again elsewhere.

There was only one thing to do now—strike somewhere else as soon as possible, just in case there was no one left alive on Precept to report the raid.

He would need an invasion force, his father had said. Gorgias made a mental note to question Myraa again about the story of the Herculean army which had fled into the Lesser Magellanic Cloud toward the end of the war. He would have to find out if this was true or just a legend; if true, he would make an effort to contact the force, or its descendants. They might have ships and weapons that would be of use to his campaign.

Passing his hand over the panel, he summoned the star charts onto the screen and began searching for a new target.

V. The Legacy

"There will always be those who must look into the dark in order to see."

—Alan McGlashan

EARTH'S SUN SETTLEMENTS sparkled across the New Zealand night, a ring of habitats encircling the planet, creating the illusion of an arch standing in the ocean. Rafael Kurbi sat with Grazia on the terrace of their seaside house. The waters were swallowing the ring as the night wore on, but there was always more coming up from the other horizon as the Earth turned.

Tightening his arm around Grazia, he thought, *I could drift off into death now and not mind.* Immediately the thought startled him, as once the idea of his own existence had surprised him. He relaxed. *I can live as long as I wish, but my life is precarious and could just as easily have not existed.*

"What is it, Raf?"

"Oh, nothing. Just bored, I suppose."

"With me?"

He looked into her dark eyes, enjoying the paleness of her skin in starlight, and wondered how long peace and satisfaction could be endured. *Strange thought, since satisfaction must by its very nature be enough, always,* he told himself unconvincingly. Perhaps there was too much order, too much tolerance and not enough conflict.

There was plenty of disorder in the planetary colonies, increasing through the Federation Snake until one reached the dark age inside the Hercules Cluster, where almost four centuries after the war the twenty worlds of the Empire were still cut off from Earth and each other.

"Well?" Grazia asked again.

"It's not you. . . ."

Three times between 2000 A.D. and 5000 A.D. the Earth had destroyed itself in war, only to be rebuilt by its nearer colonies. That kind of help might never be available again. After the great war with Hercules, the colonies began to think of themselves first, while Earth, untouched within its own solar system, was turning away from planet-based societies. Earth was becoming a garden, slowly being enclosed by the worlds of the ring, its people slowly drifting away into the skyworlds. One day the mass of the Earth and the other planets would be gone, having been used to construct the component communities of the great shell that would one day finally surround the sun, to draw the sun's energy until it was exhausted in the far future. For a time, at least, the planet would continue to belong to a humankind whose biology was relatively unchanged, to people like himself and Grazia.

I have to get back to being interested in something, he told himself, *in something other than comfort.* His friends in the surrounding communities would laugh at him when he mentioned this need for demanding work. After all, he had studied the unities of art and science, experienced the pleasures and madnesses appropriate to his five decades of life. What else did he want?

"I just feel that I should be risking something, adding to something," he said.

"That's an old-time idea; you can have it subdued."

"But I don't want it suppressed," he said.

She looked at him and smiled. "That's a strange thing to say—you wouldn't know afterward."

"Haven't you ever wondered," he said, "why we haven't found any cultures different from our own, I mean really different from the humanoid patterns we know?"

"Not really."

"Haven't you wondered why they have been only as advanced as we are, give or take a little?"

"That's just the way it is. Nothing much depends on our finding out more about it."

"Maybe there is a superior culture out there in the galaxy—
or maybe it exists only in the main group of galaxies and ours
is a backwater. We haven't gone out to look for them because
we're afraid. Maybe the war has made us distrust our curiosity?
Maybe curiosity and ambition lead to violent conflict. I don't
know. It seems wrong . . ."

"What nonsense," Grazia said, "it's enough that we're kind
and gentle and civilized."

"Look—we don't even use our subspace communications
system to search for advanced cultures, not even in our galaxy,
much less beyond. We use the system to talk to our own worlds
in the Snake. Doesn't that strike you as narrow and unenter-
prising?"

"We mind our own business, Raf."

"But look—we don't even know much about ourselves,
what we are, what life is beyond the textbook litanies."

"We're the form of living matter that asks foolish questions
about itself," she said. "There are scientific people for these
problems."

"But there aren't, Grazia. You don't know how few there
are."

"Enough, I would say."

"A few hundred. Oh, there are many technical priests who
know how to run things by looking up the answers which they
don't really understand. Too many areas of knowledge exist
only in the computer intelligences and in old books. Very little
of that lives in new human minds."

"It's there, though."

"But what about new work, new questions?"

"I think the artificial minds can do better," she said.

"They only care about knowing, not doing—they have no
drive, no instincts to use what they have learned. Once they
know, that's enough."

"I'm glad they know—it would be such a burden. We're
made for the senses, Raf, to appreciate and experience things,
not for understanding, which is an illusion anyway."

"Then maybe those who are redesigning populations in the
ring are right."

"But they're not doing what you would want, just more so
toward what I say we are. What you want was tried in Hercules,
and we got warlike, unbalanced conquerors, not knowers, or
appreciators."

"How are we to evolve further?" he asked. "We must do it

by our own hand, because natural selection is over." *Maybe it's not over*, he thought, *maybe after a million years of immortality, only the most ambitious and innovative will remain.*

"I'm glad there's a place for unchanged people like ourselves," Grazia said.

Slowly, he knew, she was going to get the better of him. But nothing she could say would rid him of the feeling that he was beginning to die, that he would continue to die no matter how often he was renewed physically, no matter how long he lived.

Julian Poincaré visited the next morning, dropping his image in from South Pole City just as Kurbi was beginning to resent the rising sun's penetration of his closed eyelids. He opened his eyes and saw the stocky man standing near the railing, looking out over the ocean.

"Julian?"

Poincaré turned around. "Ah, you're awake."

"Are you here?" Kurbi asked, sitting up on the deck cot.

"Appearance only, dear friend—no substance, no reality, at least not as much as usual. You're talking to yourself."

Kurbi looked around for Grazia, vaguely remembering that she had gotten up before dawn.

"You'll be surprised to learn," Poincaré said, "that our intelligence at the Pole has just had news that a Herculean Whisper Ship has wiped out the rim colony on Precept."

"It must be Gorgias again," Kurbi said. He stretched his long legs and stood up. "Precept? That's in the open end of the Snake, north?"

"That's right—but why should it be Gorgias? He may be dead—we haven't heard anything for more than a century. Why can't it be someone else?"

"I think he's been in stasis. There's some evidence of previous appearances and disappearances, with decades in between. If I'm right, then they have stasis capability and that means I'm right about there being a base; there would have to be to support the technology and the ship."

"And you still think he's not alone?"

"I think," Kurbi said, "that Gorgias may have a son, daughter, even brothers or relations with him." He started to pace back and forth on the terrace. "A base could support quite a few people."

"You're the expert on the Herculeans," Poincaré said.

"The corps will have something to do."

"And you too."

"What are your thoughts about this?" Kurbi asked.

"I'm worried about where the ship will turn up next. It may be soon."

"I think so too," Kurbi said. He felt wide-awake suddenly.

"As ranking intelligence officer, I'm issuing warnings—we can expect more violence."

"As long as it's out in the colonies, I don't think anyone in Chambers will care," Kurbi said.

"I'll try to throw a scare into them. I want ships and resources, and I want you. If they think the ship will pose a threat to close-in worlds, they'll give me what I want."

"Me?" Kurbi asked. He had never thought of his interest in Herculeans as resulting in any practical action. The mystery of Herculean psychology had fascinated him. He had even dreamed of time travel back into the war, just to soak up the atmosphere of those times, feel the pressure of purpose and necessity; now here was a chance to confront a living Herculean from those times.

"Julian!" Grazia said as she came out of the house. The shade screen came on over the terrace, darkening the sky and rising sun. She sat down on the deck cot.

"How are you, Grazia?"

"Fine—now tell me what you want Raf for."

"It's up to him." Poincaré shrugged, and Kurbi saw another tame wolf, like himself, among the sheep of Earth.

"Is there any doubt that it was a Whisper Ship?" he asked.

"Even Precept's simple computer slaves identified it. There's no doubt, Raf."

Grazia was looking at him, her eyes saying, *Why bother, what can it matter, my love?*

"You want to go," she said, "you want to stir up your sense of mission, destroy your equilibrium. Over what? An old war and a madman or two. Go ahead. I couldn't care less."

"Many people have died, Grazia," Kurbi said.

"You wouldn't go for that alone."

"I haven't decided yet; we're just talking."

"What if our homes were threatened," Poincaré said, "—this house; what if that ship appeared in that beautiful morning sky? What if that ocean were being beamed into steam right now?"

"I'd rather not live in such a world," Grazia said. "The

sooner they killed me the better."

"You don't mean that," Kurbi said. He took a step toward her, intending to sit down and hold her hand.

"Stop right there," she said. "Look at the two of you. You're both hoping that terrible things will happen. You may be bored with your lives, but I find ennui and changelessness quite pleasant."

"Look at it this way," Kurbi said. "All we know about the Hercules-Federation War is that we fought an implacable enemy. It's just one big enigma—no records or witnesses left, at least nothing that makes for good evidence. Here's a chance to confront an individual or individuals who still have the war mentality. They remember things and they may have records."

"We have people from then also."

"They've mostly erased their experiences, you know that."

"Well, there are Herculeans living on various worlds."

"Those survivors will never open up—they've changed."

"The simple fact of the matter," Poincaré said, "is quite clear and needs no justification—a Whisper Ship is a good-sized nuisance. It could kill more Federation citizens, it could destroy a planet under certain conditions—Earth, for example. Whatever Raf's interest, he would be useful in the hunt."

"You're just trying to scare me, Julian," Grazia said.

"I'm certainly not."

"Well, it is frightening, no matter what your motive."

"Raf, she's picking on me. Grazia, it could happen, what I say."

Grazia laughed and lay back on the cot.

The war left us a legacy, Kurbi thought, *one which must be taken up, examined, understood; to do so is a form of loyalty to the past, and truthfulness to the future.*

"Good day," Julian said and disappeared.

Kurbi looked through the space where the man's image had stood. The ocean beyond was alive with sunlight and small sailboats. He wondered what they were thinking inside the Herculean ship countless parsecs away.

"I'm going for a swim," Grazia said behind him.

VI. Target

"The savage mind deepens its knowledge with
the help of *imagines mundi*."

—Claude Lévi-Strauss

"Who is the man walking in the Way?
An eye glaring in the skull."

—Seccho

HIS SON was shaking him awake.

"We're not coming out—the ship won't come out of jump-space!"

He opened his eyes.

"I can't tell what's wrong," his son was saying, "I've tried everything."

"It's not the ship," the Herculean said, "this sometimes happens. . . ." He got up and followed his son forward through the ship.

The screen was blinking when they entered the control room, as if a storm were raging outside.

"Look," his son said, "the star analogs—they look solid

now!" In normal passage, the black places marking the positions of stars in normal space were not solid objects in relation to the ship; directly ahead of them now was a giant black sphere, its surface shiny and reflective. The ship was rushing toward it at an unknown velocity.

"I've tried to alter our course half a dozen times," his son said, "but the ship fixes on another sphere and runs toward it."

"We're not in the usual otherspace, but in a nearby parallel space. A quantum uncertainty within the ship's vibrancy matrix generator causes this sort of thing. I was warned against it. It doesn't happen very often, but it can't be helped. The old builders didn't have time to iron out the problem, and they were not sure it could even be solved without altering the fundamental laws of nature."

"But you know how to get us out?"

"I'll try."

The object ahead was now twice as large. In a few moments it covered the viewscreen. A reflection of the ship appeared in the black surface, a silver image rushing up to meet them head-on. Frozen energy, the old Herculean thought, everything that a living sun is not. The continuum flickered again, leaving a slow fading flash in the black below. Suddenly the ship's image seemed to pass into them and the vessel was flitting across a stygian plain. A mock sunrise flashed on the horizon as the continuum flickered again. *Maybe we'll die*, the older Gorgias thought. He would not have to face his son, or watch him carry out his plans.

The ghastly flickering became more frequent. The Herculean passed his hand over the glowing program plate.

The ship switched. For a moment it seemed that a more familiar jumpspace was coming into view on the screen; then the alien space flickered again and he knew that the ship had only changed position within it.

"Tell me the truth—we may never come out."

"You may be right."

"Try again."

"Here we go."

The ship switched, straining to surface into the known universe, again without success. The ship was running at another black sphere.

"What now?" his son asked. There was a trace of anger in his tone.

"Wait—try again, as often as it takes to bring us out. The uncertainty in the generator fields can't last forever by their very nature."

"Regular watches?"

"Try three times during each watch."

"I'll wait until you try once more," his son said. "Then I'll get some rest and leave you to it."

"Here we go."

The ship switched for the third time.

The screen went black.

"Now what?" his son asked.

"I don't know...."

The ship's lights flickered.

"It's as if we're not getting enough power," his son said. "Can we check anything in here?"

"No, the receiving accumulators are a sealed mechanism."

"You mean we get power from somewhere else?" his son asked.

"We've never taken on fuel, if you've noticed. For what this ship can do, it could never carry enough power or generate its own. I think we get it from the Cluster, but I don't know how. Engineering and armoring was not my strong suit. I was just an attack-force captain."

"But if the ship works, then the power source was never destroyed!" his son said.

"We're far out of our spaces—that's probably interfering with power reception."

All signs of movement were absent from the black screen; reality had solidified, freezing all motion.

The screen lightened, growing brighter, as if some titanic explosion were taking place outside. The ship was suddenly in a white space, and the stars, if they were stars, appeared as small black points.

The Herculean passed his hand over the panel for the fourth time.

The known universe recreated itself on the screen.

"We don't seem to be far from where we started," his son said, "maybe a dozen light-years from Precept."

Where hundreds lay dead in the dust. What had they known of the war? What had they ever done to my son? I should have tried to stop it.

But his doubts and tender feelings of mercy would not restore the Empire's power. His son would never accept the Empire's demise; restoration was for him the one supremely valued end, overriding all others; the effort to revive Hercules was the only way of life for him, even if in the end it might mean the death of all surviving Herculeans, including himself.

The interstellar liner drifted slowly on the screen; only minutes out of Sagan IV, it was readying to switch over into jumpspace. The Whisper Ship's beam reached out to the cylindrical hull and began pumping energy into the forward drive mass. A hole opened like a blooming flower. Gas began to spill out. The beam shifted to the midsection and another wound opened; red light and human shapes spilled out into space.

It's the only way.

His father had left the cabin a few moments before the attack. *The whole point is to do cruel and terrible things.* Silently the beam shifted and cut its third hole.

A million miles behind the rupturing vessel, the disk of Sagan IV swam in half phase. In a few minutes port tugs would be rushing out to the dying liner. He could expect a military ship or two, but they would be too late to threaten him.

There would be little for the rescuers to save. The ship would explode at any moment, as the beam's torrent of energy penetrated into vital areas. Was it true, he wondered, that power from the stars of home was finding its way into the Whisper Ship? He felt pride in the idea; Hercules was still a cluster of war stars, despite his father's weakness, despite Myraa's indifference.

The liner blossomed in space. Its hull flew apart as if driven by the magma of an exploding planet. The debris expanded, a small universe of mangled life, molten metal and hot plasma; bits and pieces would continue in all directions—into the local sun, into deep space, moving until all time ran out.

Suddenly, the magnification on his screen went up, revealing military vessels coming out from the orbital docks around Sagan IV, two near-planet defense cruisers summoned by the dying liner. Gorgias wondered if there was fear aboard the Federation ships as they examined the Herculean design on their screens. What were they thinking as they stared at the Whisper Ship, a legendary shape far out of its time?

They were coming fast now, growing in size until the screen switched to normal and they were plainly visible as bright stars no more than a few hundred kilometers away.

Automatically, the Whisper Ship began to pull away, shrinking Sagan IV to a blue point. The ship switched, blackening the stars and affixing them to a backdrop of desolate gray. The pursuers were gone.

Gorgias waited for two black dots to appear in the warp. A minute went by, two minutes; after five minutes there was still no pursuit.

"Are we running?"

He turned around and saw his father standing in the center of the cabin. Fear and sadness crowded into the older man's face, constricting his muscles as if he had been crying. The old Herculean was a disgrace to his traditions.

"The liner is destroyed, and we've lost the hunters."

His father closed his eyes. "Where are we going now?"

"I want Myraa and the others to know before we return to base."

"It will impress them, you think."

"It will inspire the others, perhaps, and she can't help being affected."

"Don't you see—it's your way of stealing courage."

"I don't see that at all."

His father walked up to him and struck him across the face with the back of his hand.

"You have no right!"

The old Herculean struck him again. The blow threw him back in the chair. "I'm going to beat you until you can't walk, until I can lock you up like a beast and not care."

"Coward," Gorgias said as he rubbed his face.

His father lunged at him and seized his throat. Gorgias felt powerful hands close on his windpipe and squeeze.

With great effort, Gorgias lifted his father by the waist and they both fell to the floor, older man on the bottom. The angry hands relaxed their hold on his throat and Gorgias struggled onto his feet.

He turned and looked at the screen. Two black dots had appeared.

"Look—hunters! I can't bother with you now. Go back to your cabin."

He sat down at the station, passed his hand over the program plate and rekindled the known universe for a few seconds, quenched it again, then searched for the sign of the pursuers.

The continuum was clear, but he knew that they would reappear in a few moments; the ship was leaving a clear trail. He would have to do something to hide it quickly.

He turned around to face his father again, but the Herculean was gone.

VII.   Awakening

"Not till we are lost . . . do we begin to understand ourselves."

—Henry David Thoreau

"THE FRONTIER SETTLEMENT on Precept," Poincaré was saying, "then the liner on the Sagan IV run. That's more than twenty thousand dead, Raf."

They sat on the sun-filled terrace, breakfast before them. Grazia was sailplaning over the ocean, a small white bird in a perfectly clear blue sky.

"They've dropped it in my lap," Poincaré said. "What do you think we should do?"

"Ask our military antiquarians."

"I'm one of them—so are you, to a degree."

"Well?"

"I say go after the ship with a small force, hunt him down, keep a larger force on call to come running when we've found him."

"What's your problem then?" Kurbi asked.

"I want you with me. I thought that much was obvious. Raf, you have a feel for Herculean civilization. I don't want this to be a completion of genocide. I think you can help me save whatever may be worth saving."

"I'd say that was a charitable way of thinking about it, considering all the carnage the Herculean has caused. Do I have a choice?"

45

"If possible," Poincaré said, "I want the Whisper Ship and its occupants captured alive. Everyone I know feels the same. They're not altruists or historians or bleeding-heart Chards—they're curious, somewhat greedy men, who want the ship and its base, just to see what's there. I wouldn't mind playing with a few Herculean war toys myself." Poincaré took a deep breath. "Besides, it's great entertainment to think of capturing these rogues. We'll exhibit them, question them, try them, inter them for life."

"The enemy's face is fascinating," Kurbi said, "especially when he is in short supply. You want me to go out and find Gorgias?"

"You still want to, don't you?"

"There's Grazia to consider—it would be dangerous. I would be giving up a life of travel and reflection."

"There'd be travel, and you can test what you've been reflecting about. You would also be helping to save lives."

Kurbi shrugged. "Does that mean so much, Julian, with so many dying by choice?"

"The ones who died out there made no choice."

"Life seems to be most precious when threatened. Take danger away, and a whole starry civilization goes to sleep."

"Exactly," Poincaré said. "You and I know that we need all the waking up we can get. This terrorist might be doing us a favor."

"I don't think he would appreciate your view of him."

"Now you're sounding like Grazia."

"I sometimes wonder if I know what I want," Kurbi said. "Life seems to possess a fundamental flaw, especially if you know it can be prolonged indefinitely."

"What flaw is that?"

"An inability to provide lasting satisfaction." He looked out across the bright morning and saw Grazia's glider come sweeping in from the ocean. In a minute or two she would pass over the house. Suddenly the craft dropped below the seaside cliffs and he could not see it. The updraft would hurl it skyward again, and she would hurtle in over the house as she had done so many times before.

Kurbi picked up the half-finished glass of grape juice and finished it. "Won't you have something with me, since you're here in the flesh?"

"No thanks. Well, what do you say?"

"I don't know right now, Julian. Let me think about it."

"I won't try and sugarcoat it—we may both get killed."

"I'm well aware of that," Kurbi said. He got up. The glider was not coming up into view.

"What's wrong?"

"The glider hasn't come up over the cliffs."

Poincaré got up also and they went to the terrace steps that led down to the path. In a moment Kurbi was running across the grass to the cliff's edge a quarter of a kilometer away. Poincaré caught up with him just in time to steady him at the edge.

"There," Julian said, pointing.

The glider was in the water, one wing broken.

"She took this updraft so many times. . . ."

"Let's get down there," Julian said. "Better still, I'll go down and you call the medics."

Kurbi turned and walked quickly up to the house, feeling that his body was not his own.

"Hurry!" Julian called after him.

She had fallen to the rocks after hitting the cliff; the sea had battered her body until she was beyond repair. There was no possibility of freezing the remains or of restarting the body's regenerative systems; only cloning remained, and he had rejected the idea. The person who would have come to him bearing Grazia's appearance and genetic structure would not have been Grazia, only her twin sister. For many others that would have been enough, but for him it would have been a mockery of his love for her.

He sat alone in the darkened living room and tried to choke his grief, compress it to a point and squeeze that point out of reality. Outside, the sky blazed, hurling spears of starlight through the clear wall between the living room and terrace. The glider sank in his mind and he reached out with invisible hands to stop it from hitting the cliff. She had been falling as he had talked with Julian, and he had known it; she might even have been conscious after hitting the sea rocks.

It would have been better, he thought, if she had been on the interstellar liner. That would have made more sense; better the explosive decompression of the void than the bloodying rocks; better murder than mindless chance. Anything was preferable to being reminded of frailty and the indifference of physical reality; the intended act was always superior to the unintended event.

Stupid thoughts, he told himself. Maybe he should go and help Poincaré trap his gadfly; maybe it would help him forget. It would be almost . . . as if he were searching for Grazia again.

He got up and went out on the terrace. The sky made him feel small. For a moment he felt that he understood the feelings of the outworlders, for whom life was joined to strenuous effort; out there living was valuable and dying meaningful. There they would laugh at the manner of Grazia's death; there life was stretched between demanding limits and did not try to be more; there life spent itself so completely that little regret was possible at its end.

He thought of his son Rik, who had not come to Grazia's funeral service, and who had refused to talk with him or share his sorrow. It would do no good to search for him among the diverse worlds of the ring; he would not recognize his son if he saw him.

Rik had never reconciled himself to the fact that he had been born of natural parents and in a fairly ancient way, while all his peers in the sun settlements were creative composites drawn from genetic-bank materials. Kurbi blamed himself for letting the boy leave Earth at an early age; in the ring he had come under the overwhelming influence of a myriad of styles. Earth could never be the same for him again.

In a way Rik was right; only a small portion of humanity lived on Earth; an even smaller portion lived the older life, which accepted leisure but little biological alteration. Perhaps, as Rik believed, the acceptance of the unmodified human form limited one's range of experiences and exercise of creative powers; while the newer, variegated humanity, Rik claimed, had overcome the old discontents.

Suddenly Kurbi was sure that he would join Poincaré, but the feeling passed; what he really wanted to do, he admitted, was to wander away from the solar system and explore the worlds of the Federation Snake. He wanted to see how people lived, and if they were happier. Julian could do without him for a time.

Grazia, he said silently. The ring of worlds in the sky blurred into a band of light as tears filled his eyes, while another part of him cursed the fact of human dependency and the insufficiency of all things.

VIII. Home

"As to what happened next...when men are desperate no one can stand up to them."

—Xenophon

THE STILLNESS in the control cabin was oppressive. The ship's motion through the gray vastness seemed to be an imprisonment within a static medium. That the ship was moving was something he *knew;* but his body felt only confinement.

His father came in and stood behind him. "Where are we going now?" he asked.

"I think we've lost the pursuers, but I don't want to lead them back to the base if I'm wrong. We're going back to Myraa—later we'll go to the base to pick up some equipment I want."

"What do you have in mind?" His father's tone was almost friendly, as if he were another person.

"What do you care?"

"I'm sorry I can't feel the way you do. Can you feel how sorry I am?"

"How can you bring yourself to care about the deaths of our enemies?"

"I can't help it—it's been so long. What can those alive now know of the old struggle?"

"I'm going to leave you at the base—unless you still want to help."

49

"If something happens to you, I will never be able to leave the base. Leave me with Myraa instead." His father's voice was almost a whisper. *He's inside me,* Gorgias thought, *I'll never get rid of him.* "I think I might like living with Myraa and the others." *Punish him, don't give him what he wants.*

"I've changed my mind—we'll go back to the base first. I'll need you to help me load and handle two or three gravitic units. You do know something about them, don't you?"

"Yes, very well," his father said, "but later you must leave me on Myraa. It's what I want now."

Gorgias turned around in his station chair.

"Must—there is little that I must do. I'll see." The old Herculean was trying to manipulate him now.

"I'll stay in the aft cabin," his father said and left the control area.

As he watched the bulkhead door slide shut, a sudden fear gripped Gorgias, as if he had been cut off from everything real. The past was shrinking away from him, leaving him alone and naked before a stone wall of infinite height and thickness, a structure that he would never be able to penetrate. He could not imagine what lay on the other side, but he knew that he desired it above everything else. He turned back to the screen and closed his eyes to shut out the timelessness of jumpspace; visualizing the wall before him, he made an effort to pierce its substance. His eyes came up against a fine texture of sandy pits and scars, where a nameless weathering had worked to breach the stone. . . .

He opened his eyes, suddenly aware that he had been dozing. The screen was filled with the gray-white light of the continuum, casting its pallor into the cabin. He looked at his hands. The skin seemed dead and dry, as if the flesh were about to fall away from the bones. *Everything in jumpspace is dead; everything that passes through dies a little.* He rubbed his hands together and they fell away from his arms. . . .

He sat up and realized that he had been dreaming about being awake. The screen was a normal gray with black stars; passage home was a quarter over and there was no sign of hunters.

He got up and paced the cabin, dreaming of the new sortie.

As the universe reappeared on the screen, the Hercules Cluster took up half the field of view ahead, a globe of fireflies exploding out from a center of concentrated light. Within a half hour the Cluster became the entire universe as the ship penetrated toward the base star inside.

Within another hour the concealing cloud was behind the ship and the dead world of the base floated on the screen. The ship brought itself in low over the scarred surface and drifted into the receiving tunnel through the sequence of locks, sliding finally into its familiar berth.

Home, young Gorgias thought bitterly, *all there is of it.*

Once, the core of the Empire had consisted of twenty worlds, all dead now. He still remembered the roll taught to him by his father: New Anatolia, Capital of the Empire; Gorgias, home of the Empire's creators; Vis and Sivat, worlds of the mental arts; Lash and Bram, planets for soldiers; Indra, the water world; Avat and Rishna, where armorers built the instrumentalities of war; Rud and Panis, shipbuilding planets, where a few inspired designers, together with a team of fleeing armorers, had built the two known Whisper Ships; Nahus and Ush, places for the arts and architecture; Ganesa, a world for poets and songsingers; Manus, a world for historians and computer libraries; Yama, the wilderness where young soldiers went to test themselves; Jas, Ulys and Mizon, outer worlds for astronomers, physicists and scientific researchers of every kind. All this within a space of fifty light-years. The Cluster's diameter of a hundred light-years contained ten thousand times as many stars as any equal volume of space. Here was room to grow, to concentrate creative energies, to create the greatest civilization in the galaxy; no wonder the Cluster had earned the Federation's envy. Here the Herculean Empire would come to be again.

He got up from the station and went aft to the side lock, which was already open. He stepped out into the stillness and looked around. The lights were still on around the stony berth. The metal door leading out from the chamber of six berths was still open. Suddenly he felt love for the base; it was strong and constant; self-maintaining, it would last forever.

His father came out and stood beside him. "What will you need me for?" he asked.

"I'll need you to help me load two gravitic units and a tug-scooter."

"Right now?"

"Yes—that's all I came for."

Gorgias led the way from the berth, through the metal door and down the long corridor into the war room, around the table to another door. Pulling it open, they went through and followed a downward-sloping passage which led into a supply warehouse composed of a hundred interlocking chambers. There were a dozen levels below this area; the lowest floor housed the life-support devices, which were powered by the thermal energy of the planet's core. As long as this world remained warm inside and the homeostatic slave intelligences continued to channel energy to the various systems, the base would live, its synthesizers producing air and foodstuffs, more than he would ever need. The berth would stock the ship with sufficient synthesizer mass and make subtle adjustments and repairs in the sealed submolar systems that received the energy to run the drive.

At times it disturbed him to know that he understood so little of the ship or the base's workings, but the great builders and armorers were gone and there was no one to teach him. Where, for example, was the power source for the Whisper Ship? Somewhere in the Cluster, but where? Where was the other ship, if there was one? Given enough time, he might come to understand more of what the base contained; but only the growth of a new population of Herculeans would be capable of retrieving the legacy of the past, bringing all the skills and knowledge out of the records and technical examples back into the container of living individuals, who could then shape new developments.

"Where would the grav units be?" Gorgias asked.

"In the wall closets," his father said. "Most were never unpacked."

The lights in the room were dim. The greenish walls rose to a height of ten feet and met a gray ceiling. The air was cool and odorless. "I was here when the base was opened," the old Herculean said, "when they were bringing in all the supplies still stored here." He went ahead to the far wall and slid open a large closet door, revealing case after case of work scooters and gravitic workhorses, each packed in a clear plastic block.

Gorgias went up to the open closet and peered in at the tools. The scooter had seats for two, hover and propulsive controls that seemed obvious and a small rack in the back; the gravitic units were featureless solid rectangles about a meter long and half a meter tall, with attachment fingers located at each right angle. On-off pressure plates were yellow and stood out from the dark green of the unit; whether the device would be used to push, pull or lift depended on the position in which it would be attached.

"How much can these handle?" Gorgias asked.

"I don't know the practical limit," his father said, "though I suspect that they could not push a planet. Anything substantially smaller, depending on where it is, on a planetary surface or in free-fall, would be fair game, I suppose."

His father seemed calmer, as if their violent confrontation had purged him of his fears and doubts. Maybe he would become his old self again and be of use after all.

"Can we use the scooter to ferry the units to the ship?"

"I think so," his father said.

"Let's unpack, then."

Together they pulled the scooter from its niche onto the floor. The plastic block was soft and gelatinous to the touch and came off easily. Gorgias peeled off the covering on the grav units and stacked them on the back of the scooter. He sat in the front saddle and his father got on in back.

"Here we go."

Gorgias pressed down on the hover-control plate gently and the scooter lifted from the floor; he pressed on the propulsion plate and the scooter moved forward. Grasping the stick, he steered the machine toward one of the marked service doors, which slid open to reveal a direct tunnel connecting to the berth area.

As the scooter carried them through the passageway, he thought of all the weapons stored in the warehouse, rooms and rooms of shelves, closets and cubbyholes turned away from the stars of home, filled with more military hardware than he could name; enough armaments to equip ten divisions.

Another door slid open and let them out into the berth chamber. Gorgias steered the scooter alongside the ship and into the open lock, stopping just past the inner door.

"We can leave it here, near the bulkhead," he said, and got off.

"What will you use the units for?" his father asked as he dismounted.

A suspicion grew in Gorgias's mind, the result of the question as well as of the older man's change in approach. Was he planning to act against him? The only way to find out was to tell him what he wanted to know and watch his reaction.

"Come with me and find out."

"Then you don't want to leave me here?"

"Tell me, why did you give me the ship if you were so worried about how I would use it?"

The Herculean did not answer immediately. At last he said, "It must be because a part of me still thinks as you do. Once all of me felt the way you do—I taught you to do so. There seemed to be no other way to live and act in the periods between stasis, especially when we thought one of our armies had escaped and might return. So much was promised by the armorers toward the end of the war—we all thought those weapons could make a difference."

"They would have if there had been time to build them."

"I think," his father said, "that I would like to live on Myraa's World. Leave me there, forget me and do as you wish, but don't leave me here. . . ."

"Very well." It would be better to agree with him now, and see what happened later. He suspected that the older man was physically ill in some way, and his mind might be affected. But what doctor from the Federation knew enough to treat a Herculean? Completely homeostatic, requiring no medical care except in serious accident cases, the race had been designed for endurance; in terms of the need for rest, recovery from infection and general vitality, a Herculean could outperform a traditional Earthborn by a factor of three to five.

Historically, Earth citizens had been shy of biological engineering, fearing the loss of versatility to specialization if the practice grew out of hand; but as the Federation grew, pockets of humankind diverged from one another, culturally and biologically, until the first settlements in the Hercules Cluster reached out for a truly improved human type, creating the long-lived Herculeans. Few were left now, he thought sadly, himself and his father and the handful on Myraa's World. He had not heard of any others. Genocide had been all but complete; but in failing to be complete, the Earthborn had made a fatal error, one which he would live to see them regret.

"Let's get going," he said to his father.

Turning from the open lock, he led the way into the control room. He sat down in the station chair and waited for the lock to close. His father came and stood at his right.

"Well, what are your plans?" There was an almost lighthearted tone in the older man's voice.

Gorgias touched the map retrieval plate and the screen lit up, revealing a solar system of twelve planets. "Here, six hundred light-years from Earth, lies New Mars, fourth planet from the twin suns. The various settlements have more than twenty million people. The planet has no heavy defenses, and no reason to expect us...."

"What's your idea?"

"I'm going to destroy most of the life on the planet," Gorgias said.

IX. The Ring

"One must somehow find a way of loving the world without trusting it; somehow one must love the world without being worldly."

—G. K. Chesterton

"...the love of a man for a woman is like an attempt at transmigration, at going beyond ourselves, it inspires migratory tendencies in us."

—Ortega y Gasset

HE WAS ALONE, going where he wished, and the fact made him feel guilty.

As he stood looking out the window of his resort room, Rafael Kurbi realized that he did not know where he was going. The green mountainside was peaceful outside his window. Here in the sun settlements of Earth's ring, a quarter of a million worlds, each a different environment and subculture, beckoned with the promise of novelty and human contact; he could change worlds as he would clothing.

From inside, the ring was a cloud of glittering insects, rivaling the stars in brightness, a milky way of human living spaces cutting across the galactic background; at the center was Earth, oasis of origins, a place to be looked at, admired, even worshipped, but not lived on. People found it strange that he had cared to dwell there so long; even though a large population

56

shared his preference, it was a tiny minority compared to the population of the ring.

The North American mountain landscape outside his window—peaks and fir trees, outcroppings and boulders—was all perfectly safe and accurate. The weather could be varied to taste, streams stocked with perfect fish, woods filled with replaceable game, the air filled with birds. If only he could order a glider with Grazia in it.

He was standing with his head toward the center of the small world; across a space of air he could see houses and roadways attached to the opposite surface fifty kilometers away. Sunlight shafted down the center of the egg-shaped air space, reflected in by a large mirror at one end of the environment; sunpower also ran the recycling plant located on the outside at the other end of the worldlet.

Less than twenty kilometers away in space hung another world, one filled with water, where visitors' hotels provided a view of aquatic human life; there one could swim to a sun window and look out at the stars.

Pulling aside the slide window, Kurbi stepped out on the terrace and took a deep breath. The air was cool and clean and stimulating. Standing there, he felt little of the stress and anguish that he knew were inside him, readying to take over.

"How are you feeling?" a familiar voice asked from behind.

He turned and said, "Hello, Julian—are you here?"

The image shook its head. "Waste of time—just dropped in to see if you'd changed your mind."

"No. Any more news of the Herculean ship?"

"Nothing at all."

"Maybe that's the end of it."

"I don't think so. I've been doing some checking—this ship has appeared before. From the scattered Herculeans still alive on more than a dozen star systems, besides those on Myraa's World, I've learned that the Whisper Ship is probably manned by an officer named Gorgias and his son of the same name. He's more than four centuries old, his son at least half that age—but much of that time may have been spent in stasis somewhere. . . ."

Like an old disease virus, Kurbi thought, *or a spore.*

"There must be an undiscovered base," Julian said. "If there is not, then the ship may very well disappear for lack of supplies and repair facilities. We were never able to capture a Whisper

Ship—the only record is of one destroying itself rather than surrendering. Some of the Herculean legends reported to me say that the ship is tied to the personality of its commanding officer in some way, and destroys itself when the officer dies. In any case, this vessel has appeared in centuries past, each time taking action against some locale in the Snake, always disappearing for long stretches of time."

"What's the point, then?"

"Revenge, from what I've managed to guess. A few of the Herculeans questioned by our operatives have shown admiration for what has happened. A thing like this could grow."

"Into what?"

"Insurrection—takeover of a world here and there."

"What do we care?"

"There is civil order to preserve—and some of the Chamber members won't stand for a Herculean survivor causing trouble. They'll do anything to quash it, out of pride."

"Let the locals do it—they do most everything else for themselves."

"Raf, what it comes down to is this—we want the ship and we want the base. It's a combination of curiosity and completing unfinished business. There may be more attacks on transports, and many worlds have no protection against attack from space—they have no need of it, since it's not the kind of thing that happens very often."

"You can do well without me, Julian. Look at the worlds around Earth—what do they care about anything that happens to old-style human types like you and me and the frontier worlds? Reality is a menu they write each morning; their bodies are clay to be molded from one generation to the next. The acts of this terrorist are part of an unpleasant game for them, one they don't care for much, so they give it to you or me. You know, Julian, these Herculeans are probably a lot like you and me, relics from another time; and they're out there kicking and screaming, getting in their licks before they're blown away."

"That's very nice, Raf, but they could destroy the Earth, the ring, most of the life in the solar system, if they can get followers. They're probably not aware of that yet but they'll catch on. It's up to those of us who have an idea of the potential danger to stop them."

Kurbi did not reply.

"It's that serious, Raf."

"You think they may have the equipment to do that?"

"If they have a base, maybe worse. They may not be aware of what they have. We don't have much will to fight back. The Whisper Ship could do quite a bit of damage if it came into our sunspace. How do you protect the ring? It wasn't made to be defensible."

"You're assuming a lot of motivation, a lot of hatred on their part."

"Raf, you know more than I do how we destroyed their entire culture—twenty worlds razed to the ground!" He paused for a moment. "It's possible none of this may happen, we may never hear of the ship again—its range is not limited and Gorgias may simply go off somewhere into the galaxy and live quietly. I don't know—but I do have a job to do as intelligence officer, and I do have some pride in how well I do it. You're a Herculean expert. It's my duty to recruit you."

"I wouldn't be much good to you now, Julian. The answer is still no."

Abruptly, Poincaré was gone. Kurbi was alone again with the perfect view, a cool breeze and the weight of a loss that could never be made good. *What in all eternity do I want,* he asked himself, knowing full well that it was involvement, a context in which he was needed. Poincaré was offering that, but it was not enough, because Kurbi would not let it be enough out of stubbornness.

Maybe there comes a time when having lived for a time is enough, and further life is useless unless one becomes a different person. The person I am must die, he told himself, but he was not sure there would ever be a successor.

On the world devoted to physical pleasure he paid to fall in love. The fee was his permission to record his memory and the time limit was three weeks; but the completeness of the illusion convinced him that more than a year had passed.

She was beautiful, brown-haired and brown-eyed, buxom and heavy-hipped—an old-style human type from before the changes; of course, she was tailor-made, to be mindwiped after his term of involvement, but he knew that only later. When she was with him, he forgot the past and believed completely. She spoke perfectly, smiled appealingly—perhaps she even understood what he said to her during those long nights when the moon never set. She was a professional, who somewhere had her own life and would return to it. In the end she helped destroy his sense of the unique, which he had gained so painfully, so completely with Grazia.

I need something constructive to do, he told himself. Julian's offer intrigued him, but he felt that he would be of no use in his present state. He wondered if he were afraid of the danger, of dying. What would it be like to confront a Herculean who had only one desire to kill those who had destroyed his world. *My past is as dead as theirs.* Again he found himself sympathizing with the Herculeans.

I want to live after all, he concluded.

On the dream world he found, and lost, Grazia three times.

One hundred kilometers long, the asteroid had been motorized and brought in from the outer solar system more than a thousand years ago. It had been bored, hollowed and honeycombed in thousands of places, creating chambers of safety for the dreamers, who lived an endless succession of dream sequences. This subculture believed in the biological history of the body and old brain—letting that history of layered impulses, instincts and images bubble to the surface of their dream lives in violent, often cruel fantasies—

—Grazia came to him in his tomb, opened the sleep crypt and asked him why he was fleeing from all that was alive. She took his hand and together they were borne up through a long tunnel, emerging at last in a sunny landscape of trees and gentle hills.

The earth smelled of flowers and dirt. Here a stiff-winged blackbird swooped toward them, seized Grazia by the torso and nearly cut her in two, carrying the remains off into the blue, cloudless sky—

TRY AGAIN.

—They waited in a garden, she looking up at the sky where the hot sun rode. Slowly its light increased, suffusing the entire sky, until the nova's heat blew away the planet's atmosphere, melting the flesh from their bodies, leaving for an instant two skeletons embracing—

AND AGAIN.

—He had come back in time to run toward the cliff edge. High over the sea, Grazia's glider was dropping toward the wall face, gaining speed as it approached the air currents near the shore. He stopped at the edge and started to wave her off, but the craft continued its approach until the sudden downdraft tumbled it out of control, smashing it up against the wall, sending it finally to the rocks and breakers below. Giant crabs scurried as the ocean retreated, and he watched them pry the body out of the cockpit and pick it clean, leaving the skeleton to bleach in the sun—

TRY AGAIN?

No, he said within himself, I'm not suited to this kind of life, I'll never be able to make it work.

WE ARE SORRY, they said, and let him go.

X. New Mars

"The Tree of Knowledge is not that of Life."

—Byron

RAFAEL KURBI arrived at New Mars with only the clothes he was wearing and his identity disk. When the shuttle from the starship touched down at Port Deimos, the captain told him over the intercom to stay in his cabin.

A few minutes later a man came to see him.

"Rafael Kurbi?" the man asked as the door slid shut behind him.

"Yes," Kurbi said and got up from his bunk.

"My name is Rensch, port commissioner for New Mars. Why are you coming here?" The man spoke Federation, but with a harsh accent that made the words startlingly unfamiliar. He was of middle height, with closely cropped black hair, slightly gray at the temples; his hands were gnarly, thick-boned. He looked at Kurbi with eyes that seemed to hide amusement, perhaps even contempt.

"To live, maybe," Kurbi said. Suddenly he became aware of his disheveled state. He needed clean clothes, a bath and a shave. The starship had not been a luxury vessel. A pervert from Earth, Rensch was probably thinking.

"Why? A Federation citizen of your rank and wealth? What would you want here? Are you an intelligence operative? I don't mind, personally and officially, but I would like to know."

He ran his hand through his coarse hair and scratched the back of his head.

"What would you know about me?" Kurbi asked, immediately regretting the challenging tone of the question. "I want to live here a while, see a little of how you live," he added before the other could answer.

"I know that you are from Earth itself, rather than from the urban ring, that you are a relatively unmodified human type, unlike the extravagantly doctored ringers. This will make you less of a curiosity to our people. Will you make official trouble if I turn you away?"

For a moment there was silence as Kurbi looked into Rensch's face. "Do you have that right?" Kurbi asked. "I'm sorry, Commissioner," he added quickly, "I shouldn't have asked that— no, I won't make any trouble for you, but I hope you will let me stay."

Rensch considered for a moment. "You'll have to work here," he said. "We don't sell much in goods or services and we don't exchange much credit with Earth—we trade mostly, for what the star freighters bring a few times a year. We're mostly self-sufficient, but improvements from the Federation have helped increase our population and it's getting harder to stay that way. Many of our people feel threatened."

"How do you mean?"

"Their way of life...."

"What can I work at?"

"You'll have to work for food and lodgings. You'll start here in the port, helping to unload what the shuttle brings down. When you're done, come to me and I'll see what else I can do. If I can't find much, you'll have to leave when the freighter goes."

"I'll be working for you, then?"

"I'm your boss as long as you're in the port."

"I hope you can help me—because I want to see more of your world. By the way, where can I stay?"

"There are a few rooms behind my office—you can stay there. Come with me now."

Kurbi followed him out of the cabin, down the shuttle's central passageway to the open lock, where a ramp led down to the unloading dock. Rensch started down ahead of him, but Kurbi paused for a moment to look out at New Mars. The port was a vast machine of black and silver metal, squatting under a sky of low, driving clouds; a drizzly rain floated down and the air smelled of ozone.

He went down the ramp to where Rensch was waiting for him.

"This is the only port we have," the commissioner said loudly. "The rest of the planet is agricultural—about twenty million people, but thinly scattered across a large land surface, three continents, all joined by passable land bridges."

"You were born here?" Kurbi asked.

"Yes—we wouldn't stand for Federation officials here."

Rensch turned and led the way across the slippery surface of the dock to a small building a hundred meters away. There was a hand-operated glass door. Inside, his office was lit by old-style fluorescent tubes; the desk and chairs were wrought iron. The commissioner crossed the room and opened a green wooden door.

Kurbi followed and looked inside.

"There's a bunk and toilet," Rensch said.

The light in the small room was dim and there was no window, only a ventilation louvre. The toilet seemed to be a simple flush device which used water; the bunk was long and narrow.

"It'll do," Kurbi said.

"There's no other place I can put you right now."

Rensch went back to his desk and sat down behind it. Kurbi followed him and sat down in one of the crude iron chairs facing the desk. The black metal was cold to the touch.

"We're not a rich planet," Rensch said, "as you can see. And we're not about to open to tourism."

"These chairs are handmade?"

"Yes—why?"

"Why don't you import high-energy generating plants, computers and autocybers, and cut down on human effort?"

"Mr. Kurbi," Rensch said, "—you don't mind if I use that form of address—"

"Not at all."

"—you see, we don't believe in life without work. I mean work that supports life, not leisure work as you would know it; we don't believe in working so well that we make ourselves obsolete . . ."

"Excuse me, Commissioner," Kurbi said, "but your hard accent and occasional unfamiliar words make it hard for me to follow you. Could you speak more slowly?"

"Yes—stop me when I use a local word. Yes—our history is made of the lives of people who came here after seeing what leisure had done to worlds nearer Earth. We work all our lives and our lives are filled up."

"Do you think this way?"

"I've had contact with offworlders. To be honest, they interest me, which is why I agreed to let you stay even though you will not fit in. . . ." He trailed off and was silent.

"When do I start?" Kurbi asked, trying to be cheerful.

"You'll have some machinery to help with the lifting, and a few co-workers, but be prepared for sore muscles during the first few weeks. Do you really want to do this?"

"I'll stay as long as you'll have me," Kurbi said.

In the first two weeks he worked under the port, in the first level below the surface, where a conveyor belt brought cargo from the shuttle as well as from ocean-going ships. Here he picked up crates with a small pincer truck and drove them to one of several warehouses near the edge of the port. There were a hundred workers toiling with him, each operating a truck.

Two men worked directly with him. One was a tall, white-haired man named Den, who was only nineteen years old, and the other was a thin, olive-skinned man with three fingers missing from his left hand. At first both men limited themselves to smiling at Kurbi; later they started to ask questions.

"Why work, offworlder?" Den asked one morning.

"I need to."

Den shrugged.

"How did you hurt yourself?" Kurbi asked the two-fingered man.

"Machine," he said and spat as he positioned a crate on Kurbi's pincer lifts.

"What's your name?"

"Two-Fingers, what else. Two will do. . . ."

Den laughed nearby.

Kurbi looked forward to driving out of the long tunnel onto the surface, where the giant iron-work warehouses stood under a cloudy sky. The sun came out in his third week, a double star more white than yellow, but it warmed him in the afternoons when he grew damp from the port's cold, basement world.

At the end of each day he ate with Rensch in the office.

Food was brought in from the workers' kitchen by one of the cooks; the meal usually included green vegetables, a piece of meat and bread. Rensch brewed a black tea himself, which Kurbi came to depend on to get him going in the cold mornings.

The commissioner would always be looking at him when they ate.

"You expect something from me, don't you?" Kurbi chewed his food and waited for an answer.

"I don't think I understand you, Kurbi. Have you come here to be as far away as you can from your past life?"

"You understand me," Kurbi said and took a sip of tea.

"Is it working?"

"I think so—otherwise I would have left."

"May I ask . . ."

"I loved someone very much—she died."

"That is why you came here?"

"You don't think it's enough, do you? You don't have to answer. I loved her too much, it might be said. But she should not have died. Isn't death frightening to you here?"

Rensch drained his tea and put the cup carefully down on his desk. "I know enough, Mr. Kurbi, to know that you would think of us as superstitious in our view of death. No, death is a way to a greater life. We believe in a merciful God."

Kurbi swallowed a mouthful of bread. "I had heard—how do you manage it?"

Rensch was not offended by the skepticism of the question. "The universe would be meaningless," he said, "if it were not a prelude to something else. Nature is a place of testing and achievement—even you believe in achievement. Otherwise life, especially immortal life, would be pointless and empty, a vastness of stars and matter and life . . . simply existing in a mindless process."

"You've been in space?" Kurbi finished the last piece of meat and took a sip of tea.

"Yes." He shrugged. "In any case, that is how most of the people here see things."

"And you?"

"I don't know. I am sure that your worlds are not committing suicide every day—they live and achieve, that much I know."

Outside, the rain came down in a sudden rush. Kurbi suddenly appreciated the pot of warm tea on Rensch's desk, and the indoor companionship of another who seemed to be interested in serious questions.

"I'd like to see the countryside," Kurbi said.

"I can probably get you a vehicle—no, that's no good, you would have to abandon it when you ran out of fuel. We refine our own, but there are severe limits. Anything advanced, you see, would change us. It might be best for you to rely on your feet; you'll see more that way. Better still, ride our freight line. It's limited, but it will get you across the continent. Also, if you stick to the line, we'll know where you are. You might get stuck somewhere."

There was a silence between them. "What's your first name?" Kurbi asked.

"Nicolai—a few people call me Nico, usually when they want something."

Kurbi became aware of voices outside, workers going home in the rain. He turned around in his chair and saw rubber-draped shapes passing the glass door.

Turning back to Nicolai, Kurbi asked, "Why, then, does this port exist? From what you say the industry here is not what you want."

"True—there are those who would like to close the port down. They want to do without the conveniences we import or manufacture here. Without the rail line, our growing rural population would have no relief in time of natural disaster, or famine, or when the need for medical care arises. Happily, we are part of the Federation, so those of us with traditional ideas cannot enforce them. The port stays because too many of us need its imports and industry, whether we like it or not. The port also stands as a way into another kind of life for the young, and it will affect individuals of each generation. . . ."

"It seems to affect you."

Nicolai sighed. "It's hard not to think of the number of worlds beyond this sky, especially when they send ships that you can see and touch. Maybe those worlds know something we don't. It's startling for me to think that on many worlds people die only when they want to. There are those here who don't believe this."

"What is the life span here?"

"Very low—one hundred thirty Earth years is the upper limit, but it can be as low as thirty-five in bad places."

"And people accept this, knowing that they might live longer?"

"They do. You see, they don't know anything, they only hear it's possible to live longer. I believe that people want to die, not only because they look forward to another life, but because life tires them out." Nicolai took a deep breath. "I can see a time when I may want to leave, Rafael."

"In order not to die?"

"I'm not afraid of dying—I don't see what I could do with a longer life, unless I changed. I can't imagine what it would be like." He paused and looked directly at Kurbi. "Would it be hard, Raf?"

"To do what?"

"To live as you have lived."

"As hard as it is for me to be here. It can be done."

"Would you help me if I . . . changed?"

"Of course, Nico."

The rain stopped its clatter. Kurbi got up and went to stand looking out the office window. Mists rose from the iron and concrete street and nearby walkways. Night had fallen during the rainstorm. Craning his neck to peer up at the overcast sky, Kurbi realized that he had not seen the stars in months.

XI. The Rock

"...everything is permitted."

—Dostoevsky

THE EXIT BEACON for New Mars was a black dot pulsing on and off in otherspace, sweeping the continuum in sections that covered a sphere once every hour, an interstellar lighthouse that could be seen by any ship, regardless of approach vector. The Whisper Ship came out automatically, asserting again its claim to being an object in Einsteinian space. A billion kilometers below the ship, the twin suns of the New Mars system floated in their fiery embrace of shared plasmas and magnetogravitic force fields.

Young Gorgias woke up only a few moments before exit, feeling empty and without the usual memory of dreams. The view on the screen shifted to a schematic of the solar system below the ship; the nonorganic intelligence was searching for an asteroid of sufficient size and orbital path, according to orders.

Gorgias watched and waited. One ellipse after another appeared, both inside and outside the orbit of New Mars. As soon as a suitable object was found, the ship would move to acquire it.

Finally all the ellipses faded from the screen except one. It intersected the orbit of New Mars at less than a million kilometers from the planet, and the object orbiting the primaries in that path was nearing the intersect point rapidly. The screen showed the orbit of New Mars in green, the rock's in red. The two bodies would be at their closest approach within a day.

The schematic map faded and the stars reappeared as the ship descended toward the orbit of New Mars. The twin stars grew brighter, filling the cabin with a yellow-white light.

Gorgias heard the door slide open and shut behind him. Turning around, he saw his father standing in front of the exit.

"I'll help, if you want," the old Herculean said.

Again, Gorgias felt suspicious. "You're still divided within yourself."

"I am still a soldier," his father said, "even if this is not a war."

"This is a different kind of war!" Gorgias shouted. "You still fail to understand that."

"I hope you are right."

"I am," Gorgias said in a lower voice. He would have to order the older man around, make some use of him. At any rate, he would not have to worry about active opposition. "You'll do your part as long as I command this ship and we're both alive."

Four hours later, the screen acquired a view of the rock, three kilometers of nickel-iron, a hilly surface pitted with small craters, veined with cracks and deep crevasses, encrusted with small mountains huddling together under the silence of stars.

The ship passed over the rock and took up a forward-station position, retreating before the flying mountain toward the rendezvous with New Mars.

The ship's intelligence threw an abstract of the asteroid on the screen; small red dots appeared, marking the places where the gravitic units would be installed in order to change the asteroid's path.

The normal view reappeared as the ship circled the rock. Laser tongues reached out to mark the surface as well as to scoop out the depressions that would receive the gravitic push-ers. Its task completed, the ship returned to the forward-station point.

Gorgias went aft to the side lock and checked the scooter. He put on the light space suit and felt the cool oxygen begin to circulate over his body. Then he turned around and saw his father putting on the other suit.

"I'll give you a hand," the older Herculean said over the intercom. "I could handle the second unit."

He wants to stop me, Gorgias thought.

"I can manage by myself."

"I'll come along as a backup, in case of accident."

"There's no time to discuss it," Gorgias said and turned to press the lock touchplate. The inner door opened and he drifted the scooter into the chamber. They both mounted the seats as the inner door closed.

The outer door opened and Gorgias ran the scooter out from the ship; fifty meters out he turned the steering stick to the right and faced the asteroid. Ahead, the rock floated against the background of the central galactic regions.

Gorgias ran the scooter forward. The asteroid grew larger. It appeared to bear down from above; in a moment, it seemed, it would crush him and his father against the ship; but the illusion passed as he oriented himself with a backward glance at the ship. He was sitting upright on the scooter; the ship was behind him, not below; the rock was ahead, and down was where his feet happened to be resting.

He turned right again and passed across the shorter face of the rock, then left as he circled around to the longer face. Three quarters of the way he noticed the red glow where the rock was still hot from the laser lash.

Turning to face the rock, he pushed the scooter toward the first marker, in the upper right quadrant. The rock wall grew to cover the whole sky, and the heated area became a staring eye. His mind quickly pictured a mouth for the face, in a faint slash cutting across the lower quadrants; a central mountain straddling the quadrant corners passed for a nose. The left eye was invisible because it was closed. In a moment the illusion fell apart as the scooter came in close.

Reorienting himself again, Gorgias turned the small craft to run parallel with the surface. The rock was glowing ahead, throwing a red light out of the crater. Gorgias stopped the scooter at the rim and dismounted. Taking one of the grav units off the rear carriage, he stepped up to the depression and went over the edge, floating down slowly in the asteroid's minimal attraction.

Reaching bottom, he knelt down on the warm rock and pushed down with the unit until the attachment fingers entered the surface slightly; in a moment, he knew, the four probes would telescope into the harder rock, expanding to form a strong hold.

Turning, he jumped out of the hole and landed near the scooter. His father was standing at the crater's edge, looking down.

"I didn't need you," Gorgias said.

"I was here if you did," his father said without turning around. He was still staring down into the hole.

"Let's go," Gorgias said and mounted the scooter.

The figure of his father turned slowly and drifted toward him, finally reclaiming its rear seat.

The scooter went straight up for a thousand meters; then Gorgias turned around and circled to the other side of the rock. New Mars floated two million kilometers away, a brown, green and blue disk slowly growing larger.

Gorgias brought the scooter level with the rock's surface and moved toward the crater's glow, stopping a meter from the edge. Again he got off and removed the grav unit from the rear. His father sat quietly in the backseat, as if reproaching him, or confirming something.

Gorgias walked up to the excavation and dropped over the edge. He touched bottom, secured the device and jumped back up to the rim.

"You didn't have to come," he said to his father.

"I'm here if you got hurt or needed help."

So you say, he thought as he clambered into the front seat. Overhead, New Mars was growing larger.

The ship passed behind the asteroid, blotting out the planet. The rock would make the ship invisible to scanners. The twin stars blazed as the vessel's motion brought them into the screen.

"It's not pushing away," his father said at his side. "The gravitics may be too weak."

Gorgias whirled his chair around and glared at the old Herculean. "You knew this would happen all the time!"

"Look, it's moving!" his father shouted.

Gorgias turned and saw the rock pulling away from the screen. The ship had activated the grav units, accelerating the asteroid. By the time it reached the planet's atmosphere, the rock would be moving at more than a hundred kilometers per second; it would strike the surface with devastating effect.

Schematics confirmed the rock's course. A map of the planet's western hemisphere flashed the point of impact: in the ocean, just off a large port city.

The asteroid continued to shrink as the ship fell behind, revealing the growing disk of New Mars.

XII. Planetgrazer

"O waste of Loss, in the hot mazes, Lost Among
  bright stars
On this most weary unbright cinder, Lost!"

—Wolfe

RAFAEL KURBI sat in the open door of the freight car and
watched the flat countryside rush by him. Once in a long while
he would see a lonely house on the horizon, its smoke a thin
wire joined to the sky. There was a sense of independence in
the sight that he admired, as well as a bit of pride. The dark
blue sky was striated with silky cirrus clouds as far as the eye
could see.

Spring had been dry, and would hurt the newly planted grain
crops if it continued moistureless. People would flock to the
railway towns to receive the Federation's relief supplies that
were stored there regularly and replenished from the port city.
Only the diehards would stay on their homesteads and use up
their own stores. Again, many would settle in the towns; slowly
the planet's culture would continue to change; the way of life
for which the planet was first settled would have to coexist
with newer ambitions.

He was more than four thousand kilometers from the port,
on the single rail line that crossed the major continent. In
addition to the two other continents, there was a group of large

73

islands in the western ocean; most of these lay below the equator and were of volcanic origin. One day in the distant future, this large continent around him would break up and the pieces would drift away from each other. It was a young world, too young for native intelligent life. Much of the larger animal life had been killed off thousands of years ago when the early colonists had arrived, during the first wave of interstellar expansion. The grass on the plain before him was originally from Earth, as was much of the vegetation, though he had been told there were native forests still flourishing untouched on the islands.

Most of the human population lived on the coastal plains, east and west, joined by this rail line. The northland was too cold, the south too hot. The central plains supported a third of the planet's twenty million people on an area of one hundred million square kilometers; the coastal settlements, with their fisheries and small farms, supported the other two thirds. The seasonal contrasts were milder on the coast, more severe on the plains.

Whenever the train slowed, Kurbi had the urge to jump off and head for the nearest house; although he had met hundreds of people in family groups, he was still curious to see how the next group lived, how they would receive him. It meant that he would have to live with them until another train came through to carry him further west or back to the port, but he did not mind; for a time, his past life would again seem far away, almost as if it had never existed. The people here lived in a great religious dream of world and sky and growing things. He could enter into their lives, and leave at any time. A part of him knew that he was using New Mars to bury his past, but he did not care; that he felt better was enough. *All the past lives in the Federation Snake*, he thought. *Worlds exist at every stage of development and its variation, each experiment and utopian scheme strives to continue, each failure struggles to survive.*

As the train slowed, Kurbi threw his rucksack out and jumped to the grass, rolling on the gentle slope. He got up, picked up his rucksack and crossed the eastbound tracks, walking back toward the house he had passed earlier.

The house was farther away than he had thought. After an hour of walking, it still seemed distant, as if defying him with its peaceful appearance. He stopped and sat down on the grass to rest. A cooling breeze passed across his back. He turned and saw the rain clouds sweeping toward him from the other side of the tracks like a curtain being drawn across the plain. Dark clouds were slipping over the horizon, bringing the much-needed rain at last. When he saw lightning brighten the prairie with its pale flash, he got up and ran.

The rain caught him while he was still a quarter-kilometer from the house. The sky flashed and the thunder rumbled, vibrating the ground. A bolt hit the grass a hundred meters to his right. He wiped the rainwater from his face as he ran, tasting its freshness on his lips; the smell of ozone was distinct as he drew a deep breath and quickened his pace.

The door of the house opened when he reached it, startling him. He stopped for a moment, then went inside.

Three women sat in wooden chairs. A man closed the door and sat down at the head of the table.

"You are welcome," the oldest-looking woman said.

"Thank you—I'm dripping water all over your floor."

"It will run through the boards," the man said. Kurbi looked at him now. His hair was black and his eyes brown; he sat with his elbows on the rough board. All four people wore the same expression as the man, a look of tolerant interest. "You are the offworlder," the man added.

"How did you know?"

"From the rail town, from those who run the train. Are you the only one?"

"I think so," Kurbi said. "You've never met an offworlder?"

"We have not," the man said as if he were proud of the fact.

Kurbi took a step forward. "My name is Rafael Kurbi."

Thunder followed, lending an absurd portentousness to his introduction.

"I live here with my wife and daughters. We do not exchange names with strangers . . . but since you have told me yours and do not know our ways, you may call me Fane Weblen."

The two younger women seemed to smile from behind their long, brown hair. The mother was without expression. Her chiseled, sun-darkened features seemed bare with her hair put up in a bun on her head. Kurbi noticed the winding gray streaks.

"Please sit down," she said in a decisive tone of voice, as if she resented his scrutiny.

Kurbi sat down in the one chair on the empty side of the table.

"Are you hungry?" she asked. "We have eaten, but there is a little meat left."

"No, thank you, I ate on the train," Kurbi said, patting his rucksack which he held on his lap. "When does the next train come by?"

"About a week," Fane said, "going east."

"You don't like the train, do you?"

"No."

"It takes from us our reliance on our bodies," the older woman said.

"But isn't it useful?" Kurbi asked.

"When?" Fane said.

"Why—when someone is sick and needs a hospital...."

"We are never sick," the woman said, "unless it is time to die."

"What about when food is scarce?"

"To be useful is not always to be right," Fane said.

The storm was dying outside. Kurbi turned and saw daylight brightening in the window.

"The rain will help," Kurbi said.

"It is welcome—but it is not enough," Fane said.

"How old are your daughters?" Kurbi asked.

"They are spoken for," Fane said.

"Do you have any sons?"

"They have gone."

"Where?"

"To the port, the rail towns—we don't know," Fane said.

Kurbi thought of his co-workers in the port, especially Den, who must have come from a family like this. A severe conflict would one day develop on New Mars, between those who would modernize according to Federation ways and those who would cling to the ideals of the original colonists. The conflict was even present in how Fane spoke to him. Quite clearly, he disapproved of offworlders and their influence, but his curiosity as well as good manners prevented him from showing his feelings overtly.

"How old are you?" the woman asked.

Her husband gave her a quick look of surprise and cut her off with another question. "How long do people live where you come from?"

"I'm from Earth," Kurbi said, "I'm fifty Earth years old. That's about thirty-five of your years, which are longer. Federation citizens can live as long as they wish depending on whether there is a rejuvenation facility nearby. Medical care is part of Federation citizenship, a right. Technically, New Mars is part of the Federation, but it's up to you what you import."

"Not every world has interstar transport facilities," Fane said, eager to show that he knew something.

"That's true," Kurbi said. He estimated that Fane was about fifty Earth years old, but he looked older.

"But I have no wish to live beyond my time," Fane added quickly. Then he looked directly at Kurbi and asked, "Don't you wish to die?"

"Sometimes—many of my people take their own lives when it comes to that."

"It was meant to be," the woman said, "the merciful God made the world to test us for another life, not for us to be happy in. If we are happy we will not learn what will be required of us later."

"How long will you live?" Fane asked.

"I don't know— past a century at least, I suppose. My wife died in a flying accident recently."

"Flying?" Fane asked.

"Gliding—for sport."

"I don't understand," Fane said.

The woman shook her head but did not speak.

"That is why you are traveling?" Fane asked.

Kurbi nodded. "May I stay here for a day or two? I've been doing chores for my food and a place to sleep. Can you use the help?"

"Yes, I can," Fane said. Kurbi sensed that the mention of Grazia's death had affected Fane, perhaps reminding him of the certainty of his wife's death, as well as of his own.

"You may stay until the next train, young man," Fane's wife said. "You may call me Slifa while you are with us."

"And your daughters' names?"

Slifa looked to her husband. Fane shrugged.

"They are Azura and Apona," she said.

"Twins?"

"Yes—they were made by God so that they might better see their faults in each other."

The two girls nodded solemnly at Kurbi, but he was still unable to see their full faces. He wondered if they were shy, or if they were supposed to wear their hair like a veil.

"I'm glad to know you, Azura and Apona."

"You must not speak of knowing them," Fane said.

"I see."

"You must not look at them long," Slifa added. "They must not become accustomed to the gaze of any other except the ones who have spoken for them."

"Very well."

Fane got up and went to the fireplace, where he added two chunks of peat to the flames. "You will sleep by the fire," he said without turning around.

Silently, the women got up. Azura and Apona went to a door at the end of the room, opened it and disappeared into a dark room, closing the wooden door firmly behind them. Slifa went to the door at the opposite end of the room at Kurbi's right, opened it and went inside, leaving it slightly ajar.

Fane prodded the fire a few times with a stick.

"Why are you really here, offworlder?" he asked as he sat down again.

"You're certainly curious about how people live elsewhere. I'm here for the same reason."

Fane shrugged and his dark eyebrows went up. "What is there to know—we know, and we know our way is right." There seemed to be a suppressed anger in the man's manner, as if the existence of other worlds were an insult to him. "I do not believe there are as many worlds as some say—certainly there are not as many as grains of sand."

Kurbi did not answer, but searched for something else to say. "I'd like to watch your sunset before I sleep," he said finally.

Fane looked at him and smiled, obviously relieved that Kurbi had not contradicted him about something he was unsure about. "Yes—but the wind gets cold," he said as he stood up. "I will leave you now."

"Sleep well," Kurbi said as the man went into his bedroom and closed the door. Kurbi heard him putting something against the door inside.

There was a muffled giggle from the bedroom at his left as he stood up to go outside. He opened the door and stepped out.

The storm was completely gone. At his right the sky was clear and blue, darkening into jet black. The twin suns were balls of molten metal, joined with a white-hot streamer of plasma. The wind from the east was cold, but there was less dust on its breath after the rain.

The suns touched the horizon and sank into the flat earth, until only an upward wash of red light was left. Abandoned, the planet seemed to shudder as the wind quickened and became cooler. Kurbi turned and went back inside, closing the wooden door quickly behind him.

He unrolled his sleeping bag by the fire, put his package of provisions aside and lay down by the warming flames. For a time he wandered in the suburbs of sleep, circling the center of rest while images of his travels came to him like actors paying curtain calls.

"If you don't return in some months," Nicolai had said, "I'll take the flyer we have and come out along the rail line looking for you—so don't wander too far from the tracks."

"I can take care of myself."

"I will come anyway."

"Suit yourself, Nico—you just want an excuse to travel. Or is it because you'll miss our talks?"

"Both."

"I'll get back, don't worry. If you feel so constricted, why don't you leave New Mars, start a new life elsewhere?"

"My family is here—I haven't faced the idea of leaving my parents permanently to go worlds away."

"You don't have a wife or children."

"No—there is a brother I haven't seen for years. It's not the same for me, Raf, as it is for you."

"I think I understand. It would be as if the Earth were not there anymore, as if something had destroyed it." He had thought of the Herculean at that moment, of Julian and his offer, and it all seemed to mean more.

A bit of moist peat crackled in the fire, jarring him into wakefulness. He felt that eyes were watching him. The floorboards creaked under him as if someone were walking across the room toward him. The planet trembled under his back slightly and he sat up, wide-awake.

The house shook a little, and the window facing east brightened. Kurbi stood up just as Fane came out of his bedroom. "Do you have quakes?" Kurbi asked.

Fane shook his head and went out the door. Kurbi followed him outside. Together they watched the eastern sky glow brighter, burning with a blue-white light that rose higher and higher, as if the planet had disgorged a bolt of light to strike the sky. The horizon flashed once, twice; the ground shook again.

"What can it be?" Kurbi asked.

"I have never seen anything like this," Fane said.

XIII. Ocean Strike

"I balanced all, brought all to mind,
The years to come seemed waste of breath,
A waste of breath the years behind
In balance with this life, this death."

—W. B. Yeats

THE ROCK became a point and disappeared into the atmosphere of New Mars. A glow appeared against the blue ocean as the asteroid hurtled in at nearly one hundred kilometers per second, a forty-billion-ton missile that would strike the ocean just off New Marsport in less than a minute. The air glowed blue from the passage a few moments before impact.

Gorgias realized that he would not be able to see the full magnitude of the ocean strike from this distance.

"Describe what is happening," he told the ship.

A violet flare appeared in the ocean below; it flashed once, twice.

SUB-NUCLEAR REACTION FROM HEAT OF IMPACT.

The screen telescoped the distance until the area of ocean took up the whole screen.

OCEAN VAPORIZED AT IMPACT POINT. CRUST PENETRATION THROUGH MANTLE. MAGMA EXPOSED.

Steam clouds covered the impact area, but the infrared glow of the wound in the ocean floor showed up clearly on the screen.

The ocean was rushing in to cool that glow, creating the steam cloud that would soon veil the whole planet.

EFFECTS:
QUAKES,
OSCILLATION OF ALL PLANETARY WATER RESULTING
IN TIDAL WAVES,
HIGH WINDS,
RAINSTORMS.
DURATION INDEFINITE.

On the edge of the continent, the city of New Marsport glowed in the infrared sensors. It disappeared as the tidal wave covered it. The sensors continued to pick up the city's fading heat as the waves cooled it. And so it would be with every coastal settlement on the planet, as the angered ocean broke upon the shores, rolling in to reclaim its ancient places.

CLIMACTIC FORECAST:
INDEFINITE WINTER RESULTING FROM CLOUD COVER.
RAIN AND WINDSTORMS INCREASING IN SEVERITY.
RECURRING TIDAL WAVES, TYPHOONS, TORNADOES, WATERSPOUTS.

All this, he thought, from the energy released by the ocean's quenching of the strike heat. A ringed waterfall as high as a mountain range was rushing in to fill the hellhole of the impact, water and steam distributing the heat energy necessary to threaten the biosphere of a world. An economical weapon, he thought, wondering if he would use it again. If he announced his responsibility for the strike, it would be difficult to repeat this form of attack; yet he wanted them to know that he had done it, rather than some mindless natural process.

"Send a message," he said to the ship, "tell them we were here."

In a few moments the communication would reach the exit beacon's warp transmitter-repeater; within minutes the Federation would know. He got up from his station and went aft to find his father.

*   *   *

All through the next day wind and rain swept across the plain. Kurbi and the Weblen family huddled in the small cellar of the house. The roof of the house had been ripped off. Kurbi feared that the cellar would flood, forcing them out into the open.

The twin girls and their mother huddled together in one corner of the wood-lined basement. Kurbi and Fane each sat in a different corner, facing the women.

"What is happening, offworlder?" Fane asked in the gloom, sounding as if he thought that Kurbi might be responsible for the disaster.

"I don't know—a volcanic eruption somewhere on the planet, maybe a large meteor strike. There's no way I can find out." He wondered if Nicolai was safe.

"My spring crop is dying," Fane said. "Nothing will grow. We are being judged."

"Death is near," Slifa said. "We must compose ourselves." Apona and Azura whimpered at her words.

"I—I can't accept this to be the will of God," Fane said.

"Do not blaspheme," Slifa said.

Thunder cracked as she spoke the words. She wailed and her daughters joined in.

"Be still," Fane shouted over the wind and thunder, "be still!"

"They can't help it," Kurbi said, "I'm fearful also."

"You—afraid?"

"Yes."

"Then we are lost."

Suddenly more water began to flow into the cellar. In a minute they were in water up to their thighs.

"Up into the house," Kurbi shouted over the rushing sound. One by one they climbed the ladder into the roofless house. Here the fireplace was a mass of wet stones; chairs, pots and pans were scattered over the floor. Overhead, the sky drove with an unbroken obscurity of rain and dirt scooped up from the land.

"Over there," Kurbi said, "There's still some cover left in that corner. Help me with the overturned table—the women can get under it if we put it against the wall."

They shoved the table into the corner and the three women crawled under it. Kurbi and Fane crouched on either side. "If the walls blow away," Fane shouted to him across the tabletop, "we'll be done."

"As long as there's a bit of wall," Kurbi answered, "there's hope."

"What if the rain doesn't stop?"

"It will," Kurbi said, "it will." It must, he thought, or the plain will flood and sweep us away. The land could only absorb so much.

"What time do you think it is?" Fane shouted.

There was no way to tell. The cloudcover had wiped out all distinction between day and night, morning and afternoon. Kurbi peered around the dark, debris-strewn floor, looking for his bedroll and rucksack.

Miraculously, the rucksack lay in the ruined fireplace, pinned down by a few stones that had fallen in from the chimney. Slowly he crawled over to the rucksack and dragged it backward.

Pulling out a few pieces of dried food, he handed them to the women under the table.

"Eat it—it's wet but we don't have much else." The stores in the basement were under water now; this was all the food that was left. Hands reached out and took what he offered.

"Pass some to Fane," he shouted.

He bit into the last piece himself, savoring the texture of synthetic protein and fruit flavor.

The light grew darker, until he could no longer see his own hands in front of his face.

I am a soldier, he thought, *my son is a terrorist.*

Everything was perfectly clear now. *If this is what it takes to survive and regain power, then I want no part of it.* A planet was dying nearby, and he had done nothing to prevent it. He would not be able to live with that knowledge.

He remembered Gorgias and Myraa playing as small children, with Oriona and himself looking on. The General would have been happy to know that his daughter, Myraa, had survived....

The old Herculean closed his eyes and lay still, overcome by the past. It was a sweet breeze of memory, enveloping him with longing and regret; he did not have the strength to struggle against it....

Gorgias, his brother Herkon and Myraa ran through the

tall grass, shouting and laughing. Oriona was smiling....

He should never have brought his son to the base, or taken him on sorties; he should never have let him use the ship's library, or taught him the roll of destroyed worlds; he should never have believed the stories of a Herculean army still at large somewhere, regardless of the evidence that such an army had escaped through the ruined gate on Myraa's World. He had failed; his whole civilization had failed. If it were to grow back, it would have to do so slowly, peacefully, out of sight of its enemies who now lived inside it in the form of hatred and the thirst for revenge. Perhaps there were irreversible things, and the Herculean Empire would never return, except maybe as something else....

Myraa, Gorgias and Herkon ran naked into his open arms, shapes out of time....

"Herkon is dead," Oriona said one day, "the others have taken him."

"How?" he heard himself ask very long ago.

His father was not in the aft cabin.

Gorgias turned and went forward again to the control room.

"Am I alone?" he asked the ship.

YES.

"When was the lock opened?"

ONE HALF HOUR AGO.

"Scan nearby space."

SCANNING. LIFEFORM AT SIX KILOMETERS.

"Overtake," Gorgias said.

The disfigured face of New Mars disappeared, to be replaced by the sight of his father and scooter directly ahead. Gorgias went aft, put on his suit and stepped into the lock. It cycled and opened just as the ship came alongside the scooter.

Gorgias reached out and pulled the scooter inside.

As the lock closed and cycled, the figure toppled from the seat, pulled down by the ship's artificial gravity. The inner door opened, and Gorgias pulled his father inside.

When he took off the helmet, he saw that the face was disfigured by lack of air pressure, eyes bulging wide open. Gorgias looked into the eyes as if he were looking across light-years, hoping that far away, at a greater distance than he had ever known, something of his father might still be alive to be recalled by a sheer act of will.

Slowly, mechanically, he stood up and took off his own suit, then his father's and hung them up in their places on the bulkhead.

Turning back to the body, he stared at it for a long time.

"You were waiting to do this," he said, "to take what remained of the past from me." He knelt down and punched the discolored face with his fist. "Coward!" For a moment the mouth seemed to turn up into the semblance of a smile, but the flesh would not stay and it turned into a sneer. "You're nothing now—you've always been nothing. Why else would you have come to this, old man?"

A wild thought came into his mind. Myraa could drag his father back, make him face what he had done, if what she said was true. He picked up the body, carried it into the aft cabin, and turned the temperature down to its lowest setting, insuring that the body would not begin to decompose for a while.

He rushed forward into the control cabin, sat down at the station and screamed an order.

"Switchover—evasive route to Myraa's World—we're being pursued by Federation cruisers."

YOU ARE MISTAKEN,
NOTHING IS VISIBLE.

He would tell Myraa that the patrol ships had appeared just after he and his father had finished attaching the gravitic units to the rock. His father had been hit by laser fire, but he had managed to get him back into the ship before he died.

"Follow orders—Myraa's World," he repeated.

When the ship was in jumpspace, Gorgias went aft and looked at his father's corpse floating in the zero-g field.

"I'll lose them," he said, "I'll get us home."

He went forward again and sat down at the screen station. The gray continuum was clear; he was safe.

Closing his eyes, he tried to push away the nagging fear that came into him. His father was dead . . . honorably, he told himself, rehearsing the lie that would have to be told.

Myraa will know the truth, another part of him said.

Myraa will know what to do, his hopes whispered.

On the third day the rain slowed to a drizzle and some light came into the sky, a pitiably feeble glow that was put to shame by the more distant lightning flashes. Kurbi opened his eyes and found himself staring at the lighter sky for a long time.

"Slifa is dead," Fane said, his voice seeming loud now in contrast to the steady rush of the endless rain. "The cold was too much for her." Azura and Apona were crying softly.

As Kurbi watched the sky, he saw a black shape appear on the horizon. He stood up, pulling the wet blanket around him, and peered through the large hole in the east wall of the house.

"There," he said pointing, but Fane and the twins paid him no attention.

The flyer came closer. "Nico," Kurbi whispered, and started toward the open doorway. He could not remember when the door had been blown away.

Kurbi leaned against the doorjamb and watched as the flyer came in low over the rails, casting a strong beam of light onto the track bed below it. In a moment it veered from the railroad and approached the house, floating to a gentle landing a hundred meters away on the rainswept prairie.

A lone figure got out and walked toward him. Kurbi shivered as he recognized Nico's stocky frame. He stumbled a few steps forward to meet him.

"Kurbi," Nicolai Rensch said as he grasped Kurbi around the wet blanket. "I knew you would be alive."

Kurbi embraced him and the other steadied him on his feet with a strong grip.

"What has happened, Nico?" he managed to ask.

"Something hit the ocean off the coast. When the storm and tidal-wave warnings came, I had only a few minutes to leave." He shook his head and looked at the ground. "I was not able to save anyone—if I had tried, they would have mobbed the flyer. I decided to look for you and help where I could do so safely and effectively. Is anyone else alive here?"

"A father and two daughters. The mother died of exposure last night. . . ."

"The flyer has a good cabin, food and medical supplies—let's take them inside and warm up."

Kurbi dropped the wet blanket from his shoulders and led the way back into the ruin of the house. There he pried the sobbing Fane away from the body of his wife and led him out toward the open lock of the flyer. Nico roused the twin girls out of their states of semishock and led them away.

Halfway to the black egg-shape of the flyer, Fane stopped and stared at the light coming out from the lock. Turning, he grabbed Kurbi's arm and looked at him with hollow eyes.

"Where are we going—what is this fearful thing you have brought me to, offworlder?" Fane's face and body trembled.

"There's food and warmth inside," Kurbi said, "we'll be safe, don't worry. My friend Nicolai came from the port and found us."

"Friend?" Fane's eyes were wide circles of darkness. "What do you know of this devil? From the city? We should not accept help after God has punished us so much. . . ."

Fane collapsed into his arms and Kurbi dragged him into the flyer.

"We can wander the planet," Nicolai said, "picking up survivors until the freighter from Earth arrives."

They sat in the control room of the flyer. On the screen the rain was coming down again and the landscape was almost completely dark. Fane and his daughters were in the midsection cabin. All three had recovered somewhat after drying out and eating some food.

"There's no link with Federation on the planet?" Kurbi asked.

"There was in New Marsport—but that's . . . gone, under water."

"Are the electrical storms affecting communications badly?"

"Pretty badly," Nico said.

"Then we'll have to get the flyer up into orbit," Kurbi said. "From there we can talk to the subspace beacon station—it'll relay a message to the nearest Federation base."

"Can you get us into orbit?" Nico asked.

"I think I can, if I study the flyer. It's the only way to get help here quickly. If we have to, we'll dock with the beacon station—there's a small installation inside, with provisions and first-aid supplies, but I don't think we'll have to try that."

"Let me show you something," Nico said. He reached over and pressed a few control areas under the screen.

A picture appeared. "I recorded this before heading west," Nico said. A column of blue air stood in the ocean. At its base the waves were turning into steam. "It was huge," Nico said. "It went up through the whole atmosphere. Something came in from space and hit us hard, Raf."

"How far away were you when you recorded this?"

"It sat on my horizon—I didn't want to get closer."

XIV.   Swimmer in Shadows

caught within ourselves
feeding inner hounds
in too tight a wood
we await the dawn

—Tymoteusz Karpowicz

IN THE POLAR MOUNTAINS of Myraa's World, Gorgias waited on a glacier. Cold white light filled the cabin through the screen. There was no sign of pursuit vessels appearing near the planet. The ship was safe; he was safe.

As he waited, Gorgias made a vow of vengeance against the Earthborn; he swore it to his father, to the twenty war stars of home and their dead worlds. The oldest Herculean had not died by his own hand; the Federation had killed him, as it had murdered his mother and brother.

He thought of his father lying cold in the aft quarters, waiting for his funeral. . . .

"We're safe," he said to the ship, "take us to Myraa." For a moment he felt brother to the ship, though it never spoke to him except through the screen readouts. He could order it to speak in a voice, now that he would be alone. *It will be strange to live now that my parents are dead, when all that was in them is in me, and nowhere else.* Whatever intelligence was buried in the vessel was also Herculean; it would die if he died; it would live as long as he lived.

The ship rose from the tilted ice-field, revealing the setting sun at one end of the glacier, creating the illusion of sunrise.

Running east, the ship reached the glacier's edge and rushed out low over the ocean, whipping up whitecaps in its wake.

"He cannot be saved," Myraa said.

As the sun set, the trees and grass in front of the house seemed to become drenched with blood; then slowly the darkness turned the red to black.

"Why not?" Gorgias asked as he turned from the windows to face her.

"He cannot enter our circle because he has already become nothing. He died too far away, Gorgias, in distance as well as in belief. He got what he expected—eternal nothingness." She paused. "I have saved many of our dead, but I can do nothing for him." She paused again. "I warn you, Gorgias, die near me—it will be the only way I can save you."

"My father was right, this is all nonsense—you can't frighten me."

"I know how he died, Gorgias."

"Stay out of my mind!"

He turned from her to the window. Herculean women might have been telepathic, his father once told him, or simply observant.

Outside, the dark countryside of hills and grass was blazing now with a million fireflies, as if invisible mourners carrying candles had gathered for a funeral. The mass of lights was concentrated in the meadow below the house, but a snaking S shape ran up the nearby hill.

Gorgias stepped closer to the window and looked out at the procession of lights. A sprinkling of stars had fallen on the darkening land, and he felt the edges of pity pushing in at him, threatening to break his self-control; beyond pity stood sorrow and guilt, avengers of the dead.

"Gorgias!"

He whirled to face her again, ready now to answer her reproaches.

"Ships are coming," she said. "I warn you to show that I am not your enemy, and that I can examine the content of minds, even at a distance."

He had expected her to blame him further for his father's death, to question again the manner of his death. Something in him had hoped that she would; instead she spoke idle prophecies.

"You will die one day, Gorgias—but remember to die here, remember. . . ."

Contempt surfaced in him, contempt for his own weakness, blotting out pity, sorrow and guilt.. He stepped up to Myraa's naked form and hit her across the face. "Get away from me!" he shouted. "Little animals, that's what you are here, animals, fools and cowards."

She only looked at him and said, "I did not have to tell you that ships are coming."

"Why did you, then? You want me to die. You said so. How would you know anyway?"

But he almost knew her answer. "I can feel them hating you as they come in their ships," she said. "How many did you kill for them to hate you that much? That many? It makes their hatred almost rational."

"It's war," he said.

"What war?"

"They killed my—our world, and my father."

"Your father killed himself."

"Stop!"

"It's true—"

"They drove him into cowardice, they took his great strength—they killed him!"

"Who's the liar, Gorgias?"

He lunged at her, grabbing her by the throat; it was soft and yielding as he squeezed. Her eyes held him in a vise. Suddenly he let her go.

"You're not worth killing," he said, hating himself for his weakness. She was too close to him, too much a part of his past to let die.

"The ships are nearer," she said. "You'd better go."

He went past her and out the back entrance. The grass was wet on the dark hillside. Fireflies exploded around him like miniature suns; he slipped a few times before he reached the bottom of the hill. He jumped into the open side lock and rushed forward as the inner door closed behind him.

"The base," he said and sat down at the screen station.

HUNTERS APPEARING IN ORBIT.

"Get us out of here," he shouted.

The ship lifted straight up through the atmosphere. Cruiser

positions registered on the screen, coming fast from dayside.

The Whisper Ship slipped into otherspace.

Gorgias saw signs of pursuit. Black dashes appeared in the grayness behind him, but he would lose them; he would lose them because he had to, because any other outcome would be unthinkable.

Ten days after Kurbi and Nicolai made orbit in the flyer, Julian Poincaré arrived with a cruiser and a dozen freighters loaded with emergency supplies. Nicolai led the freighters' lifeboats down to the tortured planet, where storms, earthquakes and tidal waves continued to rage, and where the coming fimbul winter would soon make life all but impossible for the survivors. Nico was going to try to convince as many people as possible to leave New Mars and settle elsewhere.

"It was the Whisper Ship," Julian told Kurbi in the cruiser's stateroom.

"How do you know?"

"He announced it himself—hundreds of worlds picked up the details on their relays. Most of the Snake knows by now. It was a large rock he threw at us, Raf."

"I should have guessed—my luck."

"Are you going to help me now?"

"I'd like to help Nicolai for a while—though I can see myself waking up one morning, picking up a weapon and going out to kill that monster, except—"

"What?"

"I want to see him alive—what kind of living being can destroy a planet and still live with itself?"

"He'd probably say you were taking it much too personally, since you lived through it. We did that to his world—once. Old injustices drive his life, or lives, whoever they are, and he dispenses new injustice. Who is to blame? Is there a good answer, or only answers that no one will like?"

"I would say there is no hope for them," Kurbi said, "—too much past, as you say."

Kurbi was silent for a moment. He looked around the stateroom, at the starmaps covering the walls, at the green carpeting under his dirty feet, at Poincaré sitting behind the polished ebony desk. Kurbi sat down in one of the chairs in front of the desk and said, "Julian, after what I saw down there, I think I will want to try and stop Gorgias."

"Go home first, get some rest. We've got ships looking

already—they may save you the trouble. You may not have the stomach to kill. For the terrorist, civilized behavior is a screen. He counts on the enemy's inability to behave as he does."

"You still think he's a good thing for us, Julian?"

"It wouldn't be the first time good came out of horror. Gorgias will keep us alert, interested; if we ignore him, he or his descendants will topple us one day."

Suddenly Kurbi felt very tired. Home, he thought, but all he could visualize was his small room in New Marsport, and the various houses he had slept in during his travels.

"Where do you think the Whisper Ship has gone?" he asked, trying to concentrate.

"I think he's at Myraa's World—much of his audience for his deeds is there. A harmless bunch, really. But we won't find him there. He has a base somewhere, remember? He'll be there by then."

Gorgias fled into the southern regions of the galaxy, reentering normal space and slipping back into bridgespace dozens of times; but still the hunters followed, making every turn, imitating every jump.

After a week of fleeing there was no sign of the cruisers on the gray screen, but that was only because the Whisper Ship's slightly superior speed was finally giving him a lead. At any moment the black dashes would appear on the screen.

Gorgias waited. The ship was on its own—following any evasive maneuver that became practical. He closed his eyes and tried to get some rest.

The ship switched to normal space. There was still no sign of the hunters, but directly ahead a white-hot star was streaming a tail of material into space.

BLACK-HOLE BINARY.

MATERIAL DISAPPEARING FROM NORMAL SPACE-TIME.

The ship rushed toward the empty point in space where the whirlpool of stolen star material ended. Gorgias noted the halo of debris circling the dead spot in space.

In a few minutes the ship passed the ring of captured matter and seemed to be heading directly toward the black hole.

"Explain," Gorgias shouted, wondering if something had finally gone wrong with the ship.

EVASIVE MANEUVER:
PASSAGE THROUGH BLACK HOLE ERGOSPHERE
WILL SIMULATE DISAPPEARANCE.

ONE HOUR IN ERGOSPHERE, SHIP TIME,
EQUALS ONE STANDARD GALACTIC MONTH.

HUNTER SHIPS LACK POWER FOR SKIRTING
BLACK-HOLE EVENT HORIZON.

The ship circled the dead spot in space for one hour while
Gorgias waited. Half the sky was a black lake trying to pull
him in, while in the bright universe of stars, time was rushing
forward at a furious pace. If the ship stayed here too long, all
the history of the universe would flee by him; stars would grow
old and die, all nature would become a ruin rushing together. . . .

He got up and went to the aft cabin. His father's body hung
motionless in the cold. He imagined a conversation between
himself and the old Herculean:

"Get them for me son, never rest—promise!"
I will.
"You must hate them as much as I do."
I do.
"If you are caught you must die."
I will.

He knelt before the bloated body and shivered. A new peace
came over him; he had made his vow; his father had asked him
at last, and the vow was real.

In jumpspace view, the Hercules Cluster was a mass of
black stars exploding from a black center.

Gorgias turned off the screen and dozed as the ship came
home. There had been no sign of hunters after the black-hole
maneuver, and it was now too late for pursuers to discover the
direction he had taken; they might guess that his base was in
the Cluster, but it would take centuries to check each star.

When he woke up, the ship was sitting in its berth. He got
up, went to the aft quarters and carried his father's body out
to the scooter. Securing the corpse in the backseat, he took the
forward position and floated out through the open lock.

The base lights were steady as he whisked down the passageway toward the stasis chambers. His father leaned forward

against him, cold and stiff, as the tunnel dipped into the deepest parts of the base. Gaining speed, Gorgias rushed into the underworld, emerging at last into a large circular chamber lit by one large globe of orange light.

Here the empty stasis shells waited in a circle around the room.

Gorgias stopped the scooter in front of one, took his father off the rear seat and pushed him into the shell. The field flickered as it received the body, surrounding it with a deep gloom. The shell would do as well as a tomb, he thought. He could barely make out his father's face as the darkness took him, deepening his eyes into caves that stared out into the room. The old Herculean would remain as he was for as long as the base renewed itself, for as long as power fed the accumulators, for as long as his son's hatred lived; from here the old Herculean would command all that was to come.

When he stepped into the shell at his father's right hand, Gorgias knew that two decades would pass; he could set the return for much later, if he wished, but two decades would be enough to confuse the hunters further; he would disappear from their experience for a while, enough time for them to lose interest or let down their guard. In any case, when he emerged the search would be going slower and he would have the element of surprise.

To step into the stasis field and step out at any time in the future would always be a matter of a moment. He hesitated, thinking, I never had a chance to grow up in my world, with millions like myself around me. I never had a chance to take what was mine. . . .

He stepped into a profound darkness, which became bright red.

Yellow leaves grew on trees nourished not by water but by blood; the soaked roots drank greedily, until the leaves curled scarlet and dropped to earth, each veined structure a world dying on the parched ground.

A bright sun turned the landscape white-hot, until his eyes stared into white space. A raging wind whipped him, enveloped his body with icy fingers and hurled him against invisible obstacles. Hatred froze inside him, petrifying his bones and organs; a hot wind came and coursed fire through his heart and stomach.

He opened his mouth to protest, but only curses escaped—

words like wars hurled through the doors of speech. . . .

He swam in the shadows, waiting for the iron game to resume.

BOOK TWO

THE OMEGA POINT

I.   Immortal Enemy

"What would we do without our enemies?"

—Pierre Teilhard de Chardin

"In his own unconscious every one of us is convinced of his own immortality."

—Freud

GORGIAS RAN.

Three black smudges swam in the scanner—ships creeping through his wake across the vast unreality of jumpspace. He watched, dreaming of how to lead the Earthborn to their deaths. The trackers would not overtake him for at least a week; more than enough time to lay a trap, or escape.

Suddenly the three centuries of his life shrank into an impossible instant, and there was no time to fulfill his father's vow of vengeance. A billion souls cried out from the black hole of the past, lamenting the home world's destruction. Ghosts crowded into him, wearying him with shrill pleas, and he yearned for the yellow-orange sun of Myraa's World, for the peace of the grassy plain around the hilltop house, for the warm colors of a living world to replace the sterile innards of the Whisper Ship and the ashes of jumpspace.

A hundred hours had passed since his raid on Eisen IV. He

got up from the command station and went aft, where he lay down in the small quarters and drifted through his bloodied memory, seeking oblivion. But the impossible instant of his life spun itself out into a strand of thirty decades, and he felt the tension of each long year. He wandered in the vast belly of the void, struggling to silence the reproaches of waste and loneliness.

He relived the decades of stasis in the bowels of his father's base, enduring again the torments of time-marking dreams. He cried into the shadowy echoes, demanding respite from the endless scarring—

—*starlight cut coldly into his eyes, and he saw the giant shapes of Earthborn blacking out the starfields. The figures hunched over their instruments, tracking and hating him without rest. . . .*

The black sun glowed, then blazed suddenly as the Whisper Ship winked into normal space. He had intended to emerge in the shadow of Wolfe IV, but the hunters were too far behind him for that to matter. The masses of ship and planet would merge on conventional sensors when he landed, and only the most systematic scanning of the surface would have any chance of revealing his position. Otherwise there would be no certainty that he was even on the planet. The hunters would take up orbital stations and hope to trap him when he left the surface, but he would be finished with his task long before a careful search could even begin.

The ship dropped down on the nightside, stabbed through a partial overcast and raced low over a dark ocean. Whitecaps sprang up as the glow of New Bosporus appeared on the horizon.

The port city sheltered ten million Earth Federation citizens; the planet supported sixty million humanoids, both native and recently created hybrids. Water washed half the planet, and most of the land was still frontier. Most inhabitants lived in the coastal areas of the two major continents.

The ship slowed to a hover and settled into the water. One hundred meters below the waves, the craft moved forward to within a quarter-klick of the beach and came to rest on the sandy bottom.

Gorgias thumbed a pressure point on the control board. A voice spoke on the screen audio. It was a documentary which he had recorded, the prologue to an interview with Marko Ruggerio, Earth's popular composer. The commentator's self-important tones were amusing.

"... The Herculean Empire endured for twelve hundred Earth years—A.D. 5000–6200—in the globular cluster M-13, which contains more than fifty thousand suns, at a distance of thirty-four thousand light-years from the Federation capital, Earth. The greatest concentration of stars is in the core, which is thirty light-years across...."

The distortions had come later in the year-old program. Gorgias ran the recording forward.

"... The hybrid inhabitants of the Empire were the offspring of genetically engineered crosses between Earth colonials, freed from their sunspace by the early stardrives, and the original humanoids of the Cluster. The resulting physiology was hardy and long-lived. Average height was five and a half feet, small-boned but muscular, usually dark-haired. Individuals needed, on the average, about one third the normal sleep required by Earthmen...."

The commentator had slipped over the transition years, during which hordes of invading Earthpeoples had butchered the native populations.

"... But many of the females displayed psionic powers, while the males were high-strung and emotional, giving evidence of some empathic gifts, but seldom equaling the consistent telepathic reach of the females...."

It had been the females who had seen what the Earthfolk were planning toward the end of the war, Gorgias thought bitterly, and it had been the horror of that telepathic vision which had contributed to the final collapse from within.

"... There was some variation among the planetary societies of the Cluster, but the basic model was usually military. In 4900, Gorgias the First united twenty worlds by force and shrewd alliances. By 5000 he had wiped out the original humanoids of the Cluster, leaving the hybrids dominant...."

Lies. Gorgias the First had given his life to drive out Federation interests.

"... Earth observers visiting the Empire during the following centuries came away with the impression that the hybrids were frantic workers, striving toward an impersonal future. Many historians insist that the war began as a mistake, but the Herculean reprisals were carried out with such fierce hatred of

Earthpeoples that when war was finally declared in 5148, the Federation was forced into a *de facto* policy of extermination toward the enemy; nothing less was effective...."

No one ever mentioned the Federation bases and armed, exploitative colonies which would not leave the Cluster after the formation of the Empire, refusing to accept Herculean law after centuries of existence within the Empire's bounds.

"...and in battle it was virtually impossible to take a Herculean alive. The few who were captured usually found a way to kill themselves, often taking their guards with them...."

What of the games played with prisoners, the systematic humiliations designed to drive them into senseless fury and suicide?

"...By 6200 the Empire was in ruins, following three quiet spells of about fifty years each. But many powerful renegades remained free, looting and destroying Federation colonies...."

Gorgias felt a surge of pride for those lonely survivors who warred alone.

"...The greatest of these was Gorgias and his son of the same name. The father had been a young captain when the war ended, and he was never captured. Legend has it that he was nearly five hundred years old when he died in 6600, leaving his resources and spirit of resistance to his son, who is still free, it seems, and in possession of his father's Whisper Ship...."

Was there a hint of admiration in the commentator's tone?

"...Gorgias's son has been a terrorist in the name of vaguely defined political goals. Twenty years ago it was thought that some accident had overtaken the Whisper Ship, since its attacks had stopped suddenly. Hunters go out year after year, following each new attack, at great cost and without success. It seems certain Gorgias the Fourth is the last and most resourceful of the renegades. Many doubt that he will be easily killed or captured.

"Five thousand Herculeans survived the death of their empire, fleeing from one Cluster planet to another as the worlds were sterilized. Today's Herculeans are thinly scattered across fifty star systems in the Federation Snake, where they are outcasts. A half dozen popular names have been given to them. Unlike Gorgias, they are harmless folk now, busying themselves with a religious cult which has its center on Myraa's World, a planet named after the Herculean woman who heads the revival...."

Poor Myraa, he thought, living among shadows and delusions.

"...Romantic stories say that an army of Herculeans escaped into the Lesser Magellanic Cloud, one hundred seventy thousand light-years beyond the Galactic Rim...."

I'll find them someday, Gorgias promised himself.

"...It would be an impossible task to locate them among all those far stars. But even if the army existed, how effective a force could it be today? Would the surviving generation have any desire to carry on the fight?"

The army might be in stasis, he thought, ready and waiting for a leader to set it in motion.

"...A few modern strategists insist, however, that Gorgias draws power and supplies for his ship from a hidden base. An arsenal might be cached there, posing a danger if Gorgias could raise an army. Even a small force could do a lot of damage if it were equipped with some of the Empire's legendary weapons...."

All the weapons are real, he thought, and waiting.

"...The Whisper Ship is one of the old weapons, a virtually indestructible vessel which is said to be joined to the personality pattern of the owner, and destroys itself with terrible force upon his death, or if the link is broken through some other means.

"There is no list of weapons, some of which are thought to date back to mid-Empire. It is the survival of the weapons created toward the war's end which continues to intrigue military historians...."

The decisive weapon exists, Gorgias thought, but it had come too late to be useful. He had been looking for it since his father's death, and one day he would find it.

"...One of the reasons for the utter destruction of New Anatolia, home world of the Empire, was that it had been the source of a frightening line of weaponry. The Herculean armorers had to be destroyed with their factories to shorten the war, to prevent them from releasing a weapon which might have turned the conflict in their favor...."

There were still a few places where he had not searched. It *must* exist, he thought.

"...Although an amnesty has been offered a number of times, Gorgias has not responded...."

And I never will, you fool. The amnesty was only an effort to gain control of the Whisper Ship.

"... The cult on Myraa's World deludes itself with a yearning for what is called personality fusion—a supposed step on the way to an omega point of mental development, the practical end of an observer-oriented, integrated science, so-called. The theorizing is often inarticulate, shot through with winged words, talk of a hyperpersonal society and an emergence into a new reality, as if one could waken from one dream into another. Needless to say, these claims are considered to be mere posturings, dubious at best. The cult is open only to Herculeans, but there are only a few hundred survivors on the planet, so the cult does not seem to have attracted very many from its own potential members.

"Myraa's World is far out on the Galactic Rim, off the main Federation Snake of worlds. Many stellar mappers consider the planet to be one of a chain of widely spaced bridge stars linking the spiral arms of our galaxy with the Magellanic Clouds, which are throw-offs from our main system. It has been suggested by students of Herculean civilization that Gorgias sometimes visits the planet, but there has never been any evidence for this, despite numerous stakeouts.

"Today's hunters are led by Rafael Kurbi, noted psychologist and historian, who has published works on the Herculean problem. He considers most histories of the war distorted and inaccurate. He argues that the enemy's so-called madness was only apparent, a function, perhaps, of their high but normal metabolic rate, and their social structure which rewarded certain values once quite appropriate. Since we live more slowly, Herculean behavior seemed compulsive. And he insists that Herculean actions after the opening of hostilities cannot be viewed as typical. Earth's past displays just as much madness. He is fond of citing vast quantities of Earth history, mostly pre-spaceflight and sunspace-bound, to support his views, which have gained some influence in recent years. ..."

Gorgias found himself almost sympathizing with Kurbi.

"... Still, the majority of Kurbi's peers do not take his ideas seriously. They cite the ecological catastrophe of New Mars, which had to be evacuated after a large asteroid struck the planet, bringing on a sudden ice age. Opinion is somewhat divided, however, about whether Gorgias engineered this disaster by diverting the asteroid into a collision with the planet, or took credit for a natural event. ..."

The effect of such disagreements had been to slow the search for him, so they were useful. Gorgias wondered if Kurbi realized that the Federation had fought the great war out of envy, fearful that the Cluster worlds would come to dominate the Federation in science and culture. Was he blind to the fact that Federation biologists had branded Herculeans as freaks, a mistake to be wiped out?

"... Against this colorful background, Marko Ruggerio is writing his newest work, a percussive cantata on ethical themes from the Earth-Herculean War. We'll introduce him in a moment. The performance is scheduled for the great city auditorium on Wolfe IV, a quarter-klick-high structure of plastimet, complete with perfect acoustics and environs controls. The cantata is strongly influenced by the reconciliationist sentiments of personages like Rafael Kurbi. And now let me introduce Marko Ruggerio.

"'Maestro, when do you expect to premiere your new project?'

"'A year, most likely.'

"'Do you have any special expectations about the work?'

"'Yes—I think it possible that Gorgias may come forward after the performance.'

"'Isn't that a bit optimistic?'

"'Not at all. Beauty hath power to soothe the savage beast, as they say. Seriously, I think he's tired.'

"'How can you know that?'

"'My compassion tells me so.'"

Gorgias turned on the picture and looked at the two men. Ruggerio bore the face of a weakling, with protruding front teeth and bushy eyebrows—a man who would try to gain credit for his mediocre talents by attaching them to great issues. The interviewer wore a vacant grin, and looked a bit tired from reading the background material that had been prepared for him. They were both fools; but one was an important fool who would make himself useful. Gorgias turned off the recording.

The year was over. Marko Ruggerio was here in the city. Tomorrow evening he would climb to the summit of his career. Exotics from six worlds would try to seduce him after the concert. Everyone was preparing to feel greatly edified and proud of his or her Federation citizenship.

A year ago, disguised as an immigrant seaman from Sirius, Gorgias had bought a ticket for the concert. It had not been difficult, since he shared ancestry with the Sirians, going back to ancient Asia on Earth. One had to be very early for these cultural events, he had learned.

He turned on the screen and gazed out into the dark ocean. Fish fled from his light. A crab marched across the sandy bottom and hid behind a large rock.

Gorgias waited.

II. Percussion Cantata

"...hence this tremendous struggle to singularize ourselves, to survive in some way in the memory of others...this struggle, a thousand times more terrible than the struggle for life..."

—Miguel de Unamuno

THE GREAT ARENA breathed with the voices of a quarter-million people. Rivers of speech circled the black hole of the dark stage that would soon focus the massed attention of the audience. A few stars were visible through the dome as clouds pushed in from the sea.

Gorgias sat in the end seat of the last row, next to the eastern exit. The small viewer on his right armrest, where he would see close-ups of the soloists, was still dark. Billions of Federation citizens were waiting at home, on every world in the subspace net.

He had dressed in the one-piece, close-fitting black jumpsuit once worn by soldiers of the Empire, complete with markings of rank, even on the thick black ceremonial cape. No one would notice his mockery among the great variety of attires.

In the early morning hours, he had swum ashore with his boots and cape tied in a bundle on his back. The breakers had been heavy, knocking him over a few times before he reached dry land. He had checked into a cheap hotel in the dock area, and had spent the day watching local video programs.

Just before taking his seat in the arena, he had placed a

small pulse projector below one of the rotating lenses in the ribbon of pickup cameras which would be set in motion when the concert began. Even he would be unable to predict from which direction the invisible beam would strike.

It was strange to sit among so many beings. He was an intruder at a strange ritual. Was his uneasiness visible? He was grateful for the dim lighting. He looked up and glimpsed a star just as a cloud covered it. Another revealed itself, and it seemed friendly in its remoteness. Sight of stars and gray jumpspace was the most familiar part of his life. Yet surely he was not so different from these people around him. For a moment he was a citizen of New Bosporus, with friends, position and decisions to make.

A dark-haired woman was looking up at him from two rows down, a faint smile on her lips. She turned away when he did not respond.

He looked at his timer. The light in the outer lock of the submerged ship would go on in one and a half standard hours, to aid him when he swam out from shore. He made an effort to imagine what could go wrong.

"Use your imagination," his father had told him. "Examine the wild ideas. Sudden, half-formed suspicions may save your life. But never underestimate the simple, ordinary approach; it might work better than the elaborate. Be elaborate, then be simple—don't be either for long."

The whirl of voices died. The lights dimmed into darkness, leaving only starlight.

The stage burst into sight, transfixed by a circle of beams, revealing a hundred performers sitting at their instruments.

Some sat at consoles, tilted panels sprouting oversize push-buttons and giant levers. The only novel instruments on the platform were the massive percussion batteries, dating back thousands of years to Old Earth and the First Sunspace Confederation. Two of the drums were taller than the performers who would operate the overhead hammers. Around the consoles stood celesta, xylophones, six grand pianos, giant triangles, massive bells, clickers, iron anvils and two gargantuan wooden blocks with mallets swinging freely on chains—all linked to the consoles through amplification sensors.

The fifty male performers were dressed in black one-piece suits; the females were dressed in white.

Slowly, varicolored beams bathed the stage, splashing the

musicians with a rainbow, until the kaleidoscope of transformations ended in a deep blue haze. Gorgias felt the hush of expectation in the audience.

Drums rolled through the stillness before creation—storminess struggling up from an abyss, weakening the restraining silence. . . .

White light caught Marko Ruggerio about to conduct a female soloist. She began a weary song in high soprano, childlike but powerful in its grasp of feeling; no strain showed in her face on the close-up.

The drums surged menacingly.

Gorgias felt anger at the intrusion, even as he understood. From the first, it would be a war of beauty against ugliness, good and evil; the theme was present in the black and white dress of the performers.

Despite his determination not to be swayed, Gorgias found himself surrendering to the song's charm; its endless ache glowed around his consciousness, echoing deeply within unexamined regions. He dreamed of Myraa, the loveliness of her world; he longed to caress her long brown hair. Forgetfulness sang to him.

The song was cut short by the drums. The giant mallets struck their wooden blocks with an innocence-shattering thud.

The anvils chattered like metallic teeth.

Drums unleashed their thunder.

The celesta, xylophones and triangles hurled waves of breaking glass.

Bony pianos clattered.

Strong trees splintered.

Clickers shot through the chaos of sound.

The din spent itself with a clash of cymbals. A heroic melody slipped up from below and asserted itself. It was a well-formed theme, steadfast, the massed electric strings achieving a titanic sound as the xylophones joined in—

—There was a sudden silence, as if the universe had ceased to exist—

—An inversion of the heroic theme climbed out of the silence, grew monstrous, and perished.

Heroic themes, mirror images, one for each side of the war. Gorgias smiled inwardly, contemptuous of the composer's effort at reconciliation. Who was he trying to convince? There was only one Herculean in the audience, and no one was aware of the fact. It seemed incredible that Ruggerio could mean this sort of thing seriously. And yet the naive man had been right—a Herculean had come to the concert, for whatever reason. . . .

Now the first theme returned and lumbered forward, becoming distorted and ugly; its mirror image followed suit. Gorgias strained after elements of order as they dropped away.

But the spell seized him again, and he wandered after the music, drawn to its central concerns. He closed his eyes and thought of the countless Herculeans who had been murdered at the end of the war, dying in vaporizers because the Federation had defined them as biological mistakes. He visualized massive beams scorching entire worlds. And he remembered the vow he had made before his father more than twenty-five years ago. . . .

Listless snake drums brought the end of the bleak work by a composer of poster music, whose fame would be assured not by talent but by the manner of his death.

The last drum rolled away. A distant chorus sighed. Silence spoke in the darkness.

The lights crept up halfway. Gorgias leaned forward and pressed the release on his wrist-timer. Marko Ruggerio turned on the podium while holding the hand of the soprano. The applause was enthusiastic. Gorgias watched the composer's face on the monitor as the cameras scanned the platform with their unconscious gaze.

The applause grew louder, then faltered as Ruggerio crumpled to the floor. The soloist bent over him.

The audience screamed the Federation's outrage.

The arena lights exploded into brightness. Gorgias got up. Other performers were falling as they neared the stricken maestro; the soloist collapsed over his body. Gorgias stepped into the aisle and walked up toward the exit. The weapon had not shut down, he realized, but was still stabbing with its lethal pulses as the audience watched in horror.

He hurried through the exit. The panic was just beginning; soon the exitways would be choked with people. The short downhill passage led directly to the shuttle platform. An empty car was waiting.

He stepped inside. The doors closed and the car pulled away. A minute later it rushed into the oceanfront station. The doors opened and Gorgias stepped out. The smell of brine and sewage was strong as he climbed the stairs to the surface.

The sky was overcast now. He climbed the old wooden fence and dropped to the beach. Spray cooled his face as he crossed the darkness to the breakers.

He stopped short of the foam and looked back. The only light in the dock arena came from the entrance to the underground line. The dome of the distant arena was a behemoth rising over lesser structures, spilling its brightness into the low-hanging clouds.

He dropped his cape and took off his boots. Together with the exhausted pulse weapon, there would be more than enough evidence that he had been here.

Walking into the heavy breakers, he threw himself forward and broke through, counting a hundred strokes as he swam for the ship's position.

He dived. The vessel's light lay thirty meters below him. He pulled down toward it for what seemed a long time. The lock opened when he touched it; he swam inside. It cycled and he drew a deep breath.

The inner door opened. He rushed to the control room. The ship was already sweeping through the planet's communications.

One commentator was bemoaning the tragic interruption of a great musical career; another voice accused a political faction of murder; still another was demanding an investigation of lax security. The police channels were awash with special orders.

"Into deeper waters," Gorgias ordered, feeling elation as the ship slipped away. Only another Whisper Ship could follow him into extreme depths; the hull could resist all weapons except those of the ancient Herculean masters, or the very recent planet-based Federation batteries.

The hunters waiting in orbit would soon know that he was here; his humiliation of them would make it obvious.

III. The Hunter

"You are myself, myself only with a different face..."

—Ivan Karamazov

THE PLANET SCREAMED.

Rafael Kurbi watched the screen. A million-headed organism pressed in around the stage. Ruggerio's body was being placed on a stretcher. The screaming mob parted and the composer was whisked away.

There was no doubt in his mind that Gorgias had assassinated Ruggerio, even though conclusive proof might never be found. Police were searching for the weapon; known criminals and firebrands were being picked up; but Kurbi knew that it would do no good.

He leaned forward in his command station. "All officers, attention! I suspect that the Herculean will try to leave Wolfe IV at any time now. Watch the nightside. Captain Milut, inform the authorities at New Bosporus of our suspicions, so they don't charge some innocent wretch with the killing. Ruggerio is dead, isn't he?"

"Yes," Milut said.

"This was planned some time ago."

The screen view changed to show the planet in full phase. Kurbi leaned back and tried to relax. Gorgias might attempt to leave the planet, but it was just as likely that he would try their patience by waiting.

After twenty-five years, Kurbi had learned not to be certain about anything involving Gorgias. Scores of hunters had given up in frustration and shame; others had simply accepted the quest as busywork, and had retired without caring. Kurbi was sure that he would not capture the Herculean in the Wolfe IV system; it looked too easy. Somehow, Gorgias would extricate himself; later they would understand what had happened.

Kurbi was tired. Ten years of service in relocating the survivors of the New Mars disaster, and five studying medicine at Centauri, had led to command of the hunt for the Herculean, the institutionalized stalking of an enemy who could never mount a decisive blow against the Federation, but who could still terrify a starflung civilization.

He dimmed the lights in the control room, leaving only the glow of Wolfe IV. The darkness conjured up the past as he closed his eyes; it always asserted itself when he tried to rest or sleep, and he had long ago given up trying to banish it; the dead years were an old friend who had become irritating, very much like his superior, Julian Poincaré.

He remembered how his feelings about Gorgias had changed after the ruining of New Mars. He had resolved to hunt the Herculean, even kill him if necessary; but curiosity and a deeper concern had remained part of his motives.

"I can see getting up one morning and going out to kill him," he had told Julian. "Except—"

"What?"

"I want to see him alive," he had answered. "What kind of being can destroy a planet and still tolerate itself?"

"He'd probably say you were taking it much too personally. Understandable, since you lived through it. But we destroyed his world, more than one world. Old injustices feed his life, and he dispenses new ones. Who is to blame? Is there a just answer, or only answers that no one will like?"

Fifteen years later, in a series of debates on Earth, he had finally convinced them to let him offer terms to Gorgias. The grudging decision had come during a quiet spell, when it was suspected that the Whisper Ship had met with disaster and would never be heard from again.

Gorgias remembers too much, Kurbi thought, *while we remember too little.* The Herculean's acts of the last five years had made it unlikely that a sensible peace would be concluded with him, except as a ploy to lure him into the open.

"We are not dealing with a real force," Caddas, the old historian, had said, "but with a relatively weak individual, last of his kind, however strong he seems. We will forever see the past falsely if we do not make peace with him, and hear his testimony."

The Commission, recalled to service on an *ad hoc* basis, had directed that the Herculean be taken alive; but the decision had been the result of pressures from several interests. The Historians were eager to question a survivor from the great war; he might give them caches of Herculean records and artifacts. The military gamers wanted the Whisper Ship, more valuable in their minds than the Herculean's life, or the lives of any outworlders he might kill; a peace with Gorgias might give them control of his base and all the fabled war toys that it might contain. Negotiate if possible, Kurbi had been ordered, but destroy the renegade if necessary. The commissioners had covered themselves perfectly.

Their arrogance had once made Kurbi angry; now it was simply annoying. He would do what he believed was right; whatever the outcome, no one on Earth would be able to undo it; with Gorgias a prisoner, there would be little that anyone could say.

But every new action by the Herculean made it more unlikely that a sensible peace would be concluded with him. Each side was striving to overcome a past which could not be redeemed, only silenced. The commissioners did not want a living prisoner; and Gorgias wanted a Federation reduced to ashes.

The hunters had picked up the trail from Eisen IV, where it seemed Gorgias had destroyed the jumpspace exit beacon. Kurbi had joined the trackers just before entry into Wolfe's sunspace. He might have guessed the Herculean's purpose if he had known about the composer's deluded ambitions; but it was not possible to keep up with every aspect of cultural life in a corridor of one hundred thousand worlds.

New Bosporus sparkled on the screen. Clouds floated toward the lights, heralds of the hurricane that was pinwheeling westward.

A hunter gets to know his quarry. But Kurbi wondered whether Gorgias would be as he imagined him. Would it be possible to talk face-to-face? Or would the Herculean present a twisted, unreachable otherness? Kurbi hoped for an island of sanity within the Herculean, a place unclouded by the fears and hatreds of a terrible history whose bloody tide had washed Gorgias onto the strange shore of the present. If I could reach into him, Kurbi thought, the behavior set by the past might fall away like an ancient mask of brittle clay. Would the remaining personality be a broken individual? Would it be more merciful to kill him rather than tear apart the fabric of his reality? Who could rebuild the Herculean, give him another existence as meaningful?

In an unjust universe, facts and things mingled with a small amount of free will. Justice had to be made; it was an artifact which flickered like a feeble fire, and had to be made anew constantly. . . .

Was Gorgias free to change? Was it reasonable to expect that he would give up exercising the will and power he had grown up with? He had never known anything except the vision of himself as a rogue who would topple an evil civilization.

Captain Milut's face appeared as an inset in the lefthand bottom corner of the screen. "Nothing so far," he said.

"Keep the watch," Kurbi replied. The inset faded. Milut was a good officer, but he never communicated anything of himself.

Gazing at the blue-green globe, Kurbi wondered why intelligent species could not simply turn their backs on the stars and embrace the environments of these beautiful islands swimming in the deep. The view from space, like the mood of night on a planet, invited transcendent musings, stirring one's hunger for what lay beyond the horizon of the senses. The starry everblack quickened one's interest in the abyss of death, in the rush of peril, in the urgent call that came, always ambiguously, from the other side of whatever reality chanced to be. He recalled the lines of two forgotten poets, lines which he always thought of together: "I came out of the ninth-month midnight, and one day death will be a quiet step into a sweet, clean darkness. . . ." But in this age there was a great delay between birth and death, a barrier of longevity which prevented growth beyond the known life, if such existed. . . .

There was comfort in speculating, in reaching out beyond the finitude of one's ancient, inherited self. . . .

Outworlders judged the agelessness of the Earthborn as blasphemous, an obstacle to the endless flow of newness from the process of natural reproduction. Earthborn sought to become their own posterity. Countless jokes were told about their virility, their odd medical practices and long-term outlooks; yet the outworlds were still eager to acquire Earth's skills. Outworld leaders sought political power as a means by which to escape their own natural deaths, through the importing of Earth's biotechnics. One day the entire length of the Federation Snake would live by the skills and luxuries which Earth had developed and was slowly sending out to her greedy, opinionated children.

Few in the outworlds would weep over Marko Ruggerio Gorgias had misjudged the level of pride on Wolfe IV. Petty officials would be nervous for a while, but the killing would be forgotten as soon as responsibility was dissipated.

The Herculean's target had been Earth, where the creatures of conscience still fed deeply, and would not be so easily overcome. Earth would chew on the insult, fearful that one day Gorgias would be able to do more than wound its pride.

IV.   The Fiery Cloak

"Because God put His adamantine fate
  Between my sullen heart and its desire,
I swore that I would burst the Iron Gate,
  Rise up, and curse Him on His throne of fire."

—Rupert Brooke

THE WHISPER SHIP slipped from the dark ocean and floated slowly in the high winds, held steady in the grip of its drive field. Gorgias peered ahead. The vessel entered the sunny stillness of the storm's eye and switched into jumpspace.

The hunters would be looking for a ship that would move away from the planet before entering jumpspace. Coordinate changeover was usually a dangerous procedure, given the quantum indeterminacy of distances within otherspace, but it was well within the ship's design limits.

Smudges appeared on the scanner. It had not taken the hunters long to guess what he had done.

"Switch back," he said.

The ship drifted in normal space. He counted to five.

"Back again—minimum speed."

The ship switched and he looked ahead. The hunters had gone past him in their eagerness. It would be a moment before they noticed.

"Run at the star," he ordered, expecting the ship to protest, but it obeyed.

The trick was fairly complex, and he doubted that the hunters would have the courage to follow him; even if they decided to do so, they would be too late. They would learn what he had done, but they would fail to fix his direction after he came out on the other side.

There was some danger in it; he would be playing with the star's various fields, which continued as forces even in hyperspace, but his trail would end in the heart of a furnace.

A three-dimensional chart appeared on the screen as he approached the star. Animated lines of color marked the gravito-spatial and magnetic forces belonging to the star in normal space-time, dancing to mirror the reality of the star's equilibrium between the gravitational force of collapse and that of thermonuclear expansion. In one moment the representation was a series of circles, in the next cubes within cubes with superimposed triangles. The chart was an adequate quantitative model, an example of flow geometry, necessary to the ship's navigational programs, capturing the star's essential reality.

The lines of the schematic turned red, signaling that the ship had entered the star. Gorgias gripped the armrests and tensed; he was, after all, penetrating a major stress point of reality, where even a Whisper Ship might be torn apart if something went wrong.

He watched the screen, searching for signs of instability in the transit path. The model pulsed, heartlike in its red abstraction, bloodless compared to the awesome heart of fire existing in the familiar continuum. . . .

The primary colors of the model reappeared as the pulsations slowed. The ship emerged on the other side. Gorgias relaxed, knowing that he could do it again.

"Home," he said to the ship.

All there is of it, he thought bitterly. Home was still his father's base, even after his death. It had been another universe then, yesterday and twenty-five years ago; another person had performed the burial; another person had made the vow of vengeance before stepping into the tortured sleep of the stasis field. Silently, Gorgias renewed his allegiance to the fury imprisoned within his chest; one day its full energy would be unleashed and his ancient enemies would flee before him.

The screen cleared as he looked for the marks of his pursuers; the gray screen was empty, revealing only the cavernous unreality of jumpspace, with its black suns and shifting perspectives. As he watched, the continuum turned ash-white, throwing a glare into the control room; passing through this space of skeletal reality was still a slow dying.

Gorgias tried to look forward to his arrival at the base. There he would add more memory units to the ship's intelligences; he would continue his exploration of the arsenal; perhaps this time he would find the weapon that would give him superiority over the Earthborn. The arsenal contained thousands of weapons which he had not yet mastered; one day he would be called upon to teach others their use; he would have to be ready.

He thought again of the Herculean army, wondering what life was like for it in the Lesser Magellanic Cloud. Someday he would go in search of that army, and it would become part of his offensive strategy. . . .

"If it still exists," his father's voice said within him.

The army was probably in stasis, waiting, battle-ready; with all of its equipment and twenty divisions of fighting men, it had probably settled an entire planet. . . .

Gorgias got up and went aft to his quarters, where he ate a meal from the mess dispenser and went to bed, setting the controls for zero-g.

For a time his sleep was unbroken, but later troublesome images appeared. He was poised above a great abyss, with a large weight on his back, crushing him, pushing him into the black space below; he was frozen in his dream, unable to wake up. . . .

An age passed. He was looking across the plane of the galaxy to the glowing hub. Huge fireflies clustered around it, the globular clusters in their orbits; one of those jeweled groupings contained the cinder which had once been his home. . . .

Thoughts crossed the void and struggled to enter him; he reached out, but failed to embody them completely. . . .

Myraa's eyes opened and he looked out from within her, sensing her presence around him, distinct from his mental space. Suddenly he was thrown back from her eyes, to fall endlessly toward a floor of ice. . . .

Julian Poincaré, now Earth's highest-ranking intelligence officer, appeared on Kurbi's screen. The subspace link blinked and remained steady.

"Well—has he escaped again?" he asked in a voice lower

than usual. There was no hint of the stocky man's unsettling sense of humor.

Kurbi told him about Gorgias's new maneuver. "There's almost no chance of there being a recognizable trail. He might have gone off in any direction."

The subspace image wavered again, as if Poincaré's impatience had suddenly disturbed the link with Earth.

"He'll turn up again," Kurbi said, knowing that it would mean more loss of life. "We were lucky to have confirmed his presence at all."

"Where next?"

"Myraa's World—I don't know when, but I'm certain we can catch him there sooner or later."

Julian shook his head. "You've been saying that for decades."

"We have pursued the Whisper Ship from there."

"Only once—unsuccessfully. I may believe you, but I have trouble communicating my faith to the big thumbs around me...."

The sense of urgency quickened again in Kurbi. He had to find the Herculean, talk to him face-to-face, make him understand the sense of retrieving what was still valuable in his civilization. If Gorgias died, a key to the past would perish with him. It would be difficult to understand Federation history fully without absorbing the evidence in his control; and with him would also die all the stimulating differences of culture which all civilizations needed to renew their vitality. Three centuries ago, the Federation had destroyed a proud enemy, and had turned its back on the survivors. It was this loss of Carthage that haunted Kurbi, making him feel personally cheated. The conflict had revealed only one side of Herculean culture. What about the philosophers, scientists, musicians and poets? Where was the record of their work? Gorgias might not be aware of what had survived into his keeping.

"Couldn't you have followed him through the star?" Julian asked.

"Perhaps—but by the time we would have passed through, the Whisper Ship would have been out and gone, leaving us no direction to follow. The star will have erased any of the usual signs of his passing. There might be a trace farther out, but he will be far away and covering his tracks by the time we find it."

"He's certainly put a lot of space between his tricks in the past," Julian said.

"You want to see him dead. Admit it."

"Yes—if he goes on killing. You think that yourself. There won't be any choice."

Kurbi thought of the Herculean survivors on Myraa's World. Gorgias was the kind of vigorous and intelligent leader who might pull them out of their stoicism of defeat.

"Maybe you need a rest," Julian said. "When was the last time I saw you bodily?"

"I've got to see this through to the end."

"Yours or his?"

"I'm going to Myraa's World."

"I won't stand in your way, up to a point—but if you lose a ship, or if he strikes and there is a greater loss of life, someone will have me for breakfast."

"They'll spit you out," Kurbi answered. "You'd taste too bitter."

Poincaré snorted, threw up his hands and broke the link.

Kurbi stared at his own face in the shiny gray surface of the screen. The lines were just beginning to come into his face at the age of seventy-five, but his hair was still black; his appearance would not change significantly until he was well past two hundred, if he did nothing; with rejuvenation he would stay as he was indefinitely.

He tried to imagine his life as it might be after the hunting of young Gorgias was over—the Herculean was young only by Herculean standards, yet Kurbi always thought of him as younger than himself. He thought of Grazia, dead these three long decades... frail, transparently skinned Grazia with her long black hair and large sad eyes, an exotic flower torn suddenly from the garden of Earth. He pictured her swimming gently in the pool, climbing out to lie naked on the grass; and he remembered the distant fear that had crossed his mind then, the future casting its shadow backward into a happier past—

—The glider sank suddenly toward the cliff face.

He was grateful that he had been unable to see its shape crumple up against the rock. Looking back, the chain of events leading to her death seemed inevitable, bound with an iron determinacy because there was nothing he could ever do, even in an infinity of time, to change them.

He recalled his time of wandering as he had searched for

peace in the worlds of Earth's ring, moving from one habitat to another; he might have removed the terrible memory, but that would have meant losing too much else, becoming another person.

The hunting of Gorgias had given him something useful to do, enlisting his intellect and feelings in the solving of a problem that might have no solution. The sense of urgency was always there—Gorgias was killing Federation citizens, and it was possible, though unlikely, that he might in time persuade enough outworlds to revolt against Federation authority.

The best solution would be for Gorgias to surrender, hand over his ship and base and retire to Myraa's World, where he would help revive his people's will to increase their numbers, so that one day they could return to the Hercules Cluster and rebuild their civilization along peaceful lines.

Suddenly Kurbi realized that the future he wanted for Gorgias was the sort of thing a man might want for his children, but the reality threatened to be different; Gorgias seemed as unreachable as Grazia.

Kurbi could not abandon the hunt. It would have to end in a constructive way, or with Gorgias's imprisonment, or death. That final alternative filled Kurbi with dread and sorrow. The Herculean's hatred was a natural force, self-reliant, moving by sudden inspiration, by impulses surer than intellect—admirable in its own way; but Kurbi knew that he would not shrink from killing the Herculean if it became necessary; he would kill him for what he had done to New Mars; he would kill him because he could not change him.

They would hail the act on Earth, and lament the loss of the Herculean base; the collective shoulders of the Federation would shrug at the death of a rival. *It will be my failure if we kill him*, Kurbi thought. Surely Gorgias could not forever resist capture by a starflung civilization? *He might commit suicide*. The only chance to save him would come as the result of a long personal confrontation. . . .

The screen lit up. "Still no trail," Milut said. "It's a dead end. . . ."

V. Impromptu

"O what can ail thee, knight-at-arms,
  Alone and palely loitering!"

—Keats

THE WOODED HILLS were a green blur; rain-covered leaves reflected yellow sunlight in a chain of sunbursts running before the Whisper Ship.

Three thousand light-years along the winding corridor from Earth, Izar's only navigational link with the Federation was an old-fashioned beacon—a lighthouse radiating into otherspace, guiding infrequent jumpships to what was clearly a fledgling settlement. Gorgias had noticed the signals while still in whisper drive—three concentrated beams penetrating toward the galactic perimeter; they were stationary, unlike the sweeping beams usually used for otherspace navigation; and they came from a planet, rather than from a relay in space.

Izar's possible vulnerability had caught his interest, giving him an excuse to linger. The deserted levels of his father's base could wait. Izar was inhabited by enemies—more than enough reason to scout and strike; no one would expect him here, especially if he had not planned it himself.

He felt the burden of isolation lift as the ship landed near the edge of a large clearing. He sat back and dreamed of people coming across the grass to welcome him, involving him with their looks, words and feelings.

Warm air circulated through the ship. He got up and went aft to the open side lock.

He stepped out and looked at the huge waxy leaves on the trees. The air was filled with the smell of growing things; sunlight was a veil on the greenery; wind stirred the trees with a soft rustling sound.

He looked up and saw the antiquated beacon tower standing on the mountain. There was no sign of people. He took a deep breath of the fresh, moist air. Storm clouds were moving toward the yellow sun from the south. The settlement was probably nearby, but so small that he had passed over it in a second.

He began walking across the clearing toward the wooded mountain, stretching his muscles, enjoying the feel of softness under his boots, looking at the irregularities of dirt and growing things, so new after confinement within the ship's familiar geometry.

Rain fell as he reached the trees, and he ran under the protection of the huge leaves. He looked around. Here the very shadows were green-tinted; the air's sweetness mingled with the odor of rotting things. Soon the moisture was running in rivulets from the trunks and branches, in giant drops from the overburdened leaves, accenting the smell of wet bark and minty leaf. Some of the leaves caught the water like goblets, overflowing their fill onto the path in front of him.

Quickening his pace on the well-worn trail, he came to a fork in the path. The left way led up to the tower; the right probably continued around the mountain.

He took the upward path, climbing steadily until he emerged on a flattened summit of dirt and rock. The tower stood above him, about one hundred meters of metal frame and spiral stairway with a cage at the top.

Gorgias turned and looked out over the forest. The ship sat in the clearing, its polished hull looking dull in the rain.

He turned back to the tower and noticed the wooden shelter under the spidery stairs. He hurried between the legs of the tripod and into the hut. The smell of soil was very strong inside. He saw a table, a chair and an old cot. The only window was behind him by the door. The dirt-floor hovel was probably used by maintenance people when they visited the beacon.

He sat down and wiped the wetness from his face. The chair creaked under him as he wondered whether he could readjust the beacon so that it would lead ships into Izar's sun. That would be much more enterprising than simply destroying the tower; they might replace the beacon as soon as jumpships noticed that the system was missing from their scanners.

He got up, went outside and started up the spiral, reaching the top in a few minutes. He paused and let the sun warm his face. The ship's hull glinted across the downward slope of trees.

Gorgias stepped through the entrance into a small shelter. The instrument package stood on an anchored tripod. He grasped the clear plastic covering and lifted the hemisphere back on its hinges.

After a few minutes of study, he was certain about how to make adjustments. The entire mechanism was made so that it could be taken apart easily. First he set the standard Federation coordinates for Izar's sun; then he removed the faceplate and set it to read as it had before, so that the dial would not show the change. He replaced the cover, turned and went down the spiral, his boots clattering on the rungs. It had been easy, but then what kind of security would this kind of installation ever need? Who would think that it might come into danger? Not much could go wrong with its simple design. A few ships would be lost before the beacon was repaired, but that would be enough to make his stopover worthwhile.

He reached the base of the tower and started toward the path. The sound of a snapping twig startled him, and he stopped. Someone was coming up the trail. Standing perfectly still, he listened to the gentle footsteps; then he turned, went into the hut and peered out through the rag hanging over the window.

A figure in green came up the path, grasping a tall walking stick in its hand; a wide-brimmed hat hid the face from view.

Gorgias stepped back from the window, realizing that it was too late to avoid the encounter. The figure came inside, dripping water from the hat. The person was not very tall, but thin enough to appear taller from a distance.

The girl took off her hat in a sweeping motion, throwing drops into Gorgias's face. Then she saw him and stared back in surprise, but without fear.

She looked upward, as if thinking about the beacon. He noticed her long brown hair, tied up in a bun on the back of her head. She took a step toward him and stopped, unsure of herself; then she shrugged and sat down in the chair. Gorgias relaxed, half-sure that she had not guessed the meaning of his presence.

She said something, but he did not understand the language.

Her voice was musical; he could tell that she was making an effort to be friendly.

"Id-della," she said, pointing to herself.

Gorgias nodded, unused to standing for so long in another's gaze; he could almost sense her heartbeat, feel the warmth of her skin. If she became suspicious about the beacon, he would have to destroy it. It was inevitable, he realized, that the colony would become suspicious about the beacon, whether he killed her or not, now that she had seen him.

He rushed through the door and ran down the trail. In a moment he heard her behind him, padding noisily on the packed dirt; he turned his head and saw that she was gaining, stick in hand. Suddenly he was uncertain about whether he could defend himself in hand-to-hand combat; he had never gone into a fight without weapons or the ship. His pursuer was armed with a heavy stick, and might easily crush his skull.

She was still on the slope when he reached level woodland; he heard her voice echoing from the trees when he ran out into the clearing. The sun came out, blinding him for a moment; he stumbled forward and stopped in the tall grass.

He turned around and saw her standing near the edge of the clearing, watching him as if he were a wild beast that she was hunting. She called to him, and it sounded like a question.

"She's no enemy," his father's voice said within him.

He turned away and sprinted for the ship.

The lock was warm around him as he staggered inside. He looked back and saw her running through the clearing. Voices called to her, and he saw two figures among the trees on the mountainside. She drew closer as he watched, carrying her stick like a spear, rushing through the grass with the beauty of a wild animal. She was only curious about him and the ship. *Coward,* he said to himself, hating his own fear.

"Close the lock," he said, then went forward when the door had closed, trying to ignore the absurdity of the situation. A single, powerless individual had ruined his plan.

"Lift," he said as he sat down in the control room.

In moments he was moving slowly above snow-white clouds. The ship circled and came in over the tower.

"Destroy it," he said.

Beams reached out and burned the structure. The wet trees began to smoke. The ship circled and came in again. Beams reached out again, hastening the melting; the tower seemed to sink as its metal liquified; a rain of white-hot droplets hit the trees. Gorgias regretted the loss of his jumpship trap.

"Find the town."

The ship moved away from the ruined tower, widening the circle, searching.

"On the other side of the mountain."

Gorgias leaned forward as the town came into view—one street with a dozen buildings.

"Burn it."

The ship came in low and touched fire to the roofs. Gorgias realized that the people would have time to escape if they were quick about it; he had no time for hunting individuals with a ship.

In a few moments he was over the clearing again. The girl and the two men stood in the grass, staring at the smoking mountain. One of them pointed to the smoke rising from the other side of the mountain, where their town was burning. The girl turned and looked up at the ship.

Then the clearing was behind him, and the ship was climbing starward. The drive cut in and the ship slipped into gray ashes.

There was no beacon on the screen—a small thing, but it would inconvenience his enemies; if only the girl had not come to the tower, he might have caused more damage.

She was an absurd image in his mind, laughing at him.

VI.   A Bitter Native Land

"There was a child went forth every day,
  And the first object he looked upon, that object he
    became,
  And that object became part of him for the day
    or a certain part of the day,
  Or for many years or stretching cycles of years."

—Walt Whitman

THE WHISPER SHIP flickered out of bridgespace—a broken line suddenly becoming continuous as the stars of Hercules kindled around it, throwing their light into the gas and dust of the Cluster, wrapping the myriad huddling suns in a shimmering field. These were hot suns, these fifty thousand ornaments, intense even in the lenses of faraway worlds.

The core of the Cluster, thirty light-years across, contained the greatest concentration of stars, giving the appearance of a solid mass of light, as if some cosmic craftsman were planning to create a titanic star from the compression of suns.

It had taken almost two hundred hours at full drive to get here; the ship had followed a twisting path through the plane of the galaxy, turning, winking in and out of jumpspace, doubling back to check for pursuers, finally setting a direct course for the base.

He could live out his life among these stars and not be found. As he looked at the Cluster, something like reverence came into him, as if he were looking at the beginning of all things. These stars were silent beings, ruling the galaxy from this place above the hub. The stars below circled the black hole at the galactic core; but the Cluster seemed to ride free in the night.

The screen flickered briefly as the ship passed in and out of non-space, stitching across the remaining distance to the base.

The Cluster swallowed the ship, blotting out the galaxy.

Slowly, the ship penetrated toward the center, until the cloud that hid his destination filled the screen. Here and there the cloud was suddenly pierced with light, the lances of the ruling gods outside, sentries protecting the spark inside.

The screen brightened as he neared the small, white-hot sun. Gorgias leaned forward, anticipating the sudden vista; even as a child it had never failed to move him.

The ship passed out of obscurity and the white-hot star lay before him in a pocket of space, a small desert of darkness and light. Home was here, all there was of it, the warren of war which had never been found by the Federation.

The ship slipped through the sunspace and sought the airless world.

Soon the barren, craggy surface took up half the screen; and a little later the polar mountains sprawled beneath a painted sky of star-pierced gas. The tunnel entrance gaped at Gorgias like the barrel of some huge gun set in the mountainside.

The ship floated inside; locks opened and closed as it passed through to the berth chamber far below.

Gorgias was still as the ship settled into its familiar concrete notch. Homecoming was always a time of mixed feelings. Elation would be followed by a sense of safety; later, he knew, a feeling of entombment would find him. He worried at times that the lock mechanisms might fail, trapping him here forever.

He got up and climbed the ladder to the vertical air lock. The hatches opened and he climbed out onto the ship's hull, stepping from there to the concrete block which enclosed the ship's ovoid shape on three sides.

Six berths and only one Whisper Ship. Where were the others? Somehow the question was not as insistent as it had been during past homecomings.

He turned and his footfalls echoed; he walked through the huge open door set in the cavern wall, and marched down the long dark passage until he came to the war room; the heavy door slid open and he stepped into the brightly lit chamber.

He sat down at the table of polished metal and took a deep breath. The room still held the antiseptic odor of the tireless air system.

Centuries had tumbled away and the table had not lost its mirrored luster. He looked around at the empty chairs, imagining the Herculean strategists whose faces had been reflected in the polished metal as they planned and shouted at each other across the frozen, lakelike surface....

Home. All there was of it.

The base had never been found; even now it would be able to defend itself if attacked—but that would never happen; home was a place beyond reach, beyond all danger, where all hopes were stored, as impregnable as the center of his will.

He reached over and touched the terminal next to his chair, selecting from the historical records.

The long-dead, encyclopedic voice, familiar to him throughout his life, uttered words in the dark region above the table. A misty pillar of light went up from the mirrored surface.

Gorgias had always avoided the visuals of New Anatolia's destruction; his father had described the event to him, but had always been reluctant to show him what had happened; now it was time to see, Gorgias thought, to renew his weakening will.

"These records were made with great difficulty," the voice said from the vault. "Where they are deficient, simulations have been substituted, so that the past will stand against the inevitable lies that will be told...."

A green world appeared, the plaything of a double star.

"A hundred ships from Earth," the voice continued, "built for one purpose: to strike directly at New Anatolia, to break the will of the Empire. They came out of jumpspace with their heavy lasers and sun mirrors. The entire surface of the planet had been divided up in advance, one sector for each group of ships...."

They came as if to cut grass and destroy pests, Gorgias said to himself.

Snippets of battle sequences appeared. Mobile fortresses as large as planetoids lanced energy into New Anatolia, incinerating cities, precipitating whirlwinds and earthquakes, melting the ice caps....

Floodwaters crossed continents, filling valleys as if they were ditches....

"The ground was carbonized to a depth of fifty meters, the oceans began to steam; the clouds spread across the blackened land. A billion people died. The corpses did not have time to bleed; firestorms swept the urban areas, disintegrating bone and tissue as if they were paper. Here and there a few survived, coming to the surface to breathe the fine dust and alien air, shriveling up into dry sacks filled with brittle bones. . . ."

From far out in space, New Anatolia's face was black. Sparks kindled and died. . . .

"No more," Gorgias said, seized by a sudden weary despair. The attack on New Anatolia had drawn Herculean forces home, into the final trap.

The vault filled with light as the library shut down.

Gorgias listened to the subliminal hum of the base around him. He looked at the glare of lights in the surface of the table; he looked at his fingertips touching their twins in the mirror. He wondered about the troop cylinder, imagining the small, crystal-filled casing which contained the matrix for a fully armed division of Herculean soldiers.

His father came awake inside him. *"Are you still dreaming of that?"*

"There was such a thing—I'll find it," Gorgias answered silently.

"A hundred cylinders would do no good—at best you could expect a division or two of hastily trained personnel, and you could not be sure of reviving them successfully. There might be side effects—they might all appear dead or damaged. I never saw any evidence for such a device. . . ."

Gorgias remembered the hurt in his head when his father had dreamed of the home world's death. . . .

The street.

Metal flowing down as the upper levels of the city melted.

The pain of people dying from the sudden heat in their lungs . . . exploding as the water in their bodies turned to steam.

Level after level collapsing, crushing . . .

Crowds fleeing downward into the drain tunnels . . .

A sky of red dust. Columns of energy pushing down from the armada in orbit, one column for each city, one for each unit of land. The atmosphere was blue around the frozen bolts as they pumped power into the screaming planet—energy drawn from the Cluster itself, from the very suns of home.

"Stop it!"

"The dream?" his father asked, half asleep.

"It hurts, in my head—it's so terrible."

"I'll wake up," his father said, *"and we'll take a walk down the hill."*

He remembered the walks in the tall grass on Myraa's World, the planet of exile that he had mistaken for home as a child. Time rushed forward to the present as he confronted his father:

"But I have the tripod that uses the cylinder!"

"So maybe there was one. If you find it, don't use those lives for combat...."

I have the tripod, Gorgias thought, and when I plug the cylinder into the panel...

"...use them to help our peoples to increase their numbers."

...all the power of the ship will go into reconstituting a division of Herculean fighting men.

He saw the army appearing out of nowhere, sweeping the field of battle clean of all the Earthborn, and he knew that he had to find the cylinder; it would free him from the endless cycle of striking and running; he would be able to challenge the enemy openly.

It's not here, he thought. In all the years of searching the base, he should have found the cylinder. Perhaps it had never existed. Myraa knows where it is, he thought, unable to rid himself of the long-held suspicion, but she won't tell me where to look....

There were other things he had to do while he was here. The ship's cyber-intelligence could always use more memory units, to extend its knowledge and surrogate experience. He would also have to adopt a few more weapons from the arsenal, so that he could teach their use when the time came.

He got up, went out through the automatic door and turned right into a lighted passage. It sloped gently into the depths of the base, leveling off after a quarter kilometer.

He walked into a large circular chamber. The orange globe of light was bright overhead, burning without even the smallest flicker. The mosaic of the floor was still unbroken, each stone shiny and free of dust.

He looked around at the circle of doors; each led into a weapons room, and each room led into still other rooms. The regress continued outward for many square kilometers. He had never been in all the storage chambers; it would take many years to complete the search of all the closets and corners.

He chose a door at random and went through as it slid open. The walls of the room were covered with shelves, each wall rising ten meters from the floor to form a hexagon drum fifty meters across.

He scanned the shelves, hoping to glimpse a protective case about ten centimeters square; the orange star of the Empire would probably be in one corner of the cover.

The shelves contained hundreds of hand weapons, all of the same type, each strapped to its packing board with a generous supply of power slugs laid out on both sides of the barrel. He would never have enough hands to use them, unless he found the cylinder, or contacted the army in the Magellanic Clouds. If Myraa knew where the cylinder was located, he thought, then what else did she know?

He searched room after room, stooping and climbing the shelf walls. Some chambers were filled with nothing but personal screen units, others with field-ration packs; still others contained only uniforms. Everything seemed to be duplicated into infinity. Hopeless as it seemed, he knew that the cylinder might well be here, despite his suspicions.

"You want it handed to you," his father said, *"the search is too hard."*

"Shut up!" Gorgias shouted into himself. He knew what his father would say about anything lately; the dead man's echo was growing tiresome.

Gorgias stopped looking and came out from the maze of rooms, picking up two boxes of memory cubes on the way.

The side lock was open when he reached the ship. He went through to the control room and started plugging in the additional memories. He did not know in advance what they contained, but they might prove useful in the solution of operational problems.

The prospect of not finding the cylinder wore away at him as he worked. It could very well turn out to be a sentence of death, he thought, knowing that without a large force he could not possibly win against the Federation.

The thought startled him; he had never before considered defeat or death.

Obviously, the weapon had not come into use during the war; time had run out. If it had been manufactured on a large scale, then even a small fleet of scout ships would have been able to invade one world after another, landing secretly and

deploying overwhelming forces for swift takeovers. The idea
quickened his pulse, flowering into hatred. He left the ship and
started to search again with a renewed will; but again without
success.

They would not have hidden such an important weapon, he
thought; clearly, it was somewhere else.

At last he went to the stasis chamber. The march down the
inclined tunnel helped relieve some of his tension.

The lonely orange light still shone in the chamber; the empty
stasis shells still stood in a circle against the wall, tilted like
strange sun pods to receive the orange illumination.

He walked up to the shell that held his father's body and
peered in. The shadowed face was unchanged, its cave-eyes
still staring into a mindless eternity. . . .

Gorgias saw himself emerging again and again from the
time-contracting sleep.

He turned and left the chamber.

Back inside the ship he sealed all the locks, and slept.

*Myraa listened, touching his sleeping thoughts, reaching
out to him across the island universe which swam in the fragile
bubble of space-time, which in turn floated in a greater sea of
chaos, and once every eighty billion years collapsed under the
press of darkness, only to rekindle and throw back the night.*

*"No!" his swarming thoughts cried, afraid of the black
minutes at the end.*

*She pitied his fortress self and tried to caress his spark of
awareness, but it was useless; he would have to come by himself; he could not be drawn sooner. She withdrew, leaving him
to his ghosts. . . .*

Treason and fear.

*He saw the girl who had glanced up at him in the auditorium
on Wolfe IV.*

*Her face became Myraa's, and she was singing a beautiful
song; at any moment she would stop and cry out to expose
him.*

He longed for her embrace.

*She whispered in his ear as he held her, but the words were
unclear, windlike and fearful. . . .*

*She became small and soft in his arms, completely open,
shaking slightly as he broke her in two. . . .*

Her eyes were black cavities. . . .

Five Whisper Ships sat in the previously empty berths, each vessel fully manned and equipped with troop cylinders. . . .

He woke up in a sweat, got up and went out to stand on the concrete.

He listened, trying to forget the snakelike hiss of Myraa's voice. The ancient lights in the bay chamber continued without a flicker. Invisible beings moved through the vast honeycomb of the base. The air was damp.

He imagined a din-filled base in the midst of war. Furious shouting from the war room. Weapons being brought up from the stores as ships came in and out of the bays . . .

How he wished that he might have lived then, when each moment of life had been charged with meaning and resolve, and the future lay open to courageous choices.

"But we lost," his father whispered. *"How do you explain that?"*

Suddenly the inertia of the deserted base threatened to quiet his will. Somewhere below, he knew, were luxury quarters, where he might live out a lifetime in comfort, the slave of a waking dream.

He turned, walked back into the ship and went forward into the control room. The screen came on as the ship readied itself for his command.

"Myraa's World," he said.

VII.   Ends and Means

"'What can I do to save them!' Danko thundered. Suddenly he tore open his breast, took out his heart and held it high over his head."

—Gorky

"WE'VE GOT TO CATCH HIM," Poincaré said from the screen. "They'll replace me if this goes on much longer. Some of the oldest groups have taken this up personally—the Herculean has touched their pride." He lowered his voice. "Submit a new report. Make it optimistic. I like my life as it is, Raf."

"We're doing quite a bit," Kurbi said.

"It doesn't show."

"We're ready to leave for Myraa's World. I'll beam a report in a day or two while we're in passage."

"Fine. Have the officials on Wolfe IV given you any more trouble?"

"The mayor of New Bosporus called me up and gave me a lecture on how Wolfe is entitled to protection from renegades. He made it clear that he didn't care about some two-bit composer imported by enthusiasts, but that he would not tolerate the ruin of his career. Then he went on to read me a list of his accomplishments until I cut him off."

"That's not like you."

"I'm tired, and I've been getting the feeling that all this won't mean much to me after a while. Maybe I can get it over with before that happens."

"What?"

"Oh, don't worry." Suddenly he regretted voicing his feelings to Julian. "I'll do the job as long as you're part of the Herculean Commission."

Poincaré smiled. "I know what you mean." He paused. "Maybe Gorgias will follow those Herculeans who were supposed to have escaped into the Magellanic Clouds. I personally don't care if they start another empire out there, and I don't believe we could ever find it, even if it grew to cover a thousand systems. Good luck to them—they deserve to be left alone."

"Herculeans are still human," Kurbi said, "and human beings have always had a wretched curiosity about their own kind, as well as a tendency to treat old conflicts as if they had happened yesterday. They'll come looking for us one day, unless we find them first. You've seen this kind of account-keeping in the pride of the old immortals on Earth."

"I can think of a few of them I'd never like to see again," Poincaré said. "They cling to life, Raf, and they're no wiser for their centuries of life. They're amazed that the Herculean can risk so much at his age."

"We've failed to open up the human mind as much as we've extended life," Kurbi said. "You can't have indefinite life without increasing the mind's potential for knowledge and creativity..."

"You think the Herculeans might have done something along these lines? It certainly doesn't show in Gorgias."

"Maybe there's something in the cult on Myraa's World."

"Don't let that take you in—it's just another form of stoicism, retreat from a bad war."

"You're probably right," Kurbi said. "It's just that I look at humankind's last twenty-five centuries and I see no genuine advances beyond an increase in living space—no integration of the sciences, only small technical advances, mostly a refinement of devices we've had for a millennium. No commanding art forms to mention. We've got an awesome syncretism of styles—the greatest war ever waged is our greatest originality. We're a museum display of every period from Earth's history, existing on one Federation world or another. How I wish we'd run into another starflung species as powerful as we are, so that they would take us down a few pegs, make us see ourselves from outside."

"But we had the Herculeans."

"An accident resulting from the opening up of the galaxy to our stardrives, and they were no better than us, Carthage to our Rome."

"But you're not sure that something in their culture might have been . . . different?"

"Yes. I'm sorry, Julian—you've had it with me, haven't you?"

"You make it all sound very interesting," Poincaré said. He was silent for a few moments. "You know, I think I do know how to make all this look better. Stay where you are—don't leave Wolfe's sunspace. I'm coming out there to join you."

"You'll be delaying me."

"What's a few days, a few weeks, after all the time you've put into this? I'll bring another ship, a big one, and that will get everyone here excited. Naturally, I won't say what it's for. Besides, Myraa's World is supposed to be lovely."

"It won't be any vacation if we run into Gorgias."

"Do you really think we might?"

"Maybe—we've been around a long time, waiting for a mistake on his part. He's due for one. There's something that brings him to Myraa's World, despite the danger. The surest way is to get there ahead of him, settle down and wait for as long as it takes. We've never tried it."

"Wait for me, Raf," Julian said and broke the connection.

If the war had ruined us, Kurbi thought, to the point where the Federation and the Herculean Empire had fallen apart into isolated worlds, then each world would have had a chance to go its own way, to grow and diverge for as long as the interstellar quarantine lasted. Some would view such a time as a dark age, but in fact it would have been a rebarbarization of history, a time of renewal, giving the antagonists time to digest each other's influences, undisturbed.

The Federation was still in need of such a fertilizing fragmentation.

Enemies need each other, he thought, exasperated by the idea's perverse necessity. A darkness without hope of dawn pressed in around him. The war seemed to be still raging nearby; the gestures of hate were still being made somewhere near the edge of his vision; if he turned his head fast enough, he would glimpse titanic forms locked in combat, huge limbs embracing above burning worlds, dying throats gasping for air in countless infernos. . . .

Captain Milut came into the control room and sat down.

"We're waiting here until Poincaré arrives with another ship," Kurbi said.

Milut nodded. A very reclusive officer, Kurbi thought, very careful about what was coming to him from the Service.

"Where are you from, Captain?"

"New Mars. I left long before the disaster, but . . ."

"But what?" Kurbi asked in surprise.

"It did not deserve what he did to it, even though I hated the place. . . ."

"What about your family?"

"The Federation gave me a way out."

"All your relatives were on New Mars when it happened?"

"They all died by drowning."

"Did you ask to be assigned to my command?"

Milut shrugged. "Luck of the draw."

"Are there any others here from New Mars?"

"A few, I think." He turned and looked at Kurbi with pale blue eyes. "Count me out of your suspicions, Commander. I can't speak for others, but I live in the present. My retirement and rejuvenation is coming up soon, at which time I'll change my identity and live as I please."

"What do you plan on doing?"

"I don't think it would interest you. Personally, I don't care what happens to the Herculean." Milut turned and faced the screen. "I would appreciate it, sir, if we kept things on an official basis."

"As you wish, Captain."

"One thing, Commander. I don't think that your crew's animosity toward the Herculean will help you much. It might be a handicap."

"I'm aware of that."

Suddenly Kurbi wondered whether Julian had been entirely honest with him. Was he coming out because he was afraid that his friend might fall apart under pressure? Or had Poincaré sensed success and wanted to be around for a share of the glory?

"You may go, Captain," Kurbi said, "I'll take this watch myself." Milut nodded and left the room.

Julian's trivial wit would be a welcome change.

Kurbi closed his eyes and tried to sleep. *I'm a fool*, he thought, *to have chased Grazia when she didn't want me. I wouldn't be here if she had not died. It would have been different if I had let life come to me, instead of chasing it....*

But then, things might always have been different.

He got up and paced the control room. He stopped and turned on the screen to find Earth among the stars. A map grid appeared, pinpointing the star at a distance of fifteen light-years. Why did Julian need a week to get here? What kind of ship was he requisitioning, anyway?

Kurbi sat down, and this time he slept.

VIII.   Myraa's World

"I will do such things—
    What they are yet I know not—but they shall be
The terror of the earth."

—King Lear

". . . the souls that were
    Slain in the old time, having found her fair;
Who, sleeping with her lips upon their eyes,
Heard sudden serpents hiss across her hair."

—Swinburne, *Laus Veneris*

HE SAW MYRAA and himself suspended in a clear liquid, she floating on her back below him, limbs open and long hair flowing, he a perfectly muscled body, sinewy fibers wrapped around his skeleton.

He pushed down to her, grasped her head with both hands and kissed her as she embraced him. Rings of water moved away from the intertwined bodies; the liquid plenum filled with light.

The outsider's view persisted. He held a water-filled globe in his hand, examining it against a sky of white light, watching the figures turning slowly inside. He opened his hand, watched the globe roll, fall and shatter at his feet. . . .

The laser cut through the bodies on the ground. Hands thrust

*forward from a dozen torsos. His own mouth was in the dirt;
he felt the beam touch his insides and pass through to warm
the ground under his belly.*

Blink.

*Drown, sink down, lance out as light into the sea mud,
surface into a vise of pain....*

His eyes refused to roll down from inside his head.

*He groped with a hundred hands into the white space, strain-
ing to glimpse something dark. His eyes were made of polished
marble; nerves brushed gently against their stone surfaces,
ivory wires trying to pick up something to send backstage.*

Blink.

*Inability became a fearful mass in his stomach. He closed
his eyelids, covering the white space with red capillaries. Fear
became a messenger, linking the strands of his consciousness,
preserving the matrix of his individuality, the lightning pattern
of his nervous system, entombed within his flesh....*

*The Whisper Ship blinked into normal space and rushed
into the Earth like a toy dart, blossoming into a flash—leaving
him without flesh, a pattern of naked energy....*

*He sank, passing through soil and granite into Earth's
magma-warmth, where the heat nourished his new form. He
shrugged, shifting the Earth's crust around him, and he knew
that he had filled the planet with himself. There was a thin
whisper of atmosphere at his outer edge; he felt the tidal bulge
moving, passing....*

Pulse.

He tried to wake up.

Blink.

*The cold came as he drained the planet of energy and was
left with the light of sun and stars to feed his hunger....*

Blink.

He knew vaguely that his body was thrashing around in the
cubicle, unable to break out of deep sleep; the attack would
have to run its course. The waking state seemed an undesirable
lesser state....

*He pulsed the field of Earth with a whisper of his will,
moving the planet, wrinkling its skin—*

*—and rolled it into the sun's gravity well. Earth boiled and
vaporized on the way. He shed it completely as he was borne
into the star's center.*

He filled it, but the star's power did not drain.

He remembered existing in a ship, living only half-awake, hating the Earth. . . .

Spinningspinningspinning . . .

Stop.

The enemy Earth turningturningturning . . .

Dead stop.

Billions hurled into the sky, across continents; structures knocked flat; the atmosphere seething with storms; and the sun had received the shards. . . .

He breathed in gales of hot plasma.

The sun flickered, interrupting eons of streaming. In a moment the star would not be enough.

Angrily he drew himself into a concentrated mass, shaping it—

—into a leaping shout of energy, a spark bridging the everblack to another star, abandoning the sun of his father's enemies as it collapsed into a dark, pitiable thing glowing on the edge of red and black, dying. . . .

Sirius.

Time of passage had been zero. He would be able to reach any point in the universe instantly, without experiencing the pressure of time. He bathed in the star's energy, assimilating the rhythms of its structure. . . .

He reached out and probed its orbital material.

There was no one like him here. . . .

He passed through the floor of his dream into a deadening sleep. Far away, the quiet, rational centers of his brain were grateful that the tide of megalomania had ebbed; the swirling power fantasy was frozen for a moment.

A double-pronged, misshapen finger of lightning joined the ground to the livid green sky. The sky darkened; a giant moon cast its indifferent white light through a break in the clouds and was swiftly hidden by the woolly masses, the roiling shoulders of protean night travelers moving toward the dawn. The sun crouched below the world, a fiery demon ready to lash out with a scorching tongue, but held back by the storm. The rain started as a whisper in the silence and fell in a rush of crystalline droplets which still held starlight in their structures. The thick, rich earth, loosened by the thunder, inhaled the flood; worms came to the surface and were washed pink. . . .

The starship lay like a rotting peach on the muddy plain. Rusty water ran from the hull, flowing into a deep gully cut in the red mud. The lights were bright in the open air lock; the night sky was overcast.

Gorgias watched himself walk up the gully and into the ship. Inside, in the main muster room, his father sat in a one-foot deep reptile tank. He wore a huge horned mask and large gloves. The creatures in the tank with him were in a panic. They writhed and leaped, leechlike worms, lizards, snakes and things with a hundred legs. His father grasped a snake by its head with his huge gloved hand, held it until its fangs dripped venom, then brought it up to the back of the man next in line to the tank, and forced the creature to bite him. When it was his turn, Gorgias stepped forward. . . .

A hammer blow struck stone, waking him back into the upper space of his dream.

Sirius dimmed, faltered.

He reached out to another star. There he drew a binary companion into the larger furnace, feeding on the massed energy. The star flared, gobbling up its children.

The center, the galactic hearth, drew him now. He went whispering between the stars, strong enough now to feed on the interstellar medium, breathing the galaxy's atmosphere. He went like a beggar toward the locus of endless power, knocking over garbage cans, devouring meager scraps and the smallest sparks of life on the way.

He hurried, absorbing bright stars, making them into himself. He was rushing upward through the floors of a huge iron building, past rusty girders and rotting wood, trap doors opening before him. . . .

He grasped a hundred stars in his net, a thousand, a million, as his frontier flashed outward to the edge of the galaxy. The wheel of suns became his skin as he filled it up.

The galaxy breathed with his will.

Were there others like him?

Fears crept into him as he looked out into the intergalactic dark, to the small lights beyond, and felt the hopeless cold pressing in around him.

He tried to expand into the infinite emptiness and fell back.

He began to throb, quickening the pulses as he pulled all available material into his center, flaring the globular clusters as they spiraled inward.

Pulse, breathe, pulse, breathe . . .

The starstorm spun faster and began to move, streaming suns in its wake.

In a moment of eternity he was fleeing in a monstrous red-shifted rush toward his new prey. . . .

He thrust his fist into the sky, and his grasping fingers broke through the cardboard into a white room with white walls and perfect corners. . . .

The universe collapsed into a throbbing mass inside his head.

He opened his eyes and listened to the pulse in his head. The gray of sleep quarters was a disappointment after the colors of his dream. He closed his eyes and saw the dream-mass, the glow of a collapsed universe readying to expand; his consciousness was a thin film on the edge.

He opened his eyes; the vision was gone. In a moment he was half asleep, afloat in a darkness teeming with run-on thoughts giving birth to dreams; images turned back on themselves, furious fears forced him to remember. . . .

Ratlike creatures scurried out of the drains as the rain came down and the water started to run in the huge pipes. Mists passed across the thousand-foot towers of the ancient city; wind rushed whistling through a million breaches, whooshing and shrieking until it became a howl. The raindrops became swollen as the storm reached its full force; wind and water became hammer blows, echoing in the canyons of stone, metal and plastic. Ancient girders creaked but did not fall, as if waiting for an appointed time. The drains gushed a wet foamy mass, washing out dirt and the corpses of creatures not swift enough to have escaped.

Gorgias stood next to his father in the damp maintenance storeroom beneath the first level of the city. The planet had never recovered from the war, and the Federation had abandoned it. The forests had come back to embrace the burnt-out cities, and the moist earth was beginning to cover everything in its corrosive grip.

The derelict planet made a good temporary hiding place for the Whisper Ship. The Federation's frontier was dotted with such worlds. In the mornings he would go out from the bowels of the city to the countryside, where the tall trees were thick with vines and the grassy clearings were carpeted with yellow flowers. . . .

*One morning his father had shot three human scavengers
in the street near the old center of government. . . .*

*The flapping sound of a sharp-taloned bird came up from
somewhere behind him; claws dug into his neck and a ragged
beak drank blood from his throat, leaving him to sink into a
merciful darkness. . . .*

The black and gray enigmas of jumpspace faded, revealing
an orange-yellow star. Here, at the Galactic Rim, the suns were
sparse; only the Magellanic Clouds stood out against the intergalactic black.

The water planet sparkled as the ship entered the atmosphere. Halfway around the northern hemisphere, the vessel
found the single landmass and dropped in over the eastern
continental shelf. The rocky coast came up and fell behind;
Gorgias saw rolling green country ahead. The ship turned north,
following a course for Myraa's house.

Gorgias sat back and waited, feeling peaceful, as if the past
had suddenly died within him, taking with it the weariness that
had plagued him.

As he looked across the grassy hills, the house came into
view, a lonely structure dominating its hill, attended by six
elegant trees. The familiar circular design seemed different.
The trees, he realized, were taller and thicker, the branches
heavier with curving green needles; the red cones were now a
deeper red and the grass came up closer to the panoramic
windows.

The ship circled once; he looked for signs of danger and
for human figures. The sun flashed in the windows. The ship
circled again and set down on the bottom of the hill in back
of the house.

He came out through the side lock and climbed the hill.
The sun was over the house when he looked up, but the house
soon eclipsed it as he neared the hilltop.

He paused before the back entrance. A familiar southern
breeze cooled his face. Would Myraa greet him as before?
What had it been like for her during these last decades? Were
the other Herculeans still with her? He was a stranger who had
stolen across time, from past to future; he would be the same,
but those at home would be changed. *Home?* He struggled with
the idea. Home was any place in the galaxy where others of
his kind still lived.

He stepped forward and the automatic door slid open to let him in.

"You were talking in your sleep last night," Myraa said.

"What about?" He wondered if she had dared to listen to his thoughts.

"Something about the edge of time. . . ."

He turned over. The orange sun was a ball of hot iron rising in the east window. The sky was a deeper blue than he had ever seen here. He turned his head and looked at her. The morning light reddened her tanned skin. He looked into her eyes and smiled.

"What else did I say?"

She closed her eyes and her body shuddered for a moment. "They're coming here again," she said.

"They're not sure I'm here," he answered. "You can't frighten me into leaving. They've come before, and failed."

He turned on his side to face her, and ran his hand on her hip. Her brown hair was all over the bed, longer than it had ever been. "I have loved you, Myraa."

She was silent, looking up through the skylight.

"They want the ship," he said.

"If you perish too far away from me," she said, "I will not be able to save you. All that is you will disperse. You would risk that for the ship?" She moved away from him, like a snake rearing to strike. "Gorgias, think!"

He looked at her carefully, trying to imagine the truth of her claims—that she contained within herself many personalities, among them his grandmother, his brother and his mother, as well as alien minds once native to this world. He searched her face, trying to recover the young girl he had known long ago. He still loved her, he realized, because there were few others of his kind left to love; but he could not bring himself to accept her illusions and way of life.

Myraa continued to believe that there were two kinds of survivors from the war—those with multiple-fused personalities, like herself, and those solitaries who had failed to turn inward. His brother had made the transfer moments before his death at the hands of a hunting party. They had crushed his head with a rock and left him to rot in the tall, dew-covered grass near the house. Gorgias had never known his grandmother. She had been a medical officer on one of the larger warships. The alien, Myraa claimed, had been the last of his kind. He had brought the knowledge of symbiosis to the surviving Herculeans when they had arrived on this planet; in exchange, they would always keep him with them, Myraa said.

Gorgias lay back and closed his eyes, trying to imagine what it had been like to arrive here four hundred years ago. The war was lost as hundreds of half wrecked, poorly shielded ships burned the land with their last bursts of power, leaving a yellow desert where they now decayed. The survivors of that grim landfall had marched away to find shelter from their pursuers. Most of the Herculeans died from lingering injuries; others quarreled and fought each other; the rest were hunted down for sport by bounty hunters from various colonial worlds. These raids continued for many years after the war's end, for as long as the prey struggled and fought back, until the survivors grew tired and refused to run and hide.

In those days, Myraa claimed, she had been a rescuer, a collector of souls. She sounded very believable when describing the numbers she had saved. He imagined a vast prison within her mind, where illusory personalities cried out to each other.

There could be nothing for him in her grand delusion; even the Earthborn knew that she was harmless, and left her small group alone.

She got up and stood looking out the window, her naked body obscuring the sun. Her hair appeared lighter now, her skin smoother. She stretched and turned, bathing herself in the warming glow.

"Even if personality fusion were real," he said, "I would not want it."

She turned and looked at him. "You would have to accept of your own free will."

"But it would be a turning away from the world, from everything."

"This world that you see, with all its suns and galaxies, is only the surface of a deeper ocean. You would still be able to come to the surface, but it would not be everything."

Clouds moved into view behind her. Her face was suddenly a mask, hiding a madwoman. "I cannot always judge distance," she said, "but I can feel the hunters coming!" He saw her hesitate, as if hiding something. "You . . . could stand and fight."

She wants me to die, he thought.

"I will," he said softly, horrified by the extent of her delusion, "when I find the weapon I came for. You know where it is—tell me!" If she really wanted him to die, she would tell him with the hope that it would put him in danger. He would live on as a memory in her mind, while she imagined that she had saved him.

"We hid it in the flagship after the Earthborn stripped the fleet."

He sat up. "Where?"

"First deck, third hold."

He got up from the bed and slipped into his uniform.

"Hurry!"

Her insanity saddened him; he wanted to hold her, protect her. The impulse surprised him, making him feel weak, as if his father's failure was seeping into him, sapping his will.

He went out from the bedroom to the back door; it slid open and he stepped out. The ship lay at the bottom of the hill. As he looked at the polished hull, he felt a renewed admiration for the ancient builders. He still knew very little about how the ship worked, except that its power source was not contained inside, and that nothing he had ever encountered could cut off its flow. The ship was faster than even the newest Federation vessels, and carried enough weaponry to equip a small force; its food synthesizers could turn almost any kind of raw material into edibles. Even if it were captured, opening it would be impossible. If he died, the ship would destroy itself with enough force to vaporize a planet; he would, however, have to be close enough for the ship's intelligences to pick up any violent interruption of his personality imprint. He would never be separated from the Whisper Ship; if he died, it would die with him.

Myraa came through the door and stood next to him.

"They're very near—can't you feel them?"

He stood perfectly still, listening. There was a rushing in his head, incoherent whispers mocking him. Somewhere, he knew, the hunters were hunched over their instruments, hating him. He had a sudden vision of them standing around his body, burning it into ashes with their weapons; the wind seized the ashes and blew them away....

"You're not immortal," she said, "only long-lived. You hate them, but one day you might need their services to renew your body."

"What I need I'll take," he said, puzzled by her comment.

He looked at her for a moment, then turned away and went
down the hill to the ship.

Myraa went back inside and lay down on the bed. The ship
appeared in the skylight and disappeared. She closed her eyes
for a moment, then opened them. Turning her head, she saw
a cloud obscure the rising sun; light drained from the land as
the cloud's shadow swept toward the house. . . .

The hunters were closer.

IX. Graveyard of Titans

"Their blood runs round the roots of time like rain;
  She casts them forth and gathers them again;
  With nerve and bone she weaves and multiplies
  Exceeding pleasure out of pain."

—Swinburne, *Laus Veneris*

AS THE WHISPER SHIP flashed westward toward the mountains, Gorgias watched the screen for signs of hunters. His scanners could penetrate a planet to reveal approaching vessels in normal space, but there was no way to predict a sudden appearance from bridgespace. If Myraa was right, he might only have time to retrieve the cylinder and run; he could not be sure of returning here safely in the near future.

He pictured the pursuit. A large ship would come up behind him in jumpspace, open its field-effect basket and swallow the Whisper Ship. Of course, the hunters would need an even start to have a chance of catching him, but that could happen if they surprised him.

His facial muscles tightened; fear constricted his stomach. He stared into the screen, trying to decide whether to leave the system at once or go after the cylinder. There was no visible sign of danger yet. He was so close this time. Myraa was only trying to frighten him. Once he had the cylinder, it would not matter if he ever came back here again.

He saw the snow-covered peaks that divided the continent.

The ship went over, up into thunderheads, out into blue sky; he saw grassland again as the vessel dropped lower.

The ship sped forward, pulling the horizon into the screen. At any moment, it seemed, a sudden surge would carry him over the planet's edge.

He saw the first of the spires—tall starships still pointing starward. Chained to the planet, they seemed stolc in defeat.

The ship slowed and came in low as it crossed into the desert. Four hundred years later, the land was still dead here, a sickly yellow splashed across the green plain. Only near the edges was there any sign of typical desert life. Those last intermittent bursts of lift from the emergency landfall engines of dying warships had assured that nothing would grow here for a long time to come.

The Whisper Ship eased forward between the huge vessels, hovering only a few meters above the sand. "Discarded toys," his father would have said.

An army had died here, its will broken by the sight of enemy energies tearing at the home planet, bodies slowly sickening from a lack of provisions and medical supplies.

The great ships were slipping into the sand. Drifts had accumulated in the open locks, a dry sea lapping slowly at the sinking vessels on its surface.

The enemy had sent no help to the dying, only killers not yet full of killing. When their interest had died, the survivors had been left to perish.

Twenty square klicks of desert, wind blown into sterile dunes, exposing here and there the rocky bones of the planet. The greatest concentration of ships was toward the center, around the flagship. The illness had worked its way outward from there, until the life of the planet had stopped it.

In one of these two hundred hulks, the troop cylinder held a spark of life, of power, an army from home, waiting to be summoned.

The Whisper Ship drifted through the maze, searching for the center. Finally, he saw the two largest vessels. The ship came in between them and settled on the sand.

The sun was blindingly bright when Gorgias came out through the side lock. The air was hot in his lungs. The ships towered for two hundred meters on each side of the silvery insect on the sand. So large, he thought, yet not as powerful as the Whisper Ship.

The sand was gritty under his boots. He looked around and saw chunks of carbon and fused glass. The sand-glass was multicolored, ranging from deep green and purple to crystal-clear, imprisoning small images of Myraa's sun.

He could not see between the ships to the desert; between any two hulks he saw only another, between two others still another.

He looked up. The tops of the ships were lost in the glare of approaching noon. He began to walk, hoping that the taller of the two ships would be the flagship. His feet sank in the sand, and he had to step high to keep going. He began to sweat. The air smelled of ozone. He stopped and squinted. His boot touched a piece of fused glass. He bent down and picked it up. Blue tint, clear: trapped inside was a large, centipedelike creature with a small beetle still in its pincers. He let the long-dead scene drop from his hand and continued toward the ship.

He stopped and looked up at the brown-red spire, noting that it was almost perfectly erect. For a moment he felt that it might fly again. Its engines would roar suddenly and hurl it into the clear blue sky.

He walked up to the ladder and began to climb. It was a long way up to the first lock; the rungs were hot and the hull radiated a withering heat. Sweat ran into his eyes, and he stopped to wipe his face with his sleeve.

These ships were nothing more than giant lifeboats with a few armaments, he thought as he resumed the climb. A jump-space drive attached to a hull; no gravitics, only atomic-reaction engines for landfall. The ships had been built in desperation.

He reached the open lock and climbed inside. It was cooler in the darkness. His eyes adjusted and he peered through the open inner lock. Winding stairs led upward to what were probably troop quarters in the midsection.

He looked back to the oval of the outer lock, where light spilled in from the furnace of the desert. He turned away, went inside and climbed the stairs, his footsteps echoing, disturbing the dust.

He looked up and saw daylight. When he reached the deck, he saw the massive hole in the hull.

The large doors to the hold compartments were open. He entered the first hold. It was empty, except for torn boxes and a few old crates.

The second hold was filled with bones, human and animal.

He came out quickly and entered the third hold.

It was empty.

Gorgias paused, wondering if Myraa had lied to him. He crossed to the far wall and started a careful circuit of the hold, running his hands across the metal surface.

Suddenly his hand pushed into an open area in the wall and he slipped, hitting his forehead.

Perhaps Myraa had not lied. Someone had opened this compartment and left it open. It's not here, he thought; someone found it a long time ago, when the ships were being stripped. It would have been a meaningless object to anyone not familiar with it. A crystalline rod with a metal casing, an ornament in a small box.

He felt around inside with both hands. Maybe the scavengers had missed it. It was possible that the box had been hidden long after the vessel had been stripped. His hands felt nothing but dust and bits of debris.

Leaning forward, Gorgias strained to reach the back wall of the compartment. He stopped and pulled his hand out, realizing that he would have to crawl inside to make sure that there was nothing in the back.

He lifted himself in and crawled forward. Something scurried across his right hand. He looked down, looking for an insect of some kind. Then he felt a feeble pinprick in his left hand. The insect was biting him. There was no way to tell if the creature was poisonous. Gorgias pulled his hand back and brushed the thing away with his right hand. The insect seemed large suddenly. He heard a sound as it fled.

His thumb ached as he reached the end of the dusty chamber and felt around with both hands. He peered around in the gloom. A flat shape of some kind lay at his left. Reaching out, he grasped one corner of the box and pulled. The container seemed light as he picked it up. It might be empty.

Slowly, he backed out of the storage space, pulling the flat container after him. He felt something crawl across the backs of his legs. He kicked and scrambled over the edge, landing on his feet.

He looked at his thumb. There was a red mark on the skin, nothing more.

He reached again into the compartment and pulled out the box, holding it by the bottom with his left hand. He pulled at the top, but it would not open.

Holding the box with both hands, he went to the stairs and started down. The metal creaked. Something in the structure was loose. He hurried. The spiral groaned when he reached bottom.

He went to the open lock, climbed out on the rungs with the box in his left hand and started to descend with his free hand sliding down the righthand side of the ladder, supporting his weight.

The descent was slow and painful; the metal chafed and burned his palm. He grew dizzy from the heat. Sweat ran into his eyes, but he could not wipe it away. His uniform felt as if it were floating on a thin layer of perspiration. He jumped the last two rungs and the box fell from his hand.

He lay in the sand, watching it. A depression formed around it. The sand was running away into a space somewhere below.

Gorgias lunged for the box and seized it with both hands. Crawling back, he watched the vortex deepen and stop.

The sun's position shifted, giving him a patch of shade from one of the ships. Gorgias sat up and examined the box. It was entirely black, except for the faded orange star of the Empire in the top righthand corner; a thin white line marked the lid. He pulled at it from two sides. It came up, and he saw the cylinder.

As he looked at the bright metal casing, he realized that at last he had the means to fight the hunters directly.

He looked closer; the casing was black near the top, and the orange star was bright on it. Taking the cylinder in his hand, he examined the terminals at the bottom, where it would plug into the tripod's power feed.

He took a deep breath. The cylinder had waited, safe all these years, until the time when he would need it most. He was the Empire now, armed with its greatest weapon. All surviving Herculeans would have to recognize him as their leader. He looked up at the ships around him, dreaming of a time when better vessels than these would move to his command. He looked at the Whisper Ship, imagining a hundred like it emerging from hidden bases in the Cluster.

He felt the hot sands through his uniform, and remembered Myraa's warning about the hunters. He put the cylinder carefully into its box, closed the lid and got up. The orange sun was just past noon. He hurried back to the Whisper Ship.

X. Lesser Magellanic

"... there is one thing which is terrible, and that is that everyone has his own good reasons."

—Jean Renoir

THE SHIP CIRCLED the planet. Gorgias watched the screen, but there was still no sign of hunters.

"Back to the house," he ordered.

The Whisper Ship dropped into the planet's ocean of air.

Clouds enveloped the vessel as it neared the surface, breaking suddenly to reveal the house below. Myraa stood between the trees. Her magnified image seemed to be looking directly at him. Gorgias felt her presence near the edges of his mind, circling but not daring to probe.

The ship came in low and drifted to a landing behind the house. Gorgias came out and made his way up the hill. The door opened and he went through the hallway into the main room.

Myraa stood in the center, her unclad body aglow in the afternoon sunlight.

He came up close and looked into her eyes.

"They're much nearer," she said.

"When?" he demanded.

"I can't judge distance. Soon."

"It won't do them any good." He looked up through the skylight at the clear blue sky, then out through the west window. Wind waved the tall grass. *What is she planning?* he asked himself.

"Consider that you may be putting me in danger," she said.

"You've taken good care of yourself so far," he answered without looking at her.

There was an awkward silence.

"I found the cylinder," he said as he turned to look at her again.

Her face seemed strange. "It's only a tactical weapon," she said. "If you don't win immediately, you'll have to supply and cover your force as it retreats. Where will you retreat to? You've never commanded a force."

It might have been his father speaking.

"What can they use against me here? They have no reason to suspect..."

She looked at him with icy attention. Her gaze was impenetrable, immune to intimidation.

"Come with me," she said calmly.

She turned away from him. He looked at the curve of her back, the strong muscles in her stocky thighs.

A portion of the floor slid open in front of her, revealing a stairway.

Myraa disappeared into the hill. The lights came on below. He followed. She was already a distant figure, far below.

Gorgias reached bottom and saw a long, dimly lit hallway. Myraa was a silhouette standing in the archway at the end, waiting for him.

She slipped from sight as he started toward her.

He came out into a large circular room and looked around. Parts of the granite wall and ceiling were stained where moisture had seeped in from the hill.

There was a silver plate on the floor. The polished surface rested on a platform of concrete. Gorgias stepped forward and looked into the mirrored surface.

Myraa's image joined him as she came up behind him. He took a deep breath of the damp air and turned to face her.

"It can take you," she said, "to the Lesser Magellanic Cloud and back, but only once. They left this link on their way out. Go and see what's left of them."

The survivors! It was the only thing in his mind as he stepped onto the plate. They were a reality, not just a legend.

"Have you been there?" he asked.

"I have no need."

"Then you don't know anything! They might be alive."

"You must return quickly, before all the power is gone."

He heard her warning, but she was far away, unimportant. Who was she to give him orders? He thought of the distance that he would traverse: a quarter of a million light-years. This too was accomplished by his people. What else might there be for him to find?

Myraa backed away from him. He saw the control panel on the wall. She reached back and pressed her palm against a small green square—

—darkness pushed in around him, a solid blackness threatening to crush him—

—the silence was a long shrill note, the sound of something great dying between the stars—

—Myraa had cast him into an oblivion from which he could never return—

—the starry lens of the Milky Way was rising, cut in half by a mountainous horizon.

He stood in a rocky grotto. Below him lay a barren plain, strewn with rocks. The dry, alien night was still.

He searched the sky. The planet was probably near the edge of the cloud. He might see the Magellanic stars toward morning, if there was any rotation.

He looked down into the plate and saw his faintly lit face floating in an abyss of stars.

He stepped off the receiver, wondering how long it had taken to establish it here by travel through conventional jump-space.

He walked down the rough hillside to the plain, where he stopped and looked back. The mountain was a dark mass against the intergalactic sky, its lower regions shrouded in shadow, hiding the mirror-eye whose nerve ends reached across space to the edge of the galaxy in the sky. Where else did the link lead?

He turned away and searched the horizon. There was something directly ahead, a structure of some kind. He started walking toward it.

After a few minutes he saw that it was a ship, a huge wreck lying on its side like the carcass of some huge sea creature that had been stranded at the bottom of a dry sea.

As he came closer, the derelict seemed to rise out of the

darkness toward the bright stars of the galaxy behind it. Natural conditions had not disfigured the vessel, he realized; it had been stripped. Dozens of holes had been torn in the hull, a few so large that he could see through them and across the stony plain.

He saw the first skeletons lying near the nose of the ship, jaws open in a frozen grimace.

He circled the leviathan and came upon a bone-strewn area— thousands of skeletons reclining on the bare rock—as if one day they had all lain down to rest and rotted away. The bones were very white in the starlight, protruding through the torn elbows and knees of dusty uniforms, hands and skulls a white sprinkle on the dark rock.

All have gone but me, he thought, realizing why Myraa had sent him here. *There is no one left.*

He pictured the sick soldiers lying before him, some still alive and calling out to one another, others crawling away into the darkness to take their own lives. Falling stars had whispered across the sky while the flesh of Herculeans had rotted away and the cold wind had blown through their bones. . . .

To die so far from the suns of home. He looked up at the distant galaxy, hoping to glimpse the Cluster, even though he knew that the angle was wrong for him to see it. He wanted to rip himself open and let his anger flow out to fill the universe, but there was nothing in him now except pity. He was the last flailing arm of an empire that would not let him free. He craved rest, but it would not be his until the blood of Earthmen flowed around his feet.

An ancient will to power stirred within him again, dispelling his pity and sense of weakness. A wind came up from the mountains, but he imagined that it was blowing in from beyond, from the dark belly of space-time, where it whirled the snowflake galaxies. He stood like a rock before a tide, feeling its currents pass around him, threatening to carry him off if he weakened.

A faint dawn showed itself behind the mountains, a fire kindling below the world. He saw dark clouds breaking up before the growing heat. The wind became urgent as it whipped his face.

He turned to go, knowing that in the night the skeletons possessed a kind of dignity; the harsh morning light would make them squalid and pitiable.

He walked back toward the mountain, up the stony foothill to the grotto and the mirror. There he paused and looked back at the corpse of the behemoth that had crossed the void to die here. Its dark shape lay on the plain in the gray light of morning. He heard the wind in its wounds.

This vessel had established the receiver plate, through which the soldiers arriving on Myraa's World had escaped. They were all here; there were no others. Only the cylinder remained. It might not work, he realized, or it might be empty.

He looked up at the Lesser Magellanic Cloud as it rose before the sun, a million morning stars fading in the dawn.

He turned and stepped onto the plate—

—into the room in the hill, one island universe away.

XI. Dialogue

"Is not his incense bitterness, his meat Murder?

And our hands labor and thine hand scattereth..."

—Swinburne

MYRAA WAS NOT in the underground chamber. The air was damp in his lungs as he looked around. Something was wrong.

He jumped from the plate, ran down the dark passage and climbed the stairs into the house.

A gloomy light filled the main room. Myraa was standing by the east window. The view was gone. He looked up through the skylight. The sky was a gray bowl over the house.

"There are three ships outside," Myraa said. "They've put a restraining field around the hill. There's no way out."

He rushed to the back door. It slid open and he stepped outside. The Whisper Ship was well within the field. Myraa came up behind him.

"It's still there," he said. The light from the side lock was a bright yellow in the gloom. "We won't starve."

He felt a quickening of his whole being. The sudden stress tightened his nerves and sharpened his perceptions.

"You sent me to the Lesser Magellanic to demoralize me," he said, "but it won't work."

"They'll set up a power plant outside and leave it to sustain this prison forever," Myraa said.

Gorgias gazed at the gray wall of the field. It let in only a feeble light, just enough to dilute the murkiness.

"They'll never get the ship if they do that. They'll have to drop the field, and I'll be ready."

"But even if you win here, they'll send a larger force against you. When you release the troops from the cylinder, they cannot be stored again. How will they live?"

"Once we secure the planet, we'll have ships to escape in."

"But what if you can't?"

"I can order the Whisper Ship to destroy itself. I can take the whole planet with me."

"Give them the ship," she said.

"Never." He followed her inside and into the main room.

"You'll kill us all with you," she said.

He went to the east window and peered into the grayness. They were waiting for him on the other side. He was looking forward to facing them.

Suddenly the field winked out, flooding the house with light.

Two Earthmen were coming up the hill. Three ships sat on the grassy plain behind them, three large globes casting black shadows in the bright afternoon sunlight. The taller man on the right held his left hand up in a gesture of truce. The sight of them made him restless and uneasy.

"I'll kill them as soon as they come inside."

"No—hear what they have to say," Myraa said.

"They're coming to talk because they can't do anything else. They'll try to seem generous."

"Gorgias," she said fearfully, "their thoughts are a blank wall. I can't see!"

"I don't need your way of seeing."

"They've never tried to talk with you before."

She was right. They were showing a certain amount of respect for his power. It occurred to him that he might be able to reach the ship and take off before they got to the front door. But suddenly he was curious to hear what they had to say.

He watched as they approached the front door. Myraa spoke a word and it slid open. Gorgias motioned for them to enter.

The tallest came in first. The door slid shut when they were both inside.

The taller man seemed older. His hair was a deep black.

There was a settled expression on his face. The shorter man was stocky, with streaks of white in his bushy brown hair. His eyes were a clear blue; his expression seemed to be a mixture of amusement and arrogance.

"Gorgias—may we talk?" The tall man almost smiled, as if he were greeting an old friend.

"Go ahead, talk." Gorgias stepped back. Myraa went to one of the chairs by the east window and sat down.

"We want the ship," the shorter man said. "You can have almost any kind of terms, as long as you stop all hostile actions."

The tall man gestured for his companion to be silent.

"You don't expect me to just give it to you?"

"We can give you the chance for a better life," the tall man said.

"I warn you now," Gorgias said, "the ship can defend itself without me."

"This is a truce—what do you take us for?"

Fools.

"Julian—please be quiet."

"Extermination has been your policy," Gorgias said. He regretted not having gone to the ship for a hand weapon before the two Earthmen reached the house.

The tall man seemed unimpressed by the accusation. "You know very well that hasn't happened for centuries."

"How often does it need to happen—if it's done right?"

A sad, patient look came into the tall man's face, reminding Gorgias of his father.

"There can be no agreements between us, Earthman, ever."

The tall man seemed to consider. "We are not your enemies. My name is Kurbi. My associate is Julian Poincaré. Neither of us had anything to do with the war. We're trying to clean up after what happened. We don't have to do this; we want to. As far as the Federation is concerned, it's all ancient history."

"You expect me to take what you say seriously?"

"It may be hard, but—"

"Give me back my home world," Gorgias said. He looked directly at the Earthman.

"I would if I could."

The tall Earthman was impressive. Gorgias noticed the lack of markings on his green uniform. Who was he? The meeting was not what he had imagined it would be.

"Try to consider things, Gorgias, without the past guiding your thoughts."

"The past is reliable in my case."

"It can also destroy your future, unless you choose otherwise."

"There is no future for us," his father said within him. *"All we can hope for is a personal life in the shadow of the Federation, unless we strike out for uncharted stars. Somewhere in this galaxy, or beyond it, there may be a new home for Herculeans, if we start now."*

"The facts are undeniable," Gorgias said. "The destruction of our home worlds, the hunting of my people after the war, the looting, the enslavement...."

"We agree. This is true."

Gorgias's facial muscles tightened. The man was an expert at misdirection. His visit was part of some elaborate trickery.

Kurbi looked at the floor. "Your people were brilliant," he said slowly. "Your technology and military leadership were astonishing. It was a rich culture, dominated by an absolute pragmatism. What you could do, you always wanted to do, and did as a matter of exercise. You saw yourself as the strongest, the best social organization in the galaxy. The Federation came to believe, quite honestly, that Herculeans wanted to dominate the galaxy, at least that part of it that was the Federation. By Herculean standards, you lost. You were not the strongest."

Gorgias felt a trembling inside himself.

"Who are you, Kurbi?"

"There are a few of us who don't want what's left of your civilization to perish."

"Why should you care?"

"For the same reason that we went to war to prevent the eclipse of the Federation's various cultures."

Again it was not the expected answer. Surely this was not the hunter?

Kurbi held out his hands in a pleading gesture. "Consider this, Gorgias—that this may be your last chance, that others will come if I fail, and that they will not speak or act as I do. Think—ultimately you are also descended from Old Earth, from one of the numerous families of man originating on the continents of Earth. We need not be enemies, not now. You must not die. What is left of your people must live and grow. What you know and have lived must become known. Can you see that I feel what I say?"

"What is there for me in your world?"

"Sanity—happiness, perhaps. You've never lived with a whole culture around you. Your people could become numerous again and repopulate the Cluster. It would take time, but it's possible. We would help."

Would these fools really help their enemies? Gorgias wondered. It was only a trick.

Gorgias looked into Kurbi's eyes. "You're either lying or deluded."

"But we can and would help," Kurbi said.

The man seemed to believe what he was saying. Perhaps someone was using him as a tool. Gorgias looked at the shorter man, but his face was a mask.

Gorgias turned his head and looked at Myraa, wondering if she could sense his discovery of the Earthman's trickery; but her face was expressionless. She looked away from him and gazed out the window.

Gorgias looked back to Kurbi. "My people, you say—but where are my people? Have you seen them lately? What's left are mindless freaks. Their wills are dead." He motioned toward Myraa.

Kurbi was silent for a moment. "There are others," he said finally. "You and I could gather them, bring them here."

"And what about me?"

"In time . . . you would be permitted to live here. . . ."

"Permitted! I'm free—I will not be permitted anything. You don't offer anything better than what I have now."

"You have nothing," said the stocky man.

Kurbi motioned for him to be quiet. "Gorgias, what do you have? Endless wandering . . ."

"You'll see what I have. I don't need anything from Earthmen. Get out!"

The stocky man took Kurbi by the arm and slowly led him to the door. "I'll be all right, Julian," the tall man whispered. The door opened and the Earthmen stepped through.

Gorgias followed them outside.

"Fools!" he shouted after them as they made their way down the hill. He felt the centuries of hatred uncoiling inside him like a steel snake, cutting his innards painfully, releasing the resolve that would insure his victory.

"I will destroy all of you!" he cried, his voice echoing. He imagined the bodies lying below, the ships ruined, as he went from body to body cracking heads with his boot.

"I know your game, Kurbi! You may not know it, but I know! I'll leave you all to rot here. You think you have me trapped. When I'm finished here, I'll move on Earth itself!"

Neither man showed any sign of stopping to look back, but Kurbi seemed to stumble for a moment.

"Weaklings! That's all they send against me!" Gorgias laughed.

Kurbi stopped at the bottom of the hill and turned around. "I'll give you an hour! After that it will be out of my hands. Give yourself up, Gorgias, it's your only hope."

"Hope for what? To be tried and exhibited? Look around and breathe all you can, Earthman. Today is the last day of your life!"

Gorgias caught his breath and waited for an answer.

The two men turned away and started across the grass toward the largest ship. Their shadows grew taller at their left as they moved away from the hill. A breeze waved the tall grass.

Gorgias went inside. Myraa was still in the chair, but now her feet were pulled up, arms around her knees.

"They've sent a coward to instruct me," he said. She was silent. He hated her lack of will.

He turned away from her and rushed toward the back door. He might still be able to reach the ship and take off before they put the field back over the hill.

He was finally going to meet the Herculean face-to-face. Kurbi quickened his pace.

"Slow up," Julian said behind him. "How do you know that he'll talk to us?"

"He's seen our truce sign. We're almost three quarters there and he's made no move to stop us."

Kurbi reached the bottom of the hill and started upward.

"He's probably just curious about who'd dare to come parley with him. He's flattering himself, Raf."

"Maybe—but I've got to see for myself."

They finished the climb in silence, reaching the front door together.

The door slid open. A dark shape motioned for Kurbi to

enter. Kurbi stepped inside and waited until Julian was at his side.

"Gorgias?" Kurbi asked. "May we talk?" The Herculean was powerfully built, but shorter than Kurbi had imagined him.

"Go ahead—talk." Gorgias stepped back and regarded them. The woman went to one of the chairs and sat down. Kurbi was about to apologize for the intrusion, but stopped himself.

"We want the ship," Julian said suddenly, "and for that you can have almost any terms."

Kurbi swallowed nervously. The fool. He had promised not to interfere. Kurbi motioned for him to shut up.

"You don't expect me to just give it to you."

"We can offer you the chance for a better life," Kurbi said, trying to soften the arrogance of Julian's statement.

"I warn you, the ship can defend itself without me."

Kurbi's stomach tightened. The tone of the meeting was set now; nothing was likely to change it.

"This is a truce," Julian said, "what do you take us for?"

Kurbi looked into Gorgias's eyes. The Herculean seemed to be laughing at him.

"Julian—please be quiet."

Gorgias smiled as Poincaré took a step back.

"Extermination is the policy," Gorgias said. His gaze did not waver.

"You know very well that hasn't happened for centuries," Kurbi said, feeling inadequate.

"How often does it need to happen—if it's done right?"

It's going to be impossible, Kurbi thought. Gorgias was looking at him strangely.

"There can be no agreements between us, Earthman, ever."

"We are not your enemies," Kurbi said. The words came out of his mouth without conviction. He continued speaking, but all the things he had dreamed that he would say to the Herculean seemed absurd now.

"You expect me to take what you say seriously?"

No. "It may be hard," Kurbi added to his silent assent, "but—"

"Give me back my home world," Gorgias said, looking directly at him. Suddenly the will behind his eyes seemed unbreakable. *How could I have ever thought of changing him?* Kurbi wondered.

"I would if I could," Kurbi answered.

Again the Herculean's eyes searched him strangely. *What is he looking for?*

"Try to consider things, Gorgias, without the past guiding your thoughts."

"The past is reliable in my case."

"It can also destroy your future," Kurbi said, "unless you choose otherwise." *He wants to destroy our future, and he doesn't care how he has to live to do it.*

"The facts are undeniable," the Herculean was saying. "The destruction of our home worlds, the hunting of my people after the war, the looting, the enslavement...."

"We agree. This is true," Kurbi said.

Gorgias was silent. Kurbi looked at the floor. "Your people were brilliant...." He could feel the anger rising in himself as he spoke, and he knew that this was how the destroyers of the Cluster had felt—that nothing was possible with the Herculeans except to destroy them completely.

"Who are you, Kurbi?" Gorgias demanded.

"There are a few of us who don't want what's left of your civilization to perish." The words rang falsely in his ears. How could he expect to convince Gorgias?

"Why should you care?"

"For the same reason that..." Kurbi spoke the words mechanically, feeling nothing. *I've got to make a better effort. I've got to get through.* He held out his hands. "Consider this, Gorgias—that this may be your last chance, that others will come if I fail...." *I'm failing, I'm failing.* "Can you see that I feel what I say?" *How can you? I have nothing to say.*

"What is there for me in your world?"

"Sanity—happiness, perhaps." *Sure.* "You've never lived with a whole culture around you." *That's better.* "Your people could become numerous again and repopulate the Cluster. It would take time, but it's possible. We would help." *I would help.*

Gorgias looked directly at Kurbi, "You're either lying or deluded."

"But we can and would help," Kurbi said. *I'm whining.*

Gorgias looked toward the woman before answering again.

"My people, you say—but where are my people? Have you seen them lately? What's left are mindless freaks. Their wills are dead." He motioned toward Myraa.

"There are others. You and I could gather them, bring them here."

"And what about me?"

Kurbi knew. He had always known. If Gorgias were captured, he would be tried, perhaps mindwiped, even killed; at the very least he would be imprisoned. The Earthborn immortals had a long memory, and many of them would delight in tormenting the Herculean. It was a problem without solution. Too much pride and history were involved, too much hatred; no one would accept compromises.

"In time . . . you would be permitted to live here. . . ." *Without ships or weapons. The planet would be your prison. And without medical care, your immortality would one day end. You would live with the knowledge of approaching death.*

"Permitted! I'm free—I will not be permitted anything. You don't offer anything better than what I have now."

"You have nothing," said the stocky man.

Kurbi turned and glared at Julian.

"Gorgias, what do you have?" he asked looking back to the Herculean. "Endless wandering . . ."

"You'll see what I have. I don't need anything from Earthmen. Get out!"

Julian took Kurbi's arm and guided him toward the door.

"I'm all right," Kurbi whispered. The door opened and they stepped outside.

They started down the hill.

"Fool!" Gorgias shouted behind them. The word echoed in Kurbi's ears.

"I will destroy all of you!" Gorgias cried. "I know your game, Kurbi. You may not know it, but I know!"

Kurbi stumbled and regained his footing.

"Weaklings! That's all they send against me." The Herculean laughed.

Kurbi turned at the bottom of the hill and looked up. "I'll give you an hour, Gorgias," he shouted. "After that it will be out of my hands. Give yourself up, Gorgias, it's your only hope." *I'm useless, and the hope I offer is none at all.*

"Look around and breathe all you can, Earthman. Today is the last day of your life!"

"Let's go," Julian said.

Kurbi turned away and they started back toward the large ship. "Julian," Kurbi said suddenly, "—the ship, he'll make for the ship while the field is down!"

"Don't worry. We've got scouts watching the house. If he comes out the back, up it goes. Are you all right, Raf?"

"Yes."

"We're not amateurs, and neither is he."

"I think in some ways he is," Kurbi said, "to fight such a hopeless fight."

"All the evidence he's ever had tells him that he's done well."

He's right, Kurbi thought. *If I were he, I wouldn't believe anything an Earthman told me.*

XII. Armed

"She holds her future close, her lips
Hold fast the face of things to be..."

—Swinburne, *Cleopatra*

GORGIAS RAN DOWN the hill.

The siege canopy reappeared. He stopped in the sudden, gloomy silence. His eyes adjusted and he saw that the ship was still within the circle.

He rushed toward the light of the open lock, afraid that at any moment the field's diameter would be reduced to cut him off from the ship.

He jumped into the lock and marched forward into the control room. He sat down before the screen and examined the images of the three hunter ships sitting on the grass outside. The visualizations were ghostly, but they came in despite the barrier. He wondered if the canopy's strength could be increased to blind his subspace instruments.

THERE IS A FOURTH SHIP IN LOW ORBIT.

"Are our instruments being jammed?"

YES. THE FOURTH SHIP IS INTERFERING WITH OUR NEUTRINO AND TACHYON SENSING, WITH SOME SUCCESS.

The hunters would have to lift the field and attack with a ground force to have any chance of taking him alive. He was certain that they could not have more than a hundred soldiers in the ships. After he had destroyed these three vessels, the ship in orbit would have to come down and face him or flee. That would give them something to worry about on Earth.

"Can we enter jumpspace through this field?"

THERE IS A SMALL CHANCE OF SUCCESS. NOT ADVISABLE.

It didn't matter; he would face the Earthborn at last. He thought of the dead in the Magellanic Cloud, and the cinder of the home world. All the ashes were his now, to remold as he saw fit. Even the most withdrawn Herculean survivors would recognize him after the coming victory. They would come here from all over the galaxy, from every hiding place in the Federation Snake, and he would welcome them. Myraa's World would become the staging area for the return to the Hercules Cluster. He thought of the armies that would soon be his, the fleets of ships, unimaginable weapons developed toward the end of the war. The psychological blow of the surprise itself would be enough to cripple the enemy.

Myraa would throw off the otherness which now possessed her, and take her rightful place beside him.

Kurbi had given him an hour, and that hour would be fatal to him.

Gorgias got up and went aft to the weapons closet. He wondered if Kurbi would lead the attack; of course, they would not have a chance to attack, because he would not allow things to reach that point. The Earthborn would not have a moment in which to seize the initiative.

The lights went on as he entered the weapons chamber. He looked around at the Empire's ancient arms; all were personal weapons in the light-to-heavy range. They covered the walls like ornaments.

In the center of the small floor space stood the tripod; it was complete now, with the black box containing the cylinder strapped to the control panel. Gorgias examined the assembly, trying to imagine the reality of its capabilities. Myraa was wrong. The storage of an army would include supplies, a fleet of starships, scouts—everything needed to support a large military effort.

Suddenly he was afraid. What if it didn't work after all this time? What would he do then? He would have to risk entering jumpspace through the barrier. Perhaps he should have tested the cylinder somewhere, deploying the troops in advance; but then, he realized, he would not have the element of surprise.

He would have to run if the cylinder failed. Sooner or later they would lift the canopy and he would have a chance to escape without the risk of trying to penetrate the field. Suddenly the thought of running again seemed worse than death.

"You'll die here," his father said within him. *"What do you know about commanding a large force?"*

He took a body harness from the rack and strapped it on. Next he took down a hand projector, set it for wide beam and slid it into the sheath on his chest. He strung four light-diffraction bombs around his waist, and put a pair of binocular goggles on his forehead. The controls for the personal screen went on last—a small flat rectangle which attached to the adhesion surface over his heart and was linked to the power-receiving pack on his back. The entire rig tapped into his shipboard power, giving him unlimited energy for his weapon and a high-density local screen capable of deflecting most laser weapons. The screen would not hold back the concentrated fire of ground installations, but no one would bring such power to bear on a single individual. In any case, he would not be fighting with his army; the screen and hand weapon were merely a precaution, so that he would not be vulnerable when he activated the tripod.

"You're dressing for show," his father said from deep within him.

I will command, he answered silently as he picked up the tripod, folded its legs and carried it out into the passage. The door of the weapons hold closed behind him and he continued toward the control room. He entered and saw that the screen still showed the smudged, colorless images of the hunter ships. The distortions made it seem as if a monstrous wind were raging in the pale world outside; in a moment the starships would roll toward the hill and smash against the bowl of the canopy.

Gorgias turned from the screen and carried the tripod out to the side lock. He stepped down to the ground and looked up at the house. It was brightly lit now. The canopy seemed darker with the coming of twilight outside.

He climbed the hill carefully, wondering again if the cylinder would work. He saw broken skeletons tumbling out—skulls, thigh bones and shattered pelvises emerging from a cornucopia of death. Kurbi was laughing at him, but there was regret in the tall Earthman's eyes.

He pities me, Gorgias realized as he entered the house.

Myraa was still sitting in the main room. Gorgias snapped open the tripod and set it down in the middle of the floor.

"They won't expect to be hit when they lift the canopy," he said. "They think I'm going to make a run for it in the ship. They're ready for a chase, not a fight."

Myraa was silent, staring into the obscurity of the east window. She seemed to be talking to someone or something.

He picked up the tripod. Its legs closed and he carried it out the front door. There was no use in talking to Myrra; only results would move her. He looked around as the door slid shut behind him. It seemed to be growing even darker under the canopy.

He went to the slope of the hill and opened the tripod. Setting it down, he opened the black box and removed the cylinder. Carefully, he plugged it into the round opening below the power switch. He touched the switch point and the panel lit up. The assembly was drawing power from the ship.

Gorgias stepped back and took a deep breath.

He started to pace back and forth on the grass, waiting for the canopy to lift. The grass looked black in the gloom. He looked up. The force field seemed to be pressing in around the hill, growing smaller. He stopped suddenly and peered at the perimeter at the bottom of the hill, wondering if they could reduce the size of the canopy to crush the hill and house.

He was about to go back through the house to check the ship's position when the barrier blinked out of existence. The plain below was suddenly a deep blue-green. The three starships were the heads of giants buried in the ground; their floodlights were eyes watching him.

He stepped to the tripod and touched the distance settings, so that the beam would strike beyond the ships, where the grassland rose again into gently sloping hills. His army would be recalled to life on high ground, and would sweep from there toward him and the hill.

He turned on his screen, cutting off the sound of wind and insects. The moment when the enemy might still have destroyed him and the cylinder was past, and they would never know it.

Kurbi peered at the house on the screen.

"What's he doing up there?" Poincaré said.

"What can he do?" Kurbi touched the controls and the magnification increased until the figure of Gorgias filled the screen.

"What is that thing next to him?" Poincaré asked. "And look at that harness he's wearing."

"I don't know."

"Look there." Julian pointed. "The grass around him is flattened—he's wearing a personal screen!"

"We've got to get him away from the hill," Kurbi said.

"He's drawing power from the ship."

"Look!" Kurbi shouted as a bright yellow beam reached out from the tripod and passed overhead. The screen was blind for a moment. The beam moved from right to left across the sky and disappeared.

"Commander Kurbi," a voice said over the three-ship link, "there is movement on the slopes in back of us."

"Give us a view."

The screen switched from Gorgias to darkness.

The floodlights rushed across the grass and up the slopes, searching, pushing back the darkness.

Kurbi saw the front ranks of an army—row after row of troops waiting in attack formation, as if they were toys newly taken from a box.

"No wonder he was so cocky," Julian said.

Kurbi's heart raced. He staggered over to his command station and sat down. There was a rushing in his ears, a monstrous whispering which threatened to turn into laughter.

"Where, Julian?"

"I don't know—but if we can't hold them, we'll have to flee, and then we'll never find out. I wonder how well equipped they are."

"Does he have any ships?" *Whisper Ships*, Kurbi thought, *a whole fleet. He'll destroy us completely.*

Gorgias touched the switch point and released the carrier beam. His screen went down as the yellow finger reached out, touched the faraway hills and swept from left to right. He dropped his binoculars over his eyes and watched as the wide beam painted the dark hills. Human figures flickered into existence as energy flowed across the bridge of light, instilling life into the bloodless templates of the ancient Herculean army.

Suddenly it was over; the force stood ready. The beam winked out and darkness hid the division.

The starships turned their lights toward the hills and discovered the force, ten thousand strong, armed with everything from hand weapons to heavy artillery, waiting for his command.

"Report!" Gorgias shouted into the communicator on the tripod.

There was a sputtering of static.

". . General Petro Crusus here . . . where are we . . . what are the objectives?"

"Stand by," Gorgias said.

"How goes the war, Commander? I did not receive your name."

"The war is ours to win. Take the ships in front of you."

"I see them, Commander, but what is to prevent them from lifting? Are they disabled?"

"Move on the ships!" Gorgias shouted.

"Are they Federation ships?"

"Open fire with heavy weapons. If the ships lift, track and destroy."

"Very well."

Gorgias felt a pang of sympathy for the general. Suddenly the man was active again. The Empire was still a reality for him, a night's sleep away; he had never known defeat.

The lines began to roll forward. Each figure wore a suit of black armor, a pulse-weapon backpack, a clear polarizing helmet, and a gravitational jump unit.

The front line surged forward in jumps of a hundred meters.

Gorgias searched the hills beyond for sign of his support ships, but the darkness was impenetrable.

He dropped his gaze to the starships and watched as three heavy cannon emerged from the north pole of each globe.

Behind the first line of soldiers, the second wave started down the slope.

"General Crusus—bring up your ships!"

"Ships? Stored forces have no ships, only heavy lasers. . . ."

"What?"

"I don't think we'll need more if the ships are disabled."

"Open fire!" Gorgias shouted, shaken. He peered into the darkness behind his force, trying to see the heavy units.

Six beams lashed out at the Federation ships from the blackness of the high ground, six spears suddenly pinning the enemy ships to the ground.

The third and fourth assault lines were coming down the

slope. The first wave was leaping across level grassland. Half the division was in motion now, and still Kurbi's ships had not opened fire. All the locks were still open and unprotected. What was he waiting for?

The six lasers poured energy into the Federation hulls, one beam for each hull and one for each cannon. The hulls would be breached at any moment. Gorgias felt a moment of shame inside his screen; he was safe, protected from even the sound of the coming battle.

Kurbi's lasers came to life, sweeping across the advancing army toward the Herculean heavy lasers.

The cannon on the middle starship exploded into a cluster of fireflies, and faded. The two remaining cannon were pumping energy into the hills, but there were at least six Herculean lasers on the high ground, too many for Kurbi to cover; he would not be able to destroy all of them.

The grass was on fire around the wounded ship. Black smoke rose into the night.

"Commander, can they send troops out against us?"

"I don't think so," Gorgias said. "Not enough to put against your force."

The field is mine, he thought, *the first victory on the road to rebirth.*

He turned around inside the screen and saw Myraa watching him through the window. She pointed and he turned around to see the middle ship rise above the battlefield.

"General Crusus—keep moving up. Keep hitting those hulls until they give way. Take no prisoners."

"You did not tell me that they could lift. You weren't clear . . ."

"It doesn't matter—concentrate your beams and track. We have enough power to vaporize these vessels."

"How many ships are feeding power into our weapons?" Crusus asked.

"One Whisper Ship. It's more than enough." *It draws strength from the suns of home.*

"Whisper Ship . . . you have a Whisper Ship?" The General sounded relieved. "Still, the hand weapons will have to be recharged. We'll have to retreat if we can't take the ships. . . ."

"Obey my orders! Move forward with your entire force now!"

The front lines swarmed around the globes. The locks closed. The beams locked on the hulls and held. The damaged warship hovered over its two companions. The remaining assault waves reached positions behind the vanguard and waited helplessly for the hulls to be breached.

What was Kurbi doing? His hulls could not last much longer. It was not likely that he was trying to save lives. It had to be some kind of mistake, perhaps a disagreement in the command structure. In a few minutes Kurbi would have to surrender or be destroyed.

I have commanded well.

"Be prepared if they lift," Gorgias said.

The third ship hovered.

Afterward he would kill all the Earthborn to bolster the morale of his army. They would need it after learning about the war's outcome.

My army, he thought. The words conjured up a future of fellowship. Myraa's World was secured. It was a start, a small payment toward what was rightfully his.

The Empire would live again.

The beams were not concentrating on the hovering ship. Slowly, he knew, the hulls were weakening, but the floodlights continued to bathe the field without a flicker.

He blinked—

—and found himself staring into the gray of the siege canopy.

XIII. The Field of Death

"She sees the hand of death made bare,
 The ravelled riddle of the skies,
 The faces faded that were fair,
 The mouths made speechless that were wise,
 The hollow eyes and dusty hair..."

—Swinburne, *Cleopatra*

FRESH AIR RUSHED IN around him as Gorgias turned off his screen. He took a deep breath.

"General Crusus!" he shouted into the communicator. "Report what is happening—I'm cut off from you visually."

A thunder sound erupted from the communicator.

"You didn't tell me they had another ship," Crusus said. "It's just appeared and is moving for a central position over the field...."

"Concentrate all your fire on it!"

"It's a heavy vessel—twice the size of those on the ground. Just a moment. Our beams are licking at it now," Crusus said.

Suddenly Gorgias realized that Kurbi didn't want him to see the Federation defeat.

"The big ship is holding its position," Crusus said. "I've never seen a vessel like it. How long have we been stored?"

Gorgias did not answer.

"When will you put the Whisper Ship into the air?" Crusus asked. "We may need its support."

"Later," Gorgias answered.

"The ship is firing at our lasers...I've never seen such massive beams! They've got two for each of our positions...." Crusus's voice died away suddenly.

"General—what's happening?"

"Our beams are weakening. They're running out of power. We've been cut off from our transmission source.... There, our lasers are dead, vaporized without their screens. Our force is without cover now. The only power we've left is what the soldiers have in their pulse packs."

"Fire up at the big ship!"

"With what, Commander?"

"You have ten thousand hand weapons."

"You must be mad."

The siege canopy winked off. Gorgias saw the distant fires where his ground lasers had stood. Below him, the army was firing up at the big ship, with no visible effect. One by one the small beams began to go out as their packs ran out of energy.

"We have nowhere to fall back to," Crusus said.

Gorgias wished that he could reach out with his will and crush the big ship.

The last of the individual lasers died. The army began to retreat, a huge black spider with a million legs.

"Materialize more artillery," Crusus said calmly.

"What do you mean?"

"There should be more. How many times did the cylinder cycle?"

Gorgias caught his breath suddenly. "Why—once!"

"Cycle it again. There must be more equipment. I did not have time to take inventory.... How long has it been?"

Gorgias touched the control and the yellow beam reached out again to the high ground. He dropped his binoculars over his eyes and saw three more heavy lasers, complete with crews, appear on the slopes, spaced widely as the beam swept from left to right.

The beams opened up on the big ship. The air crackled with energy. The big ship responded. Gorgias watched its lances bite into the screens of the laser cannon, but the Herculean installations continued to hurl energy without pause. There might be enough time to destroy the large globe.

The canopy went up again.

"We're without power again!" Crusus shouted, his voice full of dismay. "They're gone," he said, "our remaining lasers are gone. Isn't anyone protecting our sources?"

The canopy disappeared.

The big ship was sweeping across the troops with a wide beam, felling them as if with a huge scythe.

Gorgias pressed the controls on the tripod. The carrier beam stabbed into the dark hills and made its sweep, but the distant region of smoke and scorched ground remained without new equipment as the beam died.

The wide beam from the big ship coursed into the center of the massed men where the soldiers were pressed together, unable to move.

"There's nothing we can do!" Crusus shouted. "Where is your ship? Surely we are part of some larger operation. . . ."

Gorgias searched the high ground. Somewhere among the glowing remains of the heavy lasers, Crusus was still alive.

Again and again the deadly beam cut through the troops below, leaving clumps of ash and metal as the Herculean body armor failed. Gorgias realized suddenly that the burning would not stop until the last Herculean was dead. He *felt* the hatred that ruled the laser. Every few seconds the communicator picked up a cry of agony over the sizzling sound of the beam. The odor of ionization and burnt flesh reached him. He turned on his screen and sat down on the grass, grateful for the sudden silence. It would be useless to try to reach the Whisper Ship; as soon as he moved, the canopy would go up.

The large beam went out, its job unfinished.

"I'm sorry, Gorgias," Kurbi said from the link. "I couldn't find your subspace channel. "It was a fire-at-will order and the officer in charge . . . At least we've stopped it. Those responsible will be punished. There was nothing I could do. Gorgias?"

"You're a weakling and a coward, Kurbi. Earth sent you to preach to me, to distract me." He broke the link, feeling his face become a drawn mask as he wrapped himself in his fears.

"He won't answer," Kurbi said as he looked at the screen. Gorgias sat on the hill, staring at him. The illumination played strangely through the Herculean's screen.

"I'm going to court-martial that entire ship." He turned his chair around to face Poincaré. "You brought that ship," he said to the standing man. "You insisted on bringing it. My men were briefed in restraint. Who are they on that ship—a special death squad?"

Julian shook his head. "It won't get you anything, Raf, believe me. You'd have to work up public and judicial sympathy for a fully armed Herculean division."

"I doubt they knew what Gorgias was getting them into."

"That's incredible and you know it. How could they not have known?"

Kurbi stood up. "You don't care either."

"No one will care—they'll cheer."

"There's something not quite right about this."

"I do care, Raf. But what you and I think won't matter. It's gone too far."

Kurbi turned back to the screen and stared at the smoking battlefield. The third ship had landed again. All the locks were open and men were coming out to take prisoners and care for the wounded. The big ship was not in sight.

"What mercy do you think he would have shown us?" Poincaré asked.

"You and I know that he could not have won," Kurbi said through clenched teeth. *He would have shown no mercy,* a small voice whispered inside him.

"Hindsight—aren't you surprised by what he sent against us? If I had not brought the big ship—"

"Their weapons seemed archaic. . . ." Kurbi faced Poincaré again. "I'm still in command. I want to see the commander of that ship."

Julian was silent for a moment. "As you wish, but it won't do any good now."

I've been duped, Kurbi thought, *Gorgias was right.*

The view showed the hill again. Gorgias still sat inside his bubble. Poincaré came up and touched the controls. The hill disappeared under the inverted bowl of the siege canopy.

"Just so we don't have to chase him and his ship all over the galaxy," he said.

"It might be better to surrender now," Kurbi said into the subspace link.

"You still haven't got me," the Herculean replied quietly.

And for a moment Kurbi hoped that they would never get him.

Captain Orin Kik of the *Homestar* came into the control room and stood at attention.

Kurbi rose and stepped closer, noticing that they were of equal height.

"Why the massacre?"

"That was not my impression, sir."

Kurbi swallowed and looked at the floor. Then he looked directly at the young officer and said: "You disobeyed the order to cease fire!"

"We received no such order. The officers on my bridge will confirm this—six of them, sir."

"It was clearly given!"

"The fire-at-will was the last order we received, sir."

"Were you in control of your men?"

"Yes, I was, sir."

"Surely you could see that the Herculeans couldn't win against you, that it was senseless to keep firing after their heavy artillery was gone. You could have stood off and done nothing."

"It was a large force—no telling what they could throw against us. It was reasonable to suppose that such a force was well supported."

Failure of communications, Kurbi thought. It would be put down as such, no matter what the truth. No one had told the captain that Gorgias's division was not backed up adequately. It would have been unreasonable for him to have assumed such a thing.

"Do you have any idea, Captain Kik, who they were?"

"Herculean brigands, sir. Everyone knew that before we came out here. They deserved what they got."

"They were Herculean infantry! Soldiers like yourself."

"How is that possible, sir?"

"Captain, you are under arrest."

The youthful, thin-lipped face showed no surprise. "I did not receive any order to cease fire," it recited. "I continued as seemed necessary under the previous fire-at-will command, in anticipation of a sudden escalation in the enemy's operation. The special circumstances which you allude to were not made clear to me or to any of my officers."

I should not have agreed to let Julian bring the ship.

"It is your business to hear orders."

"I heard all orders."

There was no point in continuing the conversation.

"Under arrest, dismissed."

When the captain had gone, Kurbi sat down. Poincaré came in and Kurbi swiveled the chair around. "I know it's only a token arrest, Julian, but damn it—why did you bring that ship!"

Poincaré was silent.

"Well, Julian?"

"Just think if we hadn't been able to knock out their big artillery. They might have destroyed one or more of our ships, you know. We didn't have the troops needed to fight a whole division."

Kurbi looked into Julian's face. The stocky man was right, of course, up to a point. Kurbi felt a small measure of relief. A part of him was searching for a way out of blaming himself, he knew, and Poincaré's argument seemed convincing.

Gorgias turned off his screen and listened to the silence inside the dome of force. He stood up, lifted the now useless tripod and hurled it down the hill. The projector assembly tumbled, gouging clumps of grass and dirt out of the hill, coming to rest finally near the gray wall of the canopy. Gorgias turned and walked back into the house.

Myraa stood in the middle of the room.

"Ten thousand lives," she said.

"Without me," he said, "they would not have lived again, ever."

"They had no chance," she said. "I can hear them dying out there in the darkness, as once I listened to them perish in the Magellanic Cloud."

"Save them, then," he said. "You want us all to die anyway. They died in battle." He turned away from her. "If only I could have gotten the ship out to support them!" His voice echoed in the room.

"There is no war," Myraa said, "no home worlds to defend, no Empire. You might have let them live, to prepare."

"*I* am the Empire!" he shouted and whirled around to look at her. She came toward him, her eyes soft and caring, and it seemed suddenly that she could restore everything that he had lost.

"We'll have to lift the canopy and draw him out," Poincaré said, "before he gets any more bright ideas."

"He can't overrun us now," Kurbi said. "It's surrender or a fight."

"We'll send twenty men," Poincaré said.

"I still don't want to kill him. We haven't had any fatalities yet."

"He'd laugh in your face if he could hear you, Raf. Look how many of his own he's led to death today. How did he hide them on this world?"

Kurbi looked up at the screen. The force field seemed almost metallic in the glare of lights. He had the illusion of being in a large interior space, a titanic auditorium under a black ceiling.

"He still thinks that he can hurt us," Poincaré said. "He won't come out when we lift the canopy. We may have to go in and get him. Maybe we can taunt him?"

"We'll both lead the soldiers," Kurbi said. "I don't want the woman hurt. Maybe we can trap him."

"Calm down."

"I'll shoot the first man who disobeys an order! Tell them, Julian, tell them all very clearly."

"You tell them. You're still in command."

Kurbi remembered his visit to the large ship, where he had found Captain Kik still at liberty. The confrontation had shaken Kurbi. The memory of his own futile anger underscored his obvious loss of authority. The officers pitied him, he knew.

"You don't think we can take him alive, do you, Julian?"

"Does it matter? It will happen as it will. I know your feelings, Raf, but we both of us have lives to live, other things to return to." Poincaré stood up from the adjoining station. "We'll do it your way as much as possible. Now let's get going. I can almost hear him scheming up there."

"I'm sorry, Julian," Kurbi said, but the sense of hopelessness persisted. He spoke the words and tried to brighten his expression; a smile would have been unimaginable.

XIV.   Personal Battle

"We run carelessly to the precipice, after we have put something before us to prevent us seeing it."

—Pascal, *Pensées*

"If you do not expect it, you will not find the unexpected, for it is hard to find and difficult."

—Heraclitus

HE CAME INTO HER BODY seeking peace. He was strong, but a few times he trembled and was forced to stop. She kissed him and tightened her arms around his chest, and they floated in a timeless sea.

She opened her mind and felt her ache for him. It was also his own and he rushed to seize it. He knew that she had entered his mind to give him this double awareness, but it was unimportant beside the gift.

He melted into her, his self-consciousness dwindling.

He was afraid suddenly that he would dissolve and be absorbed into her. His nervous system was made of glass; in a moment it would shatter into a fine dust and be blown away by the wind....

He rushed upward, broke through and her pleasure was his own.

* * *

Myraa drew the dead into herself, pulling, coaxing, pleading for them to come before the darkness claimed them. They flowed in a stream from the battlefield, finding rest in the force-center of her will. . . .

The stars shone through the skylight. Gorgias lay on his back next to Myraa, her long hair covering his belly, his rage spent.

"Gorgias—the canopy is down!"

He rolled off the bed and clutched at his uniform on the floor. He stood up and stepped into it, put on his harness, checked the hand weapon and put it back into its sheath. He rushed out to the east window. The large warship now sat a thousand meters behind the three smaller craft, its lights sweeping the smoking, body-strewn ground with a nervous rhythm, as if fearful that at any moment the slain might rise to fight again.

There was no sign of survivors. *They killed them all,* he thought, and the anger rose inside him again, renewed and strong, preparing him.

Twenty armed soldiers marched down the ramp from the large ship and fanned out into a slowly advancing half-moon. They looked stocky and machinelike with their huge clear-helmets, backpacks and laser rifles held across their chests. He could not see if Kurbi was leading them.

Gorgias wondered if Crusus had survived. It would be better to kill him than to give him the news that the war was long over.

The small force was halfway to the hill now. Gorgias imagined meeting Crusus, and having to explain to the General. The thought angered him; it was the kind of thing that Myraa would place in his mind.

He turned away and ran to the back door. It opened and he scrambled down the hill toward the ship. He leaped into the open lock and rushed forward into the control room.

The screen showed that the canopy was up again. He cursed as he sat down.

"Into jumpspace!" he ordered.

NOT ADVISABLE UNDER THESE CONDITIONS.

"Do it! Get us out of here!"

As he wondered if the ship would obey him, the world outside blurred.

He was falling. The hull became transparent and he saw bright stars rushing toward him from every direction. He heard a scream. In a moment the hot stars would crush him.

Blazing suns passed through the ship, blinding him.

A rotting smell reached him.

His sight returned. He turned around suddenly and saw a decomposed body on the floor. He got up and crept toward it.

He saw himself.

As he watched, the corpse faded away. He staggered back into his command chair.

He looked around. The ship was locked in a solid gray substance.

"Back!" he ordered.

The hill reappeared.

He left the ship and clambered up the hill to the back door. He ran through the rooms and stepped out in front of the house.

The soldiers were almost halfway up the hill. He turned on his screen, drew his weapon and started down to meet them.

His anger began to throb with his pulse. He could not let them reach the house. His pace quickened.

The canopy went up behind them. They were trying to trap him inside. He aimed carefully and fired at the center of the advancing line. A screen flared harmlessly.

The sight of their confident march up the hillside infuriated him. He fired a bolt into the slope in front of them, exploding grass and dirt. The line stopped and regarded him.

He could retreat to the ship; nothing would ever be able to pry him out.

His screen flared as four beams converged.

He did not return fire; they were waiting for the instant when his screen was down.

The line started upward again. He retreated a few steps and halted. The line kept coming.

He fired and went forward. Three lasers converged on his screen and he felt the air grow warmer on his face. He pressed his energy feed to the highest setting, waited and fired.

A soldier toppled and rolled down the hill. Gorgias swept the line from right to left, channeling all his power to heat the confined spaces within the enemy's screens.

They moved toward him as his fire cut off, concentrating

their beams. He stood his ground, joined to them by nineteen arteries of fire. His screen flared and held. He waited, raging inwardly.

Their beams winked out and he fired. Another soldier fell and rolled down the hill, disappearing into the darkness beyond the reach of the house lights.

The line retreated to the bottom of the hill. Their lances blinked, as if their packs would soon be exhausted. Gorgias moved forward.

The line moved back toward the canopy.

They're stupid, he thought. *At this rate I'll pick them off one by one.*

"Gorgias!" a voice shouted through his communicator. "This is General Crusus."

"Are you a prisoner?" Gorgias asked.

"You might have let us live, given us a chance to go home and rebuild."

"Nothing is left . . ." Gorgias started to say.

"You're incompetent! Who are you, anyway?"

"You don't understand, General. . . ."

"So much time has gone by. You didn't help me understand . . . an unsupported division against ships that could have destroyed three times our number."

"They're making you say these things to distract me. I'm fighting alone!"

"Have they lied?"

The canopy disappeared and the soldiers retreated.

Lasers touched his screen and died. Gorgias moved down the hill. Maybe he could kill a few more before they reached the ships.

Retreat to the ship, he told himself. *Your screens will not hold against a ship's artillery.*

"*Coward,*" his father whispered, "*you've lost and don't know how to die.*"

The grass was black in the harsh lights. He reached level ground and fired a burst into the ground before the retreating soldiers. They stopped and stood their ground, waiting.

"Gorgias . . ." Crusus said.

"General—shut up! They're using you."

Gorgias moved forward, angry that the line had stopped its retreat.

A bolt reached out from the right end of the line. Gorgias

turned and saw a tree in front of the house catch fire. He turned back as his screen flared. They were telling him that they could destroy the house.

Gorgias hurled two bolts at the center figures, with no effect. His screen flared, but he held back, waiting for the right moment.

He touched the control over his heart. A small window opened in the screen. He hurled three light-scatter bombs and closed the opening. His screen flared on two sides as the bombs rolled on the grass and exploded. Black smoke veiled the half-moon of soldiers.

Slowly, ghostly doubles of himself appeared, twenty twins who would mirror his every move. Gorgias marched through the smoke, waiting for his doubles to draw fire.

Lasers reached out to his doubles. Gorgias swept the field from left to right, hoping to find a screen down long enough to permit a kill.

There was a sharp flash at his right. A soldier fell forward through the roiling smoke. Gorgias paused and waited for the beams to sweep across his illusory line.

The beams cut through the smoke from right to left. His screen flared and they passed. He fired again and waited.

The smoke thinned. At his left and right, his force of illusory figures was fading. One was only a floating torso now; another lacked a head, and still another had no arms. *"You did no better with them,"* his father said within him, *"than with a real force."* Gorgias shrugged. He had masked his position, had taken two lives and wasted Federation power. The fight was not over yet, he told himself as he moved forward.

His screen flared without pause. The last smoke cleared. All the remaining beams were concentrating on him. His screen began to glow, increasing its strength as he stood his ground.

He was close enough now to see faces. At the very worst, he reminded himself, he would retreat to the ship. There was nothing they could do. Even their shipboard lasers were not powerful enough to penetrate his armor, which could draw as much energy as it needed to withstand an ever-increasing concentration of force.

Suddenly the enemy lasers died. The figure in the center was holding up his hand, signaling for a cease-fire.

Kurbi. Gorgias felt a sudden anxiety. The enemy stood still, waiting, their long shadows reaching toward him across the floodlit ground.

The tall Earthman's shadow lengthened and touched Gorgias's feet. Kurbi was pointing at the house.

Gorgias looked back.

The canopy hid the hill again.

Fear cut his guts as the implications stabbed into his mind. He was separated from his ship, trapped inside the screen. The air would go bad within the field unless he blinked it to let some in. They would be waiting, weapons ready. He saw himself unconscious within the bubble; there would be no time to tear it apart. He would die, triggering the destruct cycle in the ship.

He raised his weapon and fired from left to right across the line.

What were they waiting for? Why didn't they open fire?

He swept the line again, but they did not take advantage of his vulnerable moments.

He heard a rush of air. His screen was gone. The Earthmen's shadows were spears, readying to transfix him.

His will froze; a massive weakness invaded his limbs. They had increased the strength of the siege canopy to cut him off from his shipboard power.

He pointed his weapon and fired; it sputtered and died. The ship, he knew, was trying to get power through to him. He stood perfectly still, listening to the night breeze. There was a smell of burnt flesh in the air. If the Earthmen hesitated too long, his power might come back on.

The soldiers took a few steps toward him and stopped. He aimed his beamer and it fired, but his screen did not come back on.

He fired again at the advancing line. The weapon died. Slowly, he retreated, hoping that his power would return. He glanced back at the hill; in a few moments his back would be pressed against the barrier.

He stopped and aimed at Kurbi. The beam came to life and licked feebly at the Earthman's screen. Gorgias struggled to hold the weapon steady in his shaking hands.

The beam weakened and went out.

He opened his mouth to shout an obscenity, but his throat was too dry to make a sound. His legs were stone; his body shuddered.

"Kurbi!" he rasped and fired again. The beam died. His hands were fragile glass. He dropped the weapon.

Kurbi was walking toward him alone.

Gorgias cried out and ran forward, reaching for the last light-scatter bomb around his waist. His fingers closed around it. He raised his arm for the throw.

Fire reached into his eyes, and the sun exploded in his head.

XV. The Closed Circle

"...man consists of a multitude of souls, of numerous selves...I was living a bit of myself only..."

—Hermann Hesse

THE CRESCENT OF SOLDIERS closed into a circle around the fallen Herculean, their shadows forming the spokes of a black wheel. *It's all over,* Rafael Kurbi thought as he knelt beside the charred body, *I'll be free to live other lives.* A sense of relief struggled to assert itself within him, but he held it back. He was only dimly aware of Poincaré standing at his left.

Kurbi reached out and touched the blackened corpse. It was still warm. At any moment, it seemed, the burnt flesh would blow away and the Herculean would stand up, shrugging off the ashes as easily as he had evaded his pursuers in the past. Death would be only a minor inconvenience.

"He's dead," Poincaré said, "there's no use..."

"Shut up!" Kurbi looked around at the soldiers, wondering which one had fired the final, agonizing burst. The helmets made it impossible to tell the men apart. They were all guilty, he thought, including himself.

"His ship has not destructed," Poincaré said. "The explosion he promised would have ripped the canopy apart."

Kurbi stood up. "We might have gone with it, maybe the whole planet. The fool who fired the last shot risked everything."

"You believed the threat?"

"We had no choice." Kurbi looked at the covered hill. The inverted bowl loomed above them, looking like the bald summit of a buried mountain.

"Lift the canopy," Kurbi said.

"He was obviously lying," Julian added. "He's dead and we're still here."

"Hold that order," Kurbi said suddenly. "Do not lift the canopy."

"Standing by," a distant voice said in his ear.

"What's wrong?" Julian asked.

"If there's a link between Gorgias and the ship, then maybe we screened out the destruct impulse when we cut him off from his power. We lift the canopy and the whole planet goes up."

"But there's nothing left on the body that works, Raf."

"There might be a delay in the ship sensing his death. There might be an implanted device inside the body for that. Or it might work through a simple failure of the Herculean to report in."

"I think you're giving him too much credit for cleverness. He wasn't thinking too well when we trapped him out here."

"You're probably right," Kurbi said. "Imagine yourself losing such a large force." He thought of what life would be like for the survivors.

"Do we lift the canopy or not?"

"What do you think?"

"You're still in charge, but I say go ahead."

The whole planet will go, Kurbi thought. *Gorgias will win after all.* He was startled by the realization that he was almost hoping for it to happen.

"We can't just leave things like this," Poincaré said.

Why not? Leave and never come back. "Just to be safe," Kurbi said, "we'll stand off the planet and lift the field from a distance. We have no choice. Too many lives."

"I'll send a crew to stow the body," Julian said. "We'll take it with us."

"We're out far enough," Poincaré said. "Shut off the canopy now." Kurbi sat back next to him and waited, watching the screen.

"Nothing," Poincaré said after a moment.

"Leave the other ships," Kurbi said. "We'll go down in this one."

"You were right to be cautious. We could take a shuttle this time."

"We may need the medical facilities. How are the prisoners?"

The nightside rushed up at the screen as the ship plunged into the planet's atmosphere.

"Doing well—Crusus is in good shape."

Kurbi watched the planet.

"Can I say something to you, Raf?"

Kurbi turned and looked at Julian. "What is it?"

"Can I be candid?"

"Sure, go ahead. . . ."

"You don't make it easy for a friend."

Are we friends? Kurbi asked himself, searching for an honest feeling about Julian.

"What is it?"

"It's a number of things, Raf, all mixed inside you."

"Go ahead."

"Why do you think you went hunting the Herculean?"

"Why ask me? You're going to tell me your answer."

"I think Grazia's death precipitated it. Then you saw all that dying on New Mars. Some part of you made catching Gorgias the same as saving lives. . . ."

"That's to say nothing, Julian. Gorgias killed a lot of people and had to be stopped."

"Let me finish, I'm not that obvious. Gorgias became a stand-in for Grazia. You blame yourself for not saving her. You took it on yourself to help revive a dead civilization— but neither you nor Gorgias could have done that by yourselves. . . ."

"If he could have worked with me . . ." Kurbi said.

"All your best motives got mixed in with your personal tragedy. Gorgias became a lost son to you. . . ."

"The problem had its own merits also. Besides, you pressured me into the search."

"That's true."

"It would have been better to have saved him, regardless."

"Possibly."

"There will be other things for me now."

"I'm glad to hear you say that."

The ship touched down on the darkened battlefield. The lights of the house looked almost friendly.

"I'll take a few men and investigate," Poincaré said.

Kurbi was pacing back and forth when the screen came on.

"The ship is still here," Poincaré said from the house. "So is the woman Myraa."

Kurbi nodded. Julian was sitting in the main room, alone.

"One strange thing, though."

"What?" Kurbi asked.

"It's probably nothing. Our cyberneticist is questioning the artificial intelligence in the Whisper Ship, to see if there is any hidden delay in its destruct sequence. The destruct has not been tripped. The ship is behaving as if Gorgias were still alive."

"So their technology was not infallible."

"That or it was not Gorgias who died."

It's not over. The words repeated in Kurbi's head. He felt a sudden surge of hope—and with it came the realization that Julian's view of him was correct, or as nearly correct as words could be made to express reality.

"...The ship doesn't give any sign of malfunctioning," Poincaré was saying. "It's as if it's waiting..."

"The ship is very old," Kurbi said softly.

"So, you think he's dead?"

"Yes—but send out search parties. He would have to be on foot...."

"What about the ship?"

"We'll stow it in our hold and take it with us," Kurbi said.

"What about the woman?"

"Leave her. She obviously had no part in any of this. We'd violate our agreement with the Herculeans on this world by taking prisoners. Has she told you anything?"

"They'll cheer us back home," Poincaré said.

"But I know I've failed."

"I'll let you know if we learn anything more. We'll leave the screen open."

Kurbi turned away and went to the door. It slid open and a watch officer came in to take his place. Kurbi walked into the open elevator and rode it down to the locks.

He came out into a chilly morning. A warming sun crept up from behind the mountains. Long glowing clouds streaked the sky. He wondered about the Herculean army. Maybe Myraa's people had collaborated with Gorgias to bring the force here? But from where? Myraa seemed to be at the center of something.

He took a deep breath and went back inside.

Poincaré came into the control room with a tripod on his shoulder. He opened it and set it down on the floor.

"What is it?" Kurbi asked as he stood up.

"The troops were stored in this cylinder casing, in the crystalline structure of the material inside."

Kurbi took the casing and examined it.

"We knew they were working on various things toward the end of the war," Poincaré said, "—but this!"

"So it was all Gorgias's doing," Kurbi said.

"We've examined the entire assembly," Julian said. "What's really interesting about it is that with a slight modification it might have thrown up the same army again and again, using the patterns to create an indefinite number of doubles, as long as there was energy to feed in. Gorgias did not know this at all."

"What else did Myraa tell you?"

"Crusus helped us figure out the tripod. He knows a few things about it. He's a sad person Raf, filled with doubts now."

"What else?"

"There is a base. We think the ship can take us to it. Myraa also showed me what she says is a teleport link with the Lesser Magellanic Cloud, but it's dead now, she says."

"Will the ship listen to our commands?"

"In time, she says, it might."

Kurbi found himself only half-listening as Poincaré finished his report. Despite Julian's explanation of his preoccupation with Gorgias, the future seemed empty without the hope of getting through to the Herculean.

". . . and then, Raf, her face became strange and drawn, and she looked old, as if she were staring into another universe. Raf?"

Kurbi rubbed his eyes. "That's it?"

"No—you need sleep."

"Finish what you were saying," Kurbi said.

"She wouldn't say another word to me. Well—it's not a total loss. We have the ship. We may have the base in time. Think of what we may find there—think of the archives it might contain!"

Kurbi was silent. Even if Julian was right about his tangled

motives, it would still be a long time before he could weave
another web half as meaningful. There was nothing left but
empty possibility, unconnected to him in any personal way.
He was going to become someone else, for whom none of this
would have any interest.

"You can't go on like this," Julian said.

"Hurry things along," Kurbi said, "I'm weary of this place."
Poincaré sighed.

Kurbi looked at the tripod. He stepped closer and inserted
the cylinder carefully. With these things, he thought, Gorgias
called up the past to help him, but the past came forward with
all its defects. The patterns of men long dead were rebuilt into
flesh and blood, then burned into ashes. When he had first
come to hunt Gorgias, the Herculean's life was already a mere
echo, a life which had started somewhere with groping motions,
had reached several stages of twisted development and had
settled into a wayward spiral, winding from a ruined past into
an empty future. He thought of the Federation's snaking corridor of worlds—turning, twisting as it grew, until it had reached
the Hercules Cluster, there to light the spark that gave birth to
Gorgias's people. The Herculean terrorist had been the puppet
of a greater will, growing more desperate with each failure.

Julian was speaking, but Kurbi could not listen. A cold pain
grew in his stomach. He was marching with Gorgias across a
barren waste, toward a dawn that could never come. He hated
himself.

I might have saved him, he told himself, and each word
was a star being born in a terrifying darkness.

XVI.   Galaxy of Minds

"Each consciousness seeks to be itself and to be all other consciousnesses without ceasing to be itself: it seeks to be God."

—Miguel de Unamuno

"The ego persists only by becoming ever more itself, in the measure in which it makes everything else itself . . . by slowly elaborating from age to age the essence and the totality of a universe deposited within . . .

"The only universe capable of containing . . . the person is an irreversibly 'personalizing' universe . . .

". . . however large the radius traced within time and space, does the circle ever embrace anything but the perishable?

"To satisfy the ultimate requirements of our action, Omega must be independent of the collapse of the forces with which evolution is woven.

"Thus something in the cosmos escapes from entropy, and does so more and more. It escapes by turning back to Omega . . ."

—Pierre Teilhard de Chardin, *The Phenomenon of Man*

"Under those low large lids of hers
She hath the histories of all time;
The old seasons with their heavy chime
That leaves its rhyme in the world's ears."

—Swinburne, *Cleopatra*

GORGIAS STRUGGLED to open his eyes.

"You must try to understand." Myraa's voice was all around him, soft and caressing.

"Where are you?"

"Here, near you. You're safe. They cannot hurt you now. You'll know everything soon."

He tried to move his arms.

It felt . . . as if he did not have any.

He remembered the blinding flash. His screen had been down and he had been hit. Nothing could survive a direct hit from that kind of weapon; but he was alive.

The ship. Myraa and he were safe in the ship, fleeing back to the base. Maybe the ship was still on the planet, waiting for the moment when the canopy would lift. The pain would come when the drugs wore off. He imagined that he was lying in a gel bath, waiting for the protective mass to heal his burns.

No, Myraa said. She seemed to speak from inside him.

Myraa was blocking the pain in his mind.

"Myraa! What has happened?" Suddenly he realized that he was not speaking; there was no feeling of movement in his jaw. "You promised never to enter my mind!"

"There is no other way now."

"What do you mean? Tell me!"

He tried to look around in the darkness, but his eye sockets were empty. Shadows rushed into them.

Suddenly he could see. . . .

He was in the bedroom, in what seemed to be the house. He felt himself get up against his will and walk to the window. Then he saw that it was not the same house. Below him was the white beach. Foamy waves drifted in from the warm green ocean; long-legged birds chased each other across the wet sand.

Something black pushed into the corner of his eye. His head jerked to the left, and there on the floor, in the bright afternoon light, lay a charred, unrecognizable body. He walked over and reached down to touch it, but his hand passed through to the cold floor.

"I show you an image," she said from within. *"They took the corpse with them."*

"Myraa, what are you saying?"

He looked at his right hand.

It was Myraa's.

"I could not let you die like your father." Her voice was agonizingly near. Her fingers were touching his heart, holding it, brushing it with words and warm breath. *"I could not let you dissolve . . ."*

He thought of the ship.

"They took the ship, which could not destroy itself while your mind was still whole."

He looked around the room through her eyes. The ghost of his body had disappeared. The space seemed very bright. He looked upward through the skylight at the blue sky. Everything was vivid and clear, as if he were seeing it for the first time.

I'm dead, he thought, *and she carries me inside.*

He tried to scream, to force the sound out of her throat, but it was only a thought. Her will was not his own.

"You let them take my body, to be exhibited as a trophy!"

He slipped into darkness. Myraa's thoughts were everywhere, ministering to his fears, whispering like flies. *"I could not stop them, and it was not important."*

"Traitor!" He was suddenly sickened by the idea of being imprisoned in another's body. He thought of his own arms, legs and belly, the center of his own will coiled in his loins. What was left of him?

"The old dreams are dead," she said. *"I know how they died on that world in the Magellanic Cloud. For a long time after the plague hit them, I heard their voices crying out of that dark place, out of that terrible cold, as they fought with each other. They tore at their vessels and at themselves until they died. Only a few had the strength to reach out. I saved them, but they are still not whole."*

"I am no longer whole!" He hurled the words, wishing that he could die. He wanted to bloody her from within, tear out the words that she was depositing within him. If only he could wrap himself in his own flesh again. Her soothing wounded him, and he hated her for it. How would he be able to endure an eternity of her domination? He would never be able to love her now, or have sons.

How could he kill her? He was only a thought within her, a memory. What if she chose to forget him? The chaos would take what was left of him, and he would die a second time. Could she forget him for a time, then summon him back? He would drift at the edges of her awareness, a mystery to himself, a spark struggling to grow brighter.

Somehow she was in his arms. He held her firmly as she thrust up at him.

"Liar!" he shouted.

"You lived a lie. I am still with you."

"I don't want you—I don't need you! Release me!"

"There is much more than this."

"No!"

The darkness pressed in around him, an infinite solidity that would hold him immobile forever.

"When you accept us," she said, *"you will have every-thing."*

Ages passed and she did not speak to him. The black, sunless solidity was a constant humiliation; at any moment it would close in and crush him into nothing.

The fact of his body's destruction tormented him. He felt anger and sadness, but the feelings seemed strange, echoes of their former intensity; his cries would not cry out, his rage would not swell, and a part of him held his hatred in contempt. The substructures of his body, he realized, were not there to underscore his thoughts; his feelings were beginning to fade. Perhaps he could shake off this inversion of reality, will his eyes to open in his corpse, wherever it might be, recreate his body in a sudden act. . . .

A glow enveloped his awareness . . . almost as if he had limbs again. The warmth increased and he felt his charred skin, and he knew that his nerves were signaling horror to his brain. He felt his body dying, stared through the blindness of his eyes, felt its insides beginning to decay. A distant sorrow called to him, but he could not make it his own. His body died; he could no longer feel its extremities. His self contracted to a point drifting in limbo. Anyone could pass through him now and read his most private thoughts like a roadsign.

Alien minds watched him with a cold curiosity. How could Myraa have joined with these? They had been there, he real-ized, when he had made love to her; still, he felt grateful for the attention they gave him in the darkness.

They were ancient, older than the Empire, older than the

Earth; they had survived in this way, and would continue until all the suns of space died and the universe collapsed to start the entropic decline all over again. These minds were part of a greater community, one that would not die in the final singularity; it would burst from the continuum like some great moth, newborn into the skies of some greater realm; and as it had survived from mind to mind in the universe he knew, so this being would continue to pass from realm to realm, an eternal voyager on an upward path from the infinitesimal to the infinite. . . .

The intruding vision held him, and he wondered at it. What was there to find in the upper realities?

"Who rules this mind?" he found the strength to ask. Where was Myraa? She was still someone he trusted. He would not be played with by strangers for unknown ends. Maybe Myraa was also a prisoner here, wandering in search of him, waiting for him in the darkness.

"Who rules here?" He shouted into the void, giving the words all the force that he could imagine, but again there was no answer.

The darkness became a fluid mass, carrying him along; he felt its indeterminacy at his own center. Painful sensations stabbed into him out of this chaos, emotions unattached to any specific memory.

The face of a young boy appeared. It was his brother's face. Gorgias found himself standing by the sea, and the boy had just come out of the emerald-green water. His body glistened with clear droplets. The air was fresh with spray.

"Hello, Gorgias," the boy said and hugged him around the middle with slippery arms. "You look so tired," he said looking up at him. "Tell me where you've been. You'll stay now, won't you? Come and sit with me."

The boy smiled and led him away from the water. Gorgias sat down next to him on the white sand. *How real he seems,* he thought as he looked into his brother's radiant face. *I had almost forgotten what he looked like.*

Then only the boy's face was left in the darkness, smiling at him as if their conversation had already taken place. "You'll be happy with us, Gorgias. There is such a long journey ahead of us and we'll need you. You should have come sooner. I'm sorry that Father can't be here. . . ."

"So am I," Gorgias said. "I killed him."

"Oriona will see you later."

The darkness returned, and again he felt the watchful presence of alien entities. His interest quickened, growing into a curiosity equal to his fear. What was it that had so changed Myraa and his brother?

Gorgias remembered the second time his father had brought him to Myraa's World. She had run to him across the grass and they had made love under the warm orange sun. Later, his father had spoken to them in the house on the hill. He had told them that they were fated for each other, and that the Empire's rebirth would take place only if they, and others like them, willed it. Before Herkon's death, Myraa had been a playful girl, always complaining about his father's seriousness. What was she now, he wondered? How had it happened?

He heard laughter in the dark and turned to see her coming toward him across the grassy field, her naked body bright in the sunlight. The field was dotted with thousands of yellow flowers; the cool breeze was full of fragrance. She came up to him and put her arms around his waist. "In my world," she whispered into his ear, "nothing is ever lost." Her warm breath sent a chill down his back. "You still wear your father's serious face. Don't you love me any more?" He put his arms out to hold her, but she laughed and disappeared, leaving him to embrace the void.

Another age passed before she spoke to him again. He found himself looking through blinking eyelids at Myraa's reflection in the dark window—his reflection. The room was quiet. He missed the sound of the sea washing the shore, the feel of night wind on skin which had known the sun all day, the freshness of rain.

"Hello, Gorgias," his-her reflection said to him from the window. The house seemed poised at the edge of a dark abyss.

"How long has it been?" he asked, wondering at her cruelty.

"A year since Kurbi left." She sat unmoving in the glass. "He was hurt badly by what happened here."

"No others have risen to oppose the Federation?"

"You were the last."

Her skin was milky in the black window, her breasts pointed; her long hair was invisible, blending with the night. She was sitting on the bed, her hands folded in her lap.

"How can you expect me to accept this?" he asked.

"You live—there was no other way. Now you must come to understand that you came from a lesser way of life."

"Lesser?"

"Can a child understand what it will become?"

"I am not a child."

"You are not ready to know."

"Tell me now!" he cried within her.

"Think of all the living things that die and there is nothing for them—little things with small intelligences that struggle and scream in all the corners of all the forests in the galaxy, and die so that those who come after them may do the same. Think of those living things who only dimly understand what is happening. In them intelligence flickers and fails to grow, and dies as they are dragged into death. All the good that they will ever know must be expressed in dreary effort, against the backdrop of final defeat. Think of all life, billions of sparks that fly up from a fire. The source is as generous with them as it is uncaring."

"But what has this to do with me?" he asked.

"This circle of anxious striving and repetition can be broken. You can put aside the isolation and disorder that you have known."

He felt a sudden, luxurious repose. "You will acquire the power to look outward and through all things," she said, "to fall through the bottom of mysteries, to swim in a vastness of warmth and knowing. I can help break the bonds that hold you."

He was lying on white sand; a peaceful, warm sun shone down on him and he stretched wearily. He sat up and looked toward the ocean. Myraa, her long brown hair wet on her back, splashed in the water. A young boy splashed back at her. Gorgias lay back and let the warmth of the sand creep into him. This was his universe, his world; he held it deeply within himself, a tamed chaos which expressed its order only to him.

He was a child again, standing on a hill overlooking a clearing. The tall grass was brilliant in the yellow light of late afternoon. The forest shadows were growing darker, sharper. The crystal clarity of the landscape made him feel that he knew the complexity of every blade of grass, every scrap of bark, every stone and clump of dirt; every insect was a world in itself, yet related to every other world. Everything was passing into everything else. The infinity of layers of organization seemed to glow around him, catching fire from within, yet nothing was ever consumed. The transparency of reality invited knowing. The universe trembled on the verge of revealing itself to him. . . .

He held the moment.

Something took him upward suddenly, with the power of an infinite force. He was thrust into a great lighted space, as vast as the starry void he had known. He whirled, trying to find the dark world he had left behind, anything to give him a sense of distance. . . .

There was no sense of space or time, and he knew that he might exist and perceive in a new way. He thought of his wanderings, his hatred of his enemies. The memories threatened to drag him back.

He felt a sense of expectation.

"You are not ready," Myraa said. Her words meant nothing.

He gazed into himself and saw the darkness between the suns; he drew the stars together into a dense superstar, rekindling his hatred and sense of loss.

Myraa tried to calm him, stroking him with her thoughts. "The expansion of humanity from Earth," she said, "led to dissipation, as intelligence sought to inhabit world after world, spreading itself thinly, becoming a stranger to itself. Only by turning inward can a species and an individual concentrate power, through the growing complexity of involution."

"What kind of power?"

"To continue, to be in different ways—we do not know everything," she said.

He felt suspicious, fearing her power over him. What would she do if he refused her way? He was lodged inside her. She could show him anything, and present it as some kind of reality; he would not be able to tell the difference.

"I don't want your delusions," he said.

Again she showed him the sun in a clear sky, trees and grass, the endless summer that she carried within herself. He felt her promise of renewal, drawing him into a whole underside universe of illusions, of mindscapes created by wishes. Or was it more?

"See what I see," she said.

He heard the life of the universe, felt its will uncoiling, reaching, grasping, squeezing, exploding. Voices cried in a chorus of chance. Countless living things struggled toward a fulfillment which no individual would ever know. Form after form lifted itself out of the unconscious substratum of time, demanding immortality. A myriad of suns burst into brightness and died. Empires struggled and expired, throwing off spores to start anew. Outworlds flowered, becoming flesh as populations increased. . . .

Myraa drew him further into herself.

"Illusions!" he shouted, powerless to prevent his sinking.

He felt the presence of *others* in her folds. His doubts were silenced as the great mass of minds pressed in around him. Myraa held them all, it seemed, and they held other minds— an infinity of interlocking mentalities within minds, within Myraa. . . .

There were Herculeans, his brother and mother, and grandmother; ancient minds dating from the beginning of time, aliens who had survived from the collapse of countless previous universes, entities who sang strange, joyous songs. . . .

Myraa's thoughts were radiant within his own; she seemed to be herself again, more desirable than ever.

"We are the universe," she said. "The interlocking matrix of minds is coextensive with all of nature, which is our outward face, in every stone, in every blade of grass and grain of sand. We accumulate those who return to us through death. Soulminds are returned to our matrix, into the monadic inner structure of visible reality. The material cosmos is the outward manifestation of an infinitely complex inwardness, a sentient, divine machine composed of minds within minds extending below the infinitesimal and beyond the macroscopic. All physical universes are emanations from these minds, which are also one mind, dreaming all that is beautiful and good, evil and grotesque in the eyes of lesser beings. Its creations push up like rocks from the ocean to form the world of objects. Our radiant energy is permanent, the inward power of all nature, supporting the tangential energy of entropy, which is transient, useful only for the outward workings of a fluid reality. That reality is a nursery, a place for the testing of new minds."

"I must doubt," Gorgias said halfheartedly. "I am your prisoner. You can make me see and feel anything."

"We can see anywhere," she said.

In a small lighted space he saw Kurbi, and heard his thoughts across the light-years . . . feelings of despair . . . judgments of failure . . . reproaches. Was this the man who had hunted him?

"His hunger may bring him back here," Myraa said.

A new suspicion formed in Gorgias's mind. Myraa did not fully understand this new realm. Her grouping might be only a local configuration.

Suddenly he was moving. Something was drawing him away from Myraa, along what seemed a straight line. The Myraan complex of mentalities became the hub of a wheel and he was rushing away from it along one of the spokes.

He peered ahead. The spoke seemed to be leading toward a greater center. He sensed the presence of other lines at his left and right, multiple continua converging toward some power ahead.

He slowed, humiliated by the sense of immense energy. He stopped. Churning clouds hid the place ahead. Spears of light escaped occasionally. He felt a deep sound, a rumbling bass; it passed through him, making him afraid. He might be able to master the spoke that led out from Myraa's locus, but the convergent mass, the center of centers ahead, would blind him, drive him insane.

He crept forward. Something was focusing him, opening his awareness beyond the confines that he had known. He felt suddenly that he would forget himself as he drew closer, dissolve into something larger. . . .

He began to struggle, denying the titanic will as it labored to possess him. Slowly, with great effort, he backed away from the vibrant force-center. As he retreated he felt a sense of kinship with the vast center. It was blind, but it gave consciousness all its impetus.

Long ago, he thought, intelligent beings had believed that the world was not enough, later that it was enough. If the material universe was all of reality, with nothing beyond, then intelligence was a stranger, a complexity which had coalesced by chance, a shadowed face looking into a cold, dark mirror. The loss of life within such a reality was at once irreversible and senseless; but if what he had seen so far was not an illusion, then intelligence could pass through a mirrored interface, into a vast sea inside the cosmos, below the grasping life of galaxies, into a realm of will and mind coextensive with the universe.

Gorgias turned and saw something small hanging nearby, as if it were an ornament suspended in a dark room. He came up close to it and saw it resolve into spiral galaxies composed of individual stars. The whole cosmos was wrapped in a shimmering field of force, glowing from within, ethereal and alive.

He felt it pulse with its cycle of birth and death; he felt it expand and collapse because he was part of it.

I am everywhere, he thought. *Myraa was not lying.*

He felt his will expand with the force of an explosion, radiating outward into all things, riding the spherical wave that was the power of birth and all striving, passing into quantum spaces and deep abysses, into the large and small. He looked out from a billion eyes, felt the weight of stones, leaves and trees; a galaxy lay upon his shoulders, its center swallowing itself. His consciousness flickered through the space-time he had known—

Skies,

Stormy, blue and red.

Starfields and a coiled snake.

Silence and a blood-red sun.

A vein of metal in rock,

Worn away by a hurrying stream,

Cracked by a pulling moon.

A winged thing falling

Toward its shadow.

An insect trapped in amber.

Rafael Kurbi.

I might have killed him.

I should have killed him.

There must still be a way.

—the underside of reality was filled with mirrors opening out into every place and moment. . . .

Gorgias fell back into a peaceful darkness. The effort would destroy him now, but he would grow stronger. He would be able to strike out again from this vast cave of the dead. Myraa and the others did not care for the other side of the world; for them it was only a preparation, a chancy source of new minds.

"We are free of the wheel of will," she said. "We are at peace, outside its blind tyranny." She seemed far away from him.

"You would be better off dead," he said. "You do nothing with the power that is here. This will is blind, but we might be able to direct it."

"We are not wise enough."

"You would imprison me with your ways. What wisdom do you have? None at all! What is there here for you?"

"We wait."

"For what?"

"For what is coming."

"What is that?"

"We do not know, except that it is coming."

"Fools! Circling a blind will like insects. Do you think it will speak?"

She did not answer.

Myraa sat on the bed and looked at her reflection in the night-mirror of the crystal window. She put her hands up to her breasts and held them. Soon, she hoped, Gorgias would be ready to nurture new minds, as they fled from the evolutionary cauldron of creation. . . .

Gorgias saw two pools of blue. He recognized Myraa's eyes, but he did not go up to them to look out into the room. He knew that she felt his growing strength inside her. Slowly he stretched, summoning his powers. An influx of energy twisted and turned inside him like a snake trying to swallow its own tail, and he knew that he was learning to control a will that would never die.

"Myraa!" he shouted as he stood up inside her and looked out through her creature's eyes at her reflection in the dark window. "You won't be able to fight me for long."

Her image smiled at him.

The force of her rebuff hurled him back from her eyes.

"I won't need you in time," he called to her. "How can I love you now?"

Her answer seemed warm and welcoming. "I have always loved you, Gorgias. I am stronger than you."

Her words passed into him; for a moment he began to feel that they were his own thoughts; but then he felt his strength returning as he drew himself together, coiling to strike at her self-control.

"I will go back," he shouted.

"Never," she said.

"Some things are never finished!"

He began the struggle for her body.

His will invaded her limbs, pushing into her muscles, making them his own. She froze his impulses and tightened to expel him. *The evil that returns,* she thought. *We have defeated it before and will do so again.*

He swam through her blood and lurked in the shadows of

her heart, listening to its slow, ageless beat while the rest of him wound itself around her bones and waited for her to weaken.

... Her heart burst into a sun, hurling him out into the darkness. ...

Suddenly his strength was gone.

"I am all my ancestors," he whispered, tumbling, "... and all my descendants. ... I am the Empire. ..."

"You will forget what you were," Myraa said.

BOOK THREE

MIRROR OF MINDS

I.   To Be Reborn

"That I could drink thy veins as wine, and eat
Thy breasts like honey! that from face to feet
Thy body were abolished and consumed,
And in my flesh thy very flesh entombed!"

—Swinburne, *Anactoria*

"These two things, the spiritual and the material, though we call
them by different names, in their origin are one and the same."

—Lao-tzŭ

GORGIAS DRIFTED.
  Suddenly, the flow of a muddy universe pressed cold darkness into his eyes. Pliant masses slipped into all his openings—
probes tapping his will, scattering his strength as they collected
his thoughts.
  He gulped the damp blackness, longing for a dry clearing
in the infinite substance, a warm breeze to convince him that
he still had a skin. He dreamed of a fiery explosion that would
break the vise of Myraa's dungeon.
  Fleeting images cut through his visual field. The mind-maze
was everywhere around him, falling away into pits and opening
into passages; space twisted and folded in upon itself. Moments
of pain and pleasure wandered through him like hungry vermin,
keeping his will in check.

He dreamed again of pushing himself into her limbs. Her eyes would be his eyes, her breath his own, joining him once more to the universe of his birth; but there seemed to be no way out of the prison within her.

He ached to be pulled from the darkness, as once his father had drawn him through the knothole of his mother's womb; but Myraa would never allow him to be reborn.

He dreamed of light.

He stood on a dark mirror. Shapes rose through the surface, as if they were sea creatures coming up for air. Faces, curious about him as they drew near and whisked away.

The black surface softened and gave way. He slid toward some central abyss. The softness closed around him, wrapping him in forgetfulness....

He kicked, waited and kicked again....

He peered around, shivering in a cathedral of ice.

Pale beams shot through clouded windows, illuminating a barren area on the floor far below him.

His life had been a dream; he was only a nightmare, thinking that it had been real, that it had once had a body, a purpose; the illusion of self and past, of lost power, would soon fade away with the hope of new things.

"Why was I given this?" he asked, forming the thought, thrusting it outward.

It rushed away from him, echoing back from a great distance. Then it became a grotesque, birdlike thing which cried out and flew at his eyes; in a moment it had passed into his mind and was tearing at his insides.

His throat struggled to hurl storms, but his thoughts were impotent, forming only silent words; his hatred huddled, fearful of showing itself, lest Myraa punish him.

"Myraa!" he cried as talons tore at his brain.

The silence waited within him.

"Answer me!"

Her thoughts watched him like beasts of prey, hungry but holding back. He was afraid that she would dissolve what was left of him, let it slip into nothing.

"See what you are," a pitiless thought whispered, passing through him. He was completely vulnerable. Minds rushed through him like wind through trees, exposing secret fears and shames on the way, tearing apart hopes, mocking his personal boundaries.

"Let me die." He pushed the thought outward.

There was no answer.

"Let me go! What can there be for me, like this?"

Space trembled around him. The infrastructure of reality was vibrant with minds. They nestled in folds and byways, distending the darkness, forming galaxies of consciousness.

Slowly, he became aware of a vast center, a pulsing enigma from which all nourishment flowed. He reached out, probing this heart of fire, sensing that even Myraa had no control over it.

He coiled his will and struck inward, spiraling inward into dimensionless points, held steady by his hatred. No one moved to stop him.

But his determination faltered when, after an age, he was no closer to the center.

The muddy universe closed in again, flowing into him as he struggled to throw up defenses.

"Why?" he asked, coiling tighter within himself. There had to be a way to regain control of Myraa's nervous system.

The darkness pressed in harder around him. He cried out and pushed back, but the effort filled him with pain and trembling. He coiled his will even more tightly. What he needed from the central fire was enough strength to strike out from his fortress self. Unfinished things wore away at him, insisting that if he dared enough, willed intensely enough, then he would be given the power he needed to prevail.

The darkness loosened its grip. Morning glowed around him, promising the rise of a million suns. The gathered dead within Myraa looked forward to a vague life beyond life, but he would do what no mind in nature had ever attempted. He would rend worlds, darken suns, shatter the minds of those who had taken everything from him.

"And what will it bring you?" a slippery thought asked.

"That will only be the beginning," he answered.

"Forget!" Myraa commanded, scattering the growing army of his resolve. He retreated, but she breached his walls and moved toward his center.

He shuddered and tried to resist.

"Let go what you were," she said, encamped within him. She closed herself around his heart and squeezed.

"No!" He pictured her body and hurled knives at it.

She became visible. One shoulder was bloody.

"I don't care!" he shouted, realizing that he would gladly tear her to pieces if he could.

She thrust the memory of his death into his mind. Pain surged through his lost body as the beam weapon blinded him and burned his flesh.

"I gathered you up," she said.

"Only to imprison me."

"To save you."

"For what?" he asked. Her compassion was a weapon, ready to strike if he let down his guard.

Suddenly he knew, and her fear stabbed back in confirmation. She was using the darkness to prevent him from learning how to act in this realm.

"I will be what I was!" he cried.

But without the weakening sympathies and troubled feelings of his previous self; death had taken all that from him, leaving him a new strength to explore.

II. Dark Mirror

"All, all of a piece throughout:
Thy chase had a beast in view;
Thy wars brought nothing about;
Thy lovers were all untrue.
'Tis well an old age is out,
And time to begin a new."

—Dryden

RAFAEL KURBI FELT UNEASY as he grasped the railing of his terrace and gazed out over the ocean; nothing was as it had been. He wished that the past would take him by the hand and lead him back to better times. What better times? The past was inhabited by unhappy, far-off things and lost battles. His sentiments mocked him. What would he be when he crossed the century mark? Wallowing in nostalgia. The time was coming when he would have to start erasing certain debilitating memories.

He had failed in the Herculean affair. The death of Gorgias had left him with half-asked questions, vague insights and haunting suspicions. He could still picture the impressive lines of Herculean infantry moving forward in the searchlights. The fact that Gorgias might have cycled the troop storage cylinder more than once, to materialize as many identical divisions as he might have needed, still brought a queasiness to Kurbi's stomach. The final battle had been more of a close call than anyone was willing to admit.

219

Five years.

Yet it seemed that he had seen the charred bodies only a few days ago. It still seemed to him that he might have prevented Gorgias's death. The soldier who burned him had fired without orders, on his own impulse.

"Have you become a statue?" a familiar voice asked.

Kurbi turned around. "What are you doing here?"

Julian Poincaré's image shrugged. "Can't I come see you?"

Kurbi walked through him and sat down. Julian ignored the insult. "Okay, Raf, so perhaps we're not the friends we were, but we have important matters to discuss. Will you listen?"

"Do I have a choice?"

"I'm here to do you a favor."

"Get to the point."

"We want you to go to Myraa's World . . . to look around and see what might be going on."

Kurbi felt himself tighten, as if he had just been pulled out of darkness into a harsh light. "Whatever for?" he asked, swallowing hard.

"Certain studies suggest that their mentalistic skills may pose a danger to us. There may be a weapons aspect." Julian paused and stared at him. "Well, that's what our various students say after examining the cult's claims. Something may be going on. I'll be honest. The people I work with just don't trust the Herculean survivors."

Kurbi laughed. "Troubled consciences. You're afraid that Gorgias will send his ghost to haunt you."

"Not me. I was ordered to talk to you, to ask you if you feel anything."

"Just my usual doubts and conscience." There was more to this than Julian was telling, Kurbi suspected. "Next you'll tell me they're considering rounding up the remaining Herculeans and killing them, or destroying the planet."

"That's why I want you to go and check things. If there's any kind of danger, you'll be trustworthy and we'll be sure. Raf, I fought hard for this much."

"So it's true. They want to be rid of everything that's left."

"If you care, then go see. Otherwise you'll be left out."

"And if I refuse?"

"Others will go, not so sympathetic."

"What's the use?"

"Raf, they're very sure about this. If you'd participated in the investigations of the last five years, you might feel differently."

"Do you believe it?"

"If you'd been told some of the things I have, you'd think long and hard about destroying Myraa's World while you still had a chance."

"What did they tell you?"

Poincaré sat down on an invisible chair. "They can . . . reach across stellar distances and know what you're thinking. It's possible that they can move objects against us, on a cosmic scale, project irrationalities into our minds. It would take only a few such supermen to do decisive damage."

"And what evidence have you seen for this?"

"None. But it's all implied in the Omega cult's philosophy. Look, I'll grant that our fear of the Herculeans runs deep. Maybe our guilt does also. But we've got to know. The stakes are too high to dismiss this kind of thing, whatever the evidence." He scratched a bushy eyebrow. "Belief systems that promise survival after death have always struck me as dangerous, sooner or later."

"Don't you see what you're doing to me?" Kurbi asked. "They're planning genocide . . . sorry, the completion of genocide, just so they can have certainty and be able to sleep nights. And you come here to blackmail me with the illusory hope that I can save the Herculeans!"

"Say it anyway you like, Raf. I have to get you there while you can still do some good. It's what I can do, and I'm doing it."

"You're not really concerned about me."

"I'm concerned about you too. Let me say it another way. The Old Bones are afraid. They've lived a long time. Earth is prosperous and there's a lot to lose. They're sick of having this hanging over them. Some of the oldest remember the war—they were old even then."

Long life breeds cowards, Kurbi thought.

"They want to make sure," Julian continued, "before the Herculeans grow strong and it's too late."

"A few thousand people?"

"Something is going on, I'm convinced of that."

"But it's probably nothing threatening. Just who are these researchers who are spreading this kind of superstition?"

"Then go disprove it and put an end to . . . to their demands for containing the danger. There is one bit of evidence."

"Oh, what's that?"

"All the scattered Herculean survivors are now on Myraa's World. They've been returning steadily."

"Go away, Julian. Leave me alone."

"It might have settled things more," Poincaré continued, "if we had been able to enter the Whisper Ship, if it had led us to the Herculean base. But the feeling now is that Myraa lied about quite a few things. Some believe that the ship can be activated at any time and taken from us."

Kurbi shook his head. "You've all gone insane!"

Julian smiled. "Raf, we do have *some* cause for our suspicions."

"Produce it, then, don't just refer to it!"

"We all feel uneasy, yourself included."

"You're right, but that isn't evidence for what you're talking about."

Poincaré was silent. "So, what have you been doing?" he asked after a while.

Kurbi shrugged and sat down in one of the chairs. "Thinking, reading, living a daily routine. It's easy to forget time. I try to do it more often. Don't like the residue it leaves."

"Forget, renew yourself."

"I'm not ready to let go of certain things yet. Too many bits and pieces of myself seem essential, however painful."

Julian stood up. "You're hopeless! So the universe is a bit irrational. It doesn't surprise me, since it rests on a substratum of chaos. So we're not quite cortical intellects, but that's no reason to revert to this kind of instinctive, brooding way of yours. You must enjoy it."

"Who is being instinctive, with these paranoid suspicions?" Kurbi asked. "By the way, where is the Whisper Ship now?"

"Centauri Docks, bolted down to the planet's bedrock."

"So, exactly what am I supposed to do on Myraa's World?"

"Just question her, spend some time, gather a few impressions, nothing more."

"And no action of any kind will be taken until I return?"

"I can guarantee that."

"Tell me, Julian, why should I be trusted? I was seen as being sympathetic to the Herculeans."

"So were a lot of people, but that doesn't mean they didn't see the Herculean cause as hopelessly wrong. You can be trusted because I will trust your report."

"Oh, I see."

"Cut the undercurrent, Raf. I've worked with you. We've known each other for many years. You're not a simpleton. You're a concerned, meticulous observer, whatever your wilder impulses—and you need to work, to plan for the second century of your life. We lose too many people around the century mark through self-destructiveness. It seems likely that you'll retain some continuity with your earlier self, and that will make you valuable."

"So I can take my place among the ruling Old Bones?"

Julian held up his hands. "I want this Herculean thing to be laid to rest once and for all, for your sake and for Earth's."

"One way or another. Do you believe all these speculations or not?"

"I honestly don't know. On the evidence, no. But the feeling is so pervasive..."

"So is that of a mob."

Poincaré clenched his teeth.

"I'll go," Kurbi said. "What are the arrangements?"

"You'll command your own ship," Poincaré said, rubbing his chin nervously.

Kurbi got up slowly. "I can't help feeling that you're setting me up as a stalking horse. Don't get angry, we're talking about feelings."

Julian's face became rigid. "We don't want to be wrong about this."

"Of course not."

"Why needle me? Go see for yourself. I'll trust your report."

His image disappeared.

Kurbi stepped over to the rail again. Sunlight seemed to fill the ocean, as if it had been poured into the shallows for the benefit of human swimmers. Clouds were docked on the horizon, waiting for nightfall.

The memory of the Herculeans was a dark mirror, he thought. Every time an Earthman looks into it, he scares himself witless.

III.   The Hidden Face

"Let thy chief terror be of thine own soul:
  There, 'mid the throng of hurrying desires
  That trample o'er the dead to seize their spoil,
  Lurks vengeance, footless, irresistible
  As exhalations laden with slow death..."

—George Elliot

"At the core of the romantic agony lies the monstrous recognition of life's irredeemable insufficiency."

—Anonymous

MYRAA WAS RIGID before the window. The ship from Earth was a silver ball on the grassland below the hill.

Gorgias writhed within her, stabbing into her arms and legs, burning in her belly, striving to replace her will at every nerve center in her body.

"He's here!"

"Yes," she said, striving to deny him sight.

Scalding blood coursed through her heart as she failed. Gorgias came up inside her and looked out.

"I see him!" he cried.

A tall figure walked across the grass, following a black shadow toward the hill.

Gorgias gazed at the plain behind the cruiser, where his

army of Herculeans had died. The ship sat where his own body had been burned beyond recognition. The Earthman walked the old battlefield as if nothing had happened.

The figure paused at the bottom of the hill and looked back to the ship, then turned and started upward. The ship's lock closed behind him like a cyclopean eye.

Kurbi leaned forward as he marched up the slope.

"Let him in!" Gorgias ordered.

Myraa would not move. She tried to hide her fear, but he saw at once that she was afraid for Kurbi's life.

The Earthman stopped halfway and looked out over the rolling grasslands, shielding his face from the hot afternoon sun. Then he turned again toward the house and continued his climb.

"Why is he so slow?" Gorgias said, struggling with Myraa. Finally, the figure came to the door and Gorgias hurled Myraa in front of the transparent panel. It slid open and the Earthman entered. He was unchanged from the tall, black-haired man Gorgias had first met here on Myraa's World. The same look of pity still lived in his eyes.

Myraa gazed up at him, unable to speak. Gorgias burgeoned within her, flowing with hatred for his destroyer. This was the man who had taken everything from him, leaving him as a dimensionless point within the mind of another.

"May I ask a few questions?" Kurbi said, looking around at the empty chairs in front of the windows. "Can we sit down?"

Myraa nodded.

Kurbi sat down. She took a facing chair and locked her hands together in her lap.

"Are you well?" he asked.

"Yes," she said softly, staring directly at him. "Why are you here?"

"I may be of some help." He was quiet for a moment. "What I've come for—I'll be honest—I want to dispel a few suspicions."

"He knows," Gorgias said within her. *"But how could he?"*

"What do you mean?" she asked.

"They're very nervous on Earth, especially since they failed to open the Whisper Ship after it locked us out, or locate its base."

Myraa's lips moved, but no sound came out for a moment. "We're at peace," she managed to say finally. "What can these fears have to do with us here?"

"I feel the same way. Perhaps you could return to Earth with me for a time. As leader of the survivors you could allay these suspicions."

"He must know something!"

Myraa raised walls around Gorgias, but he crumbled them. *"I won't hurt him, but let me see."*

Kurbi's face had not changed. It was still set in that patronizing stare, that look of pitying blindness.

"Tell him you'll go."

She resisted.

"Tell him!"

"All that you would have to do," the Earthman said, "is go before a group of people and repeat what you have told me—that your people wish to be left alone. I'll bring you back myself."

Gorgias wanted to leap at his throat, but he held back; there would be a better time.

Myraa felt her hands clench and unclench.

"Tell him!"

"If you don't come," Kurbi continued, "their suspicions will be increased and I will lose what influence I have. Their policies could endanger this planet." He paused. "I'm sorry to have to say this to you. Please agree to come back with me." He looked down at his feet.

"Very well," Myraa said of her own free will.

Kurbi got to his feet. "Come down to the ship when you're ready." He turned and walked to the door.

The darkness solidified around Gorgias, pushing inward to crush his awareness. Myraa had summoned help, he realized too late.

A cold morning light began to push the night away. He recognized the battlefield on Myraa's World. Herculean soldiers came out of the gloom and stood around him. He saw bodies everywhere, black from the burning.

The soldiers moved in. Their faces were burned inside their helmets, but there was no hatred in their eyes, only reproach.

"We came across time," one said, "giving up the defense of our homes to hold ourselves in readiness, when the need would be greater, and you wasted us."

"Better if you had destroyed the cylinder," another added. "We would not have suffered."

Gorgias stared back at them, realizing that he was free of

caring. They belonged to Myraa now, and should have nothing to complain about; they were alive, after all. If it had not been for him, they would have remained as bits of information inside a crystal forever.

They drew their weapons.

Beams flashed.

Gorgias felt his flesh burn and saw his right arm fall away. He sensed pain distantly, but no blood flowed.

His legs were cut off at the knees. Pain flooded into his brain. He had expected it this time, so it was more intense. He fell to the ground. They were turning him against himself, he realized as his left arm melted away.

The soldiers stood over him. They knew that he could not be killed, but they raised long metal spikes over his body.

One spike drove through his head, and he imagined its cold pass through the gray colloid of his brain. Another slid through his heart and pinned him to the black ground; blood spilled into his chest from the ruptured pump. The third shot through his guts, splintering his spine; and the last two spiked through the cartilage of his shoulders.

Myraa's World held him as he struggled to shatter the vivid impressions, but the soldiers held their spikes as he strained to lift himself.

"We are here," they said, "nothing can change that."

The sky flashed and thunder growled. Rain muddied the ground. He turned his head and saw charred bodies rising from the battlefield.

The storms were quiet inside her as she walked down to the ship. The surface of the universe was everything; sunny, grass-green, her planet wore no mask; the Earthship was a curious toy, waiting under a blue sky. The breeze blew through her long hair. She felt warm in the Herculean jump suit.

She came to the bottom of the hill and marched toward the ship. Kurbi looked out from the lock as she came into the ship's shadow and climbed the ramp.

"Your cabin is ready," he said as she stepped inside.

An abyss opened within her; she fell in and drifted over a muddy flatland. Puddles became mirrors as a white sun came out. Faces crowded to look out at her.

"This way," Kurbi said, leading her down a curving passage.

She tensed and followed as the quiet crept back into her. The faces in the puddles fell into shadow and faded, and she knew that Gorgias was still under control.

"Here we are." The Earthman turned and looked at her. "Are you well?"

She nodded and stepped to the door. "Thank you," she said as it opened and she went inside.

"We'll be leaving in a few minutes," he said as the door closed behind her and the lights came on.

The curved wall of the cabin was a depth mural of the Earth-Moon system with its ring of habitats. A small zero-g bed stood under the view. The bath was a small closet off to the right. A square locker stood at the foot of the bed.

She wondered if Gorgias could see through her eyes without her knowing it.

"Come in, General Crusus," Kurbi said.

The Herculean took a few steps into the center of the stateroom. "Do sit down," Kurbi added, shifting in his chair.

The stocky Herculean sat down and looked at him with black eyes.

"I would like to ask your impressions, if any," Kurbi began, "of the situation on this world."

Crusus shrugged. "What do you hope to find out?"

"Why haven't you decided to settle here, after your release?"

Crusus took a deep breath. "I've been asked all this before, but I'll tell you again. I have no religious feelings. I'm done with the Herculean past. There's nothing else to say."

"Is that all you can say?"

"What would you have me say? That my past threw me away? There is no past—only a few misguided individuals."

"I understand. But I have to ask these things. Do you believe there is any chance of some kind of new uprising here?"

Crusus almost smiled. "By whom? There is no force to speak of, no weapons."

"What about troop cylinders?"

"I understand there were very few of those, perhaps only one. I knew of no others when I was stored."

"But you do understand that it would take only one to start materializing the same weapons and fighting personnel over and over again? You yourself would be called up again, and each time you would be ignorant of what you know now."

"I tell you it was a fluke. You have the only cylinder. If there are others, no living Herculean has the means to find them!"

Kurbi was silent for a few moments. "I tend to agree. But, well... there is a feeling on Earth."

"I know. To settle the matter once and for all by destroying Myraa's World. The idea has a mind-settling elegance, doesn't it? We had it ourselves once, so I should know."

"You see the position I'm in."

He sighed. "Of course. You have to prove that it can't ever happen, that we Herculeans will never rise again, and you can't prove that. No one can. Not to the satisfaction of the suspicious." He laughed. "You're wasting your time, Kurbi."

"But I do care what happens."

"Do you? How can you, when I don't?"

Kurbi waited again. "What about the other survivors?"

"They've taken to Myraa's cult, even more so than the others. Just imagine yourself taken out of storage and thrown into a slaughter. And then to find out the war has been over for centuries! What do you expect? Did you have to kill nearly all of them?"

"We've spoken before, General, so you know that with me you have the most sympathetic listener possible. Better that I should find out what's going on than someone else."

Crusus raised an eyebrow. "Blackmail?"

"I have no such intention."

"Of course. Circumstances are blackmailing us both."

Kurbi took a deep breath. "What would you do in my place?"

"But there's nothing to uncover."

"It's an undercurrent. I felt it on Earth, and I feel it here."

"Isn't that to be expected?"

"Then you feel it too? What do you make of it? Please— be as explicit as you wish. No one will hold your views against you."

Crusus smiled sadly and sat back. "It means nothing, and there can be no support for any of my suspicions, nothing at all. We're talking about bad feelings, which tend to persist."

"I'd like to hear your suspicions, however unfounded."

"It's nothing specific, just something in the back of my mind insisting that it's not finished, all this, that it can't be over. Not a bit of evidence. As I said, it's just the residue left by the war. You feel the same thing. Suspicion, vague fears. It will disappear in time. Fear of the future, too."

"What do you mean?"

"That should be clear to you. If the numbers of Herculeans increase, it's inevitable that some of them will continue to resent what happened to them in the past. It seems unbelievable even now. How does a group live down such a destructive conflict, especially when people who lived through it persist? The offending generations died in past wars of this kind. The future could shrug off the past as something done by others."

"Evil didn't seem quite so bad when it could grow old and die."

Crusus was silent for a few moments. "Gorgias—what was he like, Kurbi?"

"He hated me. I stood for everything he hated. I feel that enmity even now. For a while I believed that I could reach an agreement with him. But the war had never ended for him. He believed with such force. And when he had his successes, they were terrifyingly effective. They haven't forgotten that on Earth."

"I find that hard to credit, given the erratic leadership I witnessed."

"Even great generals lose wars," Kurbi said, standing up. "Well, thank you anyway, General. What will you do after we reach Earth?"

Crusus rose. "Ship out to some obscure world and make a simpler life for myself, as far away from the past as possible."

"I wish you luck." Kurbi remembered his own wanderings among the frontier worlds of the Snake. "Will you remove any of your memories?"

Crusus looked at him. "I don't think so . . . I don't know. Thank you for the lift to Earth."

It's not finished, Kurbi thought as Crusus turned to leave.

The General stopped and faced him again. "Do you think I'll be detained on Earth for any reason?"

"I don't think so, but I can't promise. Myraa will reassure them. They'll be suspicious, but the matter may end with that. You're free to talk with her during the trip."

"Thank you. I'm not sure I want to. I've already heard what she has to offer. Do you wish me to question her? I can't find out anything that you couldn't for yourself, assuming that there is anything to learn."

"It's up to you, General."

Clearly, it was not over for Crusus, Kurbi thought as the Herculean left. It meant something to him to keep his memories, even if he wouldn't admit it to himself.

IV. The Heart of Fire

"...On every side,
spaces, the bat-wing of insanity!
Above, below me, only depths and shoal,
the silence! And the Lord's right arm
traces his nightmare, truceless, multiform.
I cuddle the insensible blank air,
and fear to sleep as one fears a great hole.
My spirit, haunted by its vertigo,
sees the infinite at every window..."

—Baudelaire, *The Abyss*

HE ROCKED THE DARKNESS back and forth, slowly trying
to open a space for himself within the rigidity of Myraa's will;
but his struggles created only a painful vibration.

He reached inward, stabbing more deeply into the infinitesimal, probing the quantum realm of softening determinisms,
collapsing lengths and fluid energies.

Again the heart of fire seemed unimaginably distant, but he
knew that he was kin to its burning assertiveness—an individual pulse shaped by the categories of space-time. If the way
out through Myraa's body was closed, then he would voyage
inward.

He moved in closer, diminishing before the unattainable
force-center of the will.

"Can you answer me?" he asked. "Do you know me?"

231

There was no answer, and he realized that it was blind, unknowing, the source of all motive, but without the power of decision.

The fools!

They worshipped it, drew their life from its outpouring, its waste.

But he would learn to use its infinite strength. Its transcendent heart would become his own.

If Myraa would not let him out, he would penetrate all that lay within and master it. Then he would shatter Myraa's control and reach out through her into the universe of decision, where everything was a facade, the masked will striving to persist, giving the world permanence.

He spiraled toward the force-center, circling endlessly, exerting all his will to draw nearer. He felt its repulsion; it pushed him back by minute degrees, slowly stealing his forward gains.

He threw himself inward, reaching out with all his longing from the endless night. He imagined that the Whisper Ship was around him, carrying him toward the fire. He shrank into a point, concentrating his strength into the tip of a spear, yearning to join his spark with the great conflagration at the heart of all things.

Suddenly a pulse stabbed into him, filling his will to the core. He was hurled away, upward, growing large swiftly, racing outward at the edge of an expanding universe.

He filled Myraa instantly, giving her no chance to resist.

Her eyes opened and he looked around the cabin.

"May I come in?" General Crusus asked over the com.

"Come in," Myraa said.

The door slid open and Crusus stepped inside.

Myraa leaped at him. She wrapped her legs around his waist and her hands locked around his throat.

"Traitor!" Gorgias shouted, digging into the windpipe.

Crusus gulped air. His arms clawed at Myraa's back, but there was nothing to grab.

Gorgias felt the windpipe collapse. Crusus fell backward onto the floor. A gurgling sound came from his throat. His eyes stared. The body twitched once, then lay still under Myraa.

Gorgias stared into the man's face as Myraa's trembling hands drew away.

"What have you done?" her voice asked faintly.

"He deserved to die," Gorgias said through the same mouth.

He looked toward the bath. "He'll fit in the disposal when I'm through with him."

"Wait—"

He pushed her away, drowning her objections in the whirl of his thoughts.

"—let me go . . ." Myraa cried faintly.

Kurbi was here on the ship.

He would die next.

Myraa gathered her forces.

He had sensed her distant actions while he was cutting up Crusus and feeding the pieces into the round waste opening. She lurked at the horizon of his mind, drawing the others into a circle around him.

He pushed the last pieces of the General's corpse into the recycler and concentrated on repelling the attack.

Bundles of energy crept over the horizon and combined to form a line of blinding white light. He spun his attention, facing in all directions at once. The circle contracted, touched him, then opened again as he pushed it away. The bright ribbon fled to the horizon and disappeared into the darkness.

Gorgias pulsed, ready to repel the next constriction.

Spears of light shot in over the horizon, making him the hub of an incomplete wheel. He concentrated and stopped the spokes halfway.

Slowly, the wheel turned around him, waiting for him to weaken, but he held the beams back. The wheel burned, straining to complete itself; the spokes yearned to bury themselves in his heart. He opened his will and threw them back into the blackness.

He looked around and saw Myraa's eyes from the inside; he came up to them and looked out into the quiet of the cabin.

Kurbi paused before the door to Myraa's cabin.

"Rafael Kurbi," he said over the com. "May I come in?"

The door slid open.

Hands reached for him as he stepped inside. They closed around his throat, tightened and pulled him down.

"Now it's your turn," Myraa said with a hiss.

Kurbi grabbed her wrists, but they were immovable. He managed to stay on his feet, gasping for breath as stars began to explode in his skull.

"What—?" he started to say as he staggered back. He saw

her eyes. There was a joyous look in them. He moved forward and fell on top of her, pinning her to the floor, but she held his throat high as he searched for a vulnerable place to grab. Her legs locked around his waist; finally, his hands found her face and he pressed his thumbs into her eyes.

Myraa's pain danced through Gorgias as she threw him back from her eyes. He slipped out of her limbs and floated in space.

The wheel appeared again around him.

"No!" he shouted as the bright spokes transfixed him.

The completed wheel pulsed, increasing strength to hold him prisoner at the hub.

Myraa's fingers loosened from Kurbi's throat. He wheezed and rolled to one side of Myraa's limp form. Breathing heavily, he looked up and saw her kneeling near him, watching, ready to pounce when he moved.

"Why?" he asked in a rasping voice.

She touched his shoulder and shook her head; then she closed her eyes and breathed deeply.

"I can tell you now," she said after a moment. She opened her eyes. "We'll be safe for a time."

The beams burned.

There could be no relief, no unconsciousness. If he had still been flesh and blood, the pain would have driven his body to its natural limits and released him. Here there was pain without physical damage, endless agony without the abyss of morphia.

The beams seemed motionless, passing into him; yet there was no body he could see—no hand to hold up to his eyes, no feet to look down at, no throat or gut to feel. He was a point in a special space, but the pain was real, a succession of aches, stabs and twists marching into his deepest places. Mountains of flesh were burned raw, bones and teeth broken, lungs and membranes ripped; bladders of memory were cut open and drained.

The wheel turned slowly, and the spokes became sharp knives. How long could Myraa's cohorts keep this up? There had to be laws and limits in these regions also, and a way to turn them to his purpose.

Kurbi took a deep breath. How could he believe what Myraa had just told him?

"You'll have to restrain me," she added.

Her attack was explained by the situation she had just described, but how to check her story?

"He'll try to kill you again," she said.

"But if this is true, I'll have to restrain you indefinitely."

"Until he can be permanently weakened, at least. We did not foresee how much strength his hatred would draw, or his will to explore and learn. He's discovering things we've only suspected."

Kurbi looked into her eyes. "Is all this true? Can it be true?"

"What would I gain by lying?" Her left hand shook.

"You tried to kill me. Perhaps this is a delusion of some kind. You may be very ill."

"You must not doubt me."

"Would it stop him if you were killed?"

"I don't know. If I were taken by another, Gorgias would persist. Perhaps he no longer needs me. But there is no one nearby to take me if I die."

"What about Crusus?"

"I took him quickly, before Gorgias could notice. Crusus will need time to recover from the shock. I have hidden him."

Kurbi gazed at her silently.

"You don't believe me," she said.

"It's not easy."

Her eyes were steady. "Lock me in this cabin."

Maybe Gorgias's death had affected Myraa more than she could admit, Kurbi thought as he stared at the grayness of jumpspace on the screen. It was all a delusion, he told himself, wondering how he would explain the General's disappearance on Earth. The situation was curious, whether Myraa was telling the truth or not; much worse if she had told the truth; Earth's fears would be confirmed. Myraa's World would be destroyed.

Searching himself, Kurbi realized that at bottom he believed what she had told him because it also confirmed his own ignorant fears. A massive struggle was going on beneath appearances.

The wheel flickered and winked out.

Free again, Gorgias searched for Myraa's eyes. They opened suddenly when he slipped into her limbs and looked out into the cabin.

"The door is locked," she said, floating in bed. "He knows everything."

"It won't do him any good," Gorgias said as he withdrew into the darkness.

V. The Listener

"...noon draws near
And fastens in the gloom. What is it brings
Such sorrow to the air,—a power, a cold
As from blown flame? Is it from plague, from strife,
Blood crying from the ground? Nay, the young life
Of centuries has hurtled overhead,
And lingers, vanquished, and not growing old,
Youth's stubborn, immature, unburied dead."

—"Michael Field" (1908)

HE WOULD NOT REPORT what Myraa had told him, Kurbi decided as the ship slipped out of jumpspace.

Earth lay ahead, an ancient jewel set in the ring of habitats. The younger worlds sparkled, but they could not compete with the awesome character of the planet. Its ocean of air concealed enigmas; its ocean of water held all the mysteries of origins. The land covered the rubble of countless civilizations, all imperfectly understood or lost. The Earth was an unconscious underworld of histories; its ring of worlds was more conscious, cortical, separate, but not completely free of the birthing place....

What could he report? There was no physical evidence that Myraa had killed Crusus. It would be easier to conclude that the General had never been on board. Her story about Gorgias would be heard with suspicion, but many would conclude that it was the delusion of one who had loved the Herculean rebel;

it was not uncommon for people to believe that they could talk to their lost loved ones. Myraa's World, home of nearly all remaining Herculeans, might be lost if Earth's fears were fed needlessly. Why add to the problem with unverifiable reports?

The existence of Myraa's World came first, he told himself as the ship made its approach to the orbital docks.

"You've told me a strange story," he said to Myraa in her cabin. "Why should anyone believe it? Whether I believe it doesn't count. If the Commission accepts what you say, it will only stir them up and put your world in danger."

"But Crusus is dead."

"I'll say he never came on board. Answer only general questions, as calmly as possible."

"But there may be danger," she insisted.

"What kind of danger?"

She looked at him. "If he gains control of me—"

"What can we do? You'll be under guard."

"A cell, physical restraints, unconsciousness. You may have to kill me!"

"How can I accept what you're saying? Even if it's true, what can he do? He'll use your body as you would. He can't make it walk through walls, or fly away. You're not armed. Don't you see? What you say may decide whether your world will continue to exist. Nothing is as important as that."

The large oval chamber was harshly lit by daylight, but Myraa did not squint, Kurbi noticed as she entered and approached the half-moon table. Poincaré, the youngest of the six-member War Dispositions Commission, sat at the left end of the table.

"What have you to say to us?" Eliade Aren asked.

The Prime Commissioner was a thin, silver-haired woman. Only a century old, she was too young to remember the war, but long-term memory imprints had given her the same gaze as that of the four members who had lived through the war with the Herculeans. She would probably add to her imprinting, Kurbi suspected, long after the other members had gone on to become other people. It was a trap well known to the memory librarians, Kurbi thought. I probably have a touch of it myself.

Myraa looked up at the Prime Commissioner. "We live our lives, we who have survived."

Aren blinked slowly. "And you are at peace?"

"We are."

Aren shrugged subtly. "But you are troubled?"

"That is our concern."

Kurbi tensed.

"When an old enemy is troubled," Aren said softly, "the victor must reconfirm victory."

"You have nothing to fear."

Aren smiled. "We shall require more than your assurance."

Kurbi stepped to Myraa's side. "I can give that, having just visited the Herculean refuge. There is nothing there to harm us, now or ever."

"And how do *you* know? Are we obliged to accept your word also? You—the sympathizer?"

"Historian, to be accurate," Kurbi replied.

Julian shifted in his seat.

"You have written," she continued, "that our extermination, as you put it, of the Herculeans might have been less complete."

"We might have gained more if some large part of their civilization had survived. We had no spoils for our effort, as many have pointed out."

"What evidence did you bring?" she asked. She did not expect to be convinced, Kurbi realized. He glanced at Poincaré. Julian's face was a mask.

"Need I remind the Prime Commissioner," Poincaré said unexpectedly, "that Rafael Kurbi tracked and cornered the Herculean renegade, thus ending the menace? He spent many years accomplishing this task, for which he deserves our respect and gratitude."

"He did so reluctantly," Aren added, gazing steadily at Kurbi.

He stared back. "To repeat, there was not as much to gain from a dead enemy as a live one. The death of Gorgias denied us knowledge of his ship and the location of his base. Major losses for a dead body."

Aren leaned forward. "I've examined these various claims of benefits from Herculean civilization. I don't find them convincing, either the cultural or the technical gains."

Julian stood up. "Then what do you expect from this hearing? Nothing, if you believe their culture was so barren, both technically and culturally. You contradict yourself, Prime Commissioner!" He sat down.

Aren seemed unsure, but she composed herself. "I did not say there was absolutely nothing for us. I said there was nothing in what had been presented. I wish to uncover what is being concealed from us."

Poincaré gestured with his right hand. "Then get on with it, and be satisfied when you find nothing but your own reflection. Otherwise there will be no end to it."

Aren glanced at him, but he ignored her.

"We will continue," she said, looking back at Kurbi, then at Myraa. "Kindly tell us something about your way of life."

"We grow our own food, build our own shelter."

"Are there children?"

Kurbi tensed again.

"Very few."

Aren's face grew taut, as if some suspicion had been confirmed. "Now tell us about your . . . beliefs."

Kurbi looked at the faces of the other commissioners. Jastov, Onell and Webst seemed bored. They had come here to assure themselves that there was nothing to Aren's fears before divesting themselves of their war memories. Ona Aren shared her sister's ideas, but that was not surprising; they were both closely allied with the Oldest, many of whom had never learned to clear their minds through forgetfulness.

"We look inward," Myraa said, "toward the center of all life. . . ."

Aren raised a hand. "No need for details. We're sufficiently familiar with many of the claims of your cult. I want to know something specific. Is there a practical basis to this Herculean inwardness, as it is described, implying certain weapons characteristics? What do you say to this?"

"Exaggerations," Poincaré said, looking upward.

Myraa was silent.

Aren looked at Kurbi. "And what do you say?"

Her hatred had told her that it had to be true, he thought. She needed for it to be true, so she could move against Myraa's World.

"No one is sure," Aren said. "You share my suspicions."

"What are you talking about!" Julian shouted.

"She knows!" Aren cried, pointing at Myraa. "Just this. The Herculean survivors are planning to field a new kind of weapon against us, one involving forces directed by a mental science which they have been nurturing for centuries."

Poincaré laughed.

"Her planet must be destroyed while we are still able to do so."

"Insanity," Kurbi said.

"Then put my fears to rest."

"How could anyone know? You've made up your mind. Prove to us that it exists, but don't burden us with having to disprove your suspicions."

"If we destroy the planet," Julian continued, "we won't prove anything, one way or the other."

"It will be safer," Aren said. "The consequences of letting the Omega cult develop may be too dangerous to take any chances. Weighing doubts may be fatal."

Gorgias listened.

The whispers had to penetrate light-years of lead, but they reached him, and their meaning gave him new strength. The last stronghold of Herculean life would be destroyed unless he acted.

Bypassing the armor of Myraa's conscious effort, he filled her musculature and looked out into the oval chamber. She struggled against him, but he held her rigid.

"We stand to lose everything," Aren was saying.

Gorgias turned and struck Kurbi across the heart. The Earthman grunted and fell to his knees.

"Yes!" Gorgias hissed through Myraa's throat. "But it's too late!"

He reached into the underwill and drew what he needed.

Aren rose, pale.

Contorting space-time, Gorgias picked her up with invisible fingers and crushed her against the floor in front of the half-moon table.

The other commissioners were getting to their feet. Gorgias glanced over at Kurbi. The Earthman was still on his knees, staring at the broken body of Aren.

Gorgias whirled around. Armed guards were taking a fix on him. He reached out to crush them, but Kurbi grabbed him around the legs. The restraining field caught them as Myraa's body hit the floor.

"Too late!" Gorgias shouted in the grayness of the inverted bell. The guards had not acted quickly enough to save the Prime Commissioner.

Kurbi wrestled with Myraa's body, trying to pin her to the floor. Gorgias looked into his eyes, then hurled the Earthman upward, pressing him against the field.

"I've waited for this," Gorgias said as he stood up. "You know what I'm going to do? Strip off your arms, legs and genitals. And then your eyes!"

Kurbi hung silently above him.

Gorgias concentrated on his right arm and wrenched it into a breaking position.

"Myraa!" Kurbi cried out.

The field winked out and Kurbi fell on him. Stunned, Gorgias concentrated his will, but the Earthman was lifted from him and the bell reappeared. He took a deep breath and got up. No matter, he would kill them all next time.

He looked around the small area of gloom, wondering if he could strike through the canopy.

"Are you hurt?" Julian asked.

Kurbi was unsteady on his feet as he looked around. "Yes," he said, struggling to control his fear.

The guards were still adjusting the shield's field strength from the portable projector. Eliade Aren was being wheeled out to the nearest freezer.

"This does it, Raf. Nothing can save Myraa's World now." He looked at the four other commissioners. They were talking together near the main exit. "My one vote won't mean a thing." Kurbi caught Ona Aren's eye, but she looked away. "I suppose you have an explanation?"

Kurbi stared at him, unable to speak. Everything Myraa had said was true.

"I know what happened," Kurbi managed to say.

Poincaré turned to the guards. "Is it secure?"

The senior officer nodded.

"Get the commissioners out of here."

When they were alone, Julian said, "We won't be able to contain this. Too many saw it." He looked at the bloody spot on the floor. "What do you know, Raf?"

"I wasn't sure until now." Kurbi told him what he had learned from Myraa.

Poincaré was silent for a few moments after Kurbi finished. "It was criminal of you not to tell me," he said, "even though I see why you were skeptical. I wouldn't have believed it. Still, we might have saved Aren from this, monster though she was."

He shook his head. "As my friend you should have told me, no matter what."

Kurbi began to pace, thinking wildly. Gorgias should have killed the entire Commission. Then no one would have known what had happened and Myraa's World might be safe. "I can't think any more about this, Julian. Worse, I don't even want to care. Why did you drag me back into all this?"

"You still know more than anyone."

"A lot of good it does. So, what do we do now?"

"Talk to whatever is inside." He stepped over to the controls and made an adjustment.

The bell of force shimmered, as if about to dissolve. Myraa's shape became visible, but it appeared deformed, huge in head and torso, small in the legs. Her mouth opened and closed like that of a huge fish gasping for air.

"Myraa?" Kurbi asked, stepping close and peering in.

"Yes," she said, her mouth a cave, "I'm here."

"We can't be sure," Julian said.

"You must not release me," she warned. "I've hurled him back, but I'm too weak to do it again."

"It must be her," Kurbi said.

"Why should he tip his hand?"

"The destruction of my world," she continued, "will do nothing to stop Gorgias."

"We may have to kill her," Poincaré said.

"It may be too late," Myraa whispered weakly. "He may be able to survive without me now."

"What should we do?" Kurbi asked.

"I can no longer advise. You should probably kill me, in the hope that he won't be experienced enough to keep himself together. He may misjudge his powers. I don't know. . . ."

"We'll keep her in the field," Julian said, "but in a cell, where we can pipe in life-support. We can't risk giving him a way out."

Kurbi nodded.

"I understand," Myraa said.

"Are you in pain?" Julian asked.

"I'm not in danger."

Kurbi looked around the chamber. He's here, he thought, slipping through the substructures of reality, rebuilding his strength, struggling toward me with a terrible hatred, an unshakable resolve.

"Leave my world to live," Myraa pleaded.

"If we could only trap him somehow," Julian said, "then we might stop the destruction of her world. But what is there to catch? A quantum ghost, more elusive than neutrinos. And we can't be sure that her death would stop him. His own certainly didn't. If all this is true."

"All that is left of him is his hatred," Myraa said.

For the first time since he had met her, Kurbi saw Myraa weep. Giant, distorted tears burst from her eyes and flowed down to the cave of her mouth.

VI. The Fortress Self

> "Mischiefs feed
> Like beasts, till they be fat, and then they bleed."
>
> —Ben Jonson, *Volpone*

GORGIAS REACHED OUT, searching for the Whisper Ship.

He visualized it, imagining that he was near the vessel.

The true nature of space-time was not the continuum of forward-flowing, relative times; he was learning an underlying unity; only adapted mental structures made distinctions, allowing for the experience of separate spaces and durations; but these seemingly external settings were mere aspects, observer-defined islands afloat on a quantum sea.

Passages in space-time were journeys across mental realms, nothing more, if the will were brave enough to break from its given categories.

He probed the Whisper Ship at its dock in the Centauri system. Energies flowed as the vessel's intelligence came to full alert.

Gorgias poised himself for the quantum transfer, leaped—

—but the ship failed to integrate him into its structure.

He dropped back into Myraa's prison.

He gathered his strength and tried again—

—and fell back, exhausted.

Myraa's mazes would hold him forever, he realized, unless he learned the patience necessary to concentrate the intensity of his conscious will enough to pass from one energy state to a higher one.

"I am in danger," he whispered as he waited, "come to me."

The ship shifted.

Far away, but also deep within him.

For an instant, the universe pulsed at his center, and he knew the possibility of engulfing galaxies, breathing at the heart of every sun, drinking the radiation of collapsing suns, feasting on the cores of imploding galaxies.

There was a direct way of doing things in the realm of unity. Myraa had tried to confine him in a maze, but she needed his cooperation to succeed. He had to force himself to think differently.

"Then forget the past," she said. "Don't let it drag you back."

"You should have let me die!" he answered. "Here I can't die, and I will rule!"

She was silent, but he felt her fear within himself.

And he felt the ship wrench itself from its dock and regain the freedom of space. The vessel came swiftly, swallowing the four light-years between Centauri and Earth; it came across the infinite inner gray of mental substance called jumpspace, which had elsewhere flowered into the facade of an external universe.

Kurbi peered into the field. Myraa had been motionless for three hours now.

Her eyes opened suddenly. "The ship has broken free. It's coming here!"

"It's beginning," Kurbi said.

"We can probably repel it," Julian said from the control unit.

"I'm not so sure. It's coming for her, and to destroy the Earth."

"Then we'll have to leave for Myraa's World at once," Julian said, "if only to draw the ship away."

Kurbi nodded, knowing that it was going to happen. "How many ships are within striking distance of Myraa's World?"

"Enough to sterilize the planet. We were right, as it turns out. We can't kill her now. We need her to draw the Whisper Ship away from Earth."

"But she *is* the ship. Gorgias is within her, controlling the vessel."

"We can't be sure, Raf. She told us herself. We can't be certain that by killing her we'll destroy the ship's command.

It might already have enough new directives to operate on its own. We can't kill our only hostage at this point." He turned away from the control unit, walked over to Kurbi and stared into the bell. "At any moment," he continued, "I will receive orders to destroy Myraa's World, especially if the medics find that Aren's brain is hopelessly damaged and can't be recovered."

Soldiers came into the oval chamber. Kurbi and Poincaré stood back as the bell was levitated out into the corridor.

"We have to board in the next few minutes, Raf. Are you coming?"

Kurbi hesitated. "What choice do I have?"

Myraa's World was a ball of ocean wrapped in a clear membrane of atmosphere. The yellow-orange sun stood guard nearby, blindly blazing away its vast store of energy. Stars are the engines of life, Kurbi thought, collapsing inward so they can radiate outward as they drive the evolution of their worlds across time, unfolding possibility and choice, finally destroying the worthy and worthless alike. Suns are insane parents.

What should have been was too hard, he told himself as he waited. *It was much easier to destroy the Herculeans then, and it is still easier now. Gorgias, where are you?* Kurbi called within himself. *Come save your world!*

One hundred ships waited for him in polar orbit.

"We've got him on sensors," Julian said next to Kurbi on the bridge. The screen turned gray. The Whisper Ship was a black smudge in the vast unreality of otherspace.

"Any moment now," Julian said.

The screen switched to a normal view. The distant stars seemed to be waiting. Kurbi felt the old curiosity and surprise at being himself and not someone else, of being contained in his own skull. Something oceanic, general, became specific and self-conscious when confined to the self's point in space.

The Whisper Ship caught the yellow-orange sunlight and seemed to burst into a small nova.

Beams lashed out from the fleet and tracked.

The vessel winked out.

"What's he doing?" Kurbi asked as the screen scanned jumpspace.

The black smudge came toward them and seemed to explode as it rushed into the screen and disappeared.

"I didn't think . . ." Poincaré said softly, stunned.

"What is it?"

"I didn't think it possible . . ."

"What's wrong?" Kurbi tensed as he watched the black stars on the gray screen.

"His ship's inside ours! Look at the readings! And there's nothing we can do."

The brig outside the force bell flickered. Distortions appeared, throwing shadows into Myraa's prison. Fearful, she pressed her face against the clouded lens of the bell and peered out. The walls of the rectangular brig were flickering very fast now.

She saw the door slide open. A guard came in, threw up his hands and disintegrated.

The flicker became imperceptible as the chamber outside the barrier exploded with white light.

The brightness faded. Myraa recognized the control room of the Whisper Ship. The Herculean vessel had passed through the Earth ship, materializing for the instant needed to snatch her and the bell from the brig.

"Too late!" Poincaré cried.

The screen blinked to normal view. Beams cut across space after the ship.

"He's thumbing his nose at us," Poincaré said. "No other reason to come out of jumpspace."

The ship winked out. The screen switched, but the smudge was already invisible against the black disk of the sun.

"Track!" Poincaré shouted.

"He'll scatter his wake through the sun," Kurbi said, "and get just far enough ahead of us so we can't catch him."

"Doesn't matter. We know where he's going."

Don't come back, Kurbi thought. *Disappear forever. There's enough galaxy out there for you to find a safe home. Leave us alone.*

Gorgias switched the ship through the star and continued on a random course through bridgespace.

He knew why the ship had accepted him completely into its own systems: Myraa's presence was now identical to his own, thus making it possible for him to flow through the artificial intelligence without abandoning her body. By rescuing Myraa, the ship had also solved the problem of integrating him into itself.

Gorgias looked into the control room. Myraa seemed unconscious inside the force bell. He reached out to the control unit and turned off the shield. Her eyelids fluttered as she struggled to remain standing. He seized her body before she could fall, walked her over to the command station and sat her down.

The ship would run its random course for a few hours, then return to the Snake.

Kurbi watched the screen.

"There," Julian said, pointing. "He's back in the Snake, on a course for Earth."

"He shows a renewed confidence," Kurbi said.

"You would too, after that maneuver. We'll have to push hard to keep up."

"Do you think Earth has enough firepower to destroy him?"

"Sure—if the ship can be tracked long enough to dump a sun's energy into it. He'll take his time getting to Earth."

Kurbi looked around the bridge. A few of the officers were staring at him from their stations. A junior officer seemed to be struggling to control his fear. One of the engineers seemed skeptical. They all knew that Gorgias was dead, Kurbi realized, but the two lunatics in command were talking as if the Herculean had risen from the dead.

Myraa opened her eyes.

"I'm free of you," Gorgias said over the ship-com.

She searched herself and found only distant echoes. Gorgias was still anchored within her, but he also flowed through the ship. She was too weak to pull him back.

"You'll see them all die," he said, laughing.

"If he answers," Poincaré said, "we'll have further confirmation that this crazy business is true." He glanced at the communications officer.

Subspace beams chased after the Whisper Ship.

Kurbi watched the gray screen.

It flickered after a few moments and Myraa's face appeared.

Kurbi waited for Gorgias to speak through her, but another

voice sounded in the Whisper Ship's control room. "You could not kill me, Kurbi! Now you'll see what I'll do to Earth!"

"He's . . . in the ship also," Myraa struggled to say.

There was a long pause. Myraa's face became a mask.

"Now he controls her and the ship," Kurbi whispered.

"Turn back now," Julian said, "or we'll destroy Myraa's World."

The featureless voice growled in anger and was silent. "Very well," it said finally and cut the link.

Kurbi shot a glance at Julian.

"What can we do, Raf? I hope it will only have to be a threat."

"The way he snatched Myraa suggests to me that he may have more in reserve than we can guess."

"A cheap trick. Impressive, but we're a hundred ships."

Kurbi shook his head. "There's more happening than we can see."

"You think he'll sweep through and kidnap us both?"

"Why not?"

"We *can* destroy him. It's not impossible."

"Assuming you can keep the ship in the beams long enough to do damage. Destroying Myraa's World won't stop him either. It'll just free him of an obligation and stiffen his resolve."

"He must believe that we *will* destroy it."

"He'll call our bluff, Julian. We're dealing with a terrorist of some experience."

"Then, we will destroy the place and follow him. What else can we do?"

"The planet is no hostage at all, therefore. The people there are innocent, so you might just as well leave it alone."

"Earth may send someone else to do it if I don't."

Kurbi glared at Poincaré. "Then let them. There may be enough time for the situation to change, so why rush into it?"

"Raf, we can't leave him a place to come back to."

"He doesn't need it! He can always retreat to his base. You know that."

Poincaré looked around the bridge. "Keep alert! He'll appear at any moment." The officers were silent, watching their instruments nervously.

Kurbi turned his chair away and stared at the screen.

VII. The Weapon

"Ourself behind ourself, concealed—"

—Emily Dickinson

THE FLEET WAITED in high orbit over Myraa's World.

Kurbi watched the sun. "He'll come out of the star," he said. *I got too close to him,* Kurbi thought. *He's never forgiven me for pitying him.*

"We'll hold him in a cross fire as long as possible," Poincaré said as ships moved off to take up positions. "What do you think he's planning?"

"He's not coming to surrender," Kurbi said.

Someone laughed behind him. Kurbi turned around. Birkut, the navigator, gave him a sheepish grin. Kurbi nodded to him, and the man returned to his scrutiny of the 3-D tank in the center of the bridge.

Kurbi turned to face Poincaré's chair again. "That one was born on New Mars after the ice age set in," the Security Chief whispered. "A hick, but a great technician."

"Gorgias must have the survivors on Myraa's World," Kurbi continued. "There's no hope for a future without them. So we must expect him to make a stand if their lives are threatened."

"He can't hope to do more than delay us in a direct confrontation. We have him now. He has no choice but to fight."

He's decided to stand and die, Kurbi thought, *rather than live without power over the people who will build the new Herculean Empire....*

"It *is* him, isn't it?" Julian asked.

"I think so."

"The ship is a menace, whether it's run by Myraa or some pattern left behind by Gorgias."

The alarm wailed.

"All ships!" Poincaré cried. "Full alert!"

The screens flickered around the control pit, filtering the glare of the yellow-orange sun. The Whisper Ship was a black spot on the bright disk.

"Here we go," Poincaré said.

Kurbi tensed in his chair. A suspicion was forming in his mind.

"Look at that," Julian said.

The ship glowed white, flared and seemed to explode.

"Jump!" Poincaré shouted as the flare expanded and rushed through the fleet. Kurbi felt a kick in his stomach.

The screens paled, but the color was not quite gray. There was a red tinge in the pallor of jumpspace, as if a fire were burning beyond the ashen veil.

Kurbi gripped the armrests and waited.

Slowly, other escaping ships entered the safety of jumpspace. They appeared slowly, straining to switch over.

"How many?" Poincaré demanded after a few moments.

"Twenty-three!" one of the officers shouted in a broken voice.

Poincaré stared at the main screen. "Come on, a few more," he whispered, but no more black globes appeared. "They've been destroyed," he admitted finally, his voice shaking. "Search for survivors in normal space."

The stars kindled into colors.

There was no debris, no lifepods, barely a residue of radiation in the home continuum.

"He'll make for Earth now," Julian said as he turned his chair to face Kurbi. "Did you notice the speed of the expansion? We couldn't react fast enough. Worlds will be nothing before a weapon of that kind." He was beginning to sweat.

So you've found it, Kurbi thought, *your ultimate vengeance weapon.*

"Alert all worlds in the Snake!" Poincaré ordered, pulling himself together; but strain showed in the stoop of his shoulders and the tightness of his face. "Should have killed her when she first told us," he said softly, shaking his head. "We waited too long, Raf." He looked up. "Follow at a safe distance," he snapped, "if there is such a thing." He sat back and spun around to face forward again. "Too long," he repeated.

The screens flashed the normal gray-white as the fleet jumped.

"We should have destroyed the place," Poincaré said as Myraa's sun blackened behind them. "It wasn't worth seventy-seven ships...."

"Why didn't you?" a voice demanded.

Kurbi turned around. It was the navigator, Birkut. Next to him, the junior officer seemed to be losing his battle against the fear Kurbi had glimpsed before. The entire eight-member bridge team seemed to be waiting for an answer. They had lost many friends, perhaps even loved ones, on the other ships.

There was nothing anyone could say to them.

He would burn worlds all the way to Earth.

A thousand planets would be no great effort, Gorgias realized. By the time he entered Earth's sunspace, he would control a flare large enough to vaporize the whole system. There seemed to be no limit to the size of the sphere he could will into existence.

The force-center flowed through him as the ship slipped through the Snake's jumpspace. There was no fatigue as he flared the ball of energy around the ship, testing the bubble's strength. The sphere expanded with the fury of his will, whether he was in normal space or not. He would avenge the death of every Herculean world fifty times over.

He would save Earth for last, to give their surviving ships time to return for a humiliating last stand.

And when the inhabited planets of the Snake were only faint traces of starstuff, he would return to Myraa's World. There he would destroy her will and take her shape for his own. He would leave her to suffer endlessly in the dungeons of his mind; in time he would forget her, and she would fade away.

It would be a universe without enemies, swept clean from Earth to the Cluster. History would begin again for his kind, and no one would challenge its course.

"But Earth will live in us," Myraa said. "We are its offspring."

Surprised, he tried to shut her out, but her thoughts shot into him like a swarm of insects, scattering into his most secret places.

He contorted her innards and forced her to bite her hands until they bled. She cried out, writhing in her seat. Her insect-thoughts died within him and he released her.

"You'll need your enemies," she said out loud and hurled her pain into him.

He twisted away, laughing.

"You are nothing without their fear."

The Whisper Ship flickered out of jumpspace, swimming again onto the surface of space-time.

New Mars lay ahead.

Gorgias listened as he swept toward the planet. The globe sang with pleas and protests. Someone had sent out a warning. He remembered the small effort he had once made to destroy it; now he would finish the job.

He watched for signs of resistance. They came at the last moment, a few beams from the exit beacon, as the edge of his expanding field whisked away the planet's atmosphere.

Heat buckled and cracked the crust.

The advancing ice age was cut short as the oceans boiled.

The globe glowed and exploded.

Gorgias passed through the shards and hot gasses. He looked back as he switched into jumpspace.

The star was alone, black in the ashes.

"It's not there," Julian said as they passed the place where New Mars had been. "Even the exit beacon is gone."

Rensch is dead, Kurbi thought.

"Psia kref!" the navigator cursed behind him. He would never go home again, Kurbi realized.

"How did we let things get this far?" the junior officer asked in a piping voice.

"Quiet!" the first officer said.

Poincaré stared at the screens. "It'll be one world after another now."

Seventy-seven ships and a world for my mistakes. Kurbi glanced at Julian. The Security Chief was sitting sideways, looking cynical and defeated.

"The old paranoids on Earth sensed it somehow," he said. "They knew!"

"I'm sorry, Julian, for whatever it's worth."

"Go back and destroy Myraa's World!" an unfamiliar voice shouted.

"Fools!" another added.

Poincaré whirled his chair around to face the speakers, but his anger died and he shrugged. "It would have taken a god to foresee this. Say what you wish. It will not be held against you, but I demand order on this ship. . . ."

How will I live with myself when Earth is gone? Kurbi asked himself. *There will be no one to take the memory from me.*

"Perhaps Myraa can still do something," Julian said. "If she's still alive."

The navigator laughed. "Fat chance! She's with them."

He'll save us for last.

"We have to follow him," Poincaré said softly. "He'll want an audience before he finishes us."

Kurbi nodded. *I'll be there.*

VIII.   Mind Net

"What value can a creature have that is not a whit different from millions of its kind? Millions, do I say? nay, an infiniture of creatures which, century after century, in never ending flow, Nature sends bubbling up from her inexhaustible springs; as generous with them as the smith with the useless sparks that fly around his anvil."

—Schopenhauer

"The inability of most people to feel the pain of others as if it were their own is what makes evil possible."

—Andrei Amalrik

GORGIAS SURGED THROUGH the ship.

He ingested its routines, penetrated systems-structures and stood before the hordes of memory. Quantum entities flashed everywhere within the leviathan of remembrance and reasoning.

Cool and abstract, the infinitesimal universe of the ship's intelligence was free of time and will; these, Gorgias realized, came in from outside, setting the ship's creatures into purposeful activity.

Observing his link to the force-center, the ship had channeled energy through him, shaping the destructive sphere of energy, treating him as a component part of itself. His capacities were an integral part of the ship now—time and will incorporated into a universe hungry for function. The vessel was his servant, but it spared him details; he was its highest function.

Better this universe, with its ties to the existence he had known, than the abasement of Myraa's interiors.

Gorgias shaped an image of himself on the screen and looked out into the control room. Myraa stared at him, unimpressed.

He heard a distant seething.

A withering wind threw him back from the screen.

He fell. Minds invaded him, gnawing at his will. Whispers cut into him like razors, drowning out his thoughts.

"... let go, let go ..."

"... what is lost cannot be reclaimed ..."

"... infinity beckons ..."

"... yet you strive to reenter the realm of preparation ..."

"... follow us ..."

"... do not look back ..."

"... look ahead to knowledge and bliss. ..."

"No!" Gorgias shouted, realizing that he had underestimated Myraa again. And he knew how much he needed to be accepted by the last Herculeans; only they could know his power and be moved, enabling him to rebuild himself, to make up for the centuries of humiliation. There was no other way. He was powerful enough to make them suffer, if necessary. They would follow him, or he would swallow them all and become the only Herculean.

"I have not finished!" he shouted. "Dead worlds still cry out!" Earth had to pay for its crimes. Centuries of failure had to be redeemed.

"You will only destroy yourself," Myraa said as the void contracted around him.

"That is no longer possible."

"I have never lied to you."

"Release me!" He struggled to draw strength.

"Come together in me!" commanded Myraa.

The whispers formed a net around him, but he broke through and fled from their deafening hisses.

Light slashed across the darkness, creating a horizon.

He flowed toward it, filled with dread at the renewed possibility of defeat. Fresh air swelled his lungs; wind combed his hair; a chill drizzle began to wash his face. He looked back and saw solid shadows dancing after him, drawing closer across the frozen waste. They were bringing him pain, elastic agonies capable of endless increase.

A shriek shot out from his throat as he strained to reach the burning horizon, where he could gaze again into the sea of fire and renew his strength.

The shadows encircled him as he ran, cutting him off from the dawn but keeping their distance. The heart of fire beckoned, but the blanket of night was too large and he would not run out from under it in time.

The circle of shapes pulled in closer around him. Long, thin blades caught the light, flashing as they struck, piercing him to make a wheel with his heart as the hub.

"Something must be wrong," Poincaré said. "The ship is drifting."

"It may be a trap," Kurbi said. "When we get closer, he'll back up and destroy a few more ships."

"Or this may be our chance! Myraa may be diverting his attention."

"I wouldn't count on it," Kurbi said. "What world is ahead of him now?"

The gray-white plenum flickered as Poincaré called up the charts. "He entered the Snake at this point, so the next system must be Izar. A rural planet, religious settlers like New Mars."

Kurbi turned his head away and closed his eyes.

Gorgias strained to break the wheel.

The blades burned in his heart. The wind howled across the wastes, and the horizon seemed unattainable.

Somewhere, he knew, the ship was adrift, vulnerable to a well-timed attack.

The wheel was rigid before his will. Pain flowed through the blades.

He set the pain aside and seized the wheel. It rolled toward the horizon and flew over the edge.

The blades withdrew as the force-center surged through him, erasing his fear and renewing his strength. The orderly mindscape of the ship's intelligence reappeared around him.

He scanned nearby jumpspace and saw that the Earth vessels were keeping their distance.

He slipped the ship into normal space and flared his will.

The bubble of force appeared and expanded, glowing white hot. He made it larger, just to see how big it could get. It rushed outward with no drop in intensity.

He stopped the field at one hundred thousand kilometers. The ship still rode at its center. He felt the lethal bubble as if it were his own skin.

He glanced into the control room. Myraa was unconscious, slumped forward in the command station, exhausted from effort.

Izar was just ahead. He nudged the planet, stripping away its atmosphere, boiling the oceans, burning the land and buckling the continents. He increased the field's intensity and vaporized the planet.

It was much too simple. He longed to see the faces of the Old Ones on Earth when they learned that their future was coming to an end, that the time would come when there would be no Earthborn in the Federation Snake. Earth's history would come to a sudden halt, reduced to microdust drifting in the void; but they had to know what was happening to them. He would have to measure his actions to make sure of that.

His own future had been taken from him before he was even born. He was the only one among the survivors who had said no to Earth, who continued to say no, and would soon say the final no; that meant more than anything. His one small self was now unique, the greatest military force in all history; not even his physical destruction had stopped him from achieving this new state.

He would sweep triumphantly into Earth's sunspace; every planet would burn; he might even destroy the sun. He would deny eternity to the old immortals of Earth; they had lived too long with the conviction that all time belonged to them.

"And then what?" Myraa asked.

He laughed. "Even your wisest did not suspect that I could do what I have done."

"You may destroy us all."

"I will not worship and cower as you do!"

"He'll grow impatient," Kurbi said. "It will take a long time to destroy all the worlds in the Snake one by one, so he'll go on to Earth."

Poincaré sighed. "He'll have plenty of time later." The Security Chief stood up and gazed at the main screen. "My impulse is to throw what we've got at him, no matter what it costs, just to do something. He'll be in range of another world soon."

"I know how you feel."

"We'll bypass him and run for Earth. Defenses have to be built up there. Maybe we can send heavier ships against him. Let's hope he doesn't tire of his butchery too soon." He sat down and stared at the gray deck.

I must be there when Earth dies, Kurbi thought, feeling a monstrous urgency stir within him.

"Suicide ships might stop him," a voice said behind him.

Kurbi turned and looked at Birkut. The navigator shrugged. "If there were enough of them."

"It might have been different," his father's voice said, "if he had been a rebel with a people behind him, to modify his aims, bring him closer to a reasonable center. Alone, frustrated, he is driven to attempt the impossible before an unforgiving enemy."

The words had lingered in the Whisper Ship's memory, waiting to strike at him like a snake from a dark cave.

Gorgias laughed. "Impossible? I've already done what the greatest Herculean generals failed to do!"

His father's words were only bits of information. There was no way to reach into the random scatter of true death to tell him what he had accomplished. He almost wished that Myraa had been able to claim him, so he could see what his son was doing.

"Did I ask to hear this?" Gorgias asked.

YES, the ship answered.

Something in him had reached out to find the words; a part of him was a betrayer.

"Ignore such requests in future."

NOTED.

Gorgias reached across the gray sea of jumpspace and examined the inhabited world of the system ahead. He caressed the planet with long bursts of exploring particles, sensing the twitching shapes of life on the obsidian surface. The harsh analogue of the world in normal space already suggested the bone-dryness of death. Passage through jumpspace had been for him a slow dying once, but now the sterile desert of jumpspace reminded him of his victory over death. Nothing could kill him now, not even if he wished it.

He recalled the pleasure of killing Commissioner Aren. The physical universe had obeyed his will. True, he needed Myraa, and the ship, but these were mere outcroppings of his will in the universe of his origin; he would not need them in time, when he learned to invade any living thing, control any thinking entity.

The planet's cities twinkled as the ship emerged from jumpspace. The ice caps were bright; the oceans caught the yellow light of the double suns on the dayside.

Gorgias threw the blister of force outward. It expanded and touched the planet. Again the atmosphere was heated and torn away; the oceans boiled, the continents baked and buckled, releasing inner fires. . . .

He pulled back.

This one he would leave to break apart by itself; too quick an end cut short agony.

He watched the burning planet. Pockets of life struggled to survive; deep places sheltered the maimed and dying. Such little sparks of will, he thought, hanging on to life as they fell into the abyss. And for them it was death, true dying, with nothing on the other side. Millions burned and fell into death as he watched. The universe was too generous with life. But what could be expected of a mindless force-center?

This was nothing compared to the coming death of Earth, he told himself, looking forward to that feast of vengeance. Kurbi and the remnants of his pitiable fleet would be there, watching in despair, awaiting their turn.

Myraa gathered the dead.

She plucked individual sparks, passing them through herself into the cradle of inwardness. Unseen to Gorgias, the trickle again became a torrent.

But she could not save them all; for that she would have needed thousands of adepts. The blood of worlds was flowing too quickly, and she had to hurry; if Gorgias were to notice, he would destroy her shape and deny her the position needed for gathering, such as it was; other adepts were too far away to be of use.

The passing dead cried out as they fell into the pull of her rescuing stream. Some were insane by the time they were picked up; all were full of fear and lamentations. A long time would pass before they emerged from the darkness within themselves.

She felt Gorgias's laughing hatred as he watched the world break into pieces, but she tried to ignore him as she worked; there was no time to oppose him now.

IX. The Old Ones

"Each of us insists on being innocent at all costs, even if he has to accuse the whole human race and heaven itself . . . Then I realized, as a result of delving into my memory, that modesty helped me to shine, humility to conquer, and virtue to oppress . . . I have accepted duplicity instead of being upset about it . . ."

—Albert Camus

ALL THESE MILLENNIA of humanity, Kurbi thought as he looked out over the ocean from his terrace. So few inner changes. Progress in government and living environments, vast potential for biological alterations, yet the human form retains its inertia, clinging to its identity, refusing to give up its evolution-imposed form and become something better. Expanded life spans, but the mind is the same, slowly filling with information which must be regularly wiped away. Forgetfulness was as real a death as any in times past, and rebirth as real a way of seizing the future as reproduction.

The Herculeans are our shame, he thought, staring up at the stars. The Cluster People were our children, our attempt at something better, but we destroyed them. Now they have sent back a single individual to topple our empire. He felt like a thief, returning to Earth to steal its last moments for himself. All those people who had left the Earth for the worlds of the Snake, about to die after centuries of living and building. We have failed to secure the future.

A dozen systems had died by the time he and Poincaré had returned to Earth. Others were dying as he stood here. He thought of his old room on New Mars, of Rensch, as if they still existed. Again, the terrible realization swept through him that Gorgias, or whatever he was now, did not crave conquest; he wished the destruction of all worlds settled by Earthpeoples; nothing else would satisfy him. And it was no longer only the wish of blind rage; he was doing it because he could do it.

And I helped him, Kurbi thought, shrinking into himself. My wishes, my feelings, my curiosities helped bring him to his greatest strength. Myraa's explorations, at first a reaction against the Herculean Empire's ambitions, had played into the hands of that past, infusing it with new strength. How stupid, Kurbi thought, to have seen her group as a mere religious cult.

Something stirred in the corner of his eye. He turned his head with a jolt, as if waking from a dream.

Dark figures waited around him. Images of the old immortals. He counted six.

"Can you do anything?" a low-pitched voice pleaded, almost growling.

"You know more than anyone," another said, quavering. "All this," he added, gesturing at the ring of sunspace settlements rising out of the dark ocean, "will perish!"

The growling voice rumbled in agreement.

Kurbi shook his head. "Nothing. The knowledge behind this weapon is beyond us. Even their Empire ignored it. Now it's in the hands of one who knows how to use it."

The dark shapes seemed to tremble.

"We cannot end!" a high voice cried out. "It cannot happen. Think! Why are you waiting? Why are you not out there?"

"Would you have us throw all our remaining forces into the fire?" Kurbi said, knowing that they did not care about the colony worlds. They would sacrifice the whole Snake to save Earth. What was life to them? A protracted endurance with pain edited out, memories rearranged, a persistence which could not imagine its own end. Where was the enlarged creativity of humankind's native longings and intelligence, where was wisdom, where happiness and satisfaction? Long life might have brought all these things, he told himself, drowning out the whisper which insisted that nothing else had ever been possible, that this was all.

One of the figures came close. The starlight showed a thin human face with chocolate skin and large eyes. Long-fingered hands reached out and passed through Kurbi's arm.

They're children, he thought as the eyes searched his face, children afraid of evil.

"Rafael," the thin lips said, "save us. You are the only one who can...."

"I don't know how."

"You do, but you haven't put your attention to it. Some part of you is holding back."

"If you can suggest..."

The other shapes glided forward and crowded around him.

"Yes," the growler said, "direct your attention and discover what must be done."

"Wishes won't work to help us," Kurbi answered, reminding himself that Gorgias had made his power fantasies a real threat. He's out there, Kurbi thought, slowed up only by his wish to be thorough.

"Discover!" the high-voiced Old One shrieked. "You must!"

We don't deserve to survive, Kurbi thought, looking into their wide, staring eyes. Their hands shook at their sides like snakes.

"Leave me alone, there's nothing I can do. Flee in your ships. Thousands of worlds wait outside the Snake."

The dark faces considered. "Yes," the high-voiced said at last, "that would be possible. Will you lead us?"

"But our Earth," the growler objected. "Our Earth will perish."

"Go settle somewhere and wipe your memory," Kurbi said impatiently.

"Wipe... Earth?" the growler asked.

Kurbi shrugged. "Might as well wipe it from your minds before it happens in reality. It will save you the pain." Then he realized that Gorgias would track those who fled. He would hunt their thoughts and probe through their amnesia. Their frightened whispers would echo in the great bell of space-time; it would be easier to hide the quasars.

The Old Ones began to wail in a sick, wrenching moan, released by a final despair; it emanated from within them, where pride born of persistence was being broken.

The six uninvited shapes faded away.

Julian appeared.

"Where are you?" Kurbi asked.

"South Pole Security. I'm going out to Ring 24. Coming?"

"I suppose we should be there in person."

"A flyer is on the way for you. What did they say?"

"They can't cope, Julian."

"I've had similar conversations. It's become clear to them that they don't control everything, or even run the world. We consult them, persuade them to agree to what must be done, but the creative impetus does not come from them. They're grateful for the continuity."

"All they have is self-consciousness and a long, selective memory. We should have been something else by now, Julian. Ours is a petrified species."

Ring 24 was a dumbbell shape made from two pyramids joined at their apexes.

Kurbi listened to the transmissions from the Snake.

"What information do you have?" one face asked.

"What kind of danger?" asked another.

"Izar is gone, ships are missing. Is this a new Herculean invasion? Please advise, can we depend on Federation forces to defend us?"

"Please confirm. . . ."

". . . twelve freighters missing . . ."

"Nothing remains in the New Mars System. . . ."

"Precept is gone!"

". . . advise what preparations to make. . . ."

"Sagan IV does not answer. . . ."

The jumpspace chatter was endless. Screens flickered, one portrait replacing another. Deep-set eyes; heavy lips; pale skins; bald heads; silent faces, animated faces—jeering, shouting, pleading; skulls containing minds unable to cope with an overwhelming fact.

"Relays are sweeping the message through the Snake," Julian said next to him, "so he's bound to pick it up."

"Why should he bother?" Kurbi said.

"He'll talk to you, I'm hoping."

What can I say? Kurbi asked himself. Shall I plead with him?

"I'm here, Kurbi," a metallic voice said over the chatter of the screens.

Poincaré raised a hand. All other receptions were blacked out.

Myraa appeared on the main screen. Her eyes were open, but she was looking inward.

Gorgias's voice came from the cabin, not from her mouth. "You've come to beg. Spare yourself the humiliation. I will destroy you along with your world and its sun."

"Would you prefer to take me prisoner?" Kurbi asked.

Gorgias laughed. It sounded like a slow drumbeat on metal.

"What would change your mind?" Kurbi asked.

"Nothing. You know that."

"There must be something we could give you. Name it."

Gorgias laughed again. "But you're about to give me everything!"

"What will you gain?" Poincaré asked.

"The satisfaction of existing in a universe without you and your kind."

"We should have destroyed Myraa's World," Julian whispered.

Gorgias heard him. "But you didn't, and now it's too late to threaten me. You hesitated because you weigh gains and losses. You can never understand the beautiful simplicity of absolute power, of not having to measure advantages."

"It takes no brains to be a glutton," Poincaré said.

Myraa's eyes blinked and closed.

Gorgias laughed faintly. "What do you hope to gain by provoking me? I am stronger than a black hole, or a quasar. A thousand of each could not stop me. Let me remind you that I have not yet destroyed as many of your worlds as you did of mine. You who took everything from me will pay everything! Have the dignity to die bravely."

He broke the link.

The cries of the Snake flooded in again.

Gorgias listened.

Someone was walking around in his mind. He pulled away from the ship's mindscape and looked into himself. Two figures came toward him from a great distance; his mother, Oriona, and his brother, Herkon.

"Go away!" he shouted.

But they drew nearer.

"You have nothing to say to me!"

Oriona shot toward him, invading his center, examining painful memories.

"You were cruel to your father," she announced, "to Myraa. You burned the homes of innocent people, and now you are destroying whole worlds. You no longer care about justice, you only wish revenge, which has no end beyond selfish satisfaction." She wrapped herself around his twinges of conscience and squeezed, seeking to give him pain.

"I don't care," he said, "pain is an old friend."

Minds of all shapes appeared within him, as numerous as stars. He felt their scrutiny, their disdain.

"You are all fools!" he shouted. "So grateful for your existence! You worship a seething blindness, and you make no difference in the world from which you came. I have learned to do more than warm myself before the force-center. Go away, or I will find a way to destroy you all!"

"Gorgias," Herkon called, "what do you have?"

"The strength of my hatred, the knowledge that it has always been justified, and now I will have the satisfaction of destroying those who murdered our kind."

"But no happiness, Gorgias."

"Happiness is vague and general. Satisfaction is specific. I will have what I have worked for!"

"And then?" Oriona asked tenderly.

"I will remake worlds, repopulate cities. I will be the heart of the reborn Cluster."

"In a perishing universe?" she asked. "It was not made for endless life, or for knowing. It is a toy for young minds, which grow into greater realms."

"I was not given what I should have had," Gorgias insisted. "I am not finished here yet. But why should you care? If what you say is true, then leave me to do as I wish."

"Turn away, son, turn away!"

"You're so certain! Then make me see what you're talking about!"

But the galaxy of minds was silent, convincing him that they had nothing to offer; they also lived in a predicament of some kind. Perhaps they needed him for a purpose?

Myraa appeared next to Oriona.

"Turn away, Gorgias," she said, "follow us."

"Go away," he repeated.

Minds crowded around him suddenly, squeezing him toward nothingness.

The force-center flowed into him, helping him resist collapse. He held his space, counterbalancing the pressure, but unable to throw it back.

Suddenly he was in a line of soldiers on a battlefield, advancing toward a house on a hill. Orders barked inside his suit helmet. Dark ships floated in the sky, cutting across the troops with massive beams. Cries burst in his ears as he was pushed into a vise of bodies.

The house on the hill was hidden by a restraining field. He was there, he realized, watching his army die; and he was here, watching a beam sizzle across the ground. It reached him and he smelled burning in his helmet. The fire cut through his armor and plunged into his body, melting his heart, penetrating deeper, pumping pain for the eternity that it would take him to die. . . .

"But I did not die," he whispered, listening to the screams of his soldiers.

"I am here," Crusus said into his ear.

So Myraa had saved him after all.

Crusus entered him with knives of revenge, twisting, plunging, cutting. "Feel what I felt, my General! I gave you everything. How did you serve me? We waited centuries to be butchered!"

Oriona hovered nearby. "He is like you," she said. "How do you like him?"

Crusus severed his head. Gorgias felt his body twitch. His mother picked up his head as he opened its eyes. Crusus was still raging over the body with his knives.

"You cannot hurt me!" Gorgias shouted, hanging by his hair from Oriona's hand.

"Gorgias, stop," Herkon pleaded.

Crusus changed into a hideous alien form. Jaws opened and crushed the headless corpse. Blood ran into the darkness.

"I am past fear," Gorgias said as Oriona lifted him high and gazed into his eyes. "The rest of you have come into this realm like beggars, but I will become its master."

She gave him a long questioning look, and for an instant her doubt became his own; then she hurled his head into the void.

He tumbled, laughing in triumph, knowing that his will was joined to the blind absolute. The force-center rose from behind the night. He fell into a close orbit around it and drew nourishment. His eyes burned, his hair flamed; the flesh flowed from his skull, but he felt no pain.

The meek could not imagine what he would dare.

X. Behind the Night

"Behind the night . . . somewhere afar
Some white tremendous daybreak."

—Rupert Brooke

"When Nero ordered the death of his teacher, Seneca, the old Stoic
went to his bath and opened his veins; but the stimulating discussion of his friends quieted his feelings and provoked his eloquence
to the point where he closed his wounds, so that he might carry
on the philosophical discussion for a time. He even dictated a
treatise before resuming his stately approach to death."

—Roman gossip

THE RING WAS THINNING.

Kurbi saw a group of worlds break formation and wink out
into jumpspace. Others, he knew, were installing pushers and
warpers. The rush for mobility would save lives in the short
run, but sooner or later Gorgias would hunt down the fugitives.

So the empire of Earth was staggering to its end, dying of
a war it had won centuries ago, he thought as he reclined on
his terrace. The death blow would come from a god without a
body, enforcing his will from beyond the grave.

*No invading hordes battering at the gates of civilization.
No complex economic struggle*. His historian's brain insisted

that Earth would fall to satisfy simple hatred, paying a thousand times the price it had exacted from the Herculeans.

What remained of the fleet was going out into the Snake, to take the Whisper Ship by surprise, if possible. The officers and crews were all volunteers, convinced that a successful defense was still possible, one way or another.

Rik was out there somewhere, fleeing with the worlds. His son had erased much of his memory by the time of Grazia's death, becoming too much of a different person to be affected by the news. *I should have sought him out sooner,* Kurbi thought, *when he would still have known me.* Rik had no past inside him; that would not save him when Gorgias caught up with the fugitive worlds. *My past will come looking for you, but you will not know it.*

"You're still determined to stay," Julian said.

Kurbi saw the image out of the corner of his eye, but did not turn his head. "I belong here."

"We'll leave together, Raf."

"And have him hunt us?"

Poincaré clenched his fists. "I can't believe that you've given up like this!"

"There's not much to live for anyway. Let him make a clean sweep."

"You've never been free of that way of thinking," Poincaré said, his voice tense and trembling. "Always ready to kick over the game board and make a quick exit."

"Game is right. Why shouldn't I rid myself of it? It throws us up against our limits as human beings too much. Is this all there is? We're appalled as we ask the question."

Julian shook his head. "I don't know...."

"Don't you see?" Kurbi asked, sitting upright. "Gorgias has broken his limits more than once now. He's almost fulfilled. By some quirk his desire has found all it needs to satisfy itself, and maybe more...."

"What? He's a strained, tormented rag of a personality, if you can still call him a person."

"He's shown us that there is more to the universe," Kurbi continued, "than the shackles we've known. The myth of our history has us breaking one chain after another, but we've only moved away from genuine possibilities. Gorgias has entered a realm which has grown from roots deep in reality. Those roots probably spring from regions deeper than we can imagine. But the important fact is that they flower *elsewhere,* beyond the sorry range of our abilities. The Herculeans found the way, and we dismissed their discovery as some kind of cult."

Julian looked exasperated. The pale light of the room from which his image was being cast emphasized the anxiety in his face.

"Don't you see?" Kurbi insisted "It's important for our peace of mind to *understand* what is happening, even if there is nothing we can do."

"You must be joking."

"It's the way I've lived my life," Kurbi added.

Julian seemed to sit down in the air. "Fine! And you want to be consistent to the end. I'm sorry, but it's just a way of quieting yourself before the death blow. That's all I see."

"Understanding is the only victory left to me," Kurbi said, sitting back again.

Poincaré took a deep breath. "Okay, Raf. I want to hear how clear you can make all this. Not very, I suspect."

"You're not really interested."

"Go ahead," Poincaré said softly.

"The universe of matter is only an aspect of youthful consciousness," Kurbi answered, "but, under certain conditions, consciousness can go on developing. Our cosmos is probably only one of many which organizes conscious intelligence out of the geometries of smaller, infinitesimal realms, and is abandoned when that intelligence matures, leaving behind an empty shell of run-down energies. Sometimes intelligence fails to make the climb and dies within the rotting fruit."

"And we're a failed universe."

"We may become one if Gorgias isn't stopped."

"I don't understand."

"He's directing his interest back into the cradle, instead of developing . . . outward. He's using directly the power which underlies all things."

"To settle old scores. Maybe there is nothing else for him out there."

"He can't see what there may be for him for some reason," Kurbi insisted. "He won't surrender his old attachments." He looked at Poincaré. The Security Chief bit his lower lip and turned away. "Perhaps it was the manner of his death," Kurbi continued. "In any case, the persistence of his hatred has blinded him. He has so much strength now that he doesn't have to be particularly crafty; it would be hard to make a mistake when you can afford to use unlimited means to kill flies. He can indulge himself."

"I'm not so sure he can't make a mistake. What about Myraa's group? Can't they do anything?"

"They haven't been able to restrain him, or convince him of their way. Maybe they don't have much to offer him. But I'm sure they've been learning for some time."

Julian gestured with his hand. "Why should you care? What's in it for you?"

"It angers me that we won't have a chance to grow, to see what they have glimpsed before he destroys us. There will be no survival, only death."

"You might not like what they've seen."

Kurbi sighed. "That's possible. I've liked to think that something in the fabric of eternity finds the destruction of conscious beings abhorrent, so it conserves and nurtures unique things, drawing them upward through the scale of things into . . . fellowship with itself."

Poincaré was silent. "Well," he said finally, "that lets out any chance of happiness in physical immortality." He was sounding more irritated. "What *can* there be in that resurrection realm which Gorgias fails to see? Maybe he's right and everyone else, including you, is being sentimental."

Kurbi smiled to himself. If only it were true, and he could forget all this as some kind of delusion. "There is a blind force-center," he continued. "It exists necessarily, is self-sustaining, and cannot be dissipated."

"Gorgias powers his weapon with that."

"Yes."

"What is Myraa's group doing with this force-center?"

"Her configuration is made up of many old, surviving intelligences, in addition to the Herculeans. Some derive from nonhuman sources. The whole group is forming an event horizon of mind around the heart of fire. The blindness will acquire awareness, they hope, much as unconscious matter evolved into intelligent life in our plenum. A god will arise at the end of history and be a product of it, not its creator."

"No Omega-god until the end? But you think this may fail."

Kurbi nodded. "I feel it within myself as a weakness, a lack of resolve."

"Well, you have given a lot of thought to this tearful and tragic stuff, but—"

"Myraa provided most of it, and it's true. The force-center

underlies everything we see and feel. Future and past are one above our level of perception."

"Raf, what are we talking about?"

"The danger that a particular species may fail to join the flowering of Omega. That's what I fear is happening to us and Myraa's group. Her physical form holds the candidate configuration together, but the mind net may dissipate if her body is destroyed. The complex may not be able to hold its developing shape if it is not weaned gradually. Gorgias himself may not be able to persist without her, despite his partial invasion of the Whisper Ship. Her mind-body focuses and concentrates. Who would collect her if she died? Are there others with her skills?"

"On Myraa's World," Julian said.

"They're too far away."

"If all this is right," Poincaré said angrily, "then we should have killed her when we had the chance. Would you let all of humanity perish to insure the survival of Omega?"

"It's not a logic I invented," Kurbi answered. "The universe is not as we would like it. I don't know. Maybe oblivion is to be preferred. But when I think of all the generations of living things which have gone into death. . . ."

"I would kill her if I could," Poincaré said. "Maybe we still can. It's our only chance. All these eschatological issues weigh on me only because you're involved, Raf, and there may be practical difficulties—"

"But you should understand. More than anything—"

"These may be realities. You talk as if they were truths long known."

"You wear blinders, Julian. Worse, you want to."

He shrugged. "Countless microcreatures make up my body. They don't interest me as long as they do their job. We can't help but be blind. All life is lived between extremes of large and small. Dig below small, or climb into large, and all experience becomes distorted as far as we're concerned."

"So you feel that we can never be more than we are?"

"We've tried to be more, Raf, and it's never worked!"

"Nothing gave us our limits except blind environment, and we haven't lived in the given environment for millennia. You blur distinctions and won't deal with the merits of what I'm saying."

"Merits!" Poincaré laughed nervously. "You're sitting here

waiting to die, and you want me to agree with you! Our ships will try to destroy the Whisper Ship one more time. If it means killing Myraa and closing some way to a distant yonder, then so be it! If it's there, we'll find it again some day. We live long enough to have the time to search."

Kurbi ignored him and looked up at the stars. There was a clear gap in the ring now, and it seemed that the arch of worlds standing in the ocean would collapse at any moment.

Gorgias reached out.

Fifty ships moved toward him through jumpspace.

So, the fools would try again. He felt their desperation, but it would be no challenge; pity that he could not rob them of the satisfaction of trying.

He looked into the cabin. Myraa stared at him from the command station. Sooner or later, he knew, she would attempt to move against him again, but he could not simply destroy her; the ship could not be all the embodiment that he would ever need. Through her, he would have to live the life which the loss of his body had denied him. By manipulating her reproductive system, he would in time be able to give birth to a copy of his previous form and occupy it.

The ships drew nearer.

He swept toward them as the field blossomed around him.

"Each life," Myraa whispered to him, "is a universe of possibility denied."

"Why else would there be satisfaction in their destruction?" he asked. "Would I waste my time on nothing? It's my future or theirs!"

The swarm of warships winked out as he passed through it. He had given them only a moment to emerge from jumpspace.

Myraa was silent.

"They're paying!" Gorgias shouted. "For my wasted centuries."

A steady breeze blew in from the ocean. Poincaré stood up and gazed into the distance for a while. Kurbi heard invisible voices around the Security Chief's image.

"They're gone, Raf," he said at last. "Now we have only the ships in Earthspace."

We created him, Kurbi thought.

"Just a moment," Poincaré said. "I'll be right back."

He disappeared.

The gap in the ring grew larger as more worlds ran for the freedom of jumpspace.

Poincaré reappeared. His image walked around and stood before Kurbi. "He's bypassing worlds now, Raf, so he'll be here very soon. You'll have to leave."

"No."

"We can leave together. It's not certain that he would find us, not certain at all."

"Tell me what we would live for and I'll go."

Poincaré's ghost approached with outstretched hands. "Why should we live for anything, Raf? Forget all your intricacies and live life as it comes. We'll flee with a small group and lose ourselves well away from the Snake, and forget all this. Raf, listen to me!"

"You could live that way. I can't. Get out and don't look back."

"Raf, I can't. . . ."

"Forget me."

XI.   The Stillness of the Will

"Now let us consider attentively and observe the powerful, irresistible impulse with which masses of water rush downwards, the persistence and determination with which the magnet always turns back to the North Pole, and the keen desire with which iron flies to the magnet, the vehemence with which the poles of the electric current strive for reunion, and which, like the vehemence of human desires, is increased by obstacles. Let us look at the crystal being rapidly and suddenly formed with such regularity of configuration; it is obvious that this is only a perfectly definite and precisely determined striving in different directions constrained and held firm by coagulation. Let us observe the choice with which bodies repel and attract one another, unite and separate, when set free in the fluid state and released from the bonds of rigidity . . . If we observe all this, it will not cost us a great effort of the imagination to recognize once more our own inner nature, even at so great a distance. It is that which in us pursues its ends by the light of knowledge, but here, in the feeblest of its phenomena, only strives blindly in a dull, one-sided, and unalterable manner. Yet, because it is everywhere one and the same—just as the first morning dawn shares the name of sunlight with the rays of the full midday sun— it must in either case bear the name of *will*. For this word indicates that which is the being-in-itself of everything in the world, and is the sole kernel of every phenomenon."

—Schopenhauer, *The World As Will and Idea*

MYRAA KNEW that she could stop Gorgias by dying.
    But her death would endanger those within her who were

not yet ready to voyage on their own.

And there was no one nearby to receive her; it would be death, the loss of personality to chaos. If it came to a choice, she realized, the death of Earth was not as important as the host of minds waiting on the inward shore, struggling to understand and unfold into the new realm. Centuries of exploration and knowledge would be lost. Let the empires of the outer world destroy themselves.

Gorgias was adept at drawing strength from the force-center. He identified with it; perhaps one day, when his hatred was spent, he would have something to teach. No one had imagined that the force-center's undisguised power might be directed back into the world of origins. All efforts had been concentrated on inquiry, with the aim of breaking the final bonds with outwardness; when all the Herculeans had been gathered, the final adept would have had to find a way to follow, or be left to die. It was thought by some that this single adept might have to live forever in the realm of galaxies, to insure the welfare of those who would voyage out into infinity, where the outward universes were only infinitesimal nodes circling the vast force-center, each nexus contributing new minds, new perspectives, in the climb toward Omega.

In reality, she could not choose to die because she was helpless within the ship. Gorgias had made sure of that.

Kurbi struggled inside Gorgias.

Earth's solar system floated defenseless over the black abyss. What had it ever been worth? he asked, whispering the Herculean's thoughts. Nothing here but a worn-out species worshiping its own identity, blind to possibility and growth. He would put it out of its misery. . . .

Kurbi opened his eyes, got up and went out on the terrace. The sky was bright with stars, but lonelier. Large sections of the ring were dark. He felt a great stillness, as if it no longer mattered whether the fleeing worlds would escape or find happiness. Oblivion seemed the perfect state; nothing would be obliged to crawl from lesser to greater to gain a sense of achievement; there would be no torment in striving and feeling empty at fulfillment; the container would not have to ache to be filled, then empty itself so it could have the pleasure of aching again; and knowledge gained through the admission of ignorance and the suspense of curiosity would not repeatedly arrive at boredom for lack of new unknowns. Perfect knowledge would be static, satisfying for only a few moments, he had always thought; but now he wondered if it might not provide an unending, secure bliss in the contemplation of final mysteries. There was no way to know.

We dwell partly in the thoughts of others, he thought, recalling his dream of being inside Gorgias. For a moment it had seemed that he would turn the Herculean away from Earth, but their thoughts had converged into a shared contempt.

He would not be able to sleep tonight.

Sleep. A vestigial fall into unconsciousness. All evolution and history struck him as the crazed effort of intellect struggling to wake up.

He went down from the terrace and wandered on the dewy hillside, as he had done countless times before when he had feared sleep. Lost, unrenewable, unable to embrace oblivion's subtleties, he preferred the strained shore of self-awareness to sleep's worrisome drift.

He stopped at the cliff's edge finally, and listened to the breakers pounding the rocks below. The white foam seemed to roll in from the ocean of stars beyond the planet's edge. There were many gaps in the arch of the ring now, yet still it seemed to stand on the horizon.

His shadow appeared on the foam below.

Kurbi turned around and saw the giant figure of Poincaré standing over the house. The grassy hillside was black from his harsh glow.

"Raf, where are you?" the figure boomed. "The Whisper Ship is at Centauri!" The image stared blindly into the darkness, then shrank toward normal size. Kurbi hurried up the hill.

Poincaré's image waited as Kurbi stepped onto the terrace. He noticed the ghostly images of flickering tank screens behind the motionless figure. "The whole sky is afire out there," the Security Chief said as Kurbi came into his field of view. "He's large enough to destroy a whole system."

"How soon?"

"A day or two, at most. You'll come with me, Raf."

"Did you think this would frighten me into fleeing? I'm staying."

"But your demise won't accomplish a thing! Do you think he'll hesitate with you here?"

"I have no illusions left," Kurbi said softly, feeling almost at peace. "Save yourself, Julian."

"Are you planning to talk to him?"

Kurbi looked up at the sea of evening. Stars twinkled silently, oblivious to the vast disturbance only four light-years away.

"It'll be a clean sweep, Raf. We have nothing to put into the field against him. The planet will be deserted within hours now."

"Everyone?"

"We can't be sure. There may be some primitives in out-of-the-way places."

"When he's finished here," Kurbi said, "he'll work his way through the remaining Snake worlds. Then he'll wait for the Herculeans to increase their numbers, in preparation for the return to the Cluster."

"And what will he be?" Julian asked. "A retired ghost. He doesn't belong in our universe. . . ."

"He'll work to fit in through Myraa, to become her as much as possible. Maybe he'll succeed."

"I hope it wears on him. Raf, you've got to come with me."

"No."

"I'll come and take you away by force."

"Don't waste your time. It will be too late for you to get to safety by the time you find me."

"I'll take that chance. I'm leaving now."

His image winked out.

Kurbi looked around. The house seemed desolate under the stars. He had taken great pride in it once, enjoying the way it fit into the hillside. He had loved the house when Grazia had loved it. The image of the broken glider came back to him. He saw Grazia being pulled by the downdraft which forced the craft against the cliff face despite all her efforts. He saw her body battered against the rocks by the breakers. He had not been there to witness the whole accident, but he seemed to remember it all.

Maybe he should have cloned her; by now her sister would have been a grown woman and he might have fallen in love with her. Grazia would have approved. The new person would have won his loyalty and affection, and he would now be living a different life. He would not have hunted the Herculean. Gorgias might not have followed so successful a course. He would still be a nuisance, struggling to reshape the ashes of the past.

Kurbi listened to the gathering silence within himself. The stars had not satisfied the hungers of humankind; as long as it held to its ancient identity, the inner hounds could not be satisfied. Social systems would only imprison these faithful guardians of adaptive evolution. The Herculeans had been the old nature's way of reasserting itself, by willing a wolf to match the growing power of intellect. Humanity had released, not its better part, but the raging beast rearmed; and the beast would live now, as surely as it cowered in the Old Ones of Earth. The past would be silenced and the future would belong to the Herculeans. They would swarm among the stars, angry at finitude and everything which was not them, transforming the stuff of worlds into more of their own kind; all that had been humanity would live in them. Hatred stirred deeply within him, and he knew that his humanity was not so different from Gorgias. . . .

A flyer appeared in the morning sky.

The oval shape landed in the open area at his right, halfway to the cliffs. A dozen men got out and marched up toward the house.

Kurbi got up from his chair and slipped away to his left. He left the terrace and ran toward the cliffs.

"Raf, wait!" Julian shouted.

Kurbi ignored him, resenting the stir which the physical effort was making within him. The ship was far to his right by the time the group started after him, and he saw that he would reach the edge well ahead of them.

There would be just enough time to cheat Gorgias and release Julian from a fatal friendship.

XII. Flower and Sword

"Only knowledge remains; the will has vanished. We then look with deep and painful yearning at that state, beside which the miserable and desperate nature of our own appears in the clearest light by contrast. Yet this consideration is the only one that can permanently console us, when, on the one hand, we have recognized incurable suffering and endless misery as essential to the phenomenon of the will, to the world, and on the other see the world melt away with the abolished will, and retain before us only empty nothingness. In this way, therefore, by contemplating the life and conduct of saints, to meet with whom is of course rarely granted to us in our own experience, but who are brought to our notice by their recorded history, and, vouched for with the stamp of truth by art, we have to banish the dark impression of that nothingness, which as the final goal hovers behind all virtue and holiness, and which we fear as children fear the darkness. We must not even evade it, as the Indians do, by myths and meaningless words, such as reabsorption in *Brahman,* or the *Nirvana* of the Buddhists. On the contrary, we freely acknowledge that what remains after the complete abolition of the will is, for all who are still full of the will, assuredly nothing. But also conversely, to those in whom the will has turned and denied itself, this very real world of ours with all its suns and galaxies, is—nothing."

—Schopenhauer, *The World As Will and Idea*

THE FIELD CONTRACTED and the Whisper Ship was alone in normal space. Behind the vessel, Centauri's three suns were missing a planet.

Earth lay ahead.

Four jumpspace units would put him at the edge of its sunspace. Gorgias felt the ship's surge of power as it slipped into the ashes.

Earth's sun grew from a black dot to a globe.

The ship resurfaced and the sun blazed. The stars looked on without interest, blind to the possibility that one of their vast number might be put out.

Mars was nearby, its red surface bright with cities. Gorgias listened, but the planet was silent, despite the lights. Then he noticed that its orbital space was nearly devoid of habitats. He clenched his will at the thought that they might have escaped him; there would be time to hunt them later.

The field blossomed around him. He stabilized it at one hundred thousand kilometers in diameter, and nudged Mars with the outer edge.

The red planet buckled. Its rotation wobbled. He brought the globe within the field. The planet broke up into pieces. These became white-hot and exploded.

Gorgias considered whether to engulf the sun and all its planets, or destroy only the inhabited inner worlds.

The bright morning sky, looking toward Mars, burned as if a hole had been opened in space, letting in the white light of eternity. Slowly, the hole grew, blotting out the stars.

"Raf, come with us!" Julian called.

Kurbi looked down at the breakers. The sliver of beach was visible in the lurid light of the sky. The air was cold in his lungs.

He turned around and saw mists rising from the black slope. "Go away!" he called to the dark figures.

They moved toward him.

"Back, or I'll jump!"

The figures halted.

"You'll die anyway," Julian said, walking forward.

Kurbi laughed. "You'd better go, or you'll cause my death directly. I'll jump anyway, just to cheat him!"

Poincaré stopped.

The sphere of force flickered and grew larger. It was already twice the size of the full moon.

"Go, Julian, while you have the chance!"

Poincaré raised his hand. The five figures behind him turned away and started back to their flyer.

"I'll stay with you," Poincaré said.

"Julian, I warn you!"

"Nothing else to do." The Security Chief walked toward him.

A cold wind struck from the ocean. Kurbi balanced himself on the edge. He had not expected Julian to call his bluff.

Kurbi looked up. A quarter of the sky was white.

"It would be nice," Julian said as he came up to him, "to believe that we are being destroyed by fresh, young barbarians who will carry out their own vision of a new future. But this is . . . another dead end throwing itself at us. It's difficult to accept that there isn't a thing we can do to stop it."

"Myraa's group is too new at this."

"Weren't there others before?"

Kurbi nodded, feeling empty. "What use would they have for the likes of Gorgias? He intrudes with brute force into the world of his birth. It probably requires many special conditions to grow out of our realm, much effort of learning and experience. There's nothing to gain by looking back. . . ."

Poincaré seemed to be breathing with difficulty. "Don't they care that he's doing harm here? I can't believe they're not trying to stop him!" His voice quavered.

"I don't know," Kurbi said. "Without Myraa we can't know anything. . . ."

The ocean was black in the white glare of Gorgias's expanding will.

"Reality is not what we thought it to be," Julian said, glancing up. Kurbi knew that he was desperate to keep the conversation going long enough to get him away from the edge. "We've lived blindly, building our understanding on the basis of operational theories, unaware—"

"How could we know?" Kurbi said. "But it's all nature still, all real, material and lawful, even the chaos which intrudes at the extremes."

Poincaré was silent. "We have no one to lead us past our deaths," he said finally.

Myraa was too far away, powerless aboard the Whisper Ship. Kurbi put his arm around his friend. Together they stepped away from the cliff's edge. "There is nothing we should concern ourselves with now, Julian, nothing."

"Just as well, if this is all we can ever be. It's not enough. Hasn't been for either of us. A long time now."

They looked up in time to see the moon blaze and disappear.

* * *

Gorgias kept his position at the orbit of Mars and expanded his will. He would take all the inner planets and the sun as well.

His will grew toward the Earth, aiming to stop at a point beyond the sun. Never again would this star's warmth drive evolution to create life.

He pushed outward. Small bits of rock and dust flared as they came into the field. He pushed easily against the solar wind, singing as he grew larger than he had ever been. There could be no limit to his size. He would be able to destroy the whole arm of this galaxy, even whole galaxies!

Earth's moon flickered and was gone.

The Earth was naked before him.

The sky flashed.

Black-white, black-white.

Something screamed inside Kurbi's head, as if it were trapped there.

Black.

The scream died, falling away into an inner abyss.

White.

Hideous monstrosities appeared in the sky, performing bestial acts. Titanic animals, like great bears, reptilian faces set in gelatinous masses, suggesting bloody afterbirths. . . .

Kurbi heard the scream again. It was a pitiable, frightening cry, turned in on itself as if determined to throw all of space-time into agony.

"The fools," he heard Julian say. "My flyer is coming back for us."

The sky became black, starless, as the scream died within Kurbi.

Gorgias fell in on himself.

He struggled to halt the collapse. Weakened by his expansion from the orbit of Mars, he could not channel enough energy to maintain his shape, much less engulf the Earth.

The force-center drew him inward, down into the infinitesimal centrality of all will.

He tried to pull back, but his resistance was gone. He managed to hover over the force-center, but the collapse into himself continued; soon he would be too small to resist the heart of fire. It had repelled and nourished him when he had been strong, but he had exceeded his capacity to control its infinite strength.

And he knew what was about to happen.

To draw on the force-center was life, but to merge with it was death, a return to the great flame of all being.

"You have made your last mistake," Myraa whispered near him.

Morning stars blazed in the sky.

"Look there," Poincaré said. "It's the Whisper Ship."

It drifted in slowly over the ocean, passed over them, and settled to the grass just below the terrace of the house. The side lock opened and Myraa rushed out.

"Myraa!" Kurbi shouted, waving at her. He started up the hillside.

"Raf, wait!"

Kurbi ignored him.

"You will be nothing!" Oriona shouted.

"Good-bye, Gorgias," his brother whispered.

The force-center bathed him with warmth as he grew smaller. He felt no pain as he spiraled in, but he cursed and began to scream. This blindly striving mass did not deserve to have him. Kurbi had earned the right to kill him, as he had earned the right to destroy all the Earthborn; but to be defeated by a mindless enemy, who had used no skill to win, was the final humiliation.

"You defeated yourself," Myraa said. "You did not trouble yourself to learn, you simply took what you desired, and one day you received more than you could handle."

"Myraa! Save me! You can save me!"

"I can, but I won't."

He cried out to her once more. She did not reply.

Myraa felt a sudden silence within herself. Gorgias was gone.

Myraa spoke quickly when Kurbi reached her.

"We must leave! The ship will now destroy itself."

"This way," Julian said, pointing to his flyer.

They ran across the hillside. "How long?" Kurbi asked, pulling next to Myraa.

"There is no way to tell. Not long."

The distance to the flyer seemed to expand. Kurbi stole a glance back at the Whisper Ship. The scream inside his head was completely gone, but he heard its echo in his memory. Gorgias was finally dead, he told himself, but the ship still served him.

They reached the flyer. Hands reached out and pulled them inside. Kurbi watched the screen as the vessel lifted. The Whisper Ship waited by the house, catching the sunrise on its silver hull.

The flyer's drive pulled hard, shrinking the house, the island, and the whole South Pacific region. The curve of the Earth appeared, and in a moment the whole planet was afloat in the night.

A point of light appeared on the island. The point grew into a circle of light, as if a second sun were rising from the depths of the planet.

The Earth shifted as the flyer pulled back, and the explosion swallowed the globe. Kurbi stared into the silent fire. Slowly, it began to fade, revealing large fragments in the sun orbit. The debris was already spreading out along the orbit, forming an asteroid belt around the sun. Now, he thought, Earth is only a coordinate in space. Gorgias had gotten what he had wanted.

"Perhaps some of the larger pieces might be useful," Julian said softly. "The habitats will be able to come back, and we still have many worlds in the Snake." -

Kurbi turned to Myraa. She explained. "Only his ignorance could stop him, and only if he made a mistake. We had to wait for him to overextend himself. There was no other way after he had grown strong."

"You deliberately waited?" Poincaré asked. -

"Our other assaults had all failed." She was silent for a moment. "Now he is part of all willing, all natural striving. But he is free of the pain of knowing. The burden of his past has been taken from him."

"He's dead, then, and can't be recovered?" Julian asked.

She nodded. "As with his father, the individual will-pattern has been scattered. Look for him in the strength of suns, in the sighs of magnetic storms, or in the swirl of galaxies. Search for him in your own wills. He is there, freed from the prison of self-awareness, riding the mindless music."

"That's the same as dead," Poincaré said.

"Akin to sleep. He deserved better, once."

Could Myraa be lying? Kurbi wondered. Perhaps Gorgias had grown beyond his hatred after Earth's destruction and had reconciled himself with her. She would hide him in return. But as he gazed into Myraa's eyes, Kurbi rejected the idea.

"But he'll never reawake," Poincaré insisted, seeking reassurance.

"Others will, in these rudimentary realms," Myraa replied, "and they will always be him."